ASULON

The Sword of Fire
Book One

William R. McGrath

PTI PRESS
FISHKILL, NY

ASULON
A PTI Press book

ASULON
The Sword of Fire-Book One
By William R. McGrath

Copyright © 2005, 2008 William R. McGrath

For information:
PTI PRESS
PO BOX 662
FISHKILL, NY 12524

This is a work of fiction. Names, characters, places and incidents either are the product of the author's imagination or are used fictitiously, and any resemblance to any actual businesses, organizations, persons, living or dead, events or locales is entirely coincidental.

Scripture verses used in the story are taken from Young's Literal Translation, The King James Bible or the Douay-Rheims Bible.

Publisher's website: www.PTIPRESS.com

Author's website: www.TheSwordofFire.com

Cover and interior artwork by Giancarlo Fusco

ISBN-13 978-0-9801058-0-3
ISBN-10 0-9801058-0-3
LCCN: 2007939968

Printed in the United States of America

Author's note: While this story is a work of fiction, most of the character and place names have a biblical, historical or mythological origin. An interesting time can be had by the reader if a name is placed in an internet search engine and seeing the results. If nothing is found, spell the word backwards and try again.

Attention churches, schools and organizations: Quantity discounts are available on bulk purchases of this book for educational, fund-raising or gift giving purposes. For information contact:

Marketing Dept, PTI Press, PO Box 662, Fishkill, NY 12524

Weights and Measures used in this story and their modern equivalents:

Fathom	Six Feet
Cubit	Eighteen Inches
League	Three Miles
Stone	Ten Pounds

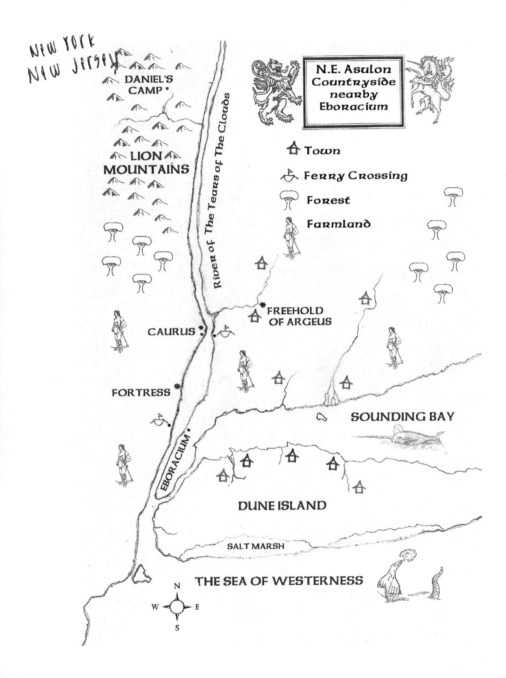

NEW YORK
NEW JERSEY

DANIEL'S CAMP •

LION MOUNTAINS

River of The Tears of The Clouds

N.E. Asulon
Countryside
nearby
Eboracium

⛪ Town

🜨 Ferry Crossing

🌳 Forest

🧍 Farmland

CAURUS •

FREEHOLD OF ARGEUS

FORTRESS

EBORACIUM

SOUNDING BAY

DUNE ISLAND

SALT MARSH

THE SEA OF WESTERNESS

N
W E
S

THE CODE OF THE PALADIN

The Warrior Virtues
DISCIPLINE
LOYALTY
COURAGE
HUMILITY

The Kingly Virtues
WISDOM
HONOR
CHARITY
JUSTICE

The Godly Virtues
FAITH
TRUTH
MERCY
LOVE

NOBILIS VOS ESTO

THE SWORD OF FIRE

"So He drove out the man; and He placed cherubim at the east of the Garden of Eden, and a flaming sword which turned every way, to guard the way to the tree of life."

-The Book of Genesis 3:24

Prologue
THE HAWK

The hawk rocked back and forth on a strong limb of the ancient oak, impatient for the rising sun to climb the mountainside and create the morning thermals. Judging the time right, the hawk stretched out its wings, took hold of the air and pulled itself aloft. Riding the warm rising draft, the hawk began its hunt, flying high above the valley running between the tall mountain and its neighbors.

A man looking skyward from that valley would have seen just a speck in the sky, which he might have guessed to be a bird of prey. However the hawk, looking down from that height with its superior eyesight, would have known the man for a man and would even have known a rabbit from a badger, were either at the man's feet.

Now, far, far below, at the edge of a clearing, the hawk spotted a man moving in a way that caused the bird to begin a slow spiral downward to investigate...

Chapter One
THE HUNTER

Seek, and ye shall find...
-The Book of Luke 11:9

The hunter stopped his slow, careful stalk through the shadows bordering the clearing and knelt behind the roots of a fallen pine. It had taken him nearly an hour in the faint light of dawn, moving no faster than a shadow across a sundial, to travel the short distance from the edge of the clearing to the downed tree. Now he waited patiently, eyes on the deer trail, ears attuned to any change in the forest's rhythm. On the border between the lowland hardwoods where the deer fed and the highland pines where they bedded down at midday, the clearing made a good place to hunt.

Gray wood ash, taken from his fire pit that morning, covered the hunter's skin, hair and beard. Over the ash, he had smeared streaks of black charcoal to break up his outline. By now, he knew how to blend in with the forest. If he did not move at the wrong time, he would appear no more dangerous to his prey than a broken tree stump.

He heard the deer just a moment before it emerged from the dark forest and entered the dawn-lit clearing. Just a twig snapping, but the sound had spoken to him of the size of the animal that made it. It was a large, mature buck, but with its antlers hidden in their velvet covering and only half the size they would reach later in the year. Not till early autumn would the antlers would be full grown, unsheathed from their velvet and sharpened by the buck upon the trunks of trees to become the weapons they were meant to be. Near the end of each winter the antlers would be shed, the breeding season over, the weapons needed for autumn's battles then just so much added weight. New antlers would begin to sprout again next spring, to start the cycle once more.

Provided the buck lived to see the spring, for death was also part of the forest's cycle.

The hunter studied the buck as it followed the feeding trail into the clearing, grazing as it walked. The buck would take a few steps, sniff the air, lower its head to graze briefly and then lift its head again to check its surroundings. The hunter watched unmoving, waiting for the buck to come within range of a sure bowshot. The buck took a few more cautious steps forward and lowered its head to inspect a mushroom.

And still the hunter waited. He had no intention of failing on so important a hunt.

To prepare for this hunt, the hunter had not eaten meat for seven days. He had built a small lodge as a steam bath, first heating rocks to a red glow, then rolling them into a pit lined with boughs of sweet balsam and quickly pouring water over the stones until the air in the lodge grew white with steam. By the morning of the hunt, he had sweated the odor of a meat eater from his body. Rising before dawn, he had washed himself in a clear mountain stream and then held his buckskin loincloth and knife sheath over a fire made smoky with green wood. He wore a flint knife newly made for this hunt, as the bone handle and sinew wrapping of his old knife would hold the scent of his last meat meal. Lastly, he had covered himself with the ash and charcoal from a fire pit made just for this purpose. He knew that if he smelled of anything at all now, it would be only of the faintest trace of wood smoke; as from a long dead fire.

And so the hunter waited behind the downed tree, his bow in hand and an arrow on the string, ready for the draw.

The buck's path took it down the trail to a point even with the fallen tree that concealed the hunter. It lowered its head again to graze upon some tender grass. The hunter drew back his bowstring, taking aim. Just as he was about to release, the buck jerked its head up and sniffed the wind, looking back down the trail.

The hunter froze, limbs straining against the heavy bow. He had missed a shot once when a deer, tense like this one, jumped aside at the release of the bowstring, quickly enough for the arrow to miss. This buck snorted, unhappy with what it had scented, and began to trot down the trail, quartering away from the hunter. Though he could have made such a shot if he had to, the hunter wanted a clean broadside through the heart that would ruin little edible meat. He parted his lips just enough to release his breath and made the bleating sound of a fawn in distress. The buck paused to turn and look back to see if whatever was attacking the fawn would pose a danger to itself.

The hunter willed the fingers of his right hand to relax and the bowstring leapt forward. The arrow flew across the clearing and struck the deer just behind the foreleg, low in the chest where the heart would be. Despite this, the buck ran, disappearing into the darkness of the forest. The hunter heard it crashing through the underbrush, then the sound of a large body falling to the forest floor. The hunter did not move; he waited as his father had taught him, making sure the deer was truly down before approaching.

A squirrel had been cracking into one of last year's acorns at the far end of the clearing when the hunter had first drawn his bow. Now it chattered noisily, alarmed by the crashing of the buck through the brush. A jay took up the cry and began to squawk.

The hunter leaned back against the fallen tree and waited for the alarm to die down. He thought how he must leave this wild country soon and that he would miss it. This was the great deep of the forest and it was very old. So thick were the ancient trees in the valleys that sunlight had not shone broadly upon the forest floor there for a thousand years. Mountains, so tall their summits were ever covered in snow, lorded, like silver-haired wise men, over the woodlands below. Among the foothills, the underlying granite bedrock lay exposed here and there, poking out of the skin of the earth, scattered like the broken bones of a giant fallen from heaven. Mountain-born streams ran cold and clear and fresh here even in midsummer. There were shy deer in the woodlands and great herds of elk in the higher meadows. Long-horned wild cattle that need flee from no bear lived here. Tawny lions prowled the mountainsides and black panthers hunted the deep valleys. Packs of wolves, so cunning and swift that even the great cats feared them, roamed at will here. The wild country was both dangerous and beautiful and the hunter loved it dearly.

After a time, the squirrel and the bird ended their alarm cries and the sounds of the surrounding forest subsided into whispered gossip. The hunter rose and made his way to the buck. It had crossed over the stream that ran just west of the clearing when it collapsed. It now lay upon the far bank, eyes staring and breath stopped, but somehow looking less dead then

11

men did when they died. A dead animal was unmoving, but still whole. A man looked shrunken, deflated somehow—if ever so slightly—in death. His father said that more left a man's body when he died than left an animal's.

The hunter looked skyward. "Thank you, Lord God, Maker of All, for this gift of meat to sustain me, skins to clothe me, bones for my tools and sinews for my bowstring: that I might hunt again."

The hunter dragged the deer back into the clearing. He would keep an eye on the trail while he cleaned the deer in case whatever the buck had scented could prove a danger to him as well.

He drew his flint knife and got to work removing the deer's organs. He worked quickly so that the blood would drain and the meat would cool. Left in the animal too long, the organs would spoil and give the meat a rancid taste. Pinching a bit of skin by the pelvis with his left hand, he inserted the tip of his knife and made a long cut up the belly, cutting through the skin and abdominal muscles. He kept his forefinger along the back of the blade so that the point would not drag through the deer's organs, spilling their contents and tainting the meat. Next he cut across the throat, severing the windpipe and esophagus, and then reached inside the chest to cut the diaphragm loose. He tilted the carcass on its side to spill out the organs. A quick shake and they fell free of their thin connections to the inside of the body cavity.

He set the liver aside on the grass, for he would eat this tonight. His father called the liver "the hunter's portion" and, on their hunts, they traditionally made a meal of the liver before returning home. As he had been taught, the hunter threw the heart as far downwind as he could. If a lion, or worse, a wolf pack, were coming up the trail, they would likely circle downwind to stalk him, stop to eat the bloody meat, and alert him to their presence. The hunter pulled up a handful of clean grass and began to wipe the blood from the inside of the carcass.

From the sky far above, a hawk cried. The hunter looked up at the bird for a moment as it circled the clearing and then returned to his work. But something about the hawk gnawed at the back of his mind. He paused. Sitting back on his heels, the hunter looked skyward, studying the bird. The hawk had tightened its path and now circled the downed deer.

"Master Hawk," he said in a low voice, "you may eat carrion in the winter, but now there is too much game in these woods for a great hunter like yourself to wait on another hunter's kill. You do not fly like you are wounded or ill. What are you about?"

As if in reply, the hawk flew down to land on a tree branch above the deer carcass. The bird looked down at the meat, then cast a glance at the hunter, shook out its wings and folded them back against its body.

Then the hawk turned its head and stared down the trail.

The hunter followed its gaze and sent his hearing out to search the forest in the way of his people. Layer upon layer of sound came to him, the calls of birds, the wind through the trees, the movements of small creatures.

And, off in the distance, there was ...silence.

Without hesitation the hunter stood, left his kill, slipped into the shadows—and listened.

Like the prow of a ship parting the waters, something was pushing a wave of silence before it, rippling through the trees, moving up the deer trail, quieting the forest creatures in its wake.

Unconcerned, the hawk flew down from its perch and landed near the deer. It turned its head this way and that, inspecting the carcass, then hopped over to the pile of organs and began to tear pieces off the liver with its sharp beak.

The hunter made his way to the pines that grew along the north side of the clearing. The lower branches of the younger trees stretched nearly to the ground, making the space underneath each pine a low and shadowed chamber. The hunter had often hidden under these trees to learn the habits of the deer that came to feed here. He checked the angle of the sun and judged it would not shine fully on the area beneath the trees for another two hours. It would be enough. He crawled into the dark space under the nearest pine and waited.

Nearly half an hour passed before the hunter caught the first sign of movement down the trail. A darker shadow emerged from the dimness of the forest. As the shadow neared, it took shape and became a tall man dressed in black traveling clothes. The wide black brim of a black felt hat hid the tall man's face. A long black cloak covered his lean frame. A long battle sword sheathed in black leather rested at his hip. The tall man lifted his head to sniff the air and hawk-like features emerged from shadow. A long aquiline nose, dark eyes and olive skin showed the man to be an Etruscan; his thick black hair, bearded chin and mustache all bore traces of silver.

He moved as a man accustomed to walking in dangerous places, with care and in silence, stopping frequently to listen to his surroundings. This was a warrior past his youth, but still strong and swift, wise in the ways of war. But the wild things did not fall silent at his approach for those reasons.

This man was a predator.

They could see it in the way the man's eyes pierced into the shadows without fear and in the way his hands seemed quick and ready, even when at rest. The animals fell silent before him as they would before the coming of a panther, hoping that the dark stalker would pass them by if only they made no sound.

The tall man made his slow, careful way into the clearing. He stopped opposite the young pine that hid the hunter and knelt to examine something on the ground. He drew a dagger from under his cloak, pierced the thing before him and held up the deer heart the hunter had thrown down the trail. The tall man turned his head to study the trees surrounding the clearing. The hunter held his breath, fearing even that slight sound might betray his presence. After a long moment, the tall man let the heart slide off his dagger. He wiped the blade on the grass and then came to his feet sheathing the dagger. As he continued across the clearing, a thin half-smile came to his lips.

The hunter let the tall man get another twenty paces past his hiding place and then slipped out from under the tree and began his stalk. He moved carefully, matching his own step with the tall man's to hide the slight sound his deerskin-clad feet made as they pressed upon the grass. Coming up from behind, his view of the man's hands would be blocked by the tall man's cloak and this worried him.

The tall man came upon the hawk feeding on the deer liver and halted.

The hunter froze.

The tall man looked from the hawk to the piled organs and then to the split deer carcass.

The hunter hesitated. He was still too far away to spring upon the tall man.

Without warning the tall man spun around, his cloak falling behind him, a flash of steel flying from his hand.

Quick as a young lion, the hunter sprang aside as the knife hissed over his head to strike, vibrating, into a tree. In one fluid motion, the hunter leapt to his feet, drawing the steel knife from the wood with his right hand and his flint knife from its sheath with his left, and charged.

The tall man calmly took a step forward to meet the attack. The hunter fell upon him, aiming a ripping stab at the taller man's throat. Without a wasted motion, the tall man stepped aside and parried the hunter's arm. As their arms struck, the hunter felt hard links of ring mail beneath the tall man's sleeve. A slash with a dagger would do nothing against the tall man's limbs or body.

The hunter drew back, switching both his knives to reverse grip, points down, and waited, arms outstretched like a mantis. He would use the knives as hooks to trap the tall man's arms and open the body to attack. Such a grip lessened the hunter's reach but doubled the power behind a stab; he would need such power to penetrate his opponent's hidden armor.

The tall man drew a dagger with his right hand and aimed a low, lunging thrust at the hunter's abdomen. As the hunter moved to parry, the tall man thrust a second blade, concealed in his left hand, at the hunter's face. The hunter tried to trap the man's arm with his own blades, but the older man evaded him like smoke, then renewed his attack, alternating between slashing and thrusting with his two blades. At the longer ranges, the older man's experience and greater reach gave him the advantage. In close, the hunter's young reflexes and strong limbs gave him the edge.

They clashed once more and the hunter's flint knife snapped in two, the thin, sharp stone too brittle to take the impact of a fight. The hunter dropped the broken blade just as the tall man lunged in.

The hunter parried the thrusting arm, caught his opponent's right hand in his left and twisted it outwards, locking the wrist. He stepped back to pull the tall man off balance and keep away from the man's other blade, while bringing the edge of his own dagger against the sleeve covering the tall man's pulse, ready to cut the wrist. Instead of resisting the lock, the tall man stepped in and threw a left thrust over the top of the locked arms. The hunter swept the thrust aside and circled his arm around his opponent's, pinning the tall man's left arm. The hunter brought his dagger up between them, pointing the tip at his opponent's throat. Now the tall man's longer reach in forward grip became a detriment, as his blade was pinned too far from the hunter's back to reach him. About to order the tall man to yield, the hunter felt three light taps on his spine. The hunter looked over his shoulder and found that the tall man had reversed his grip on his dagger and freed it to work.

The hunter smiled and released the older man.

The man took a step back, and bowed.

"Well, having a year's holiday in the woods has not slowed you down *too* much," said the tall man, sheathing his dagger.

The hunter cocked his head to the side as if the man spoke in a foreign tongue.

"Yes, Daniel, I understand," said the tall man. "After all this time alone, another man's voice must come strange to your ears."

At the sound of his name, Daniel broke into a broad grin.

"My ears may be slow to catch your words, but my eyes are glad at the sight of you!"

He stepped forward to hand the throwing knife back to its owner, resting it on an open palm, handle first, as he had been taught. "It is good to see you again, Master-Instructor Moor."

Moor did not speak in reply, but gave the half-smile that Daniel remembered so well, a smile that never seemed to include the Etruscan's eyes. Moor

17

sheathed his second dagger before taking the throwing knife and returning it to its place up his sleeve. He retrieved his cape from the ground and donned it. With its shoulders capped with hard leather, the cloak needed no clasp to keep it in place, save when riding at a gallop; yet it could be dropped with a shrug of the shoulders. That Moor did not need to unclasp his cloak before a fight was a small thing, but Moor had many small tricks like that: little things to give him even the slightest edge in a fight.

"It is good to see you also," Moor finally replied. He paused, and then added, "My prince."

"What did you call me?" asked Daniel in surprise.

"King Absalom died ten months ago," said Moor. "Absalom being without an heir, succession fell to his cousin, your father."

The Etruscan studied the young man's reaction to this news.

"Are my father and mother safe?" asked Daniel. "And the realm?"

"The realm goes better than it did," Moor replied. "And the King and Queen sleep less with their new duties, but sleep well nonetheless."

Daniel nodded his head towards the downed deer. "Tell me more of them while I finish with the buck."

They walked to the downed deer, the prince deep in thought. The hawk flew from the gut pile to land on a tree stump nearby. Daniel trimmed off the piece of liver the bird had been eating from and tossed it to the hawk.

"I think Theol has left us enough for tonight's dinner," said Daniel offhandedly as he worked.

Moor made no comment. He had eaten worse things than the leavings of a hawk.

"Master Moor, unless I am off my mark, the summer equinox is seven days away. You have come for me a week early. How did you find me?"

"Your father ordered me to return you to him earlier than the allotted time. I knew the stream where you

18

began your journey, and I knew how far you would travel in three days." He nodded towards the hawk. "Theol led me closer, for he knows the look of a man hunting and hopes for a share of the meat, as he receives on my own hunts. After that, it was just a matter of cutting your trail and following it," said Moor as if it were a small thing.

Daniel finished preparing the deer. He hoisted the carcass up onto his shoulders and led the way to his camp. Daniel thought back on the last time he had seen his teacher, nearly a year ago in the dining hall of his family's home north of Eboracium. Moor had stood next to his father as his parents gave him their blessings for his journey. That had been the first day of summer of the year he turned twenty. The appointed time had come for him to spend a year alone in the wilderness, the traditional preparation for his travel east across the ocean to the Isle of Logres, where he would study the art of governing free men with his grandfather Anak. ← angel (father of Daniel's mother) * mother is half angel

Four young men had gone out into the wilderness that year. The ship sailed north, up the Great River, "The River of the Tears of the Clouds" as the old people called it. At sunset of the third day, they set anchor for the night at the outlet of a small stream. The next morning at dawn the four young men drew straws, choosing Daniel to leave the ship first. The others laughed and slapped him on the back and said he was lucky to go first and made a brave show, but all knew that Daniel went into danger, as they would soon. Then the ship would sail north for another day and, on the morrow, it would be the turn of another. When Daniel had made his last farewell, he stripped off his clothing, stepped up on the ship's railing, dove into the cool river waters and swam ashore. For the next three days he walked, following the stream, its water his only nourishment. Each night he gathered dry tree leaves into a mound and crawled into them as both blanket and bed. The morning of the fourth day he broke his fast with fish he snatched from beneath the stream bank, cooked on a fire started by a fire bow made from a willow limb and the inner bark of a birch spun into cord. After his meal, he made a spear and a hatchet of stone and wood.

Early that same evening, at the time that animals come down to the stream to drink, he took the first of many deer that year. What meat he did not eat that night, he cut into thin strips and dried over his fire. He made the deer's sinews into bowstrings and its bones into fine tools. He took the deerskin, removed the hair and, using a paste made from the deer's brain, cured the skin over a smoky fire. From the hide he cut a loincloth and a pair of short boots. From green willow limbs he made a pack to carry his food and bone tools.

When he had finished his preparations, he set out away from the stream to find a good place to make camp. A smaller stream fed into the one that had led him inland and he followed this north for a day and a half. He made his cabin under a small rock overhang partway up the side of a hill. Here he would be protected from the wind by the hill and high enough to stay dry. Animal trails passed further down the hillside, but not close enough that his camp disturbed them greatly. If he could, he would do his hunting far from his own camp. Any game living close to his cabin would be his emergency larder; he would not hunt these unless in dire need.

He built his cabin from the broken rock that winter's frost thrust up from beneath the forest floor each year. He chose a place under the ledge with just enough room to stand upright and scraped off the top layer of soil. He built up thick walls of rock with mud and dry grass for mortar. He made a fire pit inside, near the entrance, and built up a bed of logs and pine boughs along the rear wall. That fall he would also build a small stone sweat lodge to strengthen his body against the cold. He had water close by and meadows, hardwoods, fruit trees and good hunting grounds a morning's hike away. This place would be his home for the coming year.

For the last thousand years, it had been the practice of the young men of the House of Asher to go off into the wilderness for a year of solitude to strengthen their wills and test themselves.

*****

The morning after Moor's arrival, Daniel packed the few things he would take from his camp. For himself, he kept only a flint knife, a wooden cup and buckskin shirt, pants and boots. For his father, he would bring back the black bearskin coat that had kept Daniel warm all winter; for his mother he packed two pairs of doeskin slippers and a basket of (rather hurriedly) smoked venison for their table.

Daniel and Moor dismantled the cabin, prying the stones apart with sticks and kicking the walls down. By spring, a man could walk through what had been Daniel's home for nearly a year and not know that any other man had ever trodden there. Then the two men followed the stream Daniel first used on his journey, back to the Great River where a ship awaited them.

Chapter Two
THE TRI-HEX

And it maketh all, the small, and the great, and
the rich, and the poor, and the freemen, and the servants, that it may give to them a mark upon their right
hand or upon their foreheads, and that no one may be
able to buy, or to sell, except he who is having the mark,
or the name of the beast, or the number of his name.

Here is the wisdom! He who is having the understanding, let him count the number of the beast, for the
number of a man it is, and its number is six hundred
and sixty six.

-The Book of Revelation 13:16-18

Two days later the ship bearing Daniel and
Moor came to the stone dock at the river's
edge. Perched high upon the black cliffs above them
towered the fortress of the Kings of Asulon, *Maôz-
Thabera*, 'The Fortress of the Burning'. The main gate
faced the river and could be reached only by a long
wooden stair beginning at the dock at the water's edge.
An honor guard of the King's paladins, clad in polished

armor, approached the ship. Moor stood beside Daniel and nodded to the captain.

"All hail, Prince Daniel, son of King Argeus!" called out the captain. The paladins let out a cheer and beat their swords upon their shields.

"My old home was never this loud," Daniel said, grinning.

"Best get used to it," Moor said. "The greater your status, the greater the noise at your comings and goings."

They walked down the gangway toward the cheering paladins, who formed up around Daniel and Moor and led them down the dock. At the stair, one line of men moved forward to precede them, the second followed behind. Daniel and Moor began their trek up the long wooden stair that climbed back and forth along the cliff face to the fortress. Kings of other realms would have ordered a magnificent set of stone stairs built into a cliff such as this, but the kings of Asulon thought as warriors before they thought as kings. A stone staircase, while impressive, in truth endangered a fortress. Stairs made of wood could be burned if an invader came sailing up the river, while stone stairs could not.

Over two hundred years had passed since the defeat of the last army to come close enough to the fortress that the stairs had to be burned. The kings of Asulon had long memories, though. The stairs remained of wood.

Daniel came to a landing halfway up the stair and turned to look out over the water. The mast of the ship that brought him was already far below. Other ships plied the river, carrying the commerce of Asulon.

"Do my parents make this climb every time they wish to leave the fortress?" asked Daniel, who had not been to the fortress of the king since he was a young child and remembered only the long stair.

"This is not the only way in or out of the fortress," replied Moor. In a low voice, he added, "But that is not what keeps them in the fortress now."

Daniel wanted to ask what he meant by this, but the Etruscan, never very talkative, turned and continued up the stairs. Instead, Daniel remembered his family home and felt a bit disappointed he would not see it now. He would not have time before his journey to across the sea.

His family's house sat on a thick finger of land that jutted out into a lake. Nine other homes ringed that lake, each set out into the water on a peninsula of land built for that purpose, each the home of a paladin family who could come to the aid of their neighbors quickly, if need be. The two-story, stone houses each faced a large, square inner courtyard that stayed cool in the summer and protected from the wind in the winter. Only the upper floor of these homes had windows that faced outward, but both floors had windows that faced the inner courtyard.

In Daniel's home, the lower floor held a large dining hall, kitchen and storage rooms. The upper floor housed bedchambers and a large library, which held his father's many books and maps. This latter room delighted Daniel in his youth, for many of the books told of far-off places and peoples, and the names on the maps whispered to a young boy of mystery and adventure.

Daniel missed that home. Often, after a day of training, he and his father would walk out the back door of their house, take the few steps to the lake and fish till they were called in for supper. Daniel had hoped to do that again before he left for Logres. Though he looked out over the river now, Daniel doubted he would do any fishing with his father here.

Daniel's father, Argeus, a seasoned warrior who had served in two wars; was not a violent man. Above all, he enjoyed fishing in the lake with his son and reading good books. After his release from active service, Argeus and the other elder paladins of the freehold would lead the local militia, made up of farmers and craftsmen, in military exercises once a month. That was how the older paladins spent much of their time; training others for wars they hoped would never be fought.

From the age of six until he went off to the war college at Caurus at sixteen, Daniel had spent three hours, six mornings a week, in the library with his father, learning mathematics and the sciences, the history of Asulon and of his family, the House of Asher. Afternoons were spent outside in the courtyard or forest, learning the ways of the sword and the bow. On the first day of the week, Daniel's Freehold would gather together for worship at one of their homes. Each father would take a turn reading aloud from the books of God and then leading the discussions of them. Daniel was always so proud to see the respect shown to Argeus (easily the eldest among the men of their Freehold) when it came his time to read.   *half angel*   *Angel*

Daniel's mother was Isoldé, daughter of Anak the Undying, the last of the warrior angels sent to aid mankind when the world was young, Isoldé inspired awe in common men, for the light of her father's former home in the heavens shone in her eyes. His mother had been his main teacher for the first six years of his life. As was the custom among paladin families, Isoldé had taught her son to read, write and speak fluently in the three languages he would need as a paladin. Westerness, the tongue of Asulon and the Unicorn Kingdoms, Magogian, the language of their enemy the Magog, and Cymru, the ancient tongue of southwestern Logres and spoken now by so few that it was used as a battle language among the paladins.

Daniel did not find it strange to be the son of a warrior and grandson of an angel. For the last thousand years, all the men of his house had wed the daughters of Anak, as would he when he arrived in Logres. This gave them both the right to rule in Asulon and twice the life span of common men.

Daniel and Moor reached the top of the stairs, where a line of servants waited. They cheered when they saw him.

So much for a quiet homecoming, thought Daniel.

"Prince Daniel, welcome home!" came a voice from behind the line. A thin man in his early sixties came forward to bow before Daniel. Lucan, his father's eldest servant no longer wore the homespun linen tunic and trousers Daniel remembered. The old man now dressed in rich robes of fine blue silk that would have cost him a month's pay as the servant of a retired paladin.

Daniel took the old man by the shoulders and returned him to a standing position. "Lucan, save the formalities for the throne room—though when I first saw your robes, I thought you must be the king himself."

"Me, the king!" cried Lucan, aghast. "If you think this bed sheet they have me in is good enough for the king—well, just wait till you see his majesty. But come now, young master, let us enter. Your parents know your ship has arrived and are waiting to see you."

Daniel crossed the drawbridge between the final landing and the fortress. Maôz-Thabera , so gray and imposing from the exterior, was all light and wonder inside. The walls, plastered and whitewashed, were covered in fine tapestries or painted with murals depicting great men and great battles. The brightly painted pillars carved as trees with vines spiraling upwards to the ceiling graced the great hall and throne room. Fine mosaics decorated the floors of the dining halls. Many pieces of colored glass, like living light, depicted famous kings or warriors of Asulon on each window in the fortress (high ones that faced the river and many more facing the protected inner courtyard). Servants bustled to and fro, while important men on important errands moved purposefully through the corridors.

Lucan and their escort brought Daniel and Moor into the throne room and then through it.

"The king commanded that you be brought to his chambers the moment you arrived," Lucan said. "There will be a grand feast tomorrow, but for now it's no wonder the king and queen would rather just be your father and mother and sup with you in private."

Two tall men in the black cloaks and boots of the paladins stood before an oaken door. They snapped to attention as Daniel approached. Moor raised the iron knocker and struck the door twice.

The door opened. A maidservant curtsied and said, "Welcome, Prince Daniel, Master Moor. The King and Queen await you."

They entered a plainly furnished room with a table and twelve chairs set around it. Maps of various parts of Asulon lined the wall. Daniel guessed it to be a combined meeting room and dining hall for times when the king wished to meet with his councilors less formally. A maidservant brought Daniel to his chair (Moor preferred to stand) and left through a side door. Very soon he heard voices approaching. The door swung open and a very old man in a bright green tunic entered. He struck the floor three times with his staff. "His Majesty, First of Paladins, Lion of Asulon, Defender of the Laws of the Realm, Protector of..."

"Blast it all, man," came another voice from the hall. "Save your harangue for tomorrow night."

With that, Argeus, tall and broad shouldered, strode into the room. His silver-gray mane and beard held none of the reddish-brown of his youth, but his voice remained firm and his steps sure. He wore the deep purple and gold robes of kingship.

Just behind Argeus came Queen Isoldé, bright in a dove white dress. She rushed to embrace her son.

"Oh, Daniel, Daniel," she said. "This one year has felt like one hundred."

"Come now, Isoldé, let a man look on his son," Argeus said. Father and son embraced, then Argeus held Daniel at arm's length, inspecting him.

"Aye, it is like water to a thirsty man to see you again, boy."

Daniel's mother and father looked much the same to him. His father's laugh still said all you needed

[handwritten margin notes: King Arthur, Jesus & 12 disciples]

[handwritten margin notes: family has a loving relationship]

to know about him, hale and hardy, generous to all around him. His mother's eyes still shone with the light of her father's race.

"Master Moor," the queen said, turning to the Etruscan and taking his right hand in hers. "Thank you for returning our son to us. As always, you do us service worthy of a great friend."

Moor bowed formally and said. "My queen does me honor." He turned and saluted the king. "If you will excuse me, your majesty. I have measures I must discuss with the guards concerning tomorrow's banquet."

The king nodded. Moor bowed again and left the chamber.

"Your mother prayed for you every night, Daniel," Argeus said, still grinning over his son. "Look at him, Isoldé'," he said, slapping Daniel solidly on the back. "He's as fit as a racehorse; you need not have worried."

Servants entered bearing trays and set a bowl and mug before Daniel. The bowl held a bed of boiled noodles, a poached egg and a link of sausage. Simple food for a king's home, but typical for paladins, who ate frugally as becomes warriors.

"Duck liver sausage!" cried Daniel in joy. "And milk! Oh, you do not know how long I have pined for a mug of fresh milk."

"I remember my own time of solitude," Argeus said. "The old men who trained me said that you dream of the foods of home at two times during your year alone: your first week and your last, when the time of your return draws near."

"Yes, but how did you know that I had dreamed of this?" asked Daniel.

Isoldé smiled. "This is what I used to feed you and your father when you both returned cold and wet from a winter hunting trip. So I thought it good to feed you now after so long a trip of your own."

For the next hour parents and son dined and talked and laughed.

As Argeus finished telling the tale of his first night in the fortress, when he got lost trying to find the pantry, he caught Daniel looking at his mother with tears in his eyes.

"What ails you, son?" asked the king, knowing the answer, for he had had a similar homecoming many years ago.

ails : bothers

The prince put down his mug and took hold of his parents' hands.

"I did not miss the good food of my mother's table the most while I was in the wilderness, nor the comfort of my father's house. I missed this," he said, looking at his father and mother. "I missed our laughing and talking the night away so much that my heart nearly broke with the missing of it."

we should eat with our family & enjoy the times together

Isoldé's eyes shone brightly as she looked upon her son.

"Daniel... we..." began Argeus, knowing that he should change the subject before he too came to tears, "we want you to tell us all of your adventures in the wild, from the first day to the last."

And the three of them ate and drank and laughed and cried long into the night.

* * * * *

The next day Daniel woke when a shaft of light touched his face. An old king of Asulon tried unsuccessfully to scowl down at him from the stained glass window in the wall, but the multihued sunlight came through the image too brightly for him to look menacing.

"I'm sure, sir, that you look far more fierce from the outside," said the prince with a yawn. He looked around the room and saw his buckskins set neatly on a dressing table. Daniel vaguely remembered Lucan escorting him back to his bedchamber and helping him off with his clothing. Once his mother had retired for the night, Daniel had stayed up with his father. They had toasted to each other's hunting tales (with a very good wine, if Daniel remembered right) till the cry of the night watch bade them to bed. Now Daniel also found a new set of clothing laid out near a large copper bathing tub.

A full bath will have to wait, thought Daniel, *the king's fortress is now my father's house and I must see all of it.*

He poured some cool water from a pitcher into a washbasin, washed himself quickly and donned the black cotton trousers, tall black boots and white silk shirt left for him. A black leather belt lay beside the clothes, with a buckle shaped like a round shield and set with a gemstone at its center. Daniel stared thoughtfully at the stone, brushing its surface with his fingertips. All the men of the House of Asher received such a buckle when they graduated from the war college at Caurus as *paladins,* knight-protectors of the realm. Then, Daniel had been given a buckle of silver, set with black onyx. This buckle was gold, set with a purple amethyst, signifying that he was of the king's own household.

A knock came to the door. "Enter," Daniel called out.

A servant opened the door and Lucan entered. "Good morning, my prince. Did you sleep well?"

"Yes, Lucan, very well," replied Daniel smiling at the way the old retainer said 'my prince'. "You are enjoying this turn of events, aren't you, Lucan?"

"Oh, yes, young sir. I have gone up immeasurably in my wife's eyes now that I am the prince's own chamberlain. You would think I had been made a general or some such thing."

Daniel bowed with a flourish. "Lucan, I am always pleased to contribute to your wedded bliss. Well, come now, sir general. Show a former wild man of the woods, now turned prince, what this fortress is all about."

The two left the chamber. After a stair, a corridor, and another stair, they came to a long hallway ending in

30

a stout oak door guarded by two paladins. Lucan unlocked the door and Daniel entered what, as a small boy, he had thought must be the largest room in Asulon, the throne room of the king. Tall windows of stained glass lined the south wall. The floor held a mosaic map of Asulon showing its cities, mountain ranges, grasslands, great rivers and many of the animals found in each region. The sky blue, domed ceiling had white clouds and soaring eagles painted upon it. Many spears thrust out from the top of the walls, each holding the banner of a former king of Asulon.

Lucan gestured to the banners as they walked. "There, young sir, on the north wall nearest the throne, hangs, of course, the green banner of Asa our first king, who led the House of Asher across the great ocean and brought peace to Asulon. And next to his banner hangs that of his son, Adom. Now, King Anak himself trained Adom in the art of kingship..."

Daniel saw a great *many* banners hanging from the walls and recalled how Lucan prided himself on his knowledge of Asher family history. He steeled himself for a long lecture on the subject, then remembered his training in tactics and decided to outflank his opponent through diversion.

"Lucan, tell me, do you remember when I was a young boy and played a trick on you with the hunting dogs? I took all the dogs out of their kennels and moved them into the storehouse, leaving the gate open to make it look as if they had all run off."

Lucan's brows knit in a scowl. "Do I remember it? Who was responsible for those dogs and who would lose his position if they had indeed run off? I got on my horse and rode off a' hunting after them."

"You were gone for four hours," remembered Daniel.

"And when I returned, did I not see you yourself smirking in a corner?" Lucan replied.

"Do you know what my father did with me for my little jest?" asked Daniel.

31

"I did not think it so little a jest at the time, young master," said the old man in mock indignity.

"He took me into his war room and sat me down in his huge black chair. Then, without speaking a word, he tied my wrist to the chair with this thin little bit of sewing thread and just walked away, leaving the chamber door wide open. Now, an infant could have broken that thread, but I did not dare move."

"Why not?" asked Lucan, a slight smile on his lips.

"If my father had tied me down with a strong rope, perhaps I would have tried to free myself and run off," replied Daniel. "But tying me down with the thread worried me. It was as if he dared me to break it."

"And then what happened?" asked Lucan, though he already knew the answer.

"Nothing. I just sat there dreaming up all manner of punishments my father might give me when he returned. The longer I sat there, the worse my punishment became. Do you know how long I sat there?"

"Yes, young master, I do at that," replied Lucan. "Four hours on the nose. Just as long as I spent hunting those not-missing dogs, and just long enough for your father and me to finish our third game of battle board in the dining room."

"You knew!" exclaimed the prince.

"Yes, I knew. Your father asked me what worries I had gone through searching for the dogs, and he invited me to join him for the midday meal, while he let you contemplate your crime." Lucan looked at the throne, a thoughtful expression on his face. "Your father is a wise man, who knows that to get loyalty, you must first give it. He will be a good king, I think." Just then a bell sounded. "Come, my prince," Lucan said, "time to break your morning fast."

They left the throne room and made their way past the open door of a wide dining hall. At many tables and benches, paladins, workmen, and artisans took their places with the sound of clanking pots, clinking crocks and much laughter. Daniel stopped at the doorway, scanning the crowd to find any familiar faces.

"We should not delay, my prince," Lucan said. "The king and queen will be expecting you."

Just then a voice called out from a nearby table, "Hey, look what's come floating back down the river!"

"Too late, I'm caught," said Daniel with a laugh, as a swarm of young men gathered around him with much backslapping and many questions about his adventure.

"Daniel has returned–Hurrah! Hurrah!" They picked him up on their shoulders and carried him around the room. Soon the rest of the room took up the cry. "Hurrah for Prince Daniel! Hurrah!"

Lucan stood in the doorway a moment and shook his head, but once he turned away from the chamber a grin spread across his face.

* * * * *

"The food," Daniel said at the end of the meal, "was nearly as good as seeing your ugly old faces again."

One of the young men grabbed the face of his neighbor in both of his hands, distorting it, and said, "Who are you calling old?" They all laughed.

A boy in the dark green tunic of a squire in training came up to a paladin captain, who then pointed out Daniel. The boy marched up to Daniel with a serious face and bowed. "Prince Daniel."

"Yes, lad?"

"The king wishes your presence in his chambers, your highness."

Daniel had to smile at the boy's manner. "What is your name, lad?"

"Tomkin, your highness," said the boy.

"Well, Tomkin, I am new to the fortress and need the assistance of an experienced man to guide me."

The boy stood a bit taller. "Your highness, I can guide you. I know this old place like I know my mom's own kitchen."

"Well then, Sir Guide, lead on." said Daniel, knowing Tomkin would be the hero at the table of the junior squires that night. Daniel's friends shouted their good-byes as the prince followed the boy out of the dinning hall. They made their way back past the throne room and to a large oak door at the end of a hallway. Two paladins stood guard before it, along with a servant in chamberlain's livery.

"Prince Daniel to see the king," said Tomkin, doing his best to deepen his voice.

The chamberlain looked down past his long nose at the boy and cocked an eyebrow.

"If you please, sir," added Tomkin, in a much smaller voice.

The chamberlain rapped three times with the big brass knocker set in the door, opened it and announced, "Prince Daniel to see the king."

Daniel turned to Tomkin and saluted him in the manner of the paladins, right fist over the heart.

"Thank you, Sir Guide, you have done well. Dismissed." Tomkin snapped to attention and saluted smartly, but could not keep the smile off his face. Daniel turned and entered the room.

Argeus rose from behind a large oak table.

"Well, son, have your friends filled your belly and your ears too full for you to drink and talk with your father and an old friend?"

Hanging from a peg on the wall behind Argeus was a crook-topped shepherd's staff of hickory wood, a brown leather bag and a battered sailcloth pilgrim's hat—wide brimmed, flat topped and bleached nearly white by many years in the sun.

Daniel remembered that hat.

Argeus nodded towards the other side of the room. Daniel spun round and cried out, "Simon!"

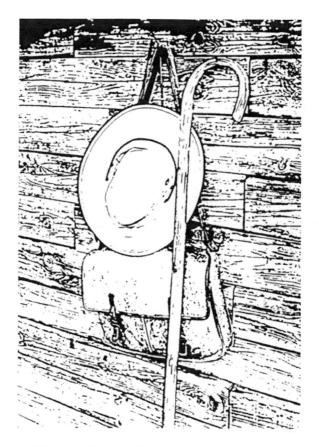

An old brown bear of a man stood by the hearth. He wore a tunic and trousers the color of ripe wheat, a wide leather belt around his thick waist and well-worn brown boots on his feet. The old man's round bald head shone above a mostly silver beard, striped here and there with strands of its original golden hue; the skin round his sapphire blue eyes crinkled like old parchment as he smiled.

"Hello, Rock-turner," replied Simon. "It's good to see you again."

Daniel rushed across the room and embraced the old man.

A priest, wise man and wanderer, Simon would rest from his travels at the home of Argeus. He always brought a gift in his bag for Daniel, sweets or a tin flute

35

when Daniel was very young, and, later, maps or books telling of far away places. Though Simon was a priest, he was tied to no formal order.

"I serve the Lord God as He pleases, not as man pleases," was how Simon explained his calling. Simon had called Daniel "rock-turner" for that was the priest's first view of him as a boy; turning over rocks to see what was underneath. Daniel spent many an hour walking with Simon, learning the names and habits of the smaller creatures of the forest. Daniel had not seen Simon since his sixteenth summer and his time at War College.

"Tankards and time to drink them!" ordered the king. Servants came, poured ale for the three men and left them.

* * * * *

"Well now, Simon," said Argeus, after half their tankards had been drained during the small talk of old friends long parted, "you told me that you had news of great import for Asulon and that Daniel should be here to hear it."

"I have grave news for you, for your house and for all of Asulon," Simon began. "Daniel, have you heard of the guild of wealthy men who call themselves 'The Builders'?"

"Yes," nodded Daniel, "they are the heads of the wealthiest houses in Asulon and the Unicorn kingdoms."

"You have spoken truly, but not completely," replied the priest. "They head many of the wealthiest houses, true, but more importantly, they head the oldest of the houses of wealth. They own of mercantile exchanges and banking houses, they make the apothecary powders that physicians use and many other things. They have become kings in their own way, for their treasuries, though less than their realm's, are ruled by fewer men. They can focus their wealth to accomplish the things they set out to accomplish. With their wealth, they build up men who agree with their goals and tear down men who would hinder them.

"They have no army, yet many powerful men heed their call. Senators and centurions, magistrates and ministers, priests and patriarchs, many who would rise to high office and, having risen, remain there, come to the Builders Guild seeking favor. And favor is given, but not without a price. Just a hint here, a suggestion there, then a demand and, finally, when the Guild have their victims addicted to their aid, a command: 'Do as we order or the gold you need to remain where you are shall disappear.'"

"And it has been thus from the founding of the first city upon the earth," agreed Argeus. "Only the king is not beholden to such men for office, but even the crown feels their power, for the Builders Guild and men like them control many in the High Senate and the Senate controls the treasury of this land."

"And yet," replied Simon, "even the High Senate knows it must please the people of Asulon to keep their seats and the keys to that treasury. So they do not do all that the Builders bid them do, at least not openly or quickly. Instead the Senators try to balance pleasing those who elect them and pleasing those who fund that election. Asulon's freedom has depended on that balance of forces for many years. But now the Builders Guild plans to upset that balance, to lay a subtle snare for the people of this land and, once that snare tightens around their necks, bring them under a cruel enslavement."

Simon took a deep breath and closed his eyes as if in silent prayer before continuing.

"King Argeus, here, then, lies the danger. The Builders Guild, these uncrowned kings of wealth, may not sit openly upon the throne here in Asulon, but they have other ways to rule. In the Unicorn kingdoms across the sea, when they have not attained the crown outright, they rule from behind the throne as firmly as if they *did* sit upon it. They mean to do the same in Asulon, but first the people must be lulled into a dependency on them. They have begun such a task in Unicornia, starting in Gaul. There, all the people bear a tattoo of their census number. The people of Gaul carry no gold or silver, but, when making a purchase, show the tattoo to the merchant and the amount is taken from the purchaser's banking house and transferred to that of the seller".

Argeus's eyebrows knit together as he heard this.

"But how can this work? How can a merchant know the amount in a man's account just from seeing a tattoo?" asked the king. "He cannot send a runner to the banking house for every purchase. The method you describe would be like taking a letter of script from a stranger. No merchant could conduct business that way."

"The Guild has found a way, though not on their own—they had help from dark places," replied Simon. "To answer your question more directly, each merchant has a black box, hexagonal in shape and about half a cubit in diameter, with a round window of red crystal set into the top. Customers place their hands atop this box. Something within the crystal then reads the number of the tattoo, sending the information—as quick as thought itself—to a similar box at both the banking houses of the customer and the merchant, transferring the amount of the purchase from the account of the customer to that of the merchant."

Surprise and more than a little wonder showed upon the king's face.

"These boxes, though strange, seem a boon rather than a cause for alarm," said Argeus. "No cutpurse could take your money unless he wanted to cut off your hand and try to buy something by passing that bloody piece of meat over these boxes."

"The danger is threefold," Simon said, "with each succeeding danger leading to the next.

"The first danger: Though the Guild will claim that they invented the device to make this type of communication possible, these boxes hold nothing but trinkets—a few mirrors and lenses, a small brass bell, some tiles of colored glass: things to fool the simple should a box be broken open. No, the boxes work because of the dark arts of sorcerers in league with the Guild.

"The second danger: The king of Gaul has forbidden the use of gold, silver or copper coin in that realm. Citizens can only buy or sell through the black boxes and the tattoos.

"And the third danger: The Guild knows that many people will not tolerate a mark upon their bodies. So they plan to begin with this."

He laid a thick bronze medallion down on the table.

"The banking houses will use these first, as a test of the black box system. People will wear these medallions and use them in place of the mark on the hand. The men of Builders Guild hope the medallions will prepare them for the eventual use of the tattoos. Look at the medallion: I am told that the three numbers at its center are always the same."

The king picked up the medallion and examined it. A puzzled look came over his face.

"What is it, Father?" asked Daniel.

"Look at this and tell me what you see," replied the king, handing his son the medallion.

Daniel felt its weight in his hand. No small amount of bronze had gone into its manufacture. It appeared about a third larger than a gold sovereign, the largest coin used in Asulon. The medallion had a small hole set near the edge, probably so that the piece could be worn around the neck, though its weight would make it cumbersome. One side of the medallion had a broad gouge running across its face, obscuring whatever design might be there, so he turned the medallion over. On this side there was a clear imprint and the sight of it caught Daniel's breath in his throat: three hexagons, descending in size, each set within the other.

Each hexagon contained six numbers, so that there were three sets of six numbers. At the center of the smallest hexagon three numbers were set apart, written in old northern runes, little used now—perhaps as a way to hide their meaning; six, six and six.

"The Tri-Hex," Daniel said, placing the medallion down on the table and pushing it away from him. "Why would they choose such a symbol?"

"Yes, why indeed," agreed Simon. "Why choose a symbol that, for all those who worship the Lord God through His son Yeshua, symbolizes the greatest evil that will ever walk among men? Why? Because the knowledge that the Builders Guild uses to power these black boxes comes from the servants of that very same evil."

"Who?" Daniel asked.

"Men who call themselves 'The Illuminati'," Simon said. "The name means 'The Enlightened Ones' and it is a name I thought had died out long before I was born. But I should have known that a name may die, but the idea behind it will live on as long as men wish it to. The Illuminati could rightly be said to have started when man first raised a tower at Babel and shook his fist at the heavens and cried out, 'You have no right to rule over me!'

"Anywhere and anytime men have gathered to oppose God, or, if they did not believe in Him, oppose the worship of Him by others, there, at that time, are the Illuminati.

"'The Enlightened Ones': an ironic name," continued Simon, "for what we call light, they call darkness, and acts we would call pure evil, they call pure freedom. The Illuminati look upon the Lord God as the Great Tyrant, while the enemy of God and man, who we know as Abaddon the Destroyer, they call Abaddon the Disenslaver. Their power comes from knowledge given to them by Abaddon in exchange for blood sacrifices...and their souls. The Black Boxes are evil, because the makers of these boxes are evil and have built evil into their very design."

"Yes," agreed Argeus, "just as the fruit of a poisoned tree will also be poison. And yet, while no Yeshuan would willingly bear the mark of Abaddon's servant; what of others? What would you say to those who do not believe as we do? Many see this as just a number and not evil."

"The great danger in this system of boxes, medallions and marks threatens even those who do not follow Yeshua," said Simon. "The information taken with these boxes can be given to anyone. One man in particular poses the greatest danger to Asulon's freedom if he acquires such knowledge."

"Who is this man?" demanded Argeus.

"The Builders Guild will offer that information to *you*, o king," replied Simon. "You would then know of every purchase made by every person in the realm. You could then say to any banking house, 'Remove authority to buy or sell from any man I consider an enemy, let not one copper's worth of credit past to them.' No one, rich or poor, great or small, could buy or sell unless he had the permission of the king. The coin of the realm would be outlawed, as would trade in silver and gold. Anyone the king deemed an enemy would face two choices, submit to the king's will or starve."

Simon watched to see what Argeus would make of this news; his reaction would show the true mettle of the man.

The king sat in silence for a long, thoughtful moment before speaking.

"Even if the use of the Tri-Hex is mere coincidence," Argeus said at last, "this system places far too much power in the hands of even a good king, and kings are not always good. The more power a king has, the more he comes to believe that he alone deserves that power. The kings of the old world thought that, since the king's judgment went unquestioned, then all that the king did was right. 'If I have done it, then it was destined to be done' became their motto. They began to think of themselves as gods. My forefather Asa once said, 'The best of governments would be one run by a good king with absolute power and the worst of governments would be one run by a evil king with absolute power.' Therefore, Asulonian freedom depends on power resting, not solely with the king, but divided equally between the throne, the Senate, the High Court and the people."

Argeus rose to his feet and paced, something he did, Simon knew, while preparing a plan of battle.

"Safety for the people's freedom lies not with absolute power in the hands of one man," said the king, "but in its being thinly spread, among as many men as possible. These black boxes of the Builders Guild concentrate power in the hands of one man, the one who controls the black box. It must not be allowed on these shores."

Simon bowed his head before Argeus.

"King Argeus, your people do well to call you 'The Wise'. Now the Builders Guild, through its Asulonian head, Sargon of the House of Stone, wishes to bring this system of commerce to your realm."

"After what you have told me, do you think I would allow that system here?"

"You may have little choice in the matter," replied Simon, "for that which has always restrained a king of Asulon from doing as much evil as he wishes, also restrains him from doing as much good as he wishes. Remember, Argeus, you invoked the king's right of the One Law when you limited the Senator's terms in office."

"Father, you have used your One Law already?" asked Daniel in surprise.

"Yes, on the very day after my coronation," replied Argues with a chuckle. "I used my One Law to order that each senator may hold no more than two terms in office. Since my law would pertain only to those elected after it was made, the old men of the Senate thought themselves safe from its effects and did not even try to raise the unanimous vote needed to forestall it. After all, has not the defeat of a sitting senator been as rare as hen's teeth for the last forty years or more?

"Well then. The elections came three months after my coronation and many new candidates came forward, saying, 'Vote for me; I am one of you.'

"And so they were, for farmers and small merchants, physicians and teachers now ran for seats that seemed not as sweet a prize to the power hungry and greedy. And the people of Asulon said to themselves, 'I think Senators Gladhand and Backslap have been at their jobs too long. They may have come to do good, but they stayed to do well and did much too well for their own purses. It is time to let some new blood into the Senate.' And that is exactly what the people did, but no one foresaw to what extent they would do so. Well, they voted out better than half of the old Senate."

The king smiled, as only a man remembering the fall of those who thought themselves invincible may smile.

"Oh, I can tell you, the weeping of eyes and gnashing of teeth was great in the halls of the High Senate when the results of that election were read. Most of these losses came from the Plebeian party- the party that claimed to love the common people, but loved levying taxes upon them even more.

The new Patrician majority, eager to show itself different from the old Plebeian leadership, proposed doing away with all the old tax laws—from the High Senate's own laws down to those of the smallest village—and making one tax law for all of Asulon, a tax upon the sale of a good or service. This eliminated the most onerous of the old laws, the tax on income, collected before a man got a single copper of his pay. This tax hindered savings, and caused many a normally honest man in Asulon to hide his income, so he could pay a reasonable amount in taxes and still have something left to raise his family.

"So then, the new tax is collected only at the sale of an item or service. The monies collected are evenly divided between the county in which the sale was made, the provincial government above that county and, finally, the realm's treasury. The new tax is simple, understandable and open and the people of Asulon have prospered for it. The common people save more and the treasury grows even as we speak.

"Not only did the new law lower the taxes on the people, it also lowered corruption at all levels of government, from the High Senate, to the provincial governments and down to the smallest county; for high taxes and high levels of corruption go so thoroughly together that it is difficult to say which is the cause and which the effect—find one and you are sure to find the other."

"But, Father," said Daniel, "do you regret using your One Law so soon into your reign?"

Argeus shook his head. "I know that most kings have saved their One Law, keeping that supreme weapon in reserve, the only law a king can make that requires a unanimous vote of the High Senate to overturn. Yes, my son, with my One Law spent, I know that if two-thirds of the Senators vote against me, they can block any law I propose. Though this restriction keeps the king weak, it also has kept us a free people.

"And because I have used my greatest weapon early in my reign, when those who might have opposed me remained unsure of my purposes, I may now call upon many new men in the Senate to put the realm's concerns before their own. Let me speak with them and find a way to defeat this plan of the Builder's Guild, the sorcerers of the Illuminati and the Evil One they both serve. We require a law that somehow forbids these black boxes without speaking of them directly. For I fear that, if the Guild gets wind of how much we know, any law we give the Senate would be doomed before the first vote."

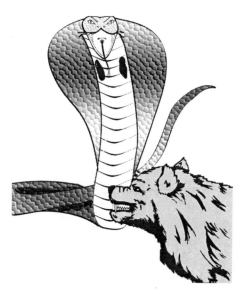

Chapter Three
THE WOLF AND THE COBRA

They sharpened their tongue as a serpent,
Poison of an adder is under their lips.
     – **The Book of Psalms**- 140:3

In a large, but otherwise unremarkable stone house in the oldest part of the city of Eboracium, the Builders Guild meets. A short, pale man with hair like a poorly constructed bird's nest speaks. He is Dew, head of the government teacher's guild. Anyone reading the faces of those present would get the impression that Dew had been speaking for quite some time—anyone, that is, but Dew himself.

"A war comes, gentlemen, a war between the old and the new, between the rough and hoary shamans of the decaying religions of the world and us, the tellers of truth, the philosophers, men of learning and of science.

"Know that we are engaged in a revolution, gentleman, but not a tumultuous revolution of the sword and the catapult. No, we fight a quiet revolution of the mind. Our battle will not be on the plains and in the valleys of Asulon, but in each and every school chamber in the land. We fight for the greatest prize of all; the future of humankind, for we wage our battle in the very minds of our children. Shall we continue teaching our children mere facts or shall we strive for something higher: to teach our children how to think and, indeed, how to act for the greater good?

"Who, then, decides what a child will learn? Her father, though he be an unschooled and illiterate farmer, or professional teachers like myself who have studied long and hard, whose very life's breath is education?

"I know what you in this room feel and I am gratified."

Dew held up his hand as if to forestall applause. He eyed each man in the silent room with the self-satisfied air of those secure in their own righteousness. He continued.

"How, then, shall we free our children from the rigid attitudes, narrow values and false beliefs taught by parents blind to the new and better path we have chosen? Parents, whose only hold over these children is the mere biological accident of their birth?

"My friends, I bring you the news that we have already won our first battle in this war, and fittingly, with barely a blow being struck, for our enemies did not deem the territory taken of any great value. We now control the schools that teach our future teachers the noble art of teaching. I am happy to report that these schools view our curriculum with the same reverence that the most rabid followers of the old religions view their 'holy' scriptures.

"The next battle will be a far greater struggle, though, for it must be waged in the schools that instruct our youth, and the enemy realizes the value of that prize. I am confident we shall prevail, however, for this battle will be fought by the very teachers we have trained, who now see themselves as apostles of a new faith—a religion of humanity based on tolerance for all things and a love of self, a religion where every person finds his or her own way and own truth, so that humankind can rise above the myths and legends of the old religions that have held us back for far too long."

Dew paused dramatically to take a slow meaningful look around the room.

"But we have enemies, gentlemen, who would try to hold back this new age of progress. Let me read to you what one Senator has said of us."

He drew a small scroll from beneath his robes, unrolled it and began to read aloud.

"My countrymen, disguise the fact as we may, there is in this country today, and in both political parties, an element which is ripe for centralized despotism. There are men and houses of vast wealth, whose iron grasp spans this whole continent, and who find it more difficult and more expensive to corrupt the thirteen provincial legislatures than one High Senate. It was said of an Etruscan emperor of old that he wished the people of his land had but one head, so that he might cut it off with a single blow. And so it is with those moneyed kings who would rule this country through bribery, fraud and intimidation. It is easy to see how; with all the powers of government centered in Eboracium they could at a single stroke put an end to Asulonian liberty. But they well understand that before striking this blow the minds of the people must be prepared to receive it. And what surer or safer preparation could possibly be made than is now being made, by indoctrinating the minds of the rising generation with the idea that ours is already a consolidated government; that the provincial legislatures have no sovereignty which is not subordinate to the will and pleasure of the High Senate, and that our Founding Laws are the mere creatures of custom, and may therefore be legally altered or abolished by custom? Such are a few of the poisonous doctrines which hundreds of thousands of Asulonian children are today drinking in with the very definitions of the words they are compelled to study.

And yet the man who dares to utter a word of warning of the approaching danger is stigmatized as an enemy to education and unfit to be mentioned as a candidate for the humblest office."

Dew looked around the room in triumph, the truth of his case obvious to him. He knew none in the room could deny his cause.

"Gentlemen, you must agree with me that these reactionaries, these obstructionists, these self-deluded men who see the phantasmal hand of conspiracy in every good work of ours, must be defeated! The next election for the members of the High Senate will be upon us before we know it. Our candidates must be properly funded in order to vanquish the foes of progress. Our cause is just. Our people stand ready. The time for action is now!"

"Thank you, friend Dew," said Sargon, leading the polite applause. It took Dew a moment to recognize the signal for him to take his seat.

One by one, other men rose to speak and various other matters were discussed. Finally the general meeting came to an end.

"Surely you see the urgency in what must be done," said Dew to Sargon, as he was guided towards the door.

"Yes, yes, of course you are correct," replied Sargon. "I will speak to the financial committee about funding your candidates this very day."

The great iron chamber door closed, echoing round the room. The members of the financial committee remained in the chamber, the inner circle of the Builders and its true leadership.

A man with silver hair spoke. "I think we should give Dew his gold, if for no other reason than to relieve us from the need to hear his twaddle again."

"If you think success will close that windy orifice he calls a mouth, then you do not know our friend Dew," said Sargon. The men around him chuckled. "But we will fund his candidates nonetheless, because his enemies are our enemies."

They agreed upon an amount. No scribe took down the vote, for no scribe ever attended a Builders Guild meeting. Later, Sargon would have a scribe write out a document authorizing the funds to be transferred from an account set up for such purposes.

Sargon knew that the teachers in the government schools adamantly opposed anyone else teaching Asulon's children; this was what had brought Dew to the meeting today. These teachers spoke loudly of the children's good, but, in truth, simple fear of economic competition fueled their furor. In recent years, parents in Asulon had taken to pooling their money to fund small private schools or to placing their children into schools run by houses of worship. Some even revived a method successful for millennia, though mocked by the government teachers, wherein parents taught their own children in their own homes.

The Builders Guild opposed these alternative methods of education for their own reasons. The Builders saw the true nature of independent education. It created a source of intellectual competition, which the men in the room could not allow if their plans for the future of Asulon were to succeed. Dew and his goals would be supported, for his enemies were indeed their enemies.

A generation ago, the Guild began a program to wrestle the government schools away from the beliefs common to the people of Asulon and toward a belief system more favorable to a world led by men like themselves. To this end, they began with the schools that taught the teachers, conditioning them to think only in certain ways and to believe only in certain things. The old ways of Asulon were mocked. Independence, faith, self-restraint, a common morality, all these were cast aside. Courses of study were watered down so that all could pass. Instead of creating independent thinkers prepared to investigate the world around them, the government schools turned out ignorant but happy sheep, who preferred soft slavery to hard freedom and the responsibilities that freedom brought. Gradually this thinking crept into the government schools at every level until it became the ruling orthodoxy among teachers across the land.

Sargon knew that, ironically, none of the men in the room had sent their own children to government schools, though they advocated such education for others. No, their own children had received private tutoring and curriculums not very different from those in the religious and private schools that their fathers publicly opposed. Learning to be sheep was good enough for the masses, but their own children would learn to be leaders.

A merchant across the table from Sargon mimicked Dew's whining pleas to the amusement of the others. Sargon rapped his knuckles on the table. "Now let us move on to something of truly immediate concern," said Sargon. He looked gravely round the room and the men became silent.

"I have received a report from a fortune-teller in my employ..."

"What? Are you listening to 'the spirits' now, Sargon?" interrupted the head of another banking house, (publicly, a sharp competitor of Sargon's) who thought himself rich and fat enough to make a jest at Sargon's expense.

"No, but many men and, in this case, one woman, foolishly speak things to those 'spirits' that they would never tell to mortals," continued Sargon. "I keep many people in my employ, including those to whom men will confide things beyond anything they would tell a wife,

50

brother or priest. Tavern owners, prostitutes and, yes, fortune-tellers have their ears open for news and their hands open for my gold. The wife of a certain senator close to Argeus recently visited one such fortune-teller."

At this news even the rival banker leaned forward with interest.

"This senator's wife came to my fortune-teller seeking counsel," continued Sargon. "It seems that the Senate will vote today on a new law dealing with the minting of coins and the Senator's wife wished the 'spirits' to tell her how she might profit from this proposed law."

"And why is this important?" asked the banker.

"It seems that Argeus has been made aware of our plans concerning the Freedom Transfer Boxes."

Sargon paused so that his next statement would hit them all the harder. He would need them fully committed to accomplish the next step in his plan.

"There is more. Argeus has seen the medallion…"

A man across the table let out a curse. Another struck the tabletop with his fist.

Sargon held up his hands for silence, "…and now Argeus proposes a law that will maintain the use of gold, silver and copper as the only metals to be used as payment in Asulon, defeating our entire plan before it has even begun. The Senate votes on the law today. I have sent word to the few senators we still control, but I fear it is too late. I could do no more than state that we did not want the law passed; I could not tell them why for obvious reasons. If we had had more warning, we could have mounted a campaign against the law–convinced the common people that the law would only benefit the rich and all the unusual rubbish they so willingly swallow. But, as things stand, I believe that this new law of Argeus's will pass."

"But how is this possible?" demanded the head of the largest shipbuilding concern in Asulon. "You assured us the medallions would not appear until we had regained control of the High Senate."

The powerful old men in the room grew angry, but fear lay under that anger. They were not young zealots willing to die for a higher cause: they fought for their own wealth and power, a cause that might now be in jeopardy.

"I have discovered the leak," said Sargon. "A low-level clerk assisting in the counting of the medallions managed to smuggle out a defective medallion, due to be melted and remade."

The fat banker shifted his great bulk back into his chair. "So tell us. Who was he working for and has he been dealt with?"

"He worked for no one, as far as we can tell," replied Sargon. "It seems that he found religion at some temple. The other clerks tell of him coming to work one morning, acting unusually cheerful and trying to convert them all to the worship of Yeshua.

"When I found that Argeus had seen one of our medallions, I ordered an investigation. This clerk was an obvious suspect. Under interrogation, he told all. It seems he believed that drivel about the Tri-Hex being an evil number, stole a medallion and turned it over to his local priest, who then apparently turned it over to that meddling cleric Simon.

"And that is why religion is such a dangerous element in society. It makes men unpredictable. They do things that defy all logic. The clerk is dead now and for what? A number on a coin?"

"But does Argeus actually believe that rot about the Tri-Hex?" asked a man who made his wealth through theaters of the cheapest type. "I would have thought an educated man such as he would not believe in those children's tales."

A tall, distinguished man rose to speak. A famous retired senator who had led a public crusade to raise taxes and "soak the rich" as he put it, he had inherited great wealth himself. It amused him that none of the laws he had ever proposed touched his own fortune, but instead prevented the very people who voted for him from becoming wealthy themselves.

"It always escapes the notice of religious fanatics that the Tri-Hex can be read from any angle and thus easily read on a coin or medallion," said the former senator. "In a device like the transfer box, even should a medallion be put on the box upside down; the box will still be able to read the central three numbers of the medallion. This way a merchant, when using the box, will know to simply turn the medallion around, rather than send the whole blasted box back to us as defective!"

"Well said, sir, well said," agreed Sargon. Sargon knew what angered the man so. The Gauls experienced this very problem two years ago, when the medallion was introduced there and did not yet bear the Tri-Hex. The creators of the box suggested adding a prefix, a three-digit entry code that could be read by the boxes whether right side up or upside down. That number turned out to be six hundred and sixty-six. If the central three digits were read as nine hundred and ninety-nine, the box would still recognize these as numbers and signal the merchant to turn the medallion around. The final medallions, and even the tattooed marks that would replace them, included the prefix.

The direction of the discussion, so far, satisfied Sargon. But would they be willing to go the distance with him? What he sought had been done only once before in his lifetime.

"It seems," continued Sargon, "that Argeus believes himself to be the moral pinnacle of Asulonian monarchy and that any king who comes after him would misuse the power that the Freedom Transfer Boxes would give the king."

"But removing coinage from society would benefit every citizen in the realm," protested the head of one of the three largest scribe services. "Outlawing coins and making transfer boxes the only means of buying or selling, will destroy every black market in Asulon. Theft will be a thing of the past. Only criminals need fear our system."

"Perhaps Argeus fears that one day things that are now legal would be made illegal," said Sargon, before someone else raised the point better.

"Balderdash!" replied the ex-senator. "New laws that outlaw formerly legal things pass the Senate every day, and you don't see the prisons overflowing with common citizens now, do you? No, the common man learns to conform to a new law like a horse to a new rider. The people do not riot, cause chaos or revolt because they know that the majority of laws are, in the end, made for their benefit. They abide by them. The few troublemakers there are, are soon found out and sent off to prison. The transfer boxes will simply mean that the foxes cannot stay underground for long."

"Do not forget," said an owner of a large western bank, "how much our houses would prosper with such a system. No more bits of parchment to be carried back and forth between merchant and banking house, no more fraudulent writs, no more 'my boy will send round your payment in the morning.' The savings to our houses on clerks alone will be monumental. We will be faster, more efficient and much more profitable".

He addressed Sargon. "And now you tell us Argeus wants to stop this progressive move that will end so much crime in Asulon and profit us all?"

Well done, thought Sargon.

"He does, and it goes beyond any prejudice to progress he has shown in the past," said Sargon. "If he succeeds, millions that should have been ours will be lost."

He fell silent, allowing that last sentence to sink into their minds and do its work.

"That man is impossible to deal with," said the shipbuilder. "This is not the first time his actions have cost us. Remember what he did to us with the Senate's terms. Only two terms per senator! Now many in the Senate think they no longer need our gold or our council. Half the old Senate gone, and what did those new fools do once they came to power? Pass that idiotic sales tax law, undoing all we have worked so hard on these many years."

The new tax system was simple, direct and fair and thus hated by many who had used the old system to gain and retain power. Men, including many in that room, who had never paid any great amount in taxes before, now had to pay the same percentage as every other person in Asulon, which rankled them to no end. Politicians, from senators to local magistrates, who had previously made millions by changing the tax laws to favor one group or another for a time and then made millions more to change the laws back again, now had no say in how taxes were collected. The powerful men in this room now had one less avenue to corrupt officials and influence policy. Argeus, in their eyes, was the ultimate author of this tax law, for he made it possible for these new senators to be elected and thus pass the law: and that was a wound they would never forgive.

Sargon looked around the room and saw men almost visibly shaking with rage. In his mind's eye he saw them as a pack of caged wolves, snarling and snapping, fangs dripping hatred, eager for the cage door to fly open so that they could tear their prey apart.

"Argeus is the wrong king for this time," said the fat banker.

"Argeus is a senile old fool and should not be king at *any* time," called out another man, giving voice to what they all had been thinking.

"Argeus's son is not yet of age to become king," said Sargon, "and Argeus himself will not step down until the prince returns from his training in Logres ten years from now. If Argeus's term ended *prematurely*, for whatever reason, Aram, his Prime Minister, would be made steward-king until the prince's return." He looked around the room. "I have it on good authority that Aram would be far more reasonable in regards to our plans than Argeus. Remember, gentlemen; a steward-king may propose a law as easily as any king."

He paused for a moment, then, giving each word careful emphasis, he said, "Just as men are not immortal, neither are their laws. What one man has brought to life, another man may *kill*."

The room grew deathly silent as each man weighed the risks of what hung unsaid in the chamber.

Then the cold hard men in the room looked into the cold hard eyes of their neighbors and found agreement.

"Are we of one mind, then, that this problem should be dealt with expeditiously?" asked Sargon.

"Yes," said the southerner. "Aye, let it be as you say," said another. One by one they gave their consent.

"I will see what can be done," said Sargon, smiling within himself.

The meeting ended and the men in the room made their way to the door without a word. The chamber door closed and Sargon had the room to himself. After a moment he heard a slight scraping of stone behind him, but did not turn around. He knew the sound of the concealed door opening. Only he and one other knew of its existence, or of the tunnel behind it.

"Sargon, you did well, but you did not do all," said a voice from the tunnel's entrance.

Sargon turned to face a man so old and gaunt that Sargon wondered, each time they met, that he could draw breath, let alone walk. The old man's thin skin stretched like parchment over his bare skull. His bony hands were all protruding knuckles and twisted blue veins. His white robes hung loosely about him and overly long in back, so that they hissed against the floor when he walked. Sargon always believed that the effect was deliberate. He reminded Sargon of a very old and angry cobra searching for one last victim to set his fangs into before he died.

Sargon bowed his head and greeted the old man in the expected manner. "Welcome, Aesculapius, Master of the Great White Brotherhood, Greatest of the Round Table of Nine, Philosopher-King of Philosopher-Kings. High Priest of the Illuminati, I greet thee."

Aesculapius bowed his head in acceptance of the praise, though he knew that Sargon was loyal to no one but Sargon.

The old sorcerer came to the council table and sat down, taking Sargon's seat at the head of the table.

"You made no mention of our agreement regarding Prince Daniel at your council with the merchants," said Acsculapius. He pronounced 'merchants' with a hiss, as if the word were distasteful to him.

"Our own discussions about the prince do not concern them," replied Sargon. "Keeping *one* secret of this size will be difficult enough without compounding the problem with *two*."

Aesculapius' eyes grew cold. "I have told you that both Argeus *and* his son represent a danger to us–the son more so, for the prophecy concerns the boy. The father merely sired him."

"Prince Daniel can be dealt with much more easily in Logres, in a hunting accident perhaps, than here with his father's guards watching," replied Sargon.

The moneylender hated these religious fanatics, but Sargon needed the Illuminati for their control of the secret of the transfer boxes. Whether, as he sometimes suspected, they stumbled upon some long dead alchemy or, as they claimed, they created it themselves, he could not say with any certainty. But he did know that they held the keys to the success of his grandest plan. He himself could never be king in Asulon, but what if he could choose and control the next king? Would that not be just as good? The transfer boxes would give him the power to do precisely that.

Aesculapius tilted his head back and closed his eyes.

Oh no, thought Sargon, *here it comes*.

The sorcerer began to speak in a low, nearly breathless voice.

In fire's ring, where angels sing,
In holies' home, sheathed in stone.
Where blood was spilt, one for all,
To make amends for the Fall.

The first of swords awaits the finding,
Of one whose oath, blood is binding.
Wisdom, strength, honor finding,
To whose arm the sword is binding.

"When we received this prophecy we were glad," said Aesculapius, "for we thought that it foretold this great weapon, the first of swords, given into our hands. But then another prophecy came. Destiny, it seemed, had given us a rival. And that second prophecy was this.'

When True West's king dies without heir,
And elder successor marries the fair.
Scion lone shall find under stone,
The first of swords, in fire's home.

Awaits your master an avenging death,
Ashes for words and smoke for breath.
In all the world there is no room,
For your prince to flee his doom.

"Yes, yes, you have told me of these prophecies from your soothsayers before," said Sargon.

Aesculapius' eyes snapped open as he turned on Sargon. "They were given in the year of Argeus' birth, though at that time we had no way of knowing that they referred to him. Now we have seen with our own eyes King Absalom die without an heir and Argeus, with a lone male offspring, take his place on the throne. We did not wish to move against the House of Asher directly, hoping that the greatest of weapons would be delivered to us before this day. But my Master does not wish to wait any longer."

"Your *master*?" Sargon was surprised. Aesculapius never before had referred to any authority in the Illuminati higher than himself.

The old man's eyes came alive. "A man, great in power and secret knowledge, like one of the Enlightened Ones of old, is our earthly prince and our strength. He must live, for if he dies my order dies with him. My Master's Master has ordained it!"

His 'Master's Master'? thought Sargon. *This old scarecrow never speaks but in riddles.* Sargon tired of Aesculapius more quickly than usual. But he smiled when he answered nonetheless.

"I did not appreciate the urgency of the matter. It will be my pleasure to see to a result that pleases you, *your* master, *his* master and any other masters you have."

"Do not even *think* to patronize me, child," snapped the sorcerer, eyes flashing. "You will do as I say to gain your precious black boxes. But know this: Prince Daniel will be dead before he leaves Asulon or you will stand before us and explain why you failed."

With that, Aesculapius turned and disappeared into the blackness of the tunnel. Sargon pressed the concealed lever and the door closed, the wall becoming a wall once more. He stood for a time staring at the wall, then, satisfied that the sorcerer would not return, closed the hidden grate that had allowed the sorcerer to hear what was said in the room.

Pity I can't have the tunnel sealed up with that snake within it, he thought.

Sargon knew he could deal with this new law Argeus proposed. In fact, it would serve him well, for it ensured that every Guild member's hands were as bloody as his. They would not dare give his name in any future investigation, lest they be caught up in the net as well. All in all, the death of Argeus would strengthen Sargon's position as leader of the Builders Guild. The Guild would never know that the king's death had been planned long in advance, and had been ordered by those outside of the Guild. To the retired senator, the fat banker and the others, it would be Sargon who had killed a king, it would be Sargon who could get big things done quickly.

Sargon found that he was suddenly very hungry. A bowl of apples, a remnant of the previous autumn's crop had been brought up from the cold cellar and set upon the council table. Sargon reached out and took the topmost apple from the pile, knocking two more apples from the bowl onto the table. About to put them back into the bowl, he stopped, held up the first apple and smiled.

Here we have useful fools like Dew, Sargon thought to himself.

He held up a second apple before him. *And here, the pack of wolves I lead, but dare not turn my back on.*

He placed both pieces of fruit in his left hand and took up a third in his right. *And here we have those lunatics of the Illuminati.*

Smiling to himself, he tossed first one apple, then the other, into the air, juggling them.

Keep this one happy, then that one, now this one here.

He kept the fruit flying through the air.

I am not a moneylender, I'm a juggler!

He threw the fruit higher and began to laugh. He tried to catch an apple in his mouth but missed. Sargon bounced the falling fruit off his knee and deftly caught it on the top of his foot where it miraculously stayed balanced. Surprised at himself, he took another apple from the bowl and began to juggle those three while standing on one foot balancing the fourth. Growing more daring, he kicked the apple from his foot into the air and tried to add it to the three but missed and all four apples fell to the floor.

"Well, sir," he said out loud, "you should know how to quit while you are ahead–and you do."

Sargon left the chamber.

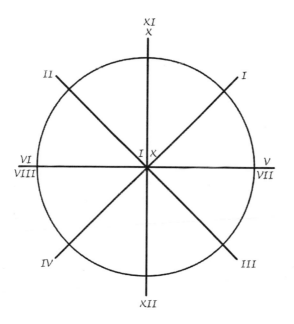

Chapter Four
SWORD AND COMPASS

Train up a child in the way he should go: and when he
is old, he will not depart from it.
-The Book of Proverbs- 22:6

The day of Daniel's departure feast arrived. Friends
and relatives, politicians and merchants had
gathered at the fortress since the day before. Most
young men of the House of Asher left Asulon for Logres
as the sons of mere paladins, not the king himself. Since
the king's very own son was making the journey to
Logres, the event would have to be worthy of the king's
house. The festivities would begin at noon and last long
into the night. A daylong tournament would be held
with contests in jousting, archery, pole-arms, and long
and short swords.

The feast traditionally ended with the departing young man showing his prowess with a weapon of his choosing. Daniel chose the sword. Now he spent his morning practicing with wooden swords against Moor in the fortress armory. When Moor broke one during an attack on Daniel, he decided it would be a good time to sit and rest a moment. Daniel reminded himself that his teacher was forty-five years old and of common blood. He could only keep this pace up for a short time compared to an Asherite. Moor poured himself a mug of the strong tea he favored and took a sip.

"Remember, Daniel, the strength of the paladin's battle sword lies in its versatility," said Moor. "Your father and the other paladins will look for that when you wield the sword."

Daniel, shirtless and sweating, nodded his head at his teacher's words. After three hours of practice, Daniel still breathed easily. The endurance of the giant sons of Anak, the Anakim, was one of the many benefits of carrying Anak's blood in one's veins. Two of the walls held weapons of various sorts. Tables lined a third, each with a shallow sand tray for drawing troop arrays and movements. The fourth wall displayed a diagram that looked like an eight-spoked wagon wheel, with four lines bisecting a circle. These lines represented the eight basic cutting angles for the sword. In various places, numbers marked the lines. Points at the bottom, center and top of the wheel signified the targets for the thrust: hips, heart and head. A similar diagram showed the eight cardinal directions of footwork. A variety of triangles, squares and diamonds on the floor showed advanced footwork patterns. A drawing of a man in full armor flanked the wheel on the wall, showing points in the armor vulnerable to attack with a sword. The training wall at Daniel's home held similar drawings.

Daniel remembered his first sword lessons with his father as a boy. His training had begun with informal footwork games soon after he could walk. By the age of two he knew the movements of sunwise and counter-sunwise by following the movements of the sundial set in the yard. He learned to turn and face the main points of the compass—north, south, east and west—by the age of three, and could point out more complex directions such as north by northwest by the age of four.

On Daniel's sixth birthday, Argeus brought him into the courtyard and sat him down. He drew two eight-spoked wheels on the wall, a large wheel in front of himself, and a smaller one before Daniel, which the boy noticed (much to his excitement), matched his size exactly. The very center of the wheel was level with Daniel's heart. Argeus drew numbers at the end of each of the eight spokes and on two of the lines themselves. Then he very solemnly told Daniel that he would begin his sword training today. Argeus explained the diagram, then had Daniel trace the lines over and over again with the tip of a stick, while Argeus did the same on the larger diagram next to him.

After Daniel could trace these lines with a reasonable degree of closeness for his age, his father presented him with a wooden sword made "just for him." Daniel remembered being very proud of his little wooden sword. Now his father had him practice his cuts and thrusts, coming close to, but not touching, the wall to gain control and accuracy. He would call out a number and Daniel would have to make that cut or thrust. To keep his young son interested, Argeus made a game of it, calling out two or three numbers at a time for Daniel to follow and then challenging the boy to call out numbers for his father to follow as well.

His father showed him basic sword blocks by drawing the shape of a house on the wall, two angled lines for the roof, two angled beams, two vertical lines for the upper floor and two for the lower. Argeus taught Daniel to move his sword parallel to the lines of the house to block his attacks.

Though training with a wooden sword, Daniel learned to treat it as a real weapon, never striking anything he did not wish to cut. After each training session,

63

Daniel wiped the wooden sword down with an oiled cloth, as if it were made of steel, and placed it upon the sword rack in the family dining hall.

At twelve, Daniel received his first steel battle sword, the sword of the paladins. As long as his arm and meant to pierce armor, the blade was balanced so that it could be wielded with either one or two hands on the grip. In close quarters the sword could also be used like a spear, with the left hand gripping the unsharpened bottom half of the blade for added control; as well as the power needed to thrust through heavy armor. Daniel learned early in his training that striking edge to edge with a sword was only done in the theater. In combat, that would destroy your sword's edge. Instead, (if you did not have your shield, your primary defense) you sought to block your opponent's sword edge with the back or side of your own blade. This required a stout blade, as too thin a blade would bend or break.

Designed as a compromise between exclusively one-handed and exclusively two-hand swords, the paladin's battle sword had a long hilt divided into two types of grip. A steel bellguard protected the right hand. What the sword smiths called a "stick and ball" handle protruded from below the bellguard. This grip was long enough for your left hand to grasp and add power to your cut, but not so long as to interfere with the movement of the sword when swung one–handed. The design of the battle sword's hilt allowed you to start the battle with a sword in your right hand and a shield in your left. Then, if your shield were destroyed during a prolonged battle (which often happened, as an indestructible shield would be too heavy to carry), you could swing your sword with both hands, adding power to your cuts and overcoming some of the advantage of an opponent who still had his own shield.

Small guards had been forged into the blade in two places, where the front edge began, to protect the owner's left hand when using the sword in a spear grip, and where the back edge began, to protect his left arm on a backhand cut. The front guard also helped prevent the sword from penetrating too far on a thrust (a man thrust through with a sword up to the hilt tended to grab his opponent's sword hand, locking the two combatants together long enough for the dying man's comrades to avenge him). The sword smiths had also forged a deep, wide groove into the blade of the battle sword. Called a "blood groove" by those unfamiliar with sword terms, the fuller's groove served two purposes unrelated to blood. On a common sword, the groove lightened the blade while maintaining its stiffness. On the paladin's battle sword, the groove also added thickness to the front and spine of the blade for more control when using the sword in a spear grip. The battle sword was a masterful balance between competing needs of the battlefield. Speed balanced with strength, control balanced with reach.

Six through sixteen: ten long years of training. But to Daniel those years were a joy because he had spent them with his father. Daniel learned his alphabet by following the lines of each letter, written large on the wall by his father, with his wooden sword. Argeus taught him that, while there were ten basic attacks with the long sword and twelve with the short, a man could deliver those attacks in many times that number of ways. He learned attacks, counterattacks and recounters in close, medium and long ranges. He learned attacks against a man stronger than himself and how to smother a faster opponent. He learned how to use a dagger in his left hand when using the short sword. He learned single and double dagger, and the empty hand arts of striking and wrestling.

65

For ten years Daniel learned all these many techniques under his father's hand and eye, until at the age of sixteen he went to the war college at Caurus.

At Caurus, Daniel and the other young sons of paladins learned not only the longer weapons they would need as soldiers: spear, halberd and mounted lance, but also the strategies of warfare needed to lead soldiers in battle. They learned higher academics, what their teachers referred to as 'soft' sciences: history, logic and politics, and 'hard' sciences: chemistry, geometry, physics, and mathematics. The boys did not chafe at their studies, though, as most boys their age would, for they learned each subject with an eye towards using that knowledge on the battlefield.

"This may save the lives of your men one day," their teachers were fond of saying to get their attention.

While most of the boys had hunted since soon after they could walk and shot a bow with deadly accuracy, they took too much time to aim their arrows for the bowmaster's liking. By the time they left Caurus, they could release an arrow at a man-size target two hundred paces away and put five more arrows into the air before the first arrow hit. They spent the first half of their training learning *how* to be a swordsman, an archer, spearman or a mounted lancer. They spent the second half of their training learning *when* and *where* to use such troops. They went from learning single combat to learning mass combat and found that, when they returned to single combat, they fought all the better. Moor, their sword instructor, told them that they learned to be a common soldier in order to be a better leader, and that by learning to be a better leader, they would, in turn, be a better soldier. Moor had many sayings about combat.

"Rightly understand single combat and you will rightly understand war; if you understand war, then you will also understand single combat" and the like. By the time Daniel left Caurus he thought he understood what Moor had meant by his sayings. He also realized that understanding how to do something and actually doing it in the heat of battle while another man tried to take your head off were two different things.

Finished with his tea, Moor crossed to the rack on the wall holding several wooden practice swords. He chose one and began to cut the air with it to test its balance.

"These never feel the same as a real sword, but they will have to do."

The Etruscan's own sword hung in its scabbard on his hip. The leather scabbard lined with metal surrounded the sword like a clam's shell, leaving the front open. This allowed for a lighting fast draw, as the sword came forward out of the scabbard rather than through the top. Moor did not carry a paladin's battle sword, though. He learned his swordsmanship in the lands of the east, and he chose an Eastern design for his sword, which the Asulonian smiths crafted for him. Moor's sword had a broad, thin blade, with a stiff spine and a razor edge, lighter than a battle sword but of the same length. It was meant more for cutting down the sudden assassin than fighting a war. The students at Caurus all called it 'Moor's razor,' (but never to his face). An inscription in Etruscan etched onto the blade read: INCERTUM EST QUO TE LOCO MORS EXPECTET

Moor had translated this to Daniel as, 'It is uncertain in what place Death awaits you.'

Moor took a helmet off a rack. "You have been taught a great deal about tactics, but you must understand strategy as well."

"But we were given many lectures on strategy at Caurus," Daniel said, remembering the long sessions in the study hall.

"Yes, and you probably slept through most of them," Moor replied. "There is a great difference between the learning of tactics and the learning of strategy that is much like the difference between knowledge and wisdom.

Tactics—*how* to swing a sword—can be easily taught.

Strategy—*when* to use such tactics—is a wisdom not so easily taught; you must learn that from experience."

Moor made another cut in the air with the wooden sword, gauging its balance.

"Your problem is that you have spent many years sparring with men of your own house, practicing to fight men who are not. Remember, not all in Anak's court will have his blood," Moor said. "Therefore, not all you meet there will have your endurance. Your current fighting strategy relies far too much on taking advantage of that endurance."

"But how can endurance be a hindrance?" Daniel asked.

Moor put the helmet on and adjusted the chinstrap. "Guard yourself and I will show you."

The older man took a position a few steps away and saluted with his sword. Daniel did likewise and began to stalk the older man, swinging his sword in easy arcs, searching for an opening. Moor stood his ground unmoving. Daniel circled him. Moor turned in place to face Daniel. The younger man tried a series of feinted attacks to draw a response from his teacher. Ever so slowly Moor lowered his sword tip to point towards the floor. Daniel recognized this bait. If he attacked with a cut, his arms would precede his sword. Moor would make a snap cut up from the floor, cutting Daniel's arms with the back edge of his blade. Daniel could counter this bait by thrusting high to the head. This would allow the point of his sword to enter the range of Moor's sword first, forcing Moor to change his snap cut into a parry. If Daniel then changed his thrust into a downward cut, he might be able to cut Moor's weapon arm before the older man could withdraw. Daniel saw all this in the blink of an eye. He did not think about it, because of his training, he just knew it.

Daniel's wooden sword shot forward with a thrust aimed at Moor's helmet. Moor raised his sword tip...and lunged forward. Daniel heard the clang of his practice sword striking Moor's helmet and, nearly at the same time, felt the impact of Moor's sword tip strike him in the chest.

Moor stood up and removed his headgear. "Now, what did you learn from that?" he asked.

"That you are getting slow in your old age," replied Daniel with a grin.

Moor stared at him, waiting.

"Well, I did hit you first," offered the prince.

"Yes," replied Moor, "but in true combat both you and your opponent would have died. Is that how you wish to fight?"

"No, but I still do not follow you."

Moor walked over to a storage cabinet near the door and removed a candle. He turned to face Daniel, extended his right arm out level with his heart, and placed the candle on the back of his hand. In a sudden blur of motion, his hand dropped out from under the candle, drew the sword and cut the candle with a rising backhand, leaving two halves spinning in the air. Before the candle halves could fall more than a hand's width, the paladin made two more cuts, making the two pieces into four and dropping them at his feet.

"No, it is not a slow hand, but a slow mind that we must correct." Moor took a towel from a rack on the wall and tossed it to Daniel. "Here, dry yourself, perhaps it will help you think more clearly."

"Yes, Master Instructor Moor," said Daniel, slipping back into the address he used for his teacher when he began training with the Etruscan five years before.

Moor took a seat at the table. "Come." He nodded to the seat opposite him. "This is a lesson you can sit for."

"Do you remember the sign I affixed over our training hall at Caurus?" Moor asked once they were seated.

"Yes, of course: *'Nobilis Vos Esto'*," Daniel replied, "'Be Noble'. My friends and I used that as a farewell after your class. It became something of a byword for us, like a secret handshake."

"And do you know why I hung those words above my hall?" Moor asked.

"You told us it was to embody all the high things of the paladin's code in just three words." Daniel said.

"Yes, it is that. It is also more," said the Etruscan. "To me, those words embody not only twelve ideals, but also one man, your father."

The older man stroked his beard for a moment in thought. "You know, your father saved me from the gallows."

"What?" Daniel looked up in surprise. "If you were charged with any capital crime, I have never heard of it."

"No, no, I committed no such offense," replied Moor. "At least, not in this country," he added with that half-smile of his. "But I would have if I had not met your father.

"When I first came to Asulon I was like a sword without a scabbard: sharp and fast and ready for use. I was thirty years of age, bitter and angry, with far too much experience in the world. I came here because I had heard that a bold, skillful man could make a fortune in Asulon. But what skills did I have but those of killing? When I landed here, I intended to hire myself out, on the surface as a bodyguard, but secretly as an assassin.

"You know that I am Etruscan by birth, but fate led me far into the East. There I did many things. I sailed with corsairs, I rode as a caravan guard on the Silk Road; I trained and led men in battle. I forged myself into a warrior just as smith would a sword, through fire and pain. Each victory fed the next. I grew proud of my skills and far too ready to prove them superior to that of any other man.

"But, still I wanted more. A desire grew in my heart to perfect my skill, so I hired myself out as an assassin. Soon my reputation grew among the powerful who wished to retain their power. I became the royal assassin for an eastern king and did his bidding for two years before even he grew to fear my skills. One day he invited me to dine with him, something he never did with his servants. I knew that either he would reward me beyond what we had agreed upon or he would poison me at diner.

"I left the country that very day.

"So I came to Asulon to make my fortune, but, before making that fortune I would first have to make a name for myself.

"I landed in Asulon at the harbor of Eboracium and entered myself in a tournament being held there. Some of your people had also entered the tournament for the sport of it, and I watched their matches before mine came up. I had heard only a little about the Asherites before I came here, so I was not sure what I was seeing at first. But then I noticed something strange about the way the men of your house fought."

"Strange," asked Daniel.

"Oh yes, very strange to my eyes back then," continued Moor. "The Asherites did not try to win; at least not at first. They would not allow themselves to lose, but they fought just hard enough to protect themselves and keep their opponent moving. They would keep at long range, defend against an attack, give a counter cut or two and then wait for their opponent's next attack. Then I saw their strategy. This back-and-forth volley would go on for a time, but eventually the commoners they fought would tire and make a mistake. Then your kinsmen would strike a true blow and end the match."

71

Daniel nodded, understanding the wisdom of such a strategy. If you had better endurance than your opponent, then it was wise to press him just hard enough to keep him moving and wait him out.

Moor continued. "The matches between your kinsmen and the commoners were interesting, but by no means beyond the norm. In the match before mine, however, I saw something that almost caused me to leave the tournament. Two men of your house paired to fight. In the beginning of their match, they looked much the same as any good swordsmen I have seen, but it was what they didn't do that unmade all my prior experience."

Daniel looked at his teacher puzzled. "And what did they not do?"

"You grew up watching the men of your house train," said Moor, "so you cannot understand the impact such things have on common men. Oh, I saw nothing unusual at first. At the command to fight, they began to circle each other looking for an opening. They clashed and it resembled the clash of many other swordsmen I've seen. Normally, when two men come together like that in battle, they exchange two or three, perhaps as many as five or six, attacks. Usually this ends the fight, as at least one of the cuts or thrusts will get past a man's defenses and strike home. If all the attacks are well met during a clash, then the two swordsmen will retreat a pace and return to circling each other looking for another opening. After a few such clashes, they retreat, as much to catch their breath as to rethink their strategy.

"Well, when your two kinsmen clashed, five quick blows were blocked and returned, then ten, then twenty. They clashed and did not stop."

Moor saw Daniel's puzzled look and said, "That is my point. *They did not stop.* For almost an hour they did not stop or slow or falter. For all that time they fought at a speed most good men can only maintain for the first few breaths of a fight. It was like watching a man run at a full sprint for ten leagues.

"Near the hour mark, one of the hickory practice swords finally broke. The two men stopped and, not waiting for the judge's decision, walked off arm in arm like brothers, laughing, neither even breathing hard."

Moor's hand came up to stroke his beard, his brows knit together, remembering that day.

"I did not know what to do. Should I fight only to lose and throw away my chance of making a name for myself? Should I join the ranks of those who forfeited matches once they saw that the House of Asher was fighting that day? Then it came to me. If I could not win by leaving the field of battle 'alive', at least I would be known as one who did not allow his opponent to survive the battle, either.

"As I said, I saw that your kinsmen did not try to win in the first moments of battle, but waited for their opponent to tire and make a mistake. I would use this as the first part of defeating them. The other part came from the fact that all their commoner opponents had tried to win. The men of Asher counted on that. While they were all good swordsmen, the Asherites were young and familiar with fighting only other good swordsmen, and so expected their opponent to make the 'right' moves in a fight. When attacked they usually just blocked, but when they did not, they would counter in such a way as to threaten a vital target of their opponent. This would force the opponent to change his attack into a block so as not to be cut. Therefore, I planned *not* to block."

"Not to block?" exclaimed Daniel. "*That* was your big plan to defeat my kinsmen."

"Essentially, yes." replied Moor. "When attacked, I would also attack. Since it is difficult to both attack and defend simultaneously with a single weapon, I hoped to cause a draw in each match. Not that I attacked blindly. At the start of each match, instead of attacking, I held my ground and waited for my opponent's attack. My opponent would throw feints and false charges to draw me out, but I just stood there. I kept my sword lowered so they could not strike it aside and enter, and just stood there. Once they saw that I would not be drawn out by feints, they would make a true attack. I did not try to block this as they expected me to, but instead made the 'wrong' attack—one that their weapon was not in position to block, but one that would also leave me open to attack.

"The first time I tried this it surprised my opponent so much that he attempted to block my sword anyway and I scored a killing point unharmed. Seeing this, my next opponent was more cautious. He charged with a midline thrust that could easily be converted to a number of different blocks. Instead of retreating, I countercharged with the same thrust. He parried my thrust, so I simply kept going, crashing into him and sending both of us to the ground. As we struggled for control of our swords, I pulled a wooden dagger from my belt and 'stabbed' him with it. Since the stab was in the heart, I thought it would count as a killing wound. It did, but not a disabling one (I did not know much about Anak's blood back then).I rose and my opponent made a cut which I only halfheartedly blocked. Such was its power that it pushed aside my block and scored a kill. So this match was a draw. One win and one draw. If I could win the next match, I would be allowed to advance to the next rank of fighters.

"By the third match, my opponent thought he knew my strategy, but knowing and defeating are two different things.

"My opponent thought he would turn the tables by trying my stratagem against me. We squared off and began our match. He made a straightforward cut towards my head. I made a thrust. Neither of us turned aside, so we both hit and 'died'—a draw for that round. He would thrust and I would thrust and we both died—another draw. Time after time we both scored and both 'died.' After it became apparent to the judges that neither of us would survive the match, they declared us both 'dead.'

"I began to remove my armor, happy at least that I was the only commoner who did not allow a warrior of Asher to pass me alive. Then one of the judges bade me stay for one more match. He pointed to an older man who sat among your kinsmen. This man had not fought, but seemed only to be accompanying the young men to the tournament. Now he donned armor, took the place opposite me and saluted. I returned the salute and lowered my sword as before. He did not wait, but charged, pulling his arm back for a thrust. I stood my ground and waited for him to get within range. I made my thrust, expecting him to impale himself on my blade as I felt his own sword point strike me in the chest. At the last possible moment two things occurred; he stopped his charge just short of my sword's tip and threw his own sword, sending it flying towards my face like a spear. The wooden sword struck me in the visor and surprised me for a moment. In that moment, my opponent sprung forward, slapped aside the flat of my blade and was on me. Instinctively, I pulled my sword arm away from him to make a disarm more difficult. As I did, he drew my own wooden dagger from my belt and stabbed me with it at the back of the neck, ending the match. He saluted and I did likewise, not knowing whether to be angry or impressed at the way he bested me. We removed our armor and he invited me to sup with him that evening.

"Do you know who that man was?"

Daniel shook his head.

"Your father." Moor said. "We ate together that night and talked until dawn. Your father told me that I did as well as I had against my first three opponents because they were young and, though well trained, were used to fighting only other well-trained men. He, on the other hand, had experienced war and had fought a variety of men, including the very frightened and poorly trained, who, in the heat of battle, often did foolish things. Both your father and I knew that even a fool's attack can kill you, if it is unexpected. Also dangerous is the overmatched, but courageous man. He knows his opponent's skills are superior to his own, but is determined not to let his be the only blood that stains the earth that day. So he makes the 'wrong' attack, one that leaves him no protection, but will likely succeed if you do not anticipate it.

"Daniel, I tell you these things as a lesson. Remember it. You cannot expect all your opponents to fight like you. You cannot always think, *What would I do in their position?*

"You are not them and they are not you. Your father learned to expect nothing and everything, and so was never surprised in battle. You must do the same."

"But how can you expect both nothing and everything at the same time?" asked Daniel.

"By looking at your opponent as both a wise man and a fool, as both hero and coward," replied Moor. "You know how to fight wise heroes, and so may be defeated by a foolish coward."

This drew a smile from Daniel.

"Oh, it is not something to grin at," said Moor. "Dead is dead, no matter who kills you.

"Soon you will be studying in Anak's fortress. You will not be the only young warrior there. Caer-Albion is one of the largest fortresses in the world and it always houses a large population within its walls. A chambermaid could work her whole life at the north side of the fortress and never meet a chambermaid who worked at the south side.

"Duels in Anak's court are rare these days, but they do still occur. Many in the Unicorn Kingdoms envy the position the House of Asher holds with Anak and would make any excuse to challenge you. Avoid these duels when you can. Remember, it is wiser to apologize to a fool than to cross swords with one. When you cannot avoid a duel, do not let them goad you into making the challenge first. Let them challenge you, so that, as the challenged party, you may choose the weapons, time and place for the duel. Choose the weapon you are most skilled with, on ground best suited for that weapon and, if known, at a time most unsuitable for your opponent."

The sword master clasped his hands behind his back and paced back and forth as he did when lecturing a class at Caurus.

"Other great houses send sons to Anak's court to study. All the kings of the west do so. There will also be craftsmen, artisans, merchants and tradesmen of all sorts at his fortress. Those not from noble houses will not normally challenge you on their own accord, but that does not mean that they might not be hired to test you while others watch to learn your fighting style. Be courteous to all, but be wary of all.

"If you must fight, remember how I fought your kinsmen in the tournament. I have tried to break you of bad habits by putting you against two or three opponents at a time in sparring, but nothing I can do in training can duplicate true combat with your life at stake. Think of any fight not as a duel between equals, but as war. Imagine that those you love most are in danger and your opponent blocks the only path to save them. Do not think time is on your side. Therefore, do not just *fight* your opponent: go *through* him, as quickly and efficiently as possible. True combat is not a game. You must cut down your opponent with a cold, controlled hatred and then immediately forget about him and move on. Do not think about winning, only cutting and moving."

While Daniel was still trying to figure out the difference between winning and cutting, he remembered something else Moor had said.

"But, wait—you said my father saved you from the gallows. How?"

Moor returned to his chair and took a long sip of tea. He stared into the mug a moment before replying.

"As I said," he began, "I planned to take up the trade of assassin when I first came to Asulon. But such men inevitably end up dead: either when a victim has better security than expected or when the authorities catch them or, as almost happened to me, when their masters come to fear them and have them killed. The night your father and I met, we talked long into the night about many things: war, politics, philosophy, religion. I told him how all the people of my village were betrayed and killed during a war. I said to him, boasted really, that because I had lost everything, I did not fear to die. I had beaten many men in combat for that very reason. They cared whether they survived the fight and I did not.

"I was a very bitter man then, for my life had no purpose, no meaning."

Moor leaned forward in his chair and focused his dark hawk-like eyes on Daniel.

"We spoke of many things that night, but one thing your father spoke of changed my life."

"What is that?" asked Daniel.

"When I first set foot upon the shores of Asulon, I knew and cared only for strength of arms," said Moor. "I grew to manhood in a world where a strong sword could change the law to suit your will, where might made right. Your father taught me another way. Not that naive tale that 'right makes might', for a sharp sword will cut through a righteous man as easily as an evil one. No, your father taught me something useful, that righteousness and truth stand alone, in and of themselves, and that they exist whether men recognize them or not, whether a good or evil man has won the day.

"Your father won me over with the logic of his argument. He described truth as being like the measurement of a tree. You might say that a tree measures five fathoms tall and I might say seven. Thus we have only two possibilities: one of us is right and the other wrong, or that we are both wrong–the tree being of some other height. In any case, my cutting off your head will have absolutely no effect on the height of that tree. Nor will that diplomatic lie that 'we can both be right' change the dimensions of our tree one bit. No, truth remains truth, no matter what men think or do or say. Our task lies in whether or not we recognize that truth when it comes before us.

"Your father told me that Asulon had begun to fall into these evil ways, where 'might made right', though here a fat purse, rather than a strong sword, became the weapon of choice.

"'But', your father said, 'there is still time for Asulon to change.' Many men in the land still thought as he did and he asked me to join them in restoring the old ways of honor, courage and virtue, the ways that said great men should serve the truth and not the other way around. What your father showed me was me a nobler way to take revenge on the kind of men who killed my family than simply becoming richer than they through the same means they used.

"Though new to Asulon, I had heard much of it in my travels. In Asulon a man could make his own destiny, no matter what his birth; in Asulon all men, rich and poor, high and low, obey the same law. I put my faith in *that* Asulon before I came here; the same Asulon your father remembered from his youth. But in this generation he could see a change coming, a change led by men of wealth and power, men whose gold came from Asulon, yet who hated Asulon. Men who thought none wiser than themselves, and believed they deserved to rule all, men who spoke of loving 'the people', but who did not trust those same people to govern themselves.

"Your father set himself against these men and their plans for Asulon. Your father strives to protect Asulon, but not just the country, the idea that a man, no matter his birth, lives free to choose his own path, to rise or fall, prosper or fail, build or travel or buy or sell, all on his own, and no other man—be he captain of wealth or king of the land—may tell him otherwise. This, then, is your father's Asulon, a land where all men stand equal in the eyes of the law."

Animated now, Moor rose from his chair and walked over to the sand table, picked up a wooden stylus and began to draw in the sand.

"Your father spoke to me about the genius of Asulon. How the founding laws set a balance between freedom and safety."

Daniel saw that Moor had drawn the four points of the compass in the sand, each marked with its respective direction.

"Your father called this theory 'Asulon's Compass.' On this compass the four cardinal points, West, East, North, and South, represent four types of government," said Moor, pointing to each.

"To the extreme West lies the land of Anarchy. Here each man rules himself and does what is right in his own eyes. Nothing in this land protects the weak from the strong. In this land of pure democracy, the majority rules," Moor's eyes glinted in what served him as a smile. "But, of course, in a pure democracy, you often have five wolves and one sheep taking a vote on what to have for dinner."

He thrust the stylus into the sand at the eastern end of the compass.

"In the extreme East we find the land of Absolute Monarchy, where one man rules over all. The people here have nothing to fear from a king perfect in wisdom and goodness, but a foolish or evil king can make this realm hell on earth. Whole peoples can be slain if one of them displeases the king."

Moor then moved the stylus to the top of his compass.

"In the extreme North lies the land of Unchanging Law. A law made here cannot be changed. This may be good when a law is well made, for it allows men to keep their heads in times of trouble. Not all the laws here will be perfect though, for men make laws and men are not perfect. An evil ruler can run afoul of his own law in this land and so takes care in what he orders, but even bad laws cannot be corrected here, no matter how flawed."

He moved the stylus again.

"In the extreme South lies the land of Ever-changing Laws. Engaging in any activity here means a daily gamble. In this land, men live in fear that they may do something illegal even though their actions were legal the day before. Men spend all their time trying to predict the ways the law will go, as a sailor in uncharted seas spends all his time predicting when a reef will appear. So they go forward slowly, if at all."

Moor lifted the stylus from the sand and began to circle it over the table.

"What, then, to do? Where shall a people live and have both freedom and safety? Go too far one way and the strong shall have freedom, but the weak shall live in fear. Go too far another and the people shall live safely for a time, but as slaves under masters who 'know better then they' how to run their lives."

Moor now thrust the stylus into the very center of the compass.

"Here, your father explained to me, in the center of all, lies the course between these extremes.

The Elder Laws of Asulon sought to take this course, to hit the target at the very center and so strike a balance between safety and freedom, progress and stability.

"To guard the weak from the strong, the Elder Laws recognize certain rights given, as your father said, 'by God to all men', as the Ten Sacred Rights, beyond the touch of government or of our fellow men. Instead of pure democracy—all the people voting on every law—elected men represent the people's interests; your senators vote on the laws of the land. But even they must still fit their laws within the framework of the Sacred Rights.

"To prevent one man from ruling all men, laws control the king. A strong king, vital in times of war, rallies the troops and gives them courage. He acts as a father figure and comforts the people in times of trouble. Yet the king does not control the treasury. He can propose a law, but only the representatives of the people can pay for the law's implementation.

"The Elder Laws also keep Asulon centered between unchanging and ever-changing law. Among the greatest works of wisdom man has written on earth, the Elder Laws can be changed if two-thirds of the people of Asulon agree to the change. Perhaps being human, the founders of this country did not hit the perfect center of their target. But having this center as a target has helped keep the people of Asulon free, and done much to prevent her leaders from straying too far in any direction.

"Above all else, your father desires to bring Asulon closer to its center. His enemies name him an extremist and say he wishes to move Asulon one way or the other, but, in truth, he intends to return it to the Elder Laws, to its center, where the weak are protected and the strong are free. In your father's vision of Asulon, I finally found a purpose for my life, an idea worth fighting for and even worth dying for."

Moor looked up at the window, judging the daylight outside. "You'll be needed at the tournament soon," he said. "Before you go I have one last piece of advice." He paused. "Recite for me the Paladin's Code."

Daniel began to recite. "Discipline, loyalty, courage and humility—practice these and you will be a good warrior. Wisdom, charity, honor and justice—practice these and you will be a good king. Faith, truth, mercy and love—practice these and you will please God."

"I know nothing about pleasing God," said Moor, "and you had best watch your father if you want to be a good king one day. But I do know something about being a warrior. Discipline, loyalty and courage are easy to explain, but have you ever wondered why humility is on that list?"

"No," replied Daniel. "The Code is so old, I never thought about why each thing in it is there."

"Well, then, I shall tell you," Moor said. "The Code does not speak of a humility that says you must go about the world with eyes downcast, believing yourself less than all others. No Daniel, you are descended from an angel and from many kings of men. You have sur-

82

vived training that would have killed a common man. These things indeed make you different from other men. No, the Code speaks of humility to remind you that, despite the fact that you have an angel's blood in your veins and kings in your ancestry and have been trained as no other men on earth have been trained, you do not, can not, know everything; not every stratagem of war nor every path through a land you have not walked."

Moor paused to study his student's face for a moment.

"I know this all seems obvious now. But the battlefields of the world are thick with the bones of men whose leaders would not heed the advice of the foot soldier who had fought this enemy before and knew which terrain suited him and which did not or the lowly shepherd who counseled against crossing the mountains in winter, less it sap the army's strength before battle.

"This, then, is the humility of a warrior, knowing that you are never too high to take advice, even when it comes from lesser men.

"So, my prince, I offer this advice to you before you leave Asulon and make your journey across the sea. Heed it, though I descend from no angels or kings.

"War is, ultimately, the art of deception and you, the honest son of an honest man, have not experienced enough of the world of men to know how to deceive. Therefore, be humble in this: you do not know all and even a lesser man can deceive you."

"Ah...yes. Thank you, sir," Daniel said, though he did not yet understand why his teacher was telling him these things.

A bell sounded from the fortress tower.

"It is time for the tournament to begin," said Moor, rising to his feet. "Your parents await you. Enough of these dry lessons. Today you shall fight!"

Chapter Five
THE TOURNAMENT

He teacheth my hands to war...
-The Book of Psalms- 18:34

Daniel sat beside his parents at the tournament grounds, with a watchful Moor a few steps away. The tournament began outdoors before the castle, where jousting runs had been built.

These days, heavily armored lancers jousted more for sport than for military practice, as current military theory did not use lancer against lancer in battle. Generals now used heavy lancers to break the lines of foot soldiers. They countered lancers, not with other heavy lancers, but lines of spear men; each in the line alternating between spear and halberd: the spears to halt the horse's charge and the halberds to pull the lancer from his horse or split him in place with the pole-mounted axe. Then men with war hammers could surround a downed lancer and punch through his armor with the spiked end of their hammers. Battles were no longer about men with equal weapons testing their skill against each other, but rather a strategy of what type of weapon countered another and where to place your troops. Modern warfare resembled a game of 'rock, paper, scissor,' and the winner was the one who successfully used his "rock" troops against the "scissor" troops of the opposition.

Battles between foot soldiers interested Daniel the most, though. Only the foot soldiers still fought troops with like weapons. Despite modern strategy where archers, lancers, charioteers, spearmen, engineers of catapult and siege tower often decided the early part of a battle, the foot soldiers always finished the job. Foot soldiers stormed the castle once the rams or catapults did their work. Foot soldiers occupied the conquered land and brought peace. Lancers might break the enemy line, but foot soldiers took advantage of the breach. Archers might start the battle, but foot soldiers finished it. And the foot soldier fought with the sword.

Daniel had always liked the sword because of the skill involved in its use. More techniques existed for the sword than any other weapon. No other weapon was as personal to a man as his sword. Archers, lancers, men with spear and halberd—all other units still had their swords at their sides. You might run out of arrows, your lance might break or your halberd might become stuck in the armor of a foe, but you could still save your life if you had your sword on your hip and knew how to use it. In times of peace when in a town, lancers went without their lance, spearmen did not carry their spears and archers left their bows tied to their saddles, but each man still had a sword on his hip to deter the thief and ruffian.

So, throughout the day, while those not fighting ate and drank, lancers jousted, halberdiers showed their cutting skills and archers shot their targets, Daniel waited for evening and the sword tournament.

Near sunset, the outdoor festivities ended and all moved indoors into the great hall. Tables lined three sides of the hall, with a raised platform occupying an open space in the center of the chamber. On the forth side of the hall, and upon its own platform, sat a lone table and Moor led Argeus, Isoldé and Daniel to their places there.

Daniel caught Moor's eyes scanning the room. "Do you fear an attack even here?"

Moor nodded his head without taking his eyes off the room. "Any time the king changes a law, it will anger someone. When the rich and powerful stand to lose a great deal of money because of that change, you have reason to be afraid."

The Etruscan had archers lining the inner balconies of the hall, with orders to slay any who approached the king or his family without leave. Soldiers stationed in the kitchens oversaw the cooks. The king's bedchamber had been swept for poisoned barbs and the like, and would be swept again later that night. Moor had positioned his most trusted men throughout the fortress. He had done all he could and yet remained uneasy.

The sword tournament would begin with the youngest boys showing their sword forms and basic drills with lightweight wooden swords. The boys marched out as a group and did their forms in unison. At the end of each form they gave their loudest battle cry. This always drew smiles and applause from the spectators, as the little ones tried so hard to look and sound fierce. Group by group, the sons of the paladins demonstrated their skills and fighting spirit for their elders.

Then sparring began with the thirteen-year-olds in full armor. As the groups grew progressively older, they wore less armor. Above eighteen years of age, the young men wore only helmets, fighting gloves and armor over their elbows, knees and groin. Some of the boys fought with the long battle sword. Some fought with a single short sword. Some of the boys fought with two short swords and several of the more experienced young men, with short sword and dagger. The daggers were the size of a paladin's camp knife, with blades no longer than a man's hand: long enough to stab, but too short to parry a sword. Sword and dagger, considered the most complex fighting style, required coordination of two weapons that fought in different ranges with different strengths and weaknesses.

The night wore on and the young men of Daniel's age fought. The prince paid extra attention to these matches, as he would be fighting one of these men during his own bout. A guard captain came with a message for Moor. The Etruscan read the parchment then leaned over to whisper something in the king's ear. Argeus nodded thoughtfully, giving his consent. Moor bowed before the king and left the chamber. Daniel wondered what that was all about as he turned back to watch the matches.

A servant came to him. "It is time, your highness."

The prince turned to his parents. "Well, I'm off." Then an idea occurred to him. "Father, may I ask you something first?"

The king caught the look in Daniel's eye and leaned forward. "Yes, my son."

"This will be the last time you see me fight for a very long time. Bless me that I do well in your eyes."

The king smiled. The request took him back to when Daniel was a young boy and his father's approval meant the whole world to him.

"Of course I will bless you, my son," said Argeus standing. "Come. Kneel before me."

Daniel knelt and Argeus placed his right hand on his son's head. He searched his mind for a blessing about honor and courage, but found himself saying these words.

> *The Lord bless thee, and keep thee.*
> *The Lord make his face to shine upon thee and*
> *be gracious unto thee.*
> *The Lord lift up His countenance upon thee and*
> *give thee peace.*

Daniel looked up at his father and, just for a moment, Argeus saw every joyous moment father and son had spent together flash through his mind. He saw his son's first toothless grin as an infant, their first fishing trip together when the boy turned three, the pride in a nine-year-old's eyes when his father had first taught him to shoot a bow. "Father, watch me," cried a twelve-year-old Daniel as he jumped his horse over a fence.

It struck Argeus hard then that ten years was a long time not to see your only son.

"Thank you, Father." Daniel rose to his feet, kissed his mother on the cheek and followed the servant off. Argeus turned to find his wife studying him.

"You are going to miss him as much as I, aren't you?" Isoldé asked her husband.

"Of course, why do you ask?"

"That was a blessing for a traveler not a fighter," she said with a smile. "Your mind must be on his journey. But now what blessing will you give him in the morning when he leaves us?"

Argeus shrugged his shoulders. "It was the best I could do on short notice. Come now, let us watch the fights."

In a side chamber, Daniel donned his helmet. The protection for his head, hands, elbows and knees had to be battle worthy, as even a wooden sword could break bones. Blows to the muscles of arms or legs were expected to be endured and the resulting bruises were considered a badge of honor among the younger boys.

A soldier at the door nodded to Daniel as he the last piece was strapped into place. "It's time, my prince." Daniel followed him out, wondering whom he would fight. He expected to see his opponent for the match in the changing room with him, one of his friends, with whom he could trade boasts before they went out to face the crowd as much as each other.

Daniel had no fear of sparring; he had done it several times a week, nearly every week for years and knew he would come away with no more than a bruise or two. But he did not wish to embarrass his father and was determined to do well in his match.

Daniel came to the sparring platform. The platform was round, about ten paces in diameter and built at chest level to the seated spectators so that they could easily see the fight. Daniel saw a tall, thickly built man in armor standing across the platform from him, also waiting for the signal to begin the match. Daniel could not tell if muscle or fat bulged beneath the loose black shirt the man wore. He guessed the former, as only a few of the very oldest paladins long retired from service would allow themselves to put on such weight.

I wonder who they have chosen for me to fight? Daniel asked himself. None of his friends were this large. Was this man an experienced soldier perhaps, to test him? A paladin to Daniel's left tied a silk ribbon of blue and red, the colors of Argeus's battle flag, to a ring made for that purpose atop Daniel's helmet. This was so that the spectators would know him in his armor. A paladin near his opponent tied a ribbon of green, white and red onto the heavy man's helmet. Daniel began to run through the battle flags of his friend's families, but could not recall these colors.

As the one leaving for Logres, Daniel got to choose the weapons used in the match. He had chosen the battle sword for the first three points, and the short sword and dagger for the last three. The wooden swords used to spar were not in true scabbards, but held on the belt by a metal clamshell clip. For advanced matches like this, the stairs to the platform were removed. On the signal, both men would leap onto the platform and begin the match. The first moments of the fight tested agility, balance and strategy as much as swordsmanship. Often the man in the best position to draw his sword the fastest won the point. One could leap unto the platform just high enough to land on one knee. This allowed for a quick draw, but, if you missed, you were not as mobile as a man who had taken the time to land on both feet.

"Blue and red," called the officiating paladin" "are you ready?"

Daniel nodded his head.

"Green, white and red, are you ready?" The man nodded.

"Salute the king." Both men turned and gave their salute.

"FIGHT!" cried out the official suddenly.

Daniel turned back and leaped atop the platform. Opting for better mobility, he landed on both feet, then drew his sword. Daniel hesitated for a moment, his opponent nowhere in sight. *He must have ducked down as soon as the fight signal had been given, while I still faced my father.* The prince had an idea where he was going, though. He turned back to face the edge of the platform and reversed his grip on his sword to deliver a downwards stab as soon as his opponent appeared from under the boards. A good trick, running under the platform to come up from behind your opponent, but one had to move quickly to make it work. Daniel waited for the man's helmet to appear from under the platform, planning to strike it just hard enough to get his opponent's attention and score a point.

A moment passed, then another and Daniel dropped, flattening himself out on the platform just in time to see a wooden dagger spinning through the air where he had stood.

THUMP, came a sound from across the platform. Now Daniel saw his opponent standing atop the platform opposite him. The man had simply ducked down at the start signal and waited for Daniel to face to the opposite side of the platform, then thrown his dagger. The man drew his sword and charged. Daniel rolled to his right, came up on one knee and aimed a horizontal cut at his opponent's right leg.

"Tricolor" (as Daniel now thought of him) pulled his leg back just enough to avoid the attack and simultaneously aimed a vertical cut at Daniel's weapon arm. Daniel changed the angle on his cut to convert it into a

90

roof block and transferred his weight onto his back leg, giving him some distance so he could come to his feet. His opponent kept the pressure on him, charging with doubled up forehand and backhand cuts followed by two-handed power cuts. Daniel took these in stride, blocking and looking for an opening. Then Daniel remembered what Moor had told him about the need to end a fight quickly during true combat. Tricolor brought his sword around for a two-handed vertical cut. Daniel made the same cut simultaneously. If neither man changed direction, they would both cut each other for a tie. At the last moment Daniel removed his left hand from his sword grip. Tricolor's sword passed where Daniel's left arm had been just as Daniel's sword cut down on Tricolor's left forearm. Daniel used the pause in his sword's momentum to change the cut into a thrust aimed at Tricolor's heart. As if he had planned the thrust himself, Tricolor turned his body to the side, allowing the thrust to glide past him and launched his own thrust at Daniel's helmet. Daniel managed to bat this away with his left hand, but he had touched the sword's edge when he did, and a real sword would have laid his hand open without an armored gauntlet.

"STOP," cried the judge. "First point tied."

The spectators applauded while Daniel and Tricolor moved to opposite sides of the platform. From now on, if either one stepped off the platform for any reason they would lose the match.

"FIGHT!" came the cry.

Now Daniel charged first. Tricolor countercharged. Daniel faked high, then flowed into a low backhand aimed at the knee. Just before their swords met at the center of the platform, Tricolor leaped into the air, coming over Daniel's head in a somersault, his sword flashing downward. Daniel barely had time to parry the cut as he dropped down under the spinning blade.

Who is this man? Daniel asked himself. He *did* everything Moor had taught him and the other trainees *not* to do. Moor had drilled the words into their heads: "Do not throw your last knife" and "Do not leap at a skilled opponent." Daniel began to wonder if his opponent were a foreigner, but had no time to consider it.

Daniel spun around, aiming a cut at his opponent's back hoping to catch him before he landed sufficiently to spring away. The man landed in a roll, but instead of rising, unwound his body, lying flat on the platform and making a two-handed thrust at Daniel's lead foot. Caught a bit by the strangeness of the technique, Daniel moved his foot back awkwardly. He thought he was safe, but his opponent released his left hand at the last moment, giving more range to his thrust and catching Daniel in the ankle. He rolled away before Daniel could make a counter cut.

"CUT!" cried the judge, pointing to Tricolor. Applause from the crowd, mixed with some laughter from the back rows. *My friends, no doubt*, thought the prince. Daniel realized that he would not be given an easy time of it just because he was the king's son. He faced an opponent quicker than Daniel would have expected for so large a frame, and evidently an experienced warrior. Down a point now, Daniel would have to catch up.

They squared off again and the judge called out, "FIGHT!"

This time Tricolor stood his ground and waited. Daniel swung his sword in slow arcs and began to circle to his opponent's left. Daniel kept his own left side open as bait. *Let us see how clever he is*, he thought. Normally, if attacked from his left, a swordsman could easily step back with his left foot, putting him in the right lead again, with more reach for his sword and just a fraction more time to decide on a counter. But Daniel stalked his opponent from the edge of the platform. If he took a step back now he would lose his balance and either fall off the platform or, at least, move awkwardly and provide an opening for his opponent to attack, while he regained his balance. He hoped that his opponent would think he had fallen back on an old habit and forgotten where he stood.

Tricolor charged with a powerful two-handed vertical cut. Instead of stepping back, Daniel stepped forward with his left foot and went into a spear grip with his sword.

As Tricolor's sword came down, Daniel raised his own sword in an angled block that deflected the force of the cut like rain off a pitched roof. He then brought the pommel of his sword down towards his opponent's helmet. Not a killing blow to an armored man, but one that could stun him even through a helmet. Tricolor shot his left forearm into Daniel's right wrist to block the attack, but this meant he now held his sword one-handed. Daniel used this opportunity to wrap his own left arm counter-sunwise around Tricolor's right, trapping his sword arm in the crook of Daniel's elbow. Daniel raised his own sword arm high and brought the butt down toward Tricolor's head again. Tricolor caught hold of Daniel's wrist to block the attack. Daniel's left arm still trapped of Tricolor's sword arm, but his hand itself was free. Daniel brought his sword arm down sunwise near his own left hand and grabbed Tricolor's right wrist, freeing Daniel's sword arm. Daniel made a backhanded slash towards Tricolor's throat. Tricolor ducked, barely missing the blade and came back up with a head butt, which rang against Daniel's helmet. Daniel released his grip on Tricolor's left arm and caught the dull back of his own sword with his left hand. Turning his wrists so that the edge of his sword faced his opponent's back, Daniel pulled the edge into the bottom of Tricolor's helmet working it into the back of his neck. Just then Daniel felt a blow to his lower back. He looked down to see that Tricolor had turned his wrist in and also taken hold of the back of his own sword with his free hand and pulled Daniel into a bear hug with the sword between his hands. Had they been using real swords, it would be too close to say which would have been severed first, Daniel's back or Tricolor's neck.

93

"STOP," cried the judge. "Both are cut. Tied point."

Daniel handed the judge his wooden battle sword, as did Tricolor. They would now fight with short sword and dagger. Daniel felt more confident now, as the intricate moves and strategy of the sword and dagger combination suited his fighting style. What made sword and dagger fighting so complex was that while the swords made their large cuts and thrusts, the smaller daggers moved in a completely different rhythm, sneaking in and out, attacking between the sword movements. Daniel thought it must be like playing a tune on one instrument with your right hand and another, much quicker tune with a completely different type of instrument with your left, the whole time coordinating the two tunes so that they complimented each other.

Daniel drew his wooden short sword and dagger and waited. He knew that, since Tricolor had thrown away his only dagger, Daniel would have a great advantage in close quarters. Tricolor drew his own short sword and began to circle to Daniel's right. The larger man turned and sprang into an attack with a flurry of quick sword cuts. Daniel met these with his sword, waiting for an opening for his dagger.

Tricolor ended a combination, withdrew and began to stalk Daniel again. Now Daniel attacked with a forehand slash to Tricolor's head. Tricolor made a wall block and quickly converted the movement into a backhand slash aimed at Daniel's neck. Only the most experienced swordsmen in the audience could follow what happened next; the rest saw one quick blur of movement. Daniel met Tricolor's cut backhand with his sword and redirected its force past him while he came up with his dagger thrusting it into Tricolor's chest. Tricolor parried the thrust with his left hand then threw a punch at Daniel's chest, which Daniel blocked with his right forearm, bringing his opponent's arm down. Daniel made a dagger thrust which pinged off the helmet between Tricolor's eyes. Off balance now, Tricolor made a forehand cut, but he was too close. Daniel made a scissoring movement, blocking Tricolor's sword arm backhanded at the wrist with his left forearm while cutting him in the sword arm with a rising backhand cut. Then he hammered Tricolor's helmet with the butt of his sword to knock him back and continued the motion with a diagonal cut to Tricolor's neck.

"CUT! POINT," cried the judge.

That is more like it, Daniel said to himself. They now had one point each. They squared off again.

"FIGHT," cried the judge. This time Tricolor did not wait to attack, throwing himself at Daniel with a series of tight multiple cuts. Daniel held his ground, blocking, evading and throwing counter cuts at his opponent. Tricolor made a backhand slash towards Daniel's head. Daniel met the blow backhanded with his own sword in his favorite scissoring move and struck Tricolor with his forearm at a nerve in the wrist. This opened Tricolor's guard for Daniel's own backhand slash. Tricolor grabbed Daniel right wrist with his free left hand to stop the slash, but Daniel was waiting for just such a mistake. His left hand shot forward and took hold of Tricolor's wrist, catching it between his own thumb and the back edge of his dagger. Daniel then slashed out with his sword, striking Tricolor across the abdomen. Still holding his opponent's left wrist, Daniel circled his right arm around and brought his forearm down on the back of Tricolor's elbow. Not enough to break the arm, the strike still sent Tricolor to his knees.

"CUT! POINT," cried the judge.

Daniel returned to his side of the platform. Tricolor waited a few moments on his knees before rising to his feet. The blow to the abdomen had taken some of the wind out of him. Daniel did not think he hit the man all that hard. None of his friends would have thought it much of a blow. It suddenly occurred to Daniel that the man *must* be a foreigner. Not only did he fight in a different style, but subtle things about the way the man moved told Daniel that he had none of Anak's blood in his veins.

Moor has substituted a foreign soldier to test me, thought the prince. As he watched the man stand at the opposite end of the platform breathing hard, Daniel knew that he must be right.

"FIGHT!" came the cry. Daniel charged forward. Tricolor dropped to one knee and reached under his shirt. Suddenly his left hand blurred as he threw something at Daniel. The prince sidestepped and saw that the projectiles were three wooden darts. Daniel did not have time to consider that this violated tournament rules, for the man sprang to his feet, drawing something from under his shirt–another wooden dagger, which he held in reverse grip. This was not a grip used in "friendly" tournaments, as a stab with this grip, even with a wooden knife, could still break a man's sternum. Daniel knew how to use a dagger in both grips, and knew the strengths and weaknesses of each. With his own dagger in forward grip, he needed to be like a wasp, quick and accurate, staying on the outside to sting and move. Using reverse grip, Tricolor was like a mantis. If Daniel closed to grapple, then the mantis would have him in his grasp and that grasp would be sharp, for the judges would still count a "cut" with the wooden dagger as a point.

The man, no longer breathing hard, circled Daniel in a very determined way. Just then Daniel caught a glint of metal on the dagger. He looked hard at the knife; the wooden blade did not look right. The dagger turned in the light and Daniel saw that it was steel, painted brown to look like wood. The edge had been sharpened after it was painted, revealing the steel beneath. Daniel just had time to think, *Assassin!* before the man charged.

Now it was a very different fight. The man, armed with two weapons, was also incredibly, impossibly, *fast*. Daniel had no time to think of an attack plan of his own;

it was all he could do to keep from getting caught by the man's dagger.

In a tournament with wooden weapons, Daniel could rely on the judge to score any "cut" he made with his wooden dagger. But his opponent had steel and could ignore a "cut" from Daniel's wooden dagger while delivering a killing thrust with his own, very real, blade. Daniel could still thrust with the wooden dagger, but it would feel like a one-knuckle punch and could not be relied upon to down a determined opponent. Daniel's hope lay in his wooden sword, which could still hit with enough force to stun, even through a helmet.

All this flashed through Daniel's mind in the time it took the man to charge towards him.

Daniel charged in response, not straight towards the man, but slightly towards his right. This made his opponent change direction just enough to slow his charge a bit. Daniel made his next four moves almost as one. He sent a backhand cut towards his opponent's head and followed it by his throwing the dagger at the man's eyes (even in a helmet, a man will blink when something comes flying at his eyes). Daniel then grasped his own right wrist with his left for more power and made a forehand cut with all his strength. The man just had time to block the cut. Daniel grabbed the man's right wrist with his left hand and rolled his sword around the block, delivering a backhand strike to the man's helmet that made the steel pot ring. Daniel followed the momentum of the backhand with his body, turning so that he had his opponent's arm extended with his elbow trapped under Daniel's armpit. Daniel then fell to the platform with the man's sword arm trapped under him. The man lay flat on his belly, his right arm stretched out and pinned by Daniel, unable to reach the prince with his dagger.

"Assassin! Guards," Daniel called out, "His dagger is real! Assassin!"

Two burly guards leapt upon the platform, disarmed the man and took hold of him. Once they had brought him to a kneeling position, the judge came forward and removed his helmet. The audience gasped and Daniel stood transfixed, his mind reeling. The assassin was Moor.

"Not too bad for a former wildman of the woods," said the Etruscan calmly. After a moment of stunned silence, a strange sound came to Daniel's ears—a single man laughing. Daniel turned. He knew that laugh.

The king, a great mirth-filled grin on his face came towards the platform followed by several guards.

"Oh, what I would not give to have an artist capture the look on your face right now," said Argeus to his son. The guards holding Moor released him and he stood. They too, grinned from ear to ear.

"Master Moor asked our leave to give you one final test before your voyage to Logres," said Argeus, "something that would seem real and put you in the right frame of mind for true combat. Well, son—did it work?"

With that, laughter again overtook Argeus, great peals of laughter that rang around the chamber. Most in the audience had gotten over their shock and now began to laugh with the king.

Daniel did not know whether to laugh or tear down the castle with his bare hands. Since laughing seemed easier, he decided he would laugh.

"Oh, father, what memories I shall have of this night. And you!" he said, turning and addressing Moor.

"Yes, my prince?" said the Etruscan, as innocently as if they discussed a particularly pleasant bit of weather.

"You have to be the most dastardly, deceitful, deceptive man in all of Asulon," said Daniel with a smile, "which makes me very glad that you are on our side."

Moor gave a slight bow. "Your father charged me with making you the best warrior that you could be. Therefore, how could I do less than all that I do?"

Moor removed his shirt to reveal the thickly padded jacket underneath, which had made him look like a much heavier man. The judge took hold of Daniel's arm and raised it high. "The winner!" he proclaimed and the crowd cheered.

The king and Daniel took their seats and the feast continued. Isoldé "gave her son an amused look.

"Mother, did you know about all this?"

"Did you think your father would have made such a play as this without telling me?" replied the queen. "Can you imagine what I would have thought when you began to cry out 'assassin' and call the guards? Your father would have heard my tongue from sundown to sunup for treating a mother's heart like that, and he knew it too. No, he made sure he told me of Moor's plan beforehand."

Daniel turned to Simon to find that the priest also had a smile on his round face."

"Simon, did you know as well?"

"Oh, yes" he replied. "Your father was concerned I might interfere otherwise, so he informed me of his little plot with Moor."

Daniel wondered how such an old man could have interfered from where he sat, but decided not to ask. He dismissed such thoughts as he found that he was suddenly, ravenously, hungry. *Well, this* is *a feast*, he thought.

After several dishes of beef and lamb and fish, stews and cheeses, sweet potatoes and salad greens, nuts and fruit and many, many toasts to his health and a good voyage, Daniel found his head swimming. Argeus had allowed him only one small goblet of wine at their family dinners at home, and now Daniel knew why. He felt lightheaded and a bit too hot. He caught Argeus appraising him out of the corner of his eye.

"Not used to it, are you?" said the king. "Good wine is usually the strongest, so don't drain your cup at every toast. That's something you should remember when you get to your grandfather's court." He winked. "Not that I've followed my own advice tonight, mind you, but then, a man's only son doesn't go sailing off across an ocean for ten years every day of the week, now does he?"

Daniel noticed that Argeus's face seemed very red. "Father, how much have you had to drink?"

"More than usual, but not more than I can hold," insisted Argeus. He stretched his arms over his head and gave a great yawn, "provided I am not called upon tonight to do anything more difficult than getting into my bed." He offered his hand to his wife and together they stood. Heralds cried out, "God save the King!" All in the great hall rose and bowed to the king and queen.

"Come, Daniel, walk with us," said Argeus. They left the feast chamber and came to the quiet passages leading to the sleeping quarters, Moor and several guards remaining a discreet distance behind as they walked.

Argeus took advantage of the passage, wide enough to walk four abreast. "Son, let us walk with you between us, so your mother and I can each see you while we speak."

He parted from Isoldé so that Daniel could stand between them. Each parent took an arm and the three moved off down the passage. It reminded Daniel of the way they used to walk when he was a young child, each parent holding him by the hand. This time he felt he was leading and protecting them, instead of the other way around. Suddenly he felt a very great reluctance to leave them.

"Tomorrow will be a busy day," said Argeus. "I won't get much of a chance to speak to you in private. I have been trying to think of some advice to give you to-night—something I have not already said. But first, I have a gift."

He drew a sheathed knife from his belt and handed it to Daniel. The prince withdrew the small, plain knife with oak handle from its plain brown leather sheath. A paladin's camp knife—its broad blade was shaped nearly like a kitchen knife, though the spine was sharpened from the midpoint back. The values of the paladins dictated that parents traditionally gave this simple blade, rather than a sword, shield or helm, to their sons before the long journey to Logres. A tool that a servant might carry, the knife reminded the young men that a warrior was a servant of his country, its people and its laws. Burned into the handle were words from the twelve virtues that all young paladins learned: three, his freehold's motto, plus a fourth virtue, one of his parents choosing. Daniel's freehold bore the words *Wisdom, Honor* and *Courage* on its banner. On the handle, Daniel found the fourth virtue, "Faith." He sheathed the knife and put it into his belt.

"Thank you, Father, Mother," said Daniel. "Whenever it is in my hand, I shall remember you both."

"We know that you will," said Argues. He paused, thinking for a moment, as if forming difficult words, then faced his son. "Well, then, I shall now give you my advice. Here it is: trust God."

"I do trust Him, Father," said Daniel, a bit surprised by his father's words.

"Oh, I you know you *believe* in God. How could you not, with your mother's stories of Anak and of his past home in the heavens? But believing and trusting are two very different things," said Argeus, resuming their walk. "All the angels believe in God, even those who oppose Him, but to serve God freely as we were created to, we must also trust Him. We must trust Him like a young child trusts his parents, trusting both in His love *and* in His wisdom. This trust believes that the Lord who made us also knows the desires of our hearts and what will bring us joy, even if the way is difficult at first. And He knows what will bring us pain, though at first it may seem right in our own eyes.

"Daniel, I worry that your life has been too easy so far, that you have not known real pain, that your faith have not been tested. Oh, you have known heat and cold, hunger and thirst and many other trials in your training, but you have not known the greatest pain of all—the pain that comes from the heart. Your faith is like your fighting skill. You have been training for years in all manner of weapons, tactics and strategies. You have sparred with other well-trained men. You have received wounds and given them. But none of it compares to real combat, facing a man trying to kill you. Tonight you may have gotten a small taste of what it feels like, but it still was not the real thing. The real test will come when you have survived true combat and must live with what follows. Just so it is with faith. You must trust God in the darkest hour of your life to know what faith really means. Trust that He loves you and knows what is best for you, no matter how deep the pit you find yourself in, or how mighty the foe set against you."

They came to the bedchamber door.

Argeus placed a hand on his son's shoulder. "So that is my advice to you Daniel: trust God. Trust that if you obey Him and have faith in Him, He will carry you through the greatest of all dangers and give to you the desires of your heart. But remember, you cannot force the Lord God, the Creator of the universe to do things the other way around. You cannot say, 'I will trust Him once He proves Himself by saving me and giving me what I desire.' Remember that, Daniel."

"Yes, sir, I will."

"You know that I am very proud of you," said Argeus, smiling his warm smile, "but you won't know how much until you have a son of your own." Argeus looked long on his son. "You don't know now. But one day, you will."

Argeus turned to his wife. "Come, Isoldé. Let us get to bed and sleep. I think I am feeling every day of my one hundred and twenty-five years tonight."

Isoldé smiled and received her son's kiss.

"Good night, Mother."

"Good night, Daniel," she said, placing a hand on his cheek. "Rest on what your father has told you."

Once they had entered the chamber, Isoldé turned to face her husband, her eyes glistening.

"Of all the battles you have won, all the great things you have done, none has made me more proud of you than what you said to our son tonight."

"Oh, well, it was just the simple truth. That's all," replied Argeus.

"Simple it may be, but not without great power," said Isoldé.

"If he heeds it," agreed Argeus, as he turned down the lamp.

Chapter Six
ASHES AT DAWN

Thou dost not murder.
-The Book of Exodus- 20:13

Daniel awoke and found that it was still some hours before dawn. Enough light came from the glowing coals in the hearth for Daniel to recognize his bedchamber. Though he had enjoyed the remainder of the evening after his match with Moor, he had been ill at ease since returning to his bedchamber and had not slept well. He decided to get dressed. "A long walk will do me good," he said to himself, hoping to shake off the nervousness he felt in the pit of his stomach. He supposed it must be a nightmare he did not now remember, but that his body still felt an echo of.

He entered the corridor and turned right, walking quickly down the hall. Without thinking, he found himself walking towards the wing of the fortress that held his parents' apartments. They were just around the corner; he could stop by and check with the guards stationed before their door. As he drew closer, he heard low voices. He turned the corner and saw Moor speaking to the guards.

"And you have heard nothing amiss all night?" Moor demanded of one of the guards. He looked up and saw Daniel. Just then Simon turned the corner at the other end of the corridor. Moor snapped his gaze from Daniel to Simon, saw the looks on both of their faces, and pushed the guard roughly aside. He knocked on the door. "Your majesty, it is Moor." He heard no reply and knocked more forcefully now. "Your majesty, it is Moor. I must speak with you."

Daniel and Simon arrived on either side of him.

"'Tis no accident that all three of us decided to check upon the king at this same moment," said Simon.

Daniel fought the wave of dread that had come over him when he saw Moor and Simon here. "I will go in to see them."

"You can't," Moor said. "The door is bolted from within." As he finished saying this, they heard the bolt sliding back. The door opened and Isoldé stood before them, binding a robe around her.

Moor bowed, visibly relieved. "My apologies for disturbing you, my queen, but we were concerned and..." He stopped speaking when he saw Isoldé's face.

She stared at Daniel with tears in her eyes.

"Mother, what is wrong?"

Isoldé did not answer, but fell into her son's arms weeping, her composure broken. Moor stepped around her and entered the room.

"Your majesty!" he called out.

Daniel looked into the bedchamber. He saw his father lying in the bed. To Daniel, he looked asleep, but Moor took the king by the hand and said softly, "Argeus." Then he laid two fingers on the artery on the side of the neck, and Daniel knew that his father was dead with a certainty that hit him in the stomach like a fist.

Moor stood by the bed with his head bowed. He took a deep breath, then turned and walked quickly back to the doorway. Daniel could sense the rage building within Moor, but the Etruscan spoke gently to Isoldé. "Lady, tell me—when did you awake and find him this way?"

Isoldé lifted her head from her son's shoulder, her eyes red and wet with tears that she did not bother to brush away. "I awoke just a short time ago. I had such a beautiful dream. Argeus and I walked together, hand in hand in a wonderful garden. And the Lord was with us, speaking to us and answering all of Argeus's questions. It seemed so real that when I woke, I wanted to wake Argeus and to tell him of it. I tried to wake him and he was...he was..."

Unable to say the word, she broke down again in tears.

Daniel knew that his mother must have woken the same time that he did. Is that why he was restless all night?

The queen's maidservants, hastily summoned, now gathered around her.

Moor turned to Daniel. "Go and escort your mother to the chamber of her head maidservant. Wait for me there." He gave a hand signal to a detachment of heavily armed guards who had arrived without Daniel noticing. Daniel nodded to the maidservants and they helped Isoldé down the hall, surrounded by eight of the guards.

Isoldé managed to keep her composure until they reached the maidservant's chamber. Once inside, she fell onto the bed and let out a wail of such utter despair that it could only come from a soul who had lost her one true love. The oldest of the maidservants rushed to her queen's side and held her as one would hold a child, rocking her back and forth as she sobbed. Daniel felt completely useless. He wanted to do something, to break something, to fight something, to have an enemy before him that he could defeat, but he could not defeat death. He looked at his weeping mother and knew he had no words that would comfort her.

Daniel could not stay there and wait, doing nothing. He turned to one of the younger maidservants. "If my mother needs me, tell one of the guards in the hall and they will fetch me." The maid nodded without speaking. She also wept. All the women in the room were crying, which made Daniel feel even more useless. He left the room and shut the chamber door behind him. The guards snapped to attention. "I am going back to my father's chamber," he told them. "If the queen needs me, I shall be there." The guard captain nodded to two of his men, who followed Daniel down the hall.

Outside the door to his father's chamber, he saw Simon speaking with Galen, the royal physician. "What have you learned?" Daniel asked the priest.

"As of this moment, nothing," replied Simon, a great sadness and weariness in his eyes. "We must do some tests which will take some time to complete. Galen and I were about to examine the king, but that is not something a son should see."

"Nevertheless, I wish to see him," said Daniel. Simon, seeing his resolve, nodded.

Daniel opened chamber door and found Argeus just as he had been when Daniel had left the room. Moor slowly pulled a thin silk scarf across one of the bedposts near Argeus's head. He barely looked up when Daniel entered, then went back to his work.

Daniel came round to the side of the bed and looked down at his father. The faintest hint of a smile lay on his lips, as if he were caught in the midst of a pleasant dream when death came for him. A lock of hair lay across Argeus's forehead and Daniel reached down to brush it back into place.

"Touch nothing!" ordered Moor, "Especially your father's body."

Stung by Moor's choice of words, Daniel snapped, "What *are* you doing with that scarf?"

Moor looked up from his work. "I am sweeping the room for poisoned barbs. Anything too small to see, but large enough to kill, can still be detected by pulling a silk scarf across the surface."

Simon and Galen, who had been waiting in the doorway for Daniel to pay his respects to his father, entered the chamber.

"What is this, a market square?" demanded Moor.

"Master Paladin, you know that we must examine the king," replied Galen.

"Moor, it is best that we test the king quickly, before his body has a chance to break down anything foreign in his system," said Simon.

Moor nodded. "Yes, of course, you are right." He rubbed his forehead with his fingertips. "Just give me a moment more. I have searched from the outside of the room in, saving the most obvious place for last."

Moor reached into a bag sitting on the floor and pulled another long silk scarf from it. This he wound around his head several times, covering his mouth and nose. He went to the head of the bed and slowly folded down the covers, bit by bit, examining the sheets closely as he did. At each turn he would take a damp cloth and swab it across the newly exposed section of sheet. When he had folded the covers all the way down, he rolled them into a ball and put them into the bag. "I did not find anything obvious, but I am not surprised in that. Poisoned barbs are unreliable to use. There is no guarantee that the targeted person will prick himself on the barb when you want him to."

"And the bed covers?" asked Daniel.

"I checked for poisoned powders. But any powder that could kill by touch or by inhalation this quickly poses the same problems as a barb: it is too easy for a servant to be poisoned by it first and the plot found out."

Moor caught the look on Daniel's face and spoke before he could ask the question. "No, I do not believe your mother to be in any danger. If the bedclothes were poisoned, your mother would have been affected by it as well."

"You assume my father was murdered?" asked the prince.

"Though not a young man, your father was in good health. Most importantly, he had recently made several
enemies among men of power. Knowing these facts, it is my job to assume the worst and then work back from there," Moor said.

Simon and Galen came forward now and stood before the king's body. They bowed three times in unison and then Galen set his bag upon a night table and began to take instruments, bottles and boxes from it. Daniel caught Simon nodding to Moor.

Moor took up his bag. "Come with me," he said to Daniel, "we shall examine the kitchens and great hall."

Reluctantly, Daniel followed his teacher out of the bedchamber.

They made their way to the kitchens to find the cooks already at work. Moor waved the chief day cook over to them.

"You are the chief cook." he said.

"For the morning and noon meals, yes, sir," replied the man.

"And do you know who I am?"

"Yes sir. You are the king's chief swordsman."

That was not Moor's official title, but Daniel thought it described him well enough.

"There has been a death in the fortress. Stop all work, but keep your people here until I release them," ordered the Etruscan. "We need to examine this room." Moor walked past the man, taking in the kitchens and the workers there. "Is there anyone here now who worked during the feast last night?" he asked the cook.

"No, sir, the night staff are all home asleep by now," replied the man.

"Then tell your people to touch nothing until I give them leave," ordered Moor. "Come with me," he said to Daniel, opening the door to the great hall.

Once in the great hall, Daniel saw that their work would be difficult. The tables had been cleaned by now and the floors swept. Moor spent some time examining the king's throne and the chair and table where he sat for the feast. He even sat in the king's chair and looked around the room from that vantage point. He began to drum his fingers on the table impatiently.

"What are you thinking?" asked Daniel.

"That I am not seeing all there is to see," replied Moor. He stood, took a lamp and his bag from table and walked to the center of the hall. He put the lamp down and began to walk in circles around it, keeping his back to the light and looking around the chamber. With the lamp behind him, Moor's shadow grew large, making a giant hawk-nosed creature appear on the wall, turning this way and that, hunting for prey. Daniel followed his gaze as his teacher swept the hall with his eyes. Tables and chairs were empty and clean. The tapestries on the walls had nothing behind them (Moor had checked) and the windows high on those walls were still dark. Moor had lit all the oil lamps on the walls when they first came in, but it was still darker than when the chandeliers with their many candles were lit during the feast. Even the fires in the hearths on each wall had burned down by now.

Daniel thought that they should leave the hall till morning and move back into the kitchens. As he was about to suggest this to Moor, the Etruscan suddenly caught sight of something and snapped his fingers. He took up the lamp and strode across the chamber to the wall behind the king's table and set his bag down by the hearth. Daniel followed. Moor opened his bag and drew from it a small hand broom and shovel, followed by a small leather sack. He began to collect the ash and bits of unburned wood from the hearth.

"Why are you collecting the ash?" asked Daniel.

"Because that is the only thing I *can* collect here," replied Moor. When he had finished his task, he placed the sack of debris, the broom and shovel back into the bag and rose to his feet, dusting himself off.

"Where do we go now?" asked Daniel.

"Not we," said Moor. "*You* will return to the royal chambers so that you can help guard your mother while I continue my search." Daniel looked about to protest, but Moor cut him off. "You cannot help me, but you can help your mother; go to her and let me work." Moor gave a whistle like a night bird and two guards came through a door.

Daniel thought of arguing, but he felt useless here with Moor. His mother might want to see him. He nodded his head and left the chamber.

Chapter Seven
BITTER FRUIT

Anyone who kills a person is to be put to death as a murderer only on the testimony of witnesses. But no one is to be put to death on the testimony of only one witness.

- The Book of Numbers- 35:30

D aniel spent the next few hours outside his mother's chambers. The guards tried to console him by saying what a good man and king Argeus had been, but that only made it worse.

Why could not an evil man have died in his place? thought Daniel.

Simon had given Isoldé a sleeping draught earlier that night. He must have known his trade, for she did not wake till well after first light. A maidservant came out of the queen's chamber and beckoned Daniel.

The prince found his mother fully dressed and more composed then he would have guessed.

Upon seeing her son, Isoldé welcomed him into her arms, but did not weep.

"Mother, are you alright?"

Isoldé stepped away from her son and held him at arm's length.

"No. My love has been taken from me and I shall not be completely *alright* until I see him again." She looked Daniel in the eye. "But we remain the king's family. This is not our time to weep. The people need us first to lead and to be strong. Later there shall be the time for us to mourn. We must not hide in a bedchamber. Come, we will go to the throne room and meet with our counselors there."

They spent the rest of that morning in counsel with ministers and advisors. They requested a report from Moor, but he sent back a message that he and Simon were still making their investigation. Late that afternoon a servant came with another message from Moor, asking to meet the queen and Daniel in the map room.

Daniel and six guards escorted the queen to the small room beyond the throne room.

As the queen entered, Moor rose from behind the long table and bowed. Simon stood beside him, looking grim.

"Do you have news for us?" asked Daniel, "Can you tell how my father died?"

"Yes, my prince, we have," said Moor, "How it happened, Simon will tell you. Who did it, I suspect but cannot prove."

"I really should do more tests before we proceed with this," said Simon.

"Friend Simon, long have I known you and long have I trusted you," said Isoldé. "Please tell me what you know now and, if you say to wait before I act, I will wait. But remember, kingdoms can be lost or won in a single day. We have many decisions that must be made."

"As my lady wishes," said the priest, bowing.

He took several vials out of a small wooden box, one by one, and lined them up carefully on the table.

Isoldé took a seat at the head of the table with Daniel at her side. Moor, as usual, stood so that he could watch the door.

"When Galen and I examined the king," began Simon, "We found no external wounds. His eyes were clear with no broken vessels, which, if present, would be a sign that he had smothered. Not that uncommon when a man has had too much to drink and buries his face while sleeping in his pillow.

Moor caught the hard look on Daniel's face. "We did not expect it to be so, but we still had to rule the possibility out."

Simon continued, "I did notice a slight bluish tint at the very tips of the king's fingers. This showed the blood not being fully rejuvenated in the lungs. Not unusual for a common man the equivalent of Argeus's age, but very uncommon to see in one of the house of Asher. I then suspected a poison. Moor searched and sampled items from the king's bedchamber, the throne room, the great hall, all the servant's quarters and the kitchens. I brought the samples to the laboratory I improvised from physician Galen's supplies and tested for every poison I could with the tools available to me."

"And you found?" asked Daniel.

"Well," said Simon, hesitating, "I have found something either a little sinister or very unfortunate. I checked the wine that was served that night. As you know, the king was fond of spiced wine. I found a glass with some wine remaining in the kitchen, where one of the cooks had been 'sampling' it. The wine contained no poison, but it did have overmuch of a spice that makes the heart beat faster: not anything unusual in a wine to be served at a celebration, just too much of it."

"I remember feeling flushed after the toasting that night. But I told myself that it was just my time to stop drinking," said Daniel. "But we all drank that wine, some men older than my father, and no one else died."

114

"In that you are correct, Daniel," said Moor. "That spice alone would not have killed your father. But listen on."

Simon continued, "Among the ashes from the great hall, Moor recovered a broken shard of pottery that would match the goblets thrown into the fire after the toast. On this shard, we found a residue of an herb that relaxes the lungs and slows the breathing, but this was not enough to kill a man, either. In any event, we don't know if this particular shard came from your father's goblet. The spice that speeds the heart and the herb that slows the breathing *would* have put a strain on his heart, though. It would have to work harder with less air, but I do not believe these things alone would have been enough to kill a man in good health. Some piece is still missing. Did he eat or drink anything else before bed that night?"

"He would eat a piece of fruit each night just before bed," said Isoldé.

"What kind of fruit did he eat recently?" asked Simon.

"Since coming to the fortress, sweet mountain apples," she replied.

Simon thought for a moment. "Did he also eat the core and the seeds within?"

"Why, yes," said Isoldé, "At our old home he would simply throw the core out the window for the squirrels to eat, but once we came to the fortress our window looked out onto the courtyard. Argeus had great respect for his crown and duties here and would not throw even an apple core upon the courtyard floor. Nor did he want to smell the core in our bedchamber all night, for it would make him hungry. So he ate it."

Simon nodded his head. "Most fruit seeds contain toxins. The Lord designed fruit to be sweet, to entice animals to eat the fruit and carry the seeds far from the parent plant, but he made the seeds themselves toxic or bitter or hard skinned to deter the animal from eating them. But the seeds from mountain apples make an unreliable poison at best. It would take a large bowl of such seeds to kill even a common man. Those of the house of Asher are harder to kill by poison than most." Simon thought for a moment. "You said he ate one fruit each night?"

"Yes. Each night, whatever was in season," replied the queen. "We were coming to the end of last autumn's apple supply from the root cellar and, of course, this summer's fruit crop had not come in yet."

"He only started eating the apple core upon becoming king, not before?"

Isoldé nodded.

"And it was only one apple a night?" asked the priest.

Isoldé's hand flew to her heart, "Yes, would that have been enough? I should have stopped him"

Simon shook his head, "One apple core a night should not have hurt him. Something is still missing here." He turned and opened his bag and took from it a small vial.

"What have you there?" asked Daniel.

"I cut a lock of your father's hair. If a toxin has built up in his system over a long time, it will show up in his hair and bones." He took an empty vial from his bag and put some of the hairs into it, then added the liquid from two other vials and held the vial over the flame of a candle. The liquid changed from a transparent red to a muddy brown.

Simon looked at the vial and frowned. "Arsenic, but Argeus would have had to eat twenty apple cores a night to be at this level. Even then, it would not have killed him."

Moor leaned forward like a hound catching a scent. "But if it was combined with the spices you found?"

"Yes, it might have weakened the king's heart enough to cause his death when combined with the other stresses placed on his body that night," nodded Simon.

"Then we must check the root cellar before someone gets a sudden hunger for all the apples that are left and our evidence vanishes," said Moor, coming to his feet.

Moor, Simon and Daniel took their leave of the queen and made their way to the lower levels of the fortress. In the root cellar, they found bins containing drying fruit and root vegetables. A small pile, perhaps half a bushel's worth, of apples remained in one bin.

"If it was murder," said Simon, "then perhaps those behind it did not believe the investigation would ever get this far."

"Oh, it was murder, of that I am certain," said Moor. "The spiced wine, the herb on the goblets and now the apples. There is a saying in my homeland: 'One time is chance, two times may be coincidence, but the third time, draw your blade."

"But we have not yet confirmed that the apples were poisoned," said Simon.

He cut three apples, took their seeds and dropped them into a small stone mortar, ground them fine and scraped the resulting paste into a vial. Simon removed from his bag the vial containing the red substance Daniel had seen him use before and added a measured amount to the crushed apple seeds. The liquid immediately turned a dark, muddy brown.

"These apples have been altered." The priest peered into the vial. "There must be ten times the amount of arsenic in these seeds as would occur naturally."

"But how could that be done without being detected?" asked Daniel. "All foodstuffs brought into the fortress were checked and sampled before going to the kitchens."

"I do not yet know," said Moor, "but I soon will." He turned to Daniel. "Return to the queen and guard her. Simon, you and I shall trace the path of these apples into the fortress."

*****

And so the investigation went, on again and off again for several days. The seventh day after the king's death, the high justices met to hear evidence in the throne room.

Members of the senate, the kings advisors, chief merchants, all who thought of themselves as important men, watched the proceedings.

On the fourth day Daniel saw Sargon enter the room.

"He dares come here!" he said in a low voice to Moor.

"He is one of the most important men in Eboracium. Men would think it strange if he did not attend."

The crier called the court to order and witnesses were called. Moor gave his testimony, explaining all that he had found. The chief gardener for the crown was called next.

"Well, sir, that's what I was told to do," the young man testified. "For three years, I apprenticed under Greenman Benmarl at the king's orchard. Then last autumn he was killed by highwaymen. That's when Master Greenman Arni took his place."

"And it was Greenman Arni who told you to fertilize the apple trees as you did?" asked the king's prosecutor.

"Yes sir, he had me pile the mash from the cider mill round 'bout all the apple trees. He said there was no profits in all that mash going to waste. I had never heard of such being used, but I was not the master then."

"And you are now?"

"Yes, sir. Master Arni's wife ran off 'bout two months ago and he left to find her. When he didn't return, I was made Master Greenman."

Simon then testified that the mash from the cider mill had been strained down to contain mostly the pulp from the apple seeds and would be unnaturally high in

118

toxins. These toxins would be drawn up into the tree and stored in the apple seeds.

The justices, five old men chosen for their positions so as to offend the least number of powerful senators, retired to deliberate.

Daniel nodded towards the chamber door behind which the justices met. "How long do you think they will take?" he asked.

"I would not expect much," replied Moor, "this is a thin trail to follow and we have not proven that it leads to any one man's door."

"But Sargon had the greatest motive."

"That we know of," corrected Moor. "Your father was king of Asulon, all who hated Asulon would have motive to kill him."

"Are you trying to tell me that Sargon was *not* behind my father's murder?" demanded Daniel.

"I am counseling that you remember your position and do nothing to jeopardize it," said Moor.

They waited for several hours until word came that the justices had reached their decision. Soon the justices entered the chamber and took their seats.

The chief justice unfurled a scroll and began to read. "First, the court would like to commend all the investigative parties for their diligent efforts on behalf of the truth. All involved have done their duties in a way commensurate with the severity of our nation's great loss."

Moor leaned in to Daniel's ear. "Beware and be strong, but do nothing no matter what you hear. When men such as these praise us overmuch, it tells me they are preparing to disappoint us."

"When a king dies suddenly," continued the chief justice, "our first thoughts run towards some evil hand at work. This is natural. All great men have enemies and, the greater the man, the greater the number of those who wish him harm. But we of the high court must look deeper. We, the High Justices of Asulon, have viewed all the evidence and reviewed all the documents brought before us in this matter.

"Therefore, it is our ruling that Argeus, King of Asulon, died in his sleep in the early morning hours of the tenth day of the sixth month of the year 1026 of an unfortunate"–at this word a murmur ran through the crowd–"accident and was not killed by any intentional act. That is the final decision of the court."

The justices rose and walked out of the room without a glance back.

"An accident!" said Daniel "Are they blind?

"What did you expect?" asked Moor. "Should they announce to the world that the king of Asulon had been assassinated, but they know not by whom and that they can do no more about it? That would have caused mayhem in the streets. Every butcher, baker and blacksmith would have had his own theory about who killed the king. Put a few such men together and you have a mob, let someone get them moving and you have a riot. Innocent men would have died and the guilty still would have gone untouched, for they would have made preparations to avoid such violence long beforehand. No, with the evidence we gave the court, it could have made no other verdict than this."

Daniel still seethed. "So we should just let this be the end of it? My father was your friend as well as your king. How can you do nothing?"

Moor nodded to a passing group of senators, then said under his breath, "I did not say *I* would do nothing, I said *you* should do nothing."

"But I am his son."

"And I am an Etruscan and we have learned that revenge is like a campfire. Build it right and you will be warm and nourished. Build it wrong and you will get burned. Men with great power who think themselves above the law should be dealt with outside the law. You will be king one day. You must represent the law." Moor looked around the room. "Come, let us leave. We can speak more on this in private."

Just then a voice rose up from behind them. "Prince Daniel, a word."

Daniel turned to find Sargon, surrounded by three large men he took to be the merchant's bodyguards, walking towards him.

"Prince Daniel, I wanted to offer my sincerest condolences," said Sargon, offering his hand. Without a word Daniel backhanded him across the nose, breaking the cartilage. Sargon staggered back against one of his bodyguards and slid to the floor.

"Hold there!" The large man on Daniel's right reached out with his left hand to grab Daniel. Without taking his eyes off the fallen merchant, Daniel took hold of the outstretched arm at the wrist and pulled the limb straight so that the man's elbow was beside Daniel's right shoulder. He snapped his body sideways, breaking the elbow joint. The man fell to the ground, howling.

The remaining bodyguard charged forward, but skidded to a stop as a flash of steel came up before him.

"Enough!" ordered Moor, his sword outstretched and ringing, humming like a hornet eager for a target to sting.

Daniel stood his ground looking down on the fallen Sargon. The prince spoke in a low voice. "I know what you did, merchant, and I will not let it pass. The next time you see my..."

The words stopped in his throat as his ribs received a blow that sent him staggering sideways, the breath gone from his lungs.

"I said enough!" said Moor in a voice as hard and unforgiving as his sword. "Daniel. Leave this chamber. *Now.*"

Gasping for breath, Daniel made his way through the shocked crowd and out of the chamber.

Moor sheathed his sword and bowed before Sargon. "My lord, I am so very sorry for that outburst."

Sargon rose, waving off the help of his two remaining bodyguards. The third lay on the floor, looking like he might vomit.

"In my day," said the merchant, a handkerchief covering his bleeding nose, "such an attack would merit time in the king's prison, no matter the man's rank."

"My lord, the boy has just returned from his year in the wilderness. I am afraid he yet has something of the wild man about him. His father has just died and he is not thinking clearly. Grieving as he is, he believes any bit of gossip that comes his way."

Sargon looked at the Etruscan measuring him. "And what of you, Master Moor, what do you believe?" he asked, wiping the blood from his face with the fine linen handkerchief.

"I believe that the high court has spoken," replied Moor. "What led to the King's death was far too complex a chain of events for any one man to put it in motion."

"So you do not believe, as the prince seems to, that I had a hand in this matter?"

Moor spread his hands in a gesture of peace. "You may have had your differences with the king, but, then, so did many men in Asulon. I know that a man of your stature would not risk all he is and all he has by soiling his hands in the death of a king. I will speak with the prince and make sure he listens to reason. You should expect a worthy gift from him in apology for his actions."

Moor nodded to some approaching guards. "In the meantime, my men will bring you to an antechamber. Please wait there and I will send the best physician we have to look after you and your man."

"It is good to see more mature minds prevailing in this matter," said Sargon. "But, as I am not mortally wounded, I shall have my own physician look after me. I suppose my man here needs more immediate care after what the prince did to him. Let your physician see to him. I must go."

"I will leave you in the care of my men, then. They will escort you out," Moor said. He bowed and left the chamber.

Sargon looked down on the injured man. "Burlos, these men will take you to a physician."

"Thank you, sir. I am sorry I could not do more."

"Yes, so am I," said Sargon. He turned to leave, then, over his shoulder, added, "Oh, by the way. You're fired."

* * * * *

"Well, that was a brilliant display," said Moor in Daniel's chambers. "Why not howl like a wolf next time you draw your bow on a deer? Why not sing aloud as you wait in ambush for an enemy? Is this what I taught you?"

The paladin paced the room, making quick, sharp gestures as he spoke, looking as if he wished very, *very* much to kill something.

Daniel sat silently at a table, rubbing liniment into the bruise forming over his ribs. The ribs were not broken, but Moor had struck him with a one-knuckle punch that more than got his attention.

"I am sorry, Master Moor. But this is the first time I have seen my father murdered. I shall strive to do better next time," replied Daniel, his voice heavy with sarcasm.

Moor shot him a hard look. "Oh, stop feeling sorry for yourself. You are going to be king one day and, as king, you must learn the skill of smiling at your enemy while your men draw daggers at his back."

Moor looked at the thin crack of light showing under the door. The guards he had stationed outside remained where he had placed them, on either side of the door, not before it, where they might possibly hear what was said within.

Moor lowered his voice. "I *had* planned to wait several months after you reached Logres safely and the rumors about the king's death spread so lean that no one man was highest in suspicion. And then," Moor smiled that thin, half-smile of his, "Sargon would have met with his own 'unfortunate accident.' But that overly hot head of yours ruined that plan. After your little performance today, if a bolt of lighting fell from the sky tonight and smote Sargon before a crowd of witnesses, all eyes would still turn to you as the killer. And if Sargon falls while you are in Logres, then they will look to those most loyal to your family—namely, to *me*—as the assassin, thank you very much."

Daniel looked up at his teacher for the first time since entering the chamber. "I am sorry, Master Moor. I did not think of it that way."

"No, the problem is you did not think in *any* way before striking," Moor said. "You saw your enemy and you reacted with no more forethought than an untrained child." He came to an abrupt halt and turned to face Daniel. "Well, at least your little performance today has brought about one good thing."

"Oh, what is that?" replied Daniel sullenly.

"I now know without a doubt that Sargon ordered your father's murder."

"How so?" asked Daniel, now very interested in what his teacher had to say.

"Sargon, the most powerful merchant in Asulon, forgave your public insult far too quickly. An innocent man would have been far angrier than he was and that anger would not have cooled so quickly. Sargon controlled his anger for a reason. Yes, Sargon ordered the king's death, and I suspect that he has sufficient intelligence to see the teeth behind the smile I gave him tonight. Therefore we have to change our plans. Pack your saddlebags, but pack light. We will leave for Eboracium tonight and will sail on the first tide for Logres."

"*We,* sir; are you coming with me to Logres?"

"Yes. Sargon cannot afford to let you live now. In his mind it would be pure self-defense to have you killed. He also knows of my loyalty to your family, so my life would be worth little here as well. So we shall go to Logres together and seek aid from your grandfather. He can avenge your father while we sit innocently in his court. Now go pack. We will leave at dawn."

"But what of my mother?" asked Daniel. "Who will be left to guard her?"

"She will be safe," said Moor, after a moment's thought. "Sargon would act against us in self-defense, not revenge. There is no profit in killing the queen and much to lose. Do not worry about her."

Just then a knock came and the chamber door opened.

"A message from the queen, your highness," said the guard, entering the room and handing Daniel a scroll. Daniel opened it and recognized his mother's own hand.

"It reads, 'Please come to the map room, we have a guest'," said Daniel.

"We should go, then," replied Moor. "Besides, I know you will not leave Asulon without first seeing your mother. You can pack when we return."

They made their way to the map room and entered. The chairs from the conference table had been moved to form a semicircle around the hearth.

Queen Isoldé sat in a chair opposite the door.

"Daniel, my son, I have someone I would like you to meet."

In one of the high-backed chairs opposite the queen, Daniel recognized the back of Simon's head. He came to his mother and kissed her in greeting, then turned to meet their guest.

A dark-haired girl of perhaps seventeen or eighteen years sat next to Simon. She rose, eyes lowered, and bowed formally in the eastern manner. Then she raised her head. Daniel looked into her eyes and...

In the space between one heartbeat and the next, the map room disappeared. Daniel saw a wilderness, a desolate place of rocky hills and stunted brush. It seemed to Daniel that he could see into this world, but floated through it and could touch nothing in it.

He could not see Isoldé, Simon or Moor, but the girl was there, kneeling at the bottom of a ravine, beside a dry streambed, in travel-worn and dusty robes. She wept and the sight of it wrenched Daniel's heart.

She cried out, *"My love, my love, will I ever see you again?"* She lifted her head and, it seemed to the prince, look right into his eyes.

"Daniel, where are you?"

The light from the dawn sun flashed on something in her hands, blinding him a moment. And then, just as suddenly as he had left it, he was back in the map room.

What was that? Daniel thought, shaken. *Was that a vision or am I going mad?*

He found that he could not take his eyes off of the girl. A great desire arose in Daniel to protect and comfort her. Certainly she was pretty, with long black hair, dark eyes and the bronze skin of those who lived in the winterless lands on the shores of the Internal Sea. But that did not keep him caught, as if in a trance. There was something about the girl's eyes, something otherworldly. The girl looked up at him, a young girl's shy smile on her face, but Daniel seemed to see something else, standing within her and almost visible. Something you could feel rather than see, like the hot coals within the ashes of last night's fire that the merest breath of wind would waken into a bright flame. It compelled him and drew him. It called out to him and spoke of wisdom and strength, knowledge and great joy. Daniel sensed all of this for the merest moment, and then, just as quickly, it was hidden from him.

Simon rose to his feet. "Prince Daniel, son of Argeus, son of Isoldé, of the House of Asher, allow me to introduce to you Rachel, daughter of Binyamin, daughter of Rebekah, of the House of Yehuda, Princess of Eretzel."

Daniel stared like a rabbit caught in torchlight.

"Son, where are your manners?" asked the queen "Welcome our guest."

"Hello" was all Daniel could get out. Moor raised an eyebrow and groaned under his breath. He did not need this kind of complication just now.

The girl smiled her shy smile and bowed again. Rising, she said formally, "I greet thee, Prince Daniel, son of Argeus, son of Isoldé, in the name of the Lord Yeshua whom I serve and in whose service I have come to offer gifts for the healing of the House of Asher."

"Hello," said Daniel again.

Moor tapped Daniel's boot with his own and broke the spell.

"And, ah, welcome to Asulon and to our home," said Daniel finally.

Rachel reclaimed her seat. Moor noticed that the prince took the chair to the left of his mother, a good spot from which to view the girl.

After servants had brought food and drink, Isoldé spoke. "This young lady has traveled very far and has been through a great ordeal to come to us. She has told Simon, who speaks her language, some of her story and he has brought her here to tell us the rest." She nodded to Rachel.

Rachel said something in a foreign tongue to Simon, who nodded. "Though she reads Westerness fairly well-she had a great love of our books as a child-it is not her mother tongue and has had only limited practice in the speaking of it," said the priest. "Therefore, she has asked me to translate her story as she tells it." Then Rachel began her tale.

Rachel had been raised in the home of Mordechai, Judge of the tribe of Yehuda, since the murder of her parents during one of the frequent Philistine raids upon Eretzel. Though an Abramim, Rachel also followed the Lord Yeshua, something which displeased Mordechai greatly. Mordechai, like most of the sons of Abram, held to the ways of his fathers in his worship of the One God. He did not consider those of his people who worshiped Yeshua to be fully Abramim. But Rachel had the gifts of true visions and healing the sick, and such gifts had to have come from God. In a vision, Rachel saw that the king of Asulon faced grave danger and would soon have need of her gifts as a healer. She asked to go to Asulon.

The vision put Mordecai in a difficult position. He thought it unwise to refuse her request, as Asulon was a great ally of Eretzel. If Asulon and its king truly needed Rachel's gifts, how could he refuse her? Yet he did not wish Rachel to go on such a long and dangerous journey alone. Mordechai called for a tournament to be held among his soldiers to choose her bodyguards. Rachel wished to leave immediately, on a cargo vessel, with only her maidservant, but Mordechai would hear nothing of it. In truth, he loved her dearly. She was like a daughter to him and Mordechai would have forbidden her to leave outright if Rachel had not been so certain of her vision.

By the time the preparations were made, the men gathered, and the tournament held, two months had passed.

Rachel stopped her narrative and a shadow of pain crossed her face. She said something to Simon in her native tongue.

Simon pulled a scroll from his cloak and handed it to Moor. "The soldiers who escorted the princess here brought this report."

Moor read silently for a moment then began to summarize the report.

"While the Eretzelian warship was still far from Asulon, they came upon a ship flying an Asulonian flag that seemed in distress, with torn sails and just a few men in rags on the deck. The warship tied alongside to give aid. Suddenly armed men came out from the ship's cargo hold. After a short battle...the captain of the warship had not ordered his men to arm before he tied alongside a strange ship...the pirates took the Eretzelian ship.

"They took the princess and her maidservant prisoner. The pirates tied the warship's wheel in place so that it would sail a straight course away from them, then poured oil onto the ship's deck. They cut the lines between the ships, throw torches onto the Eretzelian deck and the warship, under full sail, drew away."

He read down further.

"While the pirates took down their torn sails and rigged good ones from their hold, one of our own warships arrived on the scene and put together what had occurred. The pirates offered resistance, but were no match for an attacking Asulonian warship. Those pirates that survived the first assault begged for quarter. The princess was taken safely aboard, but her maidservant later died from wounds suffered during her capture."

Moor read a bit further, then smiled his half-smile.

"Ah. Good man. The captain of the warship writes:

"'I swore to those murderous scum that I would not put them to the sword if they surrendered. However, I said nothing about not putting them to the sea. The bronze tip on our bow worked exceedingly well. We gave the scoundrels the same measure of mercy that they themselves gave, and rammed their cursed ship at the waterline. We left the pirates to swim home with the sharks as their companions.'"

Moor continued, "They brought the princess to our southern naval station at Smyrna, where the royal garrison took her under its protection.

"As you have heard, she does speak some Westerness, and was able to communicate her wish to see the king. She was put on a ship bound for Eboracium and brought here."

At the end of the story the girl looked up, tears in her eyes. "All those men and my Nina died. I come too late."

"Too late for what, dear?" asked Isoldé

Rachel spoke to Simon, who translated for her. "The Lord has given me gifts of healing. I knew that the Lord wanted me to come to Asulon for a reason. Your king is dead. That must be why the dreams came, that I would come here in time, but I did not."

Rachel wept and all were silent.

Isoldé came to her and took the girl's hands in her own. "My child," said Isoldé in her kind and patient voice, "the king did not die after a long illness, but suddenly in the night. You may be able to heal, but I do not think you can bring people back from the dead. If the Lord wanted you here, it was for another reason."

Again Simon translated this and the girl replied. "But the dreams said I was to be here by the first of summer. That day has passed. I am not needed here. You have been kind, but I should return to my people. My uncle will need me."

"Well, then, allow us to show you our hospitality until we can arrange for a ship to bring you home," said the queen.

"She can sail with us!" said Daniel. "We are leaving for Logres and, from there, a ship bound for Eretzel will be easy to find."

"Oh, Daniel, there is no need to discuss the details now," said Isoldé.

Daniel looked embarrassed. "Ah...well...actually, there is, Mother. We leave for Eboracium at dawn."

Isoldé turned towards Moor. "Swordmaster, why do I feel I should look to you for an explanation?"

"Because you are wise, my queen," said Moor. "You have no doubt heard by now of the incident with Sargon after the judge's decision."

"Yes," replied Isoldé "I had left the throne room by the time Sargon was struck, but I heard soon enough." She gave her son a piercing look. "Daniel, what were you thinking? Does not the Lord say in scripture, 'Vengeance is mine?'"

"That is the problem, my queen," said Moor, casting a glance at the prince. "Daniel struck the merchant without thinking what the repercussions might be. And now we must flee Sargon's wrath to Logres. Only there will your son be safe. I shall go with him, making sure he arrives safely and staying with him for a time to watch over him."

Simon watched Rachel listen to the exchange. He was not sure how much she understood; she had needed his help with the wording of her formal greeting.

She caught his eye and motioned him closer. "Sir, they speak of taking me with them, do they not?" she said in the language of Eretzel.

"Verily, they do, little one," replied Simon in the same tongue.

"I am not sure if it is proper for me to travel with these warriors." She leaned in closer and whispered, "Besides, I think the younger one likes me."

"I believe he does at that," said Simon, smiling kindly. "But I have known him since he was a small boy and I know that he would in no wise harm thee." Simon thought for a moment. "I have told thee of myself and of my order. Princess, would it put thy mind at ease if I accompanied thee on thy journey?"

"Yes, for I know that thou art a true man of God and would see to my honor," replied Rachel.

"Good," said Simon "then let it be as thou hast said. For I see that thou were brought here at this very hour for a reason. Perhaps there will still be need for thy gifts that thou hast not foreseen."

The others had stopped speaking while Simon spoke with Rachel. Daniel saw her nod assent to Simon.

"If you will show her this kindness," said the priest, "she will sail with you to Logres. I will accompany her and then return the princess to her people."

Isoldé nodded. "Well then, as much as I dislike the idea of my son fleeing Asulon like a thief in the night, and so soon after what happened to his father, I can see the wisdom of it.

"Now, I know that you all have preparations to make."

The three men stood and bowed.

Isoldé touched her son's sleeve. "Daniel, please stay here so we can share the little time we have left."

131

* * * * *

Simon found a maidservant waiting to escort Rachel to a room. He motioned for Rachel to follow her, and fell into step behind them.

Moor caught Simon's arm. "Might I have a word with you?" He nodded towards the girl. "In private."

"Let us talk while we escort our guest to her chambers," said Simon. "We can speak in Etruscan," he added, switching to that language. "Then may you speak freely."

"That was not wise, old man," said Moor. "The girl should remain here. The journey I must make with the prince will be dangerous. Why risk the safety of the girl without need?"

"Some things you cannot see with the eyes of the flesh, but only hear with your spirit," replied Simon. "When the prince spoke of her accompanying you on your journey, the Lord quickened my heart. I heard in my spirit 'Do this, and I will guide you'."

"Oh really," said Moor, his voice mocking and cold. "Well, did your Lord tell you how I am to travel swiftly and still protect a young girl and an old priest?"

"I will look after the girl," replied Simon. "As for my welfare, you need not worry. I may be old, but I am stronger than I look."

"You will need to be strong, old man. My responsibility is to the prince. Fall behind, and you are on your own."

"Then I shall do my best to keep up," said Simon.

They came to the door of the bedchamber reserved for the girl. The maidservant knocked and another servant opened the door from within.

"I will take my leave of thee here, princess," said Simon. "Thy maidservant will wake thee in time for our travels."

Rachel leaned in whisper to Simon. "This warrior with thee," she said, "he will be our guide while we travel? I do not think I will like him."

"Yes, princess, he will guide us, but do not let him worry thee. When it comes to women, his bark exceeds his bite. Sleep well. I will come for thee at the fifth hour."

* * * * *

"Two shocks to a woman's heart in as many weeks are hard to bear, Daniel," said Isoldé. She had dismissed the servants so that they could be alone. The fire burned low in the hearth, but Isoldé had stopped her maid from adding another log before she left. The glow from the coals made a little, private sanctuary of light around them while she spoke with her son.

"I am sorry, Mother. It's my fault that I must leave so soon." Daniel looked anguished. After all she had just been through, to have their short time together taken away by his own foolishness made a bitter cup to swallow.

Why did I not think before I struck? Father was too wise and Moor is too disciplined to do such a thing. Why can I not be more like them? In my place, Father would have found a way to bring Sargon to justice and Moor himself would have brought justice to Sargon if I had not fouled things up so badly.

"Daniel, I am worried about you," said Isoldé. She held up a hand to still his protest. "No, it is not your physical safety that worries me most. I am sure Moor will see you safely to Logres. I worry more about the anger in your heart. The Lord has instructed us to leave vengeance to His own hand for a reason. It is not to protect the guilty that He has done this, but to protect the innocent."

"But, Mother, I know beyond any doubt that Sargon ordered Father's death."

"As do I," she said. "By my saying that the Lord wishes to protect the innocent, I am not speaking of protecting a man from being wrongly accused of a crime. No, when I speak of protecting the innocent, I am speaking of protecting the *victims* of that crime.

"Daniel, my son, hear me. Vengeance is a very different creature than justice. The desire for vengeance is spawned by hatred , and hatred is a hungry serpent that demands constant feeding. You feed it with your time, and with your strength, and with your will. It lies coiled around your heart and eats and eats and eats and steals from you your time and your strength and your will. You feed that serpent and it turns and churns inside you until all you can think of, every hour of every day, is vengeance.

"Then the great day comes and you set your hand to avenge the wrong done to you. If you fail at your vengeance, then the serpent turns on you like a wild creature you thought you had tamed, but which attacks once the cage door has been opened. You come to hate yourself for your failure and you live out the remainder of your life in bitterness and despair.

"But if you *do* succeed in your vengeance, then the serpent wishes to bask in its glory. It grows fat and proud and says, 'Let anyone else wrong me and they will share the same fate.' The serpent then lives its life seeking out new wrongs to avenge, taking offense at the slightest thing so it may start the cycle of vengeance again and grow even greater in pride and glory. It begins to think itself a god, for it says, 'If you can do the tasks of God, are you not then like Him?'"

"So Sargon will go unpunished while we hope for a bolt from heaven to strike him down?" asked Daniel, more sharply than he would have liked.

"Even if we do not see it, Sargon will be punished," replied Isoldé. "If not in this life, then when this life is done. But there must be a buffer between the victims and those who have wronged them. That is the king's job, to act impartially on behalf of justice. That impartial buffer, the hand of the king, makes the difference between vengeance and justice."

"And when the king himself has been wronged—what then, Mother?" asked Daniel.

"Then the king must act, but with even more restraint upon his heart than for an unknown victim. And the king's family must do the same. "

She took both his hands in her own. "Daniel, you are all I have left now. Leave Asulon as you must, but set my heart at ease first. Trust the Lord enough to leave justice to His hand. The Lord may use the thunderbolt or He may use the hangman's noose, but justice *will* be done."

She stopped speaking then, and looked off for a moment in the way that the women of their family had, as if listening for something far away.

"My son, you must wait a full year before you move against Sargon," said Isoldé. "Yes, a year will be enough. Promise me that you will wait for the Lord's justice regarding Sargon and not lift your hand against him for one full year."

Seeing the look in his mother's eyes, Daniel could do nothing but agree.

"I swear that I will wait upon the justice of the Lord," he said, "and will not lift my own hand against Sargon until a full year has passed."

"Good," said Isoldé, relieved. "Now we can speak as a mother and son should on the night before a parting. Let me tell you of my father's court..."

Chapter Eight
THE TRAVELERS

And we journey from the river Ahava, ...
to go to Jerusalem, and the hand of our God hath been
upon us, and He delivereth us from the hand of the
enemy and the lier in wait by the way;
-The Book of Ezra- 8:31

Daniel had not slept that night, preferring to spend
as much time as possible with his mother before he
left Asulon. During the night they spoke much of Argeus. Daniel recalled the small things they did together
in his youth, fishing or hiking or the quiet talks. And
now he knew that they were not small things, for he remembered them still. Isoldé spoke of his valor and yet

his gentleness toward her. While they spoke, Isoldé drew on a parchment an image of the face of Argeus, not as he was in the days before his death, but when she first met him, in the flower of his youth, when he first came to Logres. She did this, for the kings of Asulon customarily were buried in stone sarcophagi below the fortress; the stonemasons making use of the queen's drawing when carving the likeness of the king. Most kings, who died long after their tenure had ended, lay under a likeness of themselves in repose. Argeus, because he had died while king, would be shown sitting upright upon the throne, scepter in his left hand and drawn sword in his right, twice life size. The sarcophagus would be built into the base of this statue and the lid mortared in place, to be opened by none but the voice of the angel who calls the bodies of the dead to rise at the end of the age.

* * * * *

In the dim light before dawn, Moor came for Daniel in his chambers and found the prince hastily packing his saddlebags. The two men strung their bows and put them across their backs. Instead of a small hunting quiver with twelve arrows, Moor decided they each carry a war quiver holding twice that number. Moor had changed his belt insignia to that of a captain and handed Daniel a buckle as well.

"A corporal?" said Daniel, when he had seen the emblem Moor had given him. "Can I not be of higher rank than that?"

"The lower the rank we wear, the less conspicuous we will be," replied Moor. "A corporal's rank will mark you as a commoner in the crown's service and not of royal blood." He poked Daniel in the chest with a long forefinger.

"Yes, it's there," said Daniel. Moor had given him a chain mail vest earlier that night with instructions to wear it between his outer shirt and an inner padded cotton vest.

"The best armor is that which your enemy does not know about," Moor had told him. "If someone aims an arrow at you and sees no armor, it is more likely to be a broadhead made to cut flesh rather than a tapered, armor-piercing point. That will buy us some time to react—provided they do not aim for your throat, of course."

They went down to the stables to find Simon and Rachel already there. Isoldé stood beside Rachel, not wanting her last sight of her son be in the dark of night.

Three stable boys stood by, two holding the reins of an Asulonian war-horse, large chestnut stallions with black manes; the swift Mirbane for Daniel, the fierce Heofon for Moor. The third held Simon's horse, an old buckskin roan he had named Witan.

The stable master approached Rachel. "Do you know how to ride, my lady?" he asked.

"Only a little," said Rachel a bit nervously, looking up at the giant beasts.

"Take my horse, then," said Isoldé as Simon translated for the girl. "He is a gelding, very gentle, unlike these fierce stallions the men ride. He will not try to turn aside on the road should a mare pass by."

Rachel came to Isoldé, bowed before her and replied in her own tongue. "Like a mother thou hast been to me, like a daughter I will pray for thee."

Once Simon had translated this, Isoldé leaned down and kissed Rachel on the forehead.

"And when I pray for my son, I shall also pray for you," said the queen.

A stable boy led out Isoldé's horse, a straw colored gelding named Nahor, and busied himself putting a blanket and saddle upon it, and tying the saddlebags securely.

Isoldé could see Moor growing impatient waiting for Rachel's horse to be made ready.

"Swordmaster, might we speak a moment," she said, leading him a few paces away. "Moor, I know you will guard Daniel well," she said. "Still, it will ease my heart if you send word back to me that you have reached Eboracium safely."

"Do not fear overmuch for your son, my queen," replied Moor, "No man in Asulon knows this business better than I."

"Argeus would not have put so much faith in your skills were that not true," Isoldé said. "But Daniel is my only child and all in this world that I have left to me of my husband."

"I shall send word to you once we board a ship. Look for it among the kitchen staff." Moor thought for a moment. "When you hear that 'Hawkin has reached the city', then you will know that we have departed safely. I shall send you a more direct message once we reach Logres."

"Thank you," said Isoldé. "Ever have you been a friend to my family."

Moor's back straightened just a bit further. "My queen, I shall bring your son safely to your father's house or die in the attempt," he said, meaning it.

"I shall pray that it does not come to that," replied Isoldé.

Moor nodded to where Simon and Rachel stood waiting for their horses.

"Daniel and I would be all the swifter riding alone. To bring an old priest and a girl along were not part of my original plan."

"There is more to that 'old priest' than meets the eye," replied Isoldé. "He has traveled far and seen much. Argeus respected his wisdom and sought his counsel. You would do well to do the same. As for the girl, some things even your warrior eyes cannot see. My sisters and I all share our father's inner sight. I can see that the hand of God rests upon that child. For what purpose He has brought her here, I do not know, but it is the Lord's purpose nonetheless. I know you will keep a good watch over my son, but keep guard also over the girl. Even if the laws of host and guest did not hold us honor bound to see to her safety, I would still command you thus. "

Moor bowed. "As you wish, my queen."

A boy led Rachel's horse next to a set of stone steps so that she could mount. Daniel dashed over. "May I help you?" he said, offering his hand.

"I thank you," said the girl, taking his hand and mounting the horse. She patted the horse's neck. "Nahor, you will be my friend and make the ride easy, will you not?"

As if understanding, the gelding whinnied and nodded his head.

The stableman led Simon's horse toward the steps but the old priest stopped him. "No need for the stairs, my man. I am rather spry for my age." With that, he stepped into the stirrup and swung easily up into the saddle.

Daniel kissed his mother, turned away, took two quick steps and leapt onto his horse's back.

Moor looked the group over. Satisfied that all belts were tight and all bags secure, he turned to Isoldé and bowed. "Daylight is burning," Moor said, "We should go."

He mounted his horse and gave out a high bird-like cry. A similar cry cut through the gloom above. Moor's hawk, Theol, would circle high above them as they rode.

They made their way silently down the winding road that led from the highlands near the great river down into the valley to the west.

The sun crested the trees as they came to the King's Highway, the main north-south road, running parallel the river.

"The south road would be the quickest way to the ferry crossing to Eboracium," Moor said, "therefore, we shall take the northern crossing. Anyone hunting for us will not expect that." They set off on the main road, which was wide enough to ride four abreast, but Moor had them ride by twos in the center of the road. He and Daniel led; Simon and Rachel followed. They rode on as the sun rose high into the sky.

"I must go and speak to the Etruscan," said Simon to Rachel. "I will send the young man back to ride with thee." Simon's horse brought him up beside Moor.

"Daniel, I would like a word with Master Moor. Would you mind riding beside the Lady Rachel and keeping her company for a time?"

Daniel, who had been looking glum most of the morning, brightened.

"Yes, sir. I mean—no, I would not mind, sir." he said. He held back his horse to take Simon's place beside Rachel.

"Master Moor," began Simon in Etruscan, "I do not presume to know more about your business than you, but I am curious about your methods."

Moor raised an eyebrow. "Oh?"

"It seems to me that if we are being hunted as you say, then it would be wiser to have a cohort of soldiers riding with us."

"Stealth can be more effective than strength at times," replied Moor. "My people have a saying, 'ten men can keep a secret only if nine of them are dead.' If we had brought a cohort of troops with us, then invariably one of them would have bragged to some tavern girl about guarding the prince on his very dangerous journey to Eboracium. In that tavern would be a man in the employ of our enemy, keeping his ears open for such news."

"But what, then, would Sargon do?" asked Simon "Could he find enough men willing to fight twenty armed soldiers?"

"He would not need to. A half dozen men with bows, all aiming at the same target, all shooting at the same time, would virtually guarantee success," replied Moor. "With sufficient woodcraft, sheltered behind a place that horses could not swiftly cross—a section of

141

deadfalls perhaps or a steep sided creek,–they could mount their horses after their attack and make their escape without losing a man. No, we shall trust to secrecy."

As they rode on, they passed the occasional lone rider or a farmer bringing a wagonload of goods to market, but for most of the morning the road remained empty. Near midday, the land leveled out and they came to a side road that led towards the river with a sign that read 'North Ferry'.

Moor nodded to Daniel and both men unshouldered their bows, nocked an arrow and then rested these down against their left thighs to partially conceal them.

The forest thinned out as they drew closer to the river. Daniel saw the ferryman's cabin and a fenced garden of a size to give a lone man vegetables for a season. Beyond the cabin, the wooden dock held a lean-to, built to shelter those waiting for the ferry. The ferry was not in sight, no doubt on the other bank of the river. Warily, they rode out from the trees.

Moor raised his fist in a signal to halt. He pointed to the far shore of the river. Daniel could see nothing there. Then it struck him. The river was not so broad here. The ferry should have been somewhere between the dock and the far shore, but they saw no sign of it. The thick ferry rope lay limp upon the ground, one end tied to a large tree, the other end disappearing into the water. Moor dismounted, signaling the others to do the same.

"Stand between your horses. Daniel, watch the forest," Moor ordered. He held his bow low so it would not hinder his view and made his way, watchful and swift, towards the shore. Daniel would rather have accompanied Moor, but knew better than to argue with the Etruscan when the war-mind was upon him.

There were no windows in the lean-to and the opening faced the water. As he approached the dock, Moor knelt and picked up a stone with his right hand.

He slowly made his way along the dock, keeping to the ends of the boards to avoid a creak that would betray his approach. Moor reached the right side of the lean-to and stopped, listening. Slowly he crept towards the edge of the lean-to. Daniel saw him pause just before he would have come in view of anyone inside and throw the stone over the structure to the far side of the dock. The stone landed in the water with a splash as Moor stepped around the corner, disappearing into the lean-to. Daniel strained his ears, but heard only the sounds of the forest for several long moments. Then Moor emerged from the near side of the lean-to and came back to shore. He inspected the ground, evidently searching for something. At the shoreward end of the dock, he stopped and knelt to examine something at the water's edge.

He rose, shaking his head.

"Daniel, come here," Moor called out. "You should see this."

Daniel dropped the reins of his horse; Mirbane would stay in place until he saw danger and, even then, he would not go far.

When Daniel reached Moor, he saw that the paladin had pulled the ferry line from the water.

"This is really shoddy workmanship," said Moor. He held out the end of the heavy line to Daniel.

The end appeared frayed and split, as if worn down by rubbing against coarse stone.

"You see here, how the end appears to be worn away?" asked Moor. "And look here. See the small flakes of rock ground into the rope fibers?"

"The rope parted and the ferry floated downstream until the ferryman could land it?" suggested Daniel.

"The ferryman is dead," said Moor. "Look about you. This whole shore is lined with round river stones of yellow quartz, quite smooth. The stone flakes you see in the rope come from crushed gray granite, taken no doubt from the King's Highway. Do you see any granite on this riverbank? No, a sharp steel bladed severed this rope. Then it was made to look like natural wear by crushing the ends and rubbing some stone flakes into the fibers. This part of the rope would be above the water when the ferry was working. What ferryman would allow his rope to get so worn and frayed if it were in plain sight? The lazy men who did this did not wish to get wet. They should have brought the ferry halfway across the river and then cut the line. One of them would have had a long swim to shore, but their hand in this would have been harder to discover."

Daniel looked back warily towards the trees.

"We are in no danger here," said Moor. "These men act like hunters looking to take a rabbit. They plug all the holes to the rabbit's burrow but one; then they go to that one hole and set their snare. No doubt they wait for us at the southern crossing."

"What shall we do now?" asked Simon, who had joined them. "If I might suggest, we could return to the fortress and gather as many soldiers as we can find for our journey. If we will emerge from our burrow into danger, better as a bear than a rabbit."

"It would take two days to gather the men," said Moor, "and while we wait, what then? Shall we worry over every plate and goblet, wondering if our enemy has decided to do to the son what he did to the father? Perhaps he would poison us all and seek to be done with it, leaving none to take revenge. No, we will ride for the southern crossing."

"And ride straight into their trap," said Simon. "I would think the Swordmaster of Caurus would come up with a better plan than that."

"I did not say we would ride straight to them," replied Moor. "Sargon sent his men out, not knowing when we would leave the fortress. By removing this ferry, he simply hedged his bet, like any good gambler would. Now his men lie in wait, not knowing if we left the fortress or not." Moor looked up at the sun, marking its position. "By now they will be bored waiting for a prey that may not show. This is the right time for the hunted to become the hunter."

They rode off; Daniel leading Simon and Rachel, with Moor just out of sight ahead of them. When they returned to the broader King's Highway, Daniel could see Theol high in the sky, presumably flying above Moor.

After an hour passed, they saw Moor riding towards them. "Go in there," he said indicating a shadowed grove of trees within the forest. "Four men are hiding behind a deadfall half a league ahead."

"Are they the ones hunting for us?" asked Simon.

"They are not there to pick berries," replied Moor. He turned to Daniel. "A stream runs behind their position. We can use it's noise to get behind them and take them unawares."

"Wait." Simon spoke up. "Things will go better if you had a diversion."

"Ah, I did not know that your order taught military strategy as well as faith, *priest*," said Moor, stressing the last word. "How do you propose we cause this diversion? There are only two of us."

"I will ride down the road and draw their attention while you do your work," replied Simon.

"And leave the girl here alone?" said Moor "I thought she was to be under your protection while we travel."

"She will be in no danger here," said Simon. "With the sun high and hot, any bear in these parts is long into his midday nap."

Moor thought in silence for a long moment, then said, "As you wish. Having something to draw their attention will put the odds more strongly in our favor. But you must follow my instructions exactly if you want to live."

"Good," said the priest. "You shall see that even an old man can still be useful in his own way."

"We shall see," said Moor. "Daniel and I will go on ahead. Give us an hour before you mount your horse.

Half a league ahead the road bends to the right. Just after that bend, you will see that some old trees have been brought down by a storm on both sides of the road. The men we hunt hide just within the forest on the *right* side of the road. When you reach that spot, dismount and go to the *left* side of the road and sit upon a fallen tree you will see there. When you sit, place your horse between yourself and the men in the forest lest you wish to find an arrow suddenly sprout from your throat. Do you understand?"

Simon nodded.

Daniel removed his short sword from his belt. "Here, Simon, take this. You'll need something to protect yourself with."

"Thank you lad, but I am not one for such weapons. Besides, I am just the decoy. And if I do need a weapon, I have my friend here," he said, patting his staff. "I have learned a thing or two down through the years and know how to use this if need be."

Simon saw Rachel sitting on a log, waiting. "Give me a moment to speak with the princess."

He came to where she sat, hands folded in her lap, waiting patiently. "How much of our counsels couldst thou understand?"

"Thou wilt fight beside the warriors?" she asked, looking at him curiously.

"Let us pray that it will not come to that. While we are away, remain here. No danger will come to thee and we shall return soon."

"I shall trust in the Lord, who has given me into thy care," she said.

Simon nodded and then spoke a short prayer of protection over her. "I am ready," he said, turning back to Moor.

"Oh happy day," said the Etruscan under his breath.

Moor and Daniel took a moment to check their bows, then, without a sound, they made their way deeper into the forest. In such dense foliage, they disappeared from view after only a few steps.

Simon waited his hour beside Rachel, led his horse back to the road, mounted and then nudged the horse into a trot.

Moor and Daniel left the stream they had been following and moved towards the road. They made their way silently, following a deer trail as it meandered away from the stream. Moor stopped and waited for Daniel to draw close to him. Without taking his eyes off the land ahead, Moor touched the first two fingers of his right hand to Daniel's bow forming a triangle, tapped the bow twice and then pointed to the right. He gave the signal for the "Arrowhead", a simple battle plan young paladins practiced in their first week of learning to use a bow against men. Moor liked his battle plans simple; in combat, simple worked.

Once they spotted Sargon's men, Daniel and Moor would move into positions forming the base of a triangle with the enemy at the apex. This way the two paladins could fire on the same target from two different directions without risk of striking each other. Moor had signaled that Daniel would take the farther right flank, and that he would shoot first. The prince could kill one, perhaps even two, of the assassins before they took cover. Since they would be taking cover against the direction of Daniel's attack, it should allow Moor a good shooting angle from his own position. Moor would then pick off the rearmost assassin, as the man in front might miss the death of a man behind him, while watching the other direction. If Daniel kept the remaining assassins' attention by putting his arrows into the trees that protected them, Moor should be able to pick the remaining men off one by one.

Suddenly Moor stopped and put his hand behind his back, palm out. Daniel froze and waited. After a moment Moor motioned him forward. A little more than a bowshot ahead of them, Daniel could see the four assassins. Three lay stretched out on the ground before a jumble of fallen trees, while the fourth kept watch on the road. The deadfall allowed a narrow opening towards the road on the right—their likely escape route when attacked. Daniel would attack from that angle first.

The assassin on guard kicked the man closest to him and they all turned to look at the road.

Daniel saw Moor's jaw clench in anger.

Oh no! thought Daniel as he looked beyond the men to find Simon leading his horse, not to the far side of the road as instructed, but to a spot right before the men on the near side of the road. Simon tied his horse to a branch and sat down wearily on a fallen log with his back to the forest. He drew an apple from a pocket within his robes and took a noisy bite.

Daniel could see the four men whispering among themselves and knew what they were thinking. If their prey came down the road just now, either the old man or his horse would block a good bowshot. Simon sat so close that any of the men could have thrown a rock and knocked his hat off.

The tallest of the four assassins appeared to be the leader, for he said something to the other three. They nodded and moved out into the undergrowth. Daniel looked at Moor. The Etruscan shook his head and mouthed the word "*wait.*"

The three men had made off south. The tall man waited for a time, then began to move off to the north, parallel to the road, but keeping to the forest. Once all four men moved out of sight, Moor signaled Daniel to follow him. He led them straight to the pile of dead trees from which the four men had watched the road.

Daniel had a better view of Simon here, but he and Moor would have the same problem as the four men they hunted; Simon blocked their arrows here as well as he had the enemy's. He hoped Simon would move if trouble came, for the dense tangle of fallen trees offered no better opening for them to shoot from.

The old man glanced to his left and raised his hand in welcome. Through the trees Daniel could see the three men coming round the bend in the road, trudging along as if they had already walked far that day.

"Greetings, grandfather," called out one man. "This be a lonely road to be on all by yourself. I would not stay here too long, if I were you. There be highwaymen about these parts.

"Thank you, friend," replied Simon "but I am weary and need a place to rest."

"There are better places than this, old man," said the shortest of the three. "You should move down the road some."

"Oh, no," replied Simon. "These old bones are comfortable right here. I was just about to have my lunch; would you care to join me? I think I might have a spare apple or two in my pockets."

The youngest of the three, about twenty summers in age and lacking the hardness of the other two men, said, "Sir, you really ought to leave this place. There is danger here."

"No, no. I am tired of walking today. In fact, after lunch I think I will take a nap."

As one, the three men looked past Simon to where their leader had emerged silently from the trees. He walked towards them, a slight grin on his face.

He shook his head. "Ah, grandfather, you are being very stubborn today. When three men give you the same advice, you really should take it." His looked at his men, the grin leaving his face. "Kill him." The three men drew daggers and spread out, moving to surround the old man.

Simon leapt to his feet, shepherd's staff in hand. "Stay back; I do not carry this stick for naught!"

Daniel nocked an arrow, but Moor stayed his hand. "Wait for a clear shot," he whispered. "I will go north and get behind the leader."

Daniel saw the men creep closer as Simon began to swing his staff wildly and shout at the men.

Daniel's heart fell. He should not have let the old man act as a decoy. In his panic, Simon moved in the wrong direction. Instead of backing away from the men to his right, which would have drawn the men towards the opening from which Daniel could fire upon them, Simon moved towards them. The priest swung his staff without apparent skill or plan.

"Feisty for an oldster, aren't we?" said the first of the men, laughing.

"Stay away," cried Simon, "I have done you no harm. Leave me alone."

"It is too late for that, old man," said the shortest of the men. "You should have left when we warned you."

He took a step towards Simon, faking an attack to test his reaction.

Simon responded by swinging his staff in wide arcs. From where he watched in the forest, Daniel drew back his bow. He guessed these men to be highwaymen that Sargon's assassins had hired. Professionals would have ended this sooner by drawing weapons at the last moment and striking before their victim realized their intent. But Daniel knew that an old priest could not hold even mere ruffians at bay for long. *Moor, you had better hurry,* he thought, hoping for a clear shot.

The three men took their time, looking for an opening to charge all at once and overwhelm Simon. Suddenly Simon switched his line of attack from wide horizontal blows to a vertical strike aimed at the head of the short man. The man leaped back so the blow passed him. Having missed his target, Simon lost his balance, stumbled forward a step and brought his staff down upon the man's foot. "Ahhhh!" the short man howled, hopping on one foot and holding the other. "You done broke my big toe, you old fool."

The others broke into laughter. "Who's the fool?" said the first man. "I don't see him dancing on one foot."

"Enough," snapped the leader from his place by Simon's horse. "Finish this."

"Sorry, old man," said the first man, drawing his sword, "but your time has come."

The other two men drew their swords and spread out, making it hard for Simon to keep them all in his sight. The younger one tried to get to Simon's back. In doing so, he came near the opening where Daniel waited. *Just a little further*, thought Daniel, aiming his bow.

"Do not do this," said the priest. "You have one chance left to save yourselves. Once you step forward, you seal your fates."

The first man charged, attacking from Simon's right, aiming a chopping blow at his leg. Simon stepped back, moving his legs out of range while he brought his staff down upon the man's forearm, breaking the bones there. He then swept his staff up, catching the man in the throat. The man collapsed in a heap.

"You were lucky, old man," cried the short man, limping on his injured foot. "Now I owe you something for my foot."

"There is no need for this," said Simon. "Drop your swords and surrender."

The young one saw his chance and circled behind Simon. Simon saw the short man's eye flick behind him, to where his horse stood. Simon gave a short whistle and the horse kicked out, catching the younger highwayman in the body and launching him through the air like a shot from a catapult. He struck a tree and fell to the ground as if made of rags.

The short man gave a loud battle cry and charged, swinging his sword wildly, slowed by his injured leg. Simon waited until the man came within range, then struck towards the man's legs. The man tried to block the strike, but, faster than the man could react, Simon circled his staff around and brought it crashing down onto the highwayman's head. The man crumpled into the dust.

The leader of the highwaymen reversed his dagger in his hand. He drew back his arm to throw. There was too much brush there for Daniel to get a clear shot with his bow. "Simon!" he cried out. Simon spun around as the man brought his hand forward, but not in a throw. His arm came down slowly and the man toppled forward, the shaft of an arrow sticking from his back. Moor stepped out from the trees, a second arrow at the ready.

Needing no stealth now, Daniel leapt over the deadfall and ran to the road.

"You took your time with that arrow," he said to Moor.

"I did not have a clear shot until then," replied Moor, eying Simon suspiciously. "Besides, I believe our friend here knew he was in little danger from these men."

Simon smiled with all the innocence of a child. "I was just doing my part to help our journey along."

"Well, now we must sweep away the evidence of that help and be gone," said Moor. "Go collect the girl and return here. Daniel and I have work to do."

"See to them, but leave no blood," Moor ordered Daniel while he kept watch on the forest. Daniel went to the body of the leader first, drew his sword and laid it flat against the neck, feeling for a pulse. He was glad for Moor's instruction about leaving no blood, for it was the usual practice of the paladins to behead their fallen enemies; something they had learned from the sons of Anak. Daniel could see the logic of this in war, where a wounded man you thought dead could rise and slay you. "Trust that no enemy is dead, until you have taken their head," was a saying among the Anakim; begun, it was said, long ages ago when Anak had been called upon to slay monsters: but there were no monsters in the world these days. Daniel looked down at the man's dead body. He had seen many a dead animal in his time, but this was different, this was a body much like his own on the ground before him. Though he would have killed the man himself had he had an open shot at him, Daniel felt a twinge of pity for him and wondered if he had a family that he loved: probably not, for if he had he would not be lying here dead, his last thoughts those of murder. Daniel felt no pulse and so moved on to the next man. He knew why Moor did not want to leave any blood sign. If he had beheaded these men the resulting blood, and the animals it would attract, would tell any pursuer that those they hunted had passed that way. Instead he had laid the flat of his sword upon each man's neck feeling for a pulse. Nothing from the first three men, but when he came to the youngest of the highwaymen Daniel felt a slow pulse beating. "This one still lives," he called out.

Moor came, rolled the highwayman on his belly and tied his hands behind his back. The young man moaned as Moor tightened the knots. "Help me carry him into the forest," he said. "Perhaps he has information we can use."

Moor bound the young highwayman to a tree in a seated position, out of sight of the road. Daniel carried the bodies deeper into the forest and covered them with fallen pine needles and fresh aromatic branches. Daniel guessed it would take at least a full day in the heat for the vultures to pick up the scent of rotting meat and begin circling over the site.

He went to the road and collected Simon and Rachel, who were just approaching. Inside the forest, they found Moor kneeling before the bound highwayman, holding a small bottle of something apparently foul smelling beneath the young man's nose. The young man coughed and opened his eyes. It took him a moment to recognize his situation, then his eyes opened wide in fear.

"Your left arm and three of your ribs are broken," said Moor. "Do you wish me to add to that list?"

The young man shook his head vigorously in the negative.

"Good, then tell us your name."

"Nob, sir, but most just call me Spooner."

"Well, Spooner, if you wish to live another hour, tell us who hired you."

"My cousin Nester did, sir."

"Your cousin?"

"'Tis the truth, sir. He be the one whose toe the old man broke. When we were small, Nester and I would always talk of becoming pirates and having adventures. My dad's the cook at our town's tavern, and I was his apprentice these last ten years. But I did not want to be a cook all my life, sir. Last year, Nester left our village, saying he was off to seek his fortune. He was gone so long I thought he was dead. Then, just about three weeks ago, he showed up at my bedroom window and says to me that, if I wants adventure, I should follow him. We rode off and he tells me how he's become a highwayman and how he could give me all the adventure I could stand."

"It seems he did so and more," said Simon.

"Ay, sir, that he did, poor ol' Nester...not that I blame you for killing him, sir, he was going to kill you, he was. Nester always did have a mean streak in him, he did."

"Enough of your family history, boy," said Moor. "Tell us who hired you to kill us."

"Oh, no, sir, I was never hired to kill no one. Me and Nester would just jump out and hold some fat farmer at sword point while he tossed us his purse. I never killed no one in all my whole life."

"Then what of the ferryman?" demanded Moor.

"That was Odman and Dirker's doing, sir. They be the two other men you killed, sir. Nester knew them and said they were needing two more men to do a big job. Nester said they would pay us enough to keep us living high and fat all summer. It was them who done in the ferryman, sir. Me and Nester rode up with those two to the ferry without being told what for. We waited with the horses, and Odman and Dirker went to ask the ferryman about who had crossed the river in the last few days. All of a sudden, I see Dirker pull his dagger and stab the ferryman in the back. It was them who tied the body up in a sack and them that loaded that sack with rocks and then throwed the sack, ferryman and all, in the river, sir. I had nothin' to do with it."

"They did not tell you why they murdered the ferryman?" asked Moor.

"It was part of the job was all they would tell us, sir. They cut the ferry rope and we rode south. Dirker had us hide in the forest and wait, keepin' an eye out for any soldiers riding south. I don't know what we were supposed to do if we saw them. Dirker wouldn't say. I wanted to run off, but I was 'fraid of Dirker and Odman, truly I was. Dirker said that if we were caught, I would hang as sure as the rest of them would. I didn't know what to do, sir."

"Yet you drew your dagger with the others against the old man," Moor said.

"But you saw that I never came close to him. I wanted no part in murder, sir."

"Well, you have had a part, whether you wanted it or not," said Moor. "Had I the time I would turn you over to the royal guards for trial. Think now, did you ever overhear any of the others speaking about who hired them, or what their plans were if any soldiers did not appear along this road?"

"No, sir, I swear I never heard them say a thing about any of that."

"That is unfortunate," Moor said, rising to his feet and drawing his sword.

"Hold!" commanded Simon, "What are you doing?"

"He is of no further use to us," replied Moor. "We cannot leave him here to expose us to any that pursue, and we certainly cannot take him with us. He has played a part in a murder and must pay the murderer's price."

The youth's eyes went wide in terror.

"I believe he told us the truth," Simon said. "His hands were not bloodied in this. And I believe he was spared for a reason, though the others died. I think we should leave his fate in the Lord's hands."

Moor shook his head. "And if more of our enemy's men should be on this road and find him? He would be able to tell them much."

"He could tell them no more than they themselves would guess, and then they would kill him," said Simon. He looked down at the youth. "You *do* know that the men who hired Dirker would kill you if they found you: both because you had failed in your task and to ensure your silence?"

"I don't want to see any of that sort ever again, sir. Let me go and I will run straight home to my dad. I swear it, sir."

"If we let him go, he may stumble into our enemy nonetheless," Moor said.

"We can leave him tied up here," said Simon. "In the morning farmers will be going to and fro along the road and he can call out to one to untie him."

Moor sheathed his sword. "I do not like the idea, but I will respect your counsel."

"B...but you are not going to leave me tied up here for the wolves to eat!" stammered Spooner.

Moor knelt down to inspect the knots that bound the youth. "Oh, you should not worry about wolves," said the Etruscan. "There have not been any wolves this far south in many years."

Spooner's shoulders sagged in relief.

"Now bears," Moor said. "Well, that is another matter. There are bears here aplenty."

Spooner's eyes grew wide again in fear.

Moor looked him up and down. "But I would not worry too much about bears. You have no blood on you. If you remain silent tonight you should do fine."

Spooner still looked nervous, but calmed down somewhat at this news.

"Now your cousin and his friends," continued Moor, "they are all covered with blood and are just beyond that thicket, right over there. So tonight, if you

156

hear any munching and crunching of bones from that thicket, you must remain absolutely silent or the bears will have you for their dessert."

Spooner stared at the thicket as if the largest bear in all of Asulon might charge from it at any moment, fangs dripping blood and hungry for more.

"Oh, if you do manage to make it through the night," added Moor, "remember to listen carefully before hailing anyone coming down the road in the morning. You should only call at the sound of a wagon. That will be a farmer going to market. If you hail a rider on a horse, it might be Dirker's boss and he will slit your throat if he finds you. Most likely he planned to kill you and your cousin anyway, once the job was finished." Moor rose to his feet. "Remember, absolute silence tonight and call only a wagon in the morning."

The four travelers led their horses to the road.

"Moor, you are truly a cruel and dastardly man," said Simon with a chuckle.

The Etruscan bowed as if accepting a compliment. "It is a skill that has taken me many years to develop."

They continued their ride south, with Moor once again riding ahead, scouting for danger.

About the third hour of the afternoon they came upon a rise in the road. Daniel saw Moor in the distance, speaking with a man in a wagon. He waved them forward.

"This is farmer Jotham," Moor said, as they approached. "He, like us, could use some company on this road."

"Greetings, friend, and thank you," Simon said. "Might an old man and his granddaughter ride with you and rest our saddle sore, ah, seats?"

"Come on up, friend," replied the farmer. "There is not enough room on the bench for three, but the child can ride in the back, and will be more comfortable there on a sack of flour, anyway."

"The good King Argeus, the Lord bless him," Jotham went on, "cleared out many a highwaymen that used to ride this road when Absalom was king, but still some remain to worry us. It is good to have two paladins as escort."

"Just doing our job, sir," Daniel said.

"Well, we too are grateful, young man," agreed Simon.

Towards the fifth hour they came to a fork in the road. A sign pointed the way to the ferry.

"We must leave you here," Moor said, "You will be safe enough on the short road down to the ferry."

"I thank you again," said the farmer.

"Ah, yes, thank you," said Simon sleepily, apparently awoken from a nap. The old man yawned, closed his eyes and returned to his slumber.

"I traveled well with you stout lads as escort," Jotham said. He looked up at the sun. "We should arrive well before the evening crossing. And since that now gives me some time to spend at the tavern, I won't be needing this." Jotham reached under his seat, pulled out a bottle and tossed it to Moor. "Here you are, Captain, something to take the chill out of the night air."

"This will be put to good use," replied Moor. "After we go off duty, of course."

"Of course," agreed the farmer with a wink. "Git ye up!" he called out to his horse, and the wagon headed off down the ferry road.

Moor and Daniel continued south on the main road for a short time and then stopped. Moor drew the farmer's bottle from his saddlebag and they both turned off the road onto a trail that led into the woods, laughing as they did so.

Once inside the forest, they went silent, dismounted and searched the woods ahead of them. Seeing a spot that met their needs, they tied their horses to a tree in a small widening of the trail.

Moor took a length of black silk thread from his belt and tied it to a tree at knee level. He laid the thread across the trail and strung it through a forked branch he stuck into the ground behind another tree. Next he took a tin cup and plate from his pack, placed a copper coin in the cup and tied the thread to the cup's handle and placed the plate on the ground below the cup. Any pursuer following them would walk into the thread and make a sound either by jangling the cup, or, if he was too quick in his step, breaking the thread and sending the cup falling onto the tin plate. The trip line set up, Moor opened the bottle of wine and leaned it against a stone beyond the trip line to complete the picture. Moor led them fifty paces deeper into the forest then sat back against a thick tree. They waited, watching their back trail for two hours. Finally, Moor stood up and signaled to Daniel to follow. He led off silently towards the river.

After a time Daniel could hear men's voices raised in song.

He and Moor crept through the forest until they came to the edge of a high embankment, overlooking a dock that jutted out into the river. A large stone inn stood before the dock, with lantern light and laughter coming from the windows of the tavern on its first floor. At the end of the dock, tied alongside, floated the ferry. Few men could be seen outside: three young men loaded the contents of several wagons into the ferry, and an old man sat on the end of the dock, whittling. The river, at this point, grew too wide for a cable ferry, so this ferry had sails and tiller. The door to the tavern opened, a man came out and boarded the ship. A bell hung from the rail near him and the man, evidently the ferryman, rang this seven times. Other men, farmer Jotham among them, came reluctantly out of the tavern and boarded the ferry. The ferryman rang his bell three more times, cast off the lines and the ferry slipped out into the river.

The old man stopped his whittling and watched the ferry disappear into the twilight. He rose stiffly to his feet, tossed the bit of wood he had been working on into the water and sheathed his knife. Then he mounted a horse tied before the tavern and rode off up the road. Just before he would have disappeared from Daniel's view, the old man stopped his horse and sat looking into the trees. Soon a man dressed in woodsman's gray emerged from the forest. The two spoke for a moment, then the woodsman passed something to the old man, who rode off. The woodsman returned to the forest. The two paladins waited a short time and then saw a dozen men lead horses out from the forest, quietly mount up and ride away.

Moor laid his cloak out under a tree and stretched out upon it.

"And now we wait."

Moor's hawk came gliding silently through the trees and landed on a branch near its master. It put its head under its wing and settled in for the evening. Daniel sat and watched the road.

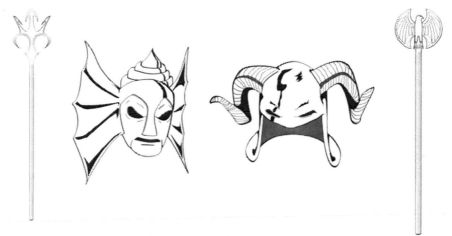

Chapter Nine
THE CITY

And it shall come to pass afterward, that I will
pour out my spirit upon all flesh; and your sons and
your daughters shall prophesy, your old men shall
dream dreams, your young men shall see visions.
- The Book of Joel 2:28

Night had fallen when Daniel heard the creaking of
wood coming from over the water.

"That would be the ferry," Moor said, rising.
"Come, we should be at the dock when the ferryman
lands. I do not think he will wait long." Moor blew softly
on Theol's beak and the hawk awoke long enough for
Moor to slip a traveling hood over its head and place the
bird upon his wrist. Moor and Daniel returned to their
horses-Daniel packing the few items Moor had used to
disguise the scene-and then they rode down to the dock.
After a short time, the ferry appeared from the gloom.
The ferryman stepped onto the dock. A short, stoutly
built man in his sixties, he looked the two paladins up
and down with a scowl as they approached.

"'Tis not safe to make this trip at night. These old eyes can't see all the flotsam in the river anymore. Might hit something, I might. 'Tis a risk to myself and my ship."

"Well, you are very kind to return for us," replied Moor. "Our duties kept us up north and we knew we would not arrive here until after you had returned to Eboracium for the night."

"'Twas not kindness that brought me back," the ferryman said with a knowing gleam in his eye. "Your friend gave me a gold crown and said I would get two more when I picked you up."

"No," Moor said, "he gave you one crown and promised we would give you *one* more when you brought us to the far shore and docked at Eboracium. I know this, for I gave him the gold and the instructions myself."

The ferryman rubbed the back of his neck with a callused hand. "I guess he did, at that. My ears tain't what they used to be. It's my age, you know."

Moor leaned in as if to include the man in a secret. "Well, friend, we carry orders to the garrison at Eboracium and, since we are on the crown's business and I am spending the crown's gold and not my own, I will give you one crown now, in addition to the one I will give you when we land at Eboracium."

"Done," said the ferryman, pleased with his bargaining skills. Moor took a coin from his belt and pressed it into the man's hand. The two paladins walked their horses aboard the ferry while the ferryman undid the dock lines. The ferryman was about to ring his bell when Moor laid his hand on the cord. "No need for that, it is just the two of us, after all."

"Oh, yes. Right you are," said the ferryman. He let out his sail and set course for the far shore. Daniel could see a few small lights shining. As the lights grew brighter, he began to make out several docks, some for ships and the southernmost for the ferry. Beyond the dock, a flat plaza paved with cobblestones led to a row of warehouses and taverns. In times gone by, no lights would have shone from the waterside of Eboracium at night, to conceal the city from pirates. But that was a long time ago. The House of Asher had brought the Asulonians together to fight their common enemy and end the raids; now lights shown merrily from the many windows that faced the river.

The ferry came to its dock and the ferryman set his lines for the night.

"Here you are, friend," said Moor, handing the ferryman a coin. "And to help warm you when you reach home..." He reached into his saddlebag, brought forth the farmer's bottle of wine and handed it to the ferryman.

"Why, thank yee, Captain," nodded the ferryman grinning. "This will sure do nicely to take the damp out of these old bones tonight." He pointed to a tavern across the way. "Your friends be in that tavern there."

"Thank you, sir," said Moor. "We have kept you long enough. Now you should take yourself home and enjoy your evening."

The two paladins walked their horses the short distance across the plaza and tied them to the rail before the tavern.

The tavern's street level windows had been cut from the bottom of old wine jugs: tinted green to start with, years of smoke had made them impossible to see through.

"I will go first and move to the hinge side," said Moor, "You go to the lock side and remember not to silhouette yourself in the doorway."

"Yes, sir," said Daniel, thinking his teacher overcautious. The door hinged on the right, so Daniel would go left when he entered.

In one motion, Moor opened the door and slipped past the threshold on the hinge side of the door, opening the door wide enough that anyone lying in ambush behind it would be pinned against the wall.

163

Daniel took one step into the room then one left, his back near the wall. Moor closed the door behind them. They moved smoothly, so that only a well trained eye would catch the significance of their entry.

A small lantern on each of its dozen tables lit the tavern's main room dimly. Daniel liked this type of tavern. The air smelled of smoke, roasted meat, fresh bread and beer. Local men, farmers and merchants by their look, sat in small groups. A few glanced up, but, not recognizing the newcomers, went back to their tankards.

A portly man in a stained leather apron came up to them beaming. "Table, gents?" he said.

"We are looking for some friends," replied Moor, looking over the man's shoulder, "and there they are."

Simon and Rachel sat at a table along the far wall. Rachel had the hood of her cloak up, keeping her face in shadow, but Simon had laid his hat on the table and leaned back in his chair, enjoying a tankard.

"Timing, in peace as well as war, is everything," he said, downing the last of his beer as Moor and Daniel came to their table. "Shall we go?" said Simon, placing a coin on the table. He stood and stretched his arms overhead. "It will be good to sleep in my own bed tonight." He tipped his hat to the tavern keeper. "Remember what I said about that poultice for your knee."

"Aye, I'll do that. Much obliged, sir."

"You pick an odd time to make friends," Moor said to Simon once they were outside.

"Sometimes the best way to hide is to look like you have nothing to hide," replied Simon. "Besides, while I spoke to the tavern keeper, I also had a good view of the door and all who entered. Nothing seemed amiss while we waited for you."

A high wall, covered in so many centuries worth of vines that it looked like an ancient cliff face, separated the dock area from the city proper. The gate, its iron doors open, stood in the center of the wall. Moor nodded to the two city guards flanking the gate.

"Evening," said the older of the guards, as he waved them through. Daniel knew that, even without the paladin's insignia he and Moor wore, they still would have entered without much in the way of questioning. Eboracium was a city of commerce, not of security, and in these peaceful days, the city fathers permitted little to interfere with that commerce. The four travelers emerged from the wide tunnel beyond the gate and came upon a long, broad street running north and south. On each side of the street was a thick wall of crushed stone, laying there so long the stones were now fused together, with houses and shops cut into the wall. Grass grew from the tops of the walls. To the birds of the air, the city must have looked like a grassy plain with regular stone-lined valleys running north and south. Moor led them north, towards the garrison. As they rode, they passed cross tunnels, cut at regular intervals.

They passed through one such cross tunnel, up a street and through another tunnel. When Moor felt satisfied that no one followed them, he doubled back south.

"We will go to the deep water docks," said Moor. "At a tavern there we should find a captain with a ship bound for Logres."

"What tavern should we try first?" asked Daniel, as casually as he could.

"I was thinking of the Seven Fathoms," Moor said, eyeing the prince. "Why, would you recommend another?"

"Ah, no," replied Daniel "I just thought that, the closer we go to the docks, the better our chances of finding a ship leaving on the next tide."

"The Fathoms will be close enough," Moor said.

Moor had chosen quiet streets so far, with the shops closed for the night and the owners, no doubt, home for their suppers. Since entering the city, they had passed only a lamplighter going about his business. As they continued, Daniel saw that more and more of the shops had iron bars built into their windows. Daniel knew that the southern tip of the island that made up Eboracium housed the poorer classes and rougher types.

"Spare a copper, sirs?" called out a gray-bearded old beggar.

Daniel stopped his horse. "Here you are, friend," he said, dropping a coin down to the beggar. As his parents had taught him, Daniel always kept a few coppers in his bag for those less blessed than he, but this beggar reminded him somehow of Argeus—perhaps because of his age and thick beard. Daniel had reached into his main pouch and dropped a silver piece into the man's hand.

"Now promise me that you will use at least some of this for what sits on a plate rather than in a tankard," Daniel said.

"I promises, sir," said the old man, staring at the coin in disbelief.

"We do not have time for this," Moor said.

"There is always time to give a kindness to the unfortunate," said Simon, "for you are doing the Lord's work when you do so."

Moor just stared hard at Daniel until the prince touched heels to his horse's flanks and they moved on.

After a time, the travelers turned west into another tunnel. Now they could hear the sounds of many voices, some in laughter and some in song. They emerged into a well-lit street with sailors swaggering, carriages rumbling and merchants strolling up and down the cobbles. Taverns lined both sides of the street. Moor led them south again to a tunnel that had been converted into a stable. A thick wood fence stood across the tunnel, bearing a sign that read, "Aleway Stable." Pictures of a horse and a coin had been painted below the words for those who could not read Westerness. Another sign listed the rates. Daniel had forgotten how expensive it was to stable a horse in the city. If they stayed the night, stabling for their four horses would cost a day's wages for most men. The travelers dismounted, Simon helping Rachel from her saddle.

"Let us not advertise our identities too much while we look for our ship," Moor said quietly, indicating to Daniel that they should leave their long swords in their saddle scabbards.

Moor rang the miniature ship's bell that hung from the gate. A brown-haired boy of about sixteen years came out from the back of the stable wiping his hands on his smock.

"Evenin', gentlemen. Be leaving your horses with us tonight?"

"Not all night, lad," replied Moor. He reached into his belt for a silver crown, handing it to the boy. "Just an hour or two. Brush them down and let them cool. I want you to give them water, but no oats. When all this is done, I would like them re-saddled and placed in stalls near this gate, so we won't have long to wait when we return."

The boy looked down at his hand and saw a full silver crown rather than a half—twice the regular fee—and nodded his head, a sly grin coming to his face as he would pocket the remainder. He led the animals inside.

The street noise had awakened Moor's hawk. The paladin removed the bird's hood, gave a low whistle and pointed to the grassy roof of the stable. The bird stretched out its wings and, in two flaps, landed on the roof. Moor took his saddlebags off the horse and slung them over his shoulder. Daniel had nothing of any great value in his, so he left them with his horse, as did Simon and Rachel. They headed further south until Daniel saw a familiar sign, a fathomer's rope, with seven knots tied along its length.

"Ah, here we are," Moor said, loud enough to be heard over the din on the street.

"Perhaps something nearer the docks would be better," Daniel said.

"Nonsense," replied Moor. "Besides, I've heard the beer here is especially good."

Moor motioned Daniel closer. "For secrecy's sake, I should give you a traveling name for tonight.

Let's see now, the people of this city like to name their sons after animals, so we shall call you...Hawkin. Hmm, no, too common. Bullkin? No, sounds fat. Wolfkin? No, that won't do either, too memorable." He snapped his fingers, "Ah, I have it—Bearkin."

Simon did not know why, but Daniel blushed red up to his ears.

Moor opened the door and nodded for Simon and Rachel to enter first, then Daniel. As he entered, Daniel brought the hood of his cloak over his head.

Larger than it appeared from the outside, the tavern included the adjoining shops, bought years ago and the dividing walls demolished. Long tables, crowded with laughing, shouting men from many nations, stood in rows in the center of the room. Barrels lined the left wall, ready for tapping. Serving girls went to and fro, half a dozen full tankards in each hand. A cheery fire blazed in a hearth set into the back wall.

"Help you, gents?" said the alewife, approaching them.

"Yes. A table on the platform," said Moor, handing the woman a coin.

The woman led them through the tables to a low platform set against the tavern's right-hand wall. Here the tables were smaller, seating four to six, with high-backed chairs rather than the benches that flanked the long tables on the main floor. A waist-high railing separated the platform from the main floor. Merchants did much of their business with the ship captains on this platform, where distance and the din of the crowded room would keep their conversations private. They would be charged more for this table, but Moor would not sit confined on a bench in case they had to move quickly.

"Will this do?" asked the alewife, leading them to a table at the corner of the platform.

"Yes, perfect," replied Moor.

"I'll send one of my girls to you smartly, then," said the alewife and hurried off.

Daniel started to sit in the nearest chair, with his back to the room, but Moor barred his way.

"Why, Bearkin, where are your manners? You should let your grandfather and cousin sit first." He held out the chair Daniel had chosen for Rachel. Simon sat next to her, not knowing Moor was up to, but willing to follow along. Daniel sat down hurriedly along the wall. As Moor sat beside him, he pulled Daniel's hood back. "Keep your hood off," said the paladin. "It would look strange to wear it indoors. Besides, have I not taught you that hoods interfere with your side vision?"

A serving girl came up to them. "Good evening to you all. What will you have tonight, light or dark?" She looked up and suddenly her face brightened. "Bearkin, you've come back!" She ran to Daniel, took hold of his face in both her hands and gave him a kiss that would have sucked all the air from a blacksmith's bellows.

"Where have you been?" she said. "You've been gone more than a year."

Daniel, blushing scarlet, gave a fairly good impression of a landed fish, his mouth was working, but no sound coming out.

"We have been away on business," Moor said. "And we must be away again. But, before you know it, we shall be back and ready to enjoy your beer and the company of the beauty who brings it."

"Oh my, yes, the beer—I forgot," said the girl. "Bearkin, I know you likes your dark. And for you, sirs?"

"Dark for me and my grandfather here," replied Moor. "My cousin is too young for a tankard. But I know that your mistress keeps a big kettle of tea hot to keep you girls going on long nights. Please bring my cousin a mug of tea. And charge us the price of a tankard, to keep your mistress happy."

The girl curtsied with a giggle in Daniel's direction and hurried off.

"Well, 'Bearkin', you seem well known here," said Simon disapprovingly. Rachel kept her eyes downward, biting her lip to keep from smiling. Daniel said nothing, preferring to suffer in silence while he prayed for a mountain to fall from the sky and hide him.

Simon nodded for Moor's attention. "This situation was not unknown to you," he said in Etruscan.

"Of course," replied Moor in the same tongue. "There is little about those under my command that I do not know. The boy began coming here once a month nearly two years ago."

"I hope he has not done anything improper with the girl," said Simon.

"No, it has not gone that far," said Moor. "As you know, the men of the house of Asher differ from other men, for the blood of Anak runs in their veins.

"I believe that, because their lifespan is twice of a normal man, they go through puberty at a much later age—one of the reasons they spend a year of solitude in the deep forest when they come to their twentieth year. A common man will go through this change over the course of a year as he enters his teens, but the change to manhood comes upon Asherites all at once as their teen years pass. They become so restless that the best place for them is in the wilderness."

"And yet, before that, you allow them to come to a place like this?" asked the priest.

"Young Asherites often come to the city looking for adventure," replied Moor. "But, though they appear to be men fully grown, they remain boys at heart when it comes women. I usually send an older man to secretly keep watch over them and see that they do not get into more trouble than they can get themselves out of. Since the boy's father was my friend, I took it upon myself to watch over him. He would come here, buy a beer, and sit for hours making puppy-dog eyes at the serving girl you just saw. But at that time he posed no more danger to her virtue than a ten-year-old boy."

"And now?" asked Simon.

"And now his blood runs just as hot as any other young man," said Moor, "though the Asherites tend to fall in love with the first girl they meet when they come of age. That is why their parents send them to Logres as soon as their year in the wilderness ends. It is also the main reason that I am so against this foreign girl joining us; her presence runs the risk of our young friend becoming infatuated with her, when he will wed a princess of Logres."

"But he is not betrothed to any one girl, as yet," Simon said.

"Not to any in particular, but the sons of his house have wed the daughters of Anak for a thousand years. Anak would take it as a great insult if the boy wedded a commoner," Moor said. He leaned in slightly and lowered his voice further. "For reasons beyond the political, the boy must marry one of Anak's daughters."

The serving girl returned, having brought beer to all the other tables in her section first so that she would have some free time at Bearkin's table.

"Here you are, friends," she said placing the tankards before the men and the mug of tea before Rachel, whom she eyed suspiciously.

"Oh, Bearkin, it is *so* good to see you again," she gushed, turning to Daniel. "You must tell me of *all* your adventures."

Daniel looked like a deer surrounded by a wolf pack, not knowing which way to run. Moor decided to show him some mercy.

"All in good time, lass," said the Etruscan. "First I would speak to your master. Please ask him to come here."

"Yes, sir," said the girl reluctantly and hurried off.

"This is one of the larger taverns in town," Moor said. "Odds are there will be a dozen sea captains in the room tonight and half of those will command ships bound for Logres."

The tavern keeper came threading his way through the tables.

"Yes, sir, how may I be of service? The beer is to your liking, I trust."

"None better in all Eboracium," said Moor jovially, using the pretext of shaking the tavern keeper's hand to slip a coin into the man's palm. Lowering his voice he said, "We seek a ship bound for Logres on the next high tide. I know you pride yourself on knowing your customers. I am sure you can help us."

The tavern keeper glanced at the contents of his hand and smiled.

"Oh, I know I can, sir."

The tavern keeper went to a man smoking a pipe across the room. He bent down to whisper into the man's ear. The man shrugged his thick shoulders, then rose and followed the tavern keeper to Moor's side.

"This is Captain Njorthr of the good ship Prydwen," said the tavern keeper. "It may be that he can aid you."

"Captain, please join our table," said Moor. "I have a business proposition for you."

The captain swung a chair over from the next table and sat down. "I am listening," he said, waving the serving girl over. "Just long enough to down the tankard you will be buying me."

The girl brought the beer and Moor and Njorthr began their negotiations. Spying a free moment, the serving girl sat down very close to Daniel.

"Now, you must tell me all about the adventures that kept you from me for so long."

Daniel spent the next several minutes trying to use as many words as possible to say as little as possible. Rachel sipped her tea and watched in silence.

Daniel was searching his mind for something more to say when a shadow fell upon the table—a big shadow. Daniel looked up to see a very large and very angry sailor, a Scandian by his golden hair and gray eyes, looming over them on the platform.

"When I asked you to sit with me, you said no," said the sailor to the serving girl. "Why is he better than me?"

Moor's right hand was already under his cloak. With his left hand, he laid a silver piece on the table. "My friend, the young are foolish and do not appreciate a man of your obvious quality. Let me buy you a tankard so you can forget their foolishness."

The sailor angrily swept the coin off the table.

"Come with me, dear," Simon said to Rachel, leading her away. Njorthr, who had seen his share of tavern brawls and could see this one coming like a mid-day storm, followed. The serving girl shrank against Daniel, clutching his arm. "Ranulf, I can sit where I please," she said.

The sailor ignored her. "Get up," he growled to Daniel, his breath smelling of too much beer and too few teeth. The sailor was breathing hard now, his chest heaving, his fists clenched, building himself up for an attack.

Moor stood up. "Friend, you do not want to do this. You will not like the result."

"I said get up!" shouted the sailor.

Daniel shrugged off the serving girl as he came to his feet. As he did so, having little experience with tavern fights, he scraped his chair loudly against the floorboards in that particular way guaranteed to turn every head in the room towards them. The serving girl ran weeping off the platform and into the arms of the alewife, who led her away.

The tavern went deathly silent as all stopped and turned to watch the fight brewing. A pause hung in the air like a cold fog.

"You should return to your table... now," Moor said to the sailor, no longer caring to hide the sound of oncoming death in his voice.

The sailor's eyes flicked down to Moor's belt buckle. "I am no soldier. I do not take orders from you." He lunged forward, took hold of Moor's cloak and pulled upwards, intending to catch the lighter man in the throat with the cloak's clasp or chain, but this cloak had neither, only hard leather shoulder caps. The cloak came up and Moor disappeared.

The sailor looked at the empty garment, bewildered for a beer-clouded moment, then his face contorted as he screamed out in pain. The sailor dropped the cloak and up from the floor came Moor, clothed in the color of night, a paladin revealed in his wrath.

Moor stepped back, pointed a long forefinger at the sailor and commanded in a fell voice, "STA! IN PERICULUM MORS!"

The sailor seemed frozen in place as he stood staring at Moor.

Without warning Moor leaned in and slapped the sailor across the face. The man let out a bellow of rage and took a step towards the paladin.

Moor took a step back and commanded, 'STA! INFLEXIO POTORIS!"

And again the sailor screamed out in pain at the words of the paladin. He grabbed his left leg in both hands, but did not advance any further.

Once more Moor took a step towards the sailor and slapped the larger man across the face. As before, the man roared out in anger and began to charge the paladin when...

"STA! INSCITUS NAUTICUS!" commanded Moor. The man seemed to hit an invisible wall and fell back a step, screaming.

Daniel had moved away from behind the table, the better to see around Moor for any other attackers. A quick glance down showed Daniel what stopped the sailor's charge. Moor's fallen cloak partially obscured it, but Daniel could see the hilt of one of Moor's daggers protruding from the top of the sailor's boot, the blade pinning the man's foot to the floorboards.

Moor came at him again and slapped the sailor another stinging blow in the face.

The man leapt as before, but this time the dagger must have pulled loose, for the sailor charged forward like an enraged bull. Moor sidestepped and slapped the man hard across the ear. The sailor crashed into the table and fell to the floor as if dead. Moor reached down to retrieve his cloak, hiding his dagger in the folds as he did so.

"All right then, gentlemen," called the tavern keeper, hurrying over to the table. "That's more than enough activity for tonight."

The tavern keeper checked the sailor for a heartbeat. Satisfied that the man would live and he had no need for the city guards, the tavern keeper nodded for some nearby men to carry the sailor away.

"What did you do to him?" asked the tavern keeper, eyeing Moor suspiciously.

"Nothing fatal," replied Moor. He whispered something in the tavern keeper's ear and handed him a gold coin.

"I'll take care of it, sir," said the tavern keeper, satisfied. His storeroom doubled as an infirmary for the frequent brawls that ensued whenever men and alcohol met. He would bind the sailor's wounded foot there. The tavern's patrons, having seen all there was to see, returned to their tankards. The tavern resumed its regular noise level.

"You handled that well," Njorthr said, returning to his seat. He did not see the dagger, but had deduced how the trick must have been done.

"Better to make an example of one man than to have a whole table of drunken fools come at you," said Moor. "Now, about your fee, I think you can bring it down by twenty crowns..."

The two men had just agreed on a price when a loud commotion came from the door leading to the kitchen. Eight angry Scandian sailors poured forth, heading straight for Moor.

"Well, they figured that out sooner than I expected," Moor said, standing.

He took hold of a tankard in each hand while the captain moved away, putting his back to a wall.

"No blades," Moor said to Daniel. "We do not need the city guards called for this."

Daniel kicked the table over to act as a temporary barricade just as the first of the sailors reached the platform. One lunged at Moor's throat with his left hand, drawing back his right for a blow. Moor batted the hand away with one tankard while smashing the sailor in the face with the other. The paladin kicked the stunned man into the path of another sailor just as a third sailor charged forward. This man tossed the heavy table behind him as if it were a footstool and came at Daniel with a right punch. Daniel parried the punch with his left hand, striking the man's biceps with his right fist, numbing the arm. Using the man's own arm as a lever against him, Daniel spun the sailor around and kneed him in the kidney. That took the wind out of his sails and the sailor collapsed at Daniel's feet. The prince took a step back so that the next man would have to step over his fallen comrade to attack.

Daniel stole a glance to see how Moor fared, but he need not have worried. The older man was like a whirlwind. The tankards Moor had been holding had not lasted for more than a broken head or two, but Moor still had the handles and used them as palm sticks, striking out to hammerfist one man in the temple, then hooking another man in the jaw. With no wasted motion, Moor would strike an opponent and then send him crashing into his neighbor to block another's charge. A man threw a punch. Moor parried the fist with his left arm and struck it with his right elbow. After a satisfying crunch, the man howled, clutching his broken hand. Daniel knew Moor wore light chain mail, the outer forearms padded by thick leather with a triangular steel rib sewn into it. Strong enough to stop a sword cut, this armor would be devastating to the bones in a man's hand.

Moor grabbed the man by the hair and pulled him down into the path of another sailor charging forward. The two fell in a tangle. Moor had lost his palm sticks, so he picked up a chair and brought it crashing down upon the two fallen men.

Another sailor leapt over the rail at the far end of the platform and drew a knife. Daniel saw that Moor had already thrown every small object within reach, so Daniel charged before the man could do so. Though not what he had expected, the sailor set his feet firmly and readied himself to take the attack. Three quick steps carried Daniel across the platform. A fourth would put in range of the sailor. Instead Daniel kicked the front of table nearest the sailor towards the rail. Spying a chance to gain higher ground and an advantage, the sailor leaped upon a chair, then took one step onto the rail and the other onto the table—whereupon Daniel kicked the sailor's leg out from under him. The man fell, battle-anger still written on his face; until he realized that he straddled a waist-high rail. That meant that the first things to hit the rail would be his...

The sailor's testicles hit the rail with the full weight of the sailor upon them. The sailor gave a small, defeated moan and fell back into the crowd. Something heavy hit the floorboards behind Daniel. He spun and barely had time to parry a vicious thrust as another dagger-wielding sailor came at him. He struck the man in the temple with an elbow, then grasped the attacker's knife hand and twisted it outward in a wrist lock. The sailor's head must have been too hard to fall to a single strike, for he threw a wild punch with his free hand. In one motion, Daniel parried through the punch and circled his arm around the sailor's, locking the man's left arm. Daniel disarmed the man, took hold of the knife himself and brought the blade up to the sailor's throat.

"Stay back!" he shouted to the two sailors advancing towards the rail.

They hesitated only a moment, then drew their own knives.

Well, that didn't work for long, thought Daniel as he brought the sailor's head crashing down onto the table. He ran the dazed man over the rail and into his fellows.

The sound of wood methodically being broken four times came to Daniel above the din of the fight. Four sailors, not part of the first group, must not have liked the way the fight was going and had decided to join in. They had broken off four table legs to make heavy clubs.

The new four pushed others out of their way in their eagerness to get at the two men on the platform. Daniel transferred the sailor's knife to his left hand. Despite Moor's instructions, his right hand moved to grip his short sword and prepare to draw.

The men surged forward and ...just came to a halt. One by one, every man in the room stopped his attack. Arms dropped heavily to sides, weapons clattered to the floor and eyes slowly blinked once, twice, and then closed. To Daniel, the air felt heavy and sweet, as if he stood in a meadow at high summer.

And, as if swept by an unseen hand, all the lamps in the room flickered out.

The tavern went silent.

Then a song drifted out from the darkness.

Daniel slowly turned his head (the air felt as thick as honey) and saw Rachel and Simon standing before the glowing coals of the hearth. Rachel sang, her hands moving before her as if weaving the words in the air. She sang in a language unlike any Daniel had ever heard, yet he felt as if he should know it.

As he watched, the stone wall behind Rachel shimmered and faded away, revealing a sunlit jungle, wild and beautiful. He could hear the singing of many birds and the sound of a waterfall in the distance. The song ebbed and flowed, riding over and under the sounds of the jungle.

Like a whisper, a passage of the song came to him, and while it was his ears that heard the words of the song, it was his heart that knew their meaning.

Eden died slowly
between the Fall and the Flood

For those born in Paradise
Did not die soon or swift

In those born in Paradise
Still lingered the Gift

In a clearing at the center of the jungle, as yet untouched by the Fall of Man, a single flower could be seen—a blue rose, the last of the living gems of the Garden. A song came from the Rose, for all living things had voice before the Fall.

Men entered the clearing, the king and court of a sea-coast people out on a hunt. The Sea King caught sight of the Rose and, awestruck by its beauty and by its song, ordered his men to build a shrine round about the flower.

Then the song revealed the scouts of the king of the mountain people, coming upon the shrine and its worshipers. They returned to the Mountain King, who became enraged at the tidings, for he counted the jungle as part of his domain. The Mountain King gathered his army to expel the foreigners from his territory. He chased off the Sea King and his people. Enraptured by the Rose, he, too, made camp before the shrine. The Sea King soon returned with his own army and the two fought.

Blood was spilt and men killed. This tormented the Rose.

"It wounds my heart," she cried
But no man heard
For past were the days
When men took heed of voices
Other than their own

Such things lay with Paradise

179

And Paradise lay shattered on the ground

As the blood of men reddened the earth, her own color faded.
> *Her petals were blue*
> *but her blood was red*
> *and redness covered the ground*

The rose cried out a final time before she withered and died.
> *In later years, mighty men*
> *Men of renown*
> *Would make quest for a flower such as she*
> *But they found her like not again*

> *Such things lay with Paradise*
> *And Paradise lay shattered on the ground*

The men around her fought on, oblivious to her death. Storm clouds rolled in. Rain fell.

* * * * *

Daniel awoke with a start, finding himself on the busy street outside the tavern. Rachel stood before him, holding his hand, concern written on her face.

"Are you well?" she asked shyly.

"Yes, I think so," replied Daniel, still feeling a bit unsteady. Moor leaned against a wall next to him, disbelief and belief warring in his eyes.

"What happened in there?" asked Daniel.

"I do not know," replied the girl. "Such a thing has never happened to me before."

Simon stood nearby, watching the two men recover. He looked up and snapped his fingers. "I've almost forgotten our friend the captain." He dashed inside and returned a moment later, guiding the still dazed Njorthr.

Moor breathed deeply to clear his head. His eyes kept shifting back and forth from Simon to Rachel.

"Come," he said finally. "We must retrieve our horses from the stable and make for the docks. Your ship sails on the morning tide, correct, Captain? Captain?"

Njorthr, a very puzzled look upon his face, felt around the top of his head, searching for the lump from a blow he did not remember taking, but decided he must have suffered.

"What...oh, yes, on the morning tide we sail," said Njorthr, abandoning his search. He looked skyward to check the few stars strong enough to be seen through the lights of the city. "You should make haste, the night is nearly over." He waved a passing coach painted with a yellow stripe indicating it was for hire, and boarded.

"The Prydwen is at dock seven. Gather your horses and meet me there while I see to the extra supplies I now need. You cannot miss the Prydwen. Tallest ship on the dock, long and lean, three-masted she is, with a figure of a woman painted blue, carrying sword and shield, carved into her bow." He signaled the driver. "Do not be late!" he called as the coach moved off.

* * * * *

The two men hiding in the shadows of a doorway diagonally across the street waited patiently. They had thought it strange when the tavern had gone from bright and noisy to dark and silent, so they had lingered to investigate.

They watched as three men and a girl exited the tavern, two of the men staggering out from the tavern— not as men drunk, but as those just woken from a deep sleep. One of the watching men checked a square of parchment he had recently been ordered to carry with him at all times. On it were drawn the likenesses of a young man and a bearded man of about forty. He showed it to his partner, who agreed that they might indeed have found the men they were ordered to kill. The

181

two waited while the ship's captain rode off in a coach, then they followed the remaining four.

* * * * *

Moor rang the stable bell impatiently. The stable door was shut and locked from within.

"Alright, alright. Keep your britches on!" came a voice from the other side of the door. A small shutter opened and the stable boy's face appeared in the opening.

"Oh, it's you, sir. Returning a bit late, are we? The beer was better than you expected, I'll wager."

He brought the horses already saddled, as Moor had instructed. The four travelers rode east and then south, heading for the deep-water docks. As they rode the streets became more and more deserted.

Just before they crossed through yet another tunnel, Moor raised his hand.

"Hold," he said. "Someone has put out the lamps." Both Moor and Daniel drew short handled torches from their saddlebags and set them afire from the lamps still lit on the street. Moor considered the tunnel a moment. "Here, make yourself useful," the Etruscan said, handing Simon his torch. The paladin then strung his bow and nocked an arrow upon it.

They entered the tunnel. It was empty. Nothing seemed amiss save the unlit lamps. A smaller tunnel intersected the main tunnel at its midpoint. This tunnel had a locked gate set back a half pace, and angled slightly downward for the short distance they could see in the torch light.

"What smells so bad?" asked Rachel.

"Truly you are a princess, if you do not know that smell," replied Moor. "That tunnel leads to the city sewers. It is said that, once, an entire city existed beneath this present one. Now, only deep tunnels, used as the city's sewer system, remain."

Four silhouettes moved across the mouth of the tunnel ahead. Moor brought them to a halt.

"Stay away from me!" A panic-stricken voice echoed down the tunnel.

Daniel recognized the old beggar he had given a coin to earlier that night. Three men, steel glinting in their hands, surrounded him. They tried to herd the old man into the tunnel, the better to do their work in darkness.

Suddenly the rage that had been building within him since his father's death swept over Daniel like a storm. He spurred his horse into a gallop and charged forward.

"Wait you, fool!" growled Moor in frustration as he kicked his horse to follow.

As he neared the mouth of the tunnel, Daniel dropped his reins to his saddle horn and unhooked his cloak, but kept it in hand. The three men just barely had time to notice the sound of hoofbeats before Daniel fell upon them. He threw his cloak into one man's face, his torch at another and then spun his horse around in a circle, spurring it to kick and hold the men at bay.

"Run!" he shouted to the beggar. The old man blinked his beer befogged eyes for a moment (it appeared that he had not kept to his earlier promise) and took off, running south.

Daniel leapt off his horse, drawing his short sword and dagger in one motion. The three robbers surrounded him, angry that their prey had gotten away.

They held long butcher knives in their left hands and heavy woolen cloaks in their right. The bottoms of the cloaks ended in rough tassels. Daniel had heard of this trick and knew there would be fish hooks hidden there. The robbers circled him, swinging their cloaks, keeping their right legs forward to give them more reach. Daniel held his dagger in reverse grip, the better to catch the heavy wool of the cloaks.

The robber on his left attacked first, swinging his cloak at Daniel's head to blind him. The prince blocked the cloak with his left arm, impaling it on his dagger. The robber pulled on the cloak, drawing Daniel towards him. Instead of resisting, Daniel charged in, getting some slack in the cloak. He had kept his sword close to his left hip, so that the robber's own cloak hid it from the man's view. Daniel now swept the sword upward, severing the robber's hand at the wrist and, before the man could let out the shocked scream rising in his throat, beheaded him with a backhand cut.

The two remaining robbers attacked together. The man on Daniel's right was slightly closer, so Daniel chose to deal with him first. The man sent his cloak at Daniel's legs in a forehand sweep. Daniel blocked this with his sword, then stepped on the cloak, pinning it to the ground. The robber charged in, aiming a thrust with his knife at Daniel's heart. The prince parried the thrust with his dagger arm and stepped in, cutting low to the back of the knee with his sword, hamstringing the man. The third robber charged in to aid his partner. Daniel plunged his dagger into the second robber's back and pushed him into the path of the third man. The third robber staggered back from his falling comrade. With red hatred in his eyes, he charged at the prince, flailing with his cloak. Daniel took a step back to gauge his timing, then counterattacked, cutting at the cloak with rising cuts.

The robber's thick woolen cloak, held by only one end, took the sword cuts well, the blade barely marking it. Daniel changed his tactics. He switched his dagger into a forward grip. As the man leapt forward for another attack, Daniel ducked under the cloak. A treble hook caught Daniel's right sleeve and the robber grinned evilly, seeing his prey caught. The robber pulled, readying his knife for a thrust, but made a fatal mistake. He had counted on the fact that his butcher knife was longer than his opponent's dagger, so he thought he could beat him to the punch. As the robber pulled, Daniel stepped in, moving his left leg forward. Both men released their thrusts at the same exact moment. The robber's eyes widened in surprise as Daniel's dagger hit him in the armpit, his own knife still a blade length from his opponent's heart. The force of Daniel's thrust staggered the robber. With his remaining strength, the man renewed his thrust. Daniel, leaving his own dagger stuck in his opponent, parried the knife thrust with his left arm and caught the robber's knife hand in a lock.

The robber locked eyes with Daniel. The dying man tried to work up enough saliva to spit in his opponent's face as a last act of defiance, but his mouth had gone dry. Then the look of hatred on his face changed to one of fear and denial. He sank to his knees. His head fell forward, his neck too weak to support its weight. The robber looked down at the cobblestones before him; his own blood ran in rivulets between the stones and into the gutter. That was his last view of this world as Daniel swung his sword and beheaded the man.

"Are you finally done with this?" Moor appeared out of a shadowed doorway, bow in hand. In his focus on the robbers, Daniel had not noticed the paladin.

Moor returned an arrow to his quiver. "That took too long."

"I do not see any of your arrows in them," replied Daniel, breathing harder than he ever had in training.

Moor came to him. "If you could not handle three such as these, then all your years of training have been wasted. I thought it better to watch the street for others."

He noted Daniel's breathing and his voice lost some of its hardness. "So now you understand. To kill a man is a far different thing than a friendly sparring match with your friends. But do not worry. The next time you spill blood, you will not react as much. By the third time, it becomes just another unpleasant job that must be done."

Simon and Rachel rode out from the tunnel. She stared down at the bodies of the dead men. "Follow me, child," said Simon, leading her away. He knew what the paladins would do next.

"Clean up this mess and let us be away," said Moor.

Daniel removed his dagger from the body of the third robber and wiped the blood from the blade on the dead man's cloak. Moving to the second robber, he beheaded the body, and tossed the head into the darkness of the tunnel. He had collected the other two heads and threw the last into the tunnel just as he heard hoofbeats and booted feet coming up the street from the south. Simon and Rachel sat upon their horses, looking south and blocking Daniel's view in that direction.

Simon put his fist behind his back, opened and closed it twice, then held his thumb out once.

"Ten men and an officer," said Moor. "Daniel, get into the tunnel and wait for my signal."

Daniel dashed off as Simon led their horses in front the tunnel entrance.

Now Moor could see the men approaching. A group of city guards quick marched up the street led by a mounted marshal.

The paladin stood his ground as they approached.

"Hail to you, friend," said Moor.

"Evening, Captain," returned the marshal, seeing Moor's rank, though he eyed him carefully. "What has passed here? Are the king's paladins now come to collect our city's trash?" The marshal saw the cloaks and long knives near the bodies and knew the robbers for what they were.

"My companions and I came upon a young man being set upon by the three robbers you see lying here. Before I could ride to his aid, the young man dispatched all three. I wanted to question him, but he leapt upon his horse and galloped away north."

"He did all this and took the heads of the three men with him?" asked the marshal.

"No," replied Moor. "The heads he threw into the tunnel."

"Do not the paladins behead the men they kill?"

"Yes, but, by the way he fought, I do not believe the young man was a paladin." He caught the look the marshal gave his clothing. "Marshall, if I did this deed I would say so, it being a service to the city to remove vermin like these, but you see no blood on me, do you?"

"But I *do* see three of you and four horses, one with an empty saddle."

"That horse belongs to one of my men," said Moor. "He had a bit too much fun down on the street of taverns, so I left him there to recover while I returned his horse to our garrison."

"But your garrison is to the north, beyond those taverns," replied the marshal growing more suspicious of this paladin captain by the moment.

"Yes, but I must first escort the two you see with me to their home before I return north."

While Moor and the marshal spoke, Simon's horse began to whinny nervously. Simon dismounted to sooth it. One by one, he went to each of the traveler's horses and whispered words of comfort into their ears, which seemed to calm them. He remounted his horse and began to whistle a mischievous tune, which he sent merrily out into the night.

"Does all this amuse you, sir?" asked the guard marshal.

"He is my grandfather," said Moor, "and unfortunately he is not altogether, *all together*, if you get my drift," He rubbed his temple in a circular motion with his fingertips to get his point across.

"Ah, yes, I see" nodded the marshal, "and the girl?"

"Is my niece," said Moor. He lowered his voice. "It is not exactly regulation to be escorting them, but they are family and, as you well know, the streets are not safe for them to travel at night alone."

* * * * *

Unseen by Moor and the marshal, two heads ducked back from the other end of the tunnel. The two assassins had made it to the tunnel entrance in time to witness Daniel's fight with the three thieves. Like the thieves, the assassins carried long butcher knives under their cloaks, but, unlike those amateurs, they also carried an assortment of smaller butcher knives, sharpening stones and other tools in their bags. If stopped by the city guards, they knew enough about a butcher's trade to pass themselves off as such.

They had decided to wait in the shadows until the matter sorted itself out. Perhaps the thieves would do their work for them and they would be able to collect their gold without any risk to their own skins. Then they saw how quickly the prince had killed the men and thought that perhaps their own attack could wait. In the next moment, they saw the young man running down the tunnel towards them. At first they thought they had been spotted, but their target disappeared into the sewer entrance. They knew these tunnels well and remembered the locked gate set about a cubit back from the main tunnel, making a hiding place just large enough to be hidden from the street, but far too small to protect a man from their kind of attack.

They crept silently along the dark wall. Each man carried a short metal tube in his belt, which held a feathered dart, the tip of which had been dipped in the venom of the Bothrops, the most potent viper in Asulon. Though no snake's bite could kill one of the House of Asher, the assassins knew that this venom would numb the limbs and dull the mind of their victim long enough for the two of them finish off the prince with their long knives. The two professionals had worked out a plan for killing in these tunnels beforehand. When they drew even with their target, the taller of the two men would take three steps forward, draw the target's attention, then turn and release his dart from there.

Simultaneously, the shorter man would kneel and send his own dart, catching their victim from two sides and two heights. They crept closer.

Then they heard a new voice came from the far end of the tunnel and saw a mounted city marshal and several guardians. They stopped, but decided that this new element really wouldn't hinder them. They moved silently down the tunnel, then paused as a silhouette, the merest sliver of a head, peered out from the sewer entrance. This must be their target, his attention focused on watching the guard marshal.

So much the better, the assassins thought as they neared their point of attack.

* * * * *

"Will you please *stop* that whistling," said the marshal, beginning to lose patience with the old man. Even the marshal's horse seemed unhappy with the sound, for it acted nervous, stomping a hoof and snorting.

The marshal returned his attention to the paladin. "I think, Captain, that you should come with me and make a report to my superiors. They are paid enough to sort this all out."

"I shall do as you ask, Marshal," replied Moor. "Just let me return these two to their home and I'll be at your commander's door at dawn."

The marshal's instincts said make the man come now, but then. he *was* a captain in the king's paladins and must have powerful connections, even if, by the look of him, he was a foreigner and not of royal blood himself. The marshal's instincts won out in the end and he decided to take the three into custody. As he wondered how to accomplish this with the least chance of damage to his career, a strange sound came to him out of the depths of the tunnel. It reminded him of the sound of dry leaves blowing along the cobblestones, mixed with a high-pitched murmuring that he knew he should be able to identify, but couldn't. Then came a sound that he did recognize, the sound of running boots. A young man, his clothes smeared with blood, came charging out of the tunnel and leapt upon the riderless horse beside the old man.

"Hold there!" ordered the marshal. "Where do you think you are going?"

"Far from here, and so should you," cried the young man, galloping away.

The marshal turned to give chase when, like the sudden bursting of a dam, what seemed to be every rat in Eboracium came pouring forth from the mouth of the tunnel, running in every direction, scurrying between the hoofs of the marshal's horse, dashing between the legs of his men, climbing up the walls near by. The marshal's horse reared in panic. The guardsmen scattered, trying to get away from the squeaking, clawing, leaping gray flood.

Moor had swung onto his horse at the first appearance of the rats, hands clenched tight on his reins to keep his horse from bolting, but the rats flowed around his, Simon, and the girl's horses like a stream around a stone, never getting closer than a cubit to them. Their horses had remained calm, content to watch the chaos unfold around them.

"Ride!" Moor ordered, spurring his horse. Simon took hold of Rachel's reins and followed.

They found the prince waiting for them in the next tunnel.

"Follow me." Moor said.

The paladin led them up and down, in and out the streets of Eboracium. When he knew no one followed, he brought them to the deep-water docks an hour after dawn. They came to dock seven and found the Prydwen and Njorthr, scowling down from the ship's deck.

"Good *afternoon*, gentlemen," called Njorthr. "You took your time arriving. I was beginning to think you had changed your mind."

"Not with the deposit I left you, Captain," replied Moor.

"Well, come aboard then," Njorthr said, waving them up. "My cargo arrived late anyway, so no true harm done."

A young junior officer from the harbormaster's office supervised the loading of supplies onto the ship and counted them off on a parchment that the captain would sign before he set sail.

Moor wrote out a message and gave it to the man along with a coin.

"Can you see to it that this goes to the head cook at the fortress? We escorted his son down to the city on his first trip here, and I wanted to let his father know that he arrived safely."

The young man shot a quick glance at the color of the coin in his hand, gave a slight nod of his head and returned to his task.

Men continued to load the ship for the long voyage to Logres. Sailors led complaining goats up the gangplank and others came aboard carrying cackling chickens in wicker cages—fresh meat and eggs for the journey. Barrels containing beer, beef preserved in brine and cabbages came next, food that would store well for use when the livestock had run out. Then came bag after bag after bag of oats.

When he had spoken to the tavern master earlier that night, Moor had asked for a cargo ship carrying horses bound for Logres—common enough in Eboracium. Passenger ships were not so common though. So few made the dangerous journey across the ocean that such a ship would be unprofitable. Only naval vessels carrying troops exclusively carried passengers across the sea, and Moor had not wanted to trust to so obvious a method. Fortunately, most cargo ships had a compartment or two with extra bunks that could be hired out for passengers, and used for storage otherwise. Moor had chosen a ship carrying horses, as this would be the swiftest of the cargo ships—as horses did not take well to long sea voyages–and so would not be so heavily laden as one carrying hard goods.

"'Hoy, there," hailed an approaching sailor with bare feet and skin so tanned as to look like old leather.

"Call me Scupper," said the sailor, "Captain says you're to be sailin' with us. Come below wit' me and I'll show you your quarters."

As they followed Scupper below, Moor came near to Simon and said in a low voice, "You and I must have words later."

Simon nodded. "I did not think you put much value in the words of an old man, but we will speak."

They came to a small room with a table and two benches, all fixed securely to the floorboards so they would not move as the ship rode the waves.

"This here is our ship's mess, where you'll be takin' your meals," said Scupper. "The captain will come down to see you in a bit, but he told me to make ye comfortable till then." He took a kettle from where it hung above a lamp's flame and poured tea into four wide-bottomed mugs. "Here ye go then, hot fresh tea."

The sailor handed a mug to Daniel. When the prince reached out to take it, he winced and sucked in his breath.

"Mind yer hand, the tea's hot."

"No, it's not the tea," said Daniel. "I just felt a odd pain in my back."

"What?" said Moor. "Stand up, we didn't have time to check you for wounds after..." He looked hard at Daniel, then let his eyes dart towards the sailor. "...your fall. Take off your shirt."

"Ouch!" said Daniel as he began to remove the shirt.

Rachel looked up, her face showing concern, but she remained silent.

"Wait a moment," said Simon, standing. "Turn around." He felt at the shirt, found something, then bent down to examine it more closely. "Yes, here is the problem. You have a fishhook stuck in you, lad."

"A fishhook," said Scupper. "Oh, I know how to deal with a stuck hook."

He went into a cupboard and took out a wire cutter. "We just cuts the eye off and push the rest of it through and out."

"I'm afraid that won't do the job this time," said Simon. "The point is embedded in a rib." He reached into a pocket and brought out a bit of twine. "But there is another way."

Rachel could not follow all that was being said, but she knew that Daniel was injured in some way. She reached out and touched Simon's sleeve.

"Grandfather," she said in Abramim, using the polite term in that language for an older man, "May I help."

"No, child," replied Simon in the same tongue. He, too, shifted his eyes to the sailor and back. "It is a trifling wound. It is best that thou dost not reveal thyself without need. I can deal with this small thing myself."

He switched back to Westerness. "I'll take that cutter, if you please, Scupper. It will be useful in getting the hook through the shirt at least." Simon cut the eye from the hook and Daniel took the shirt off. The hook passed through his mail vest and padded shirt to show itself lodged in his skin, halfway up the bend. Simon tied the two ends of the twine together to form a loop and put one end around the bend of the hook and the other end around his wrist.

"This may sting a bit, but it will be over quickly," he said.

Daniel saw the concern written on Rachel's face and said easily, "It will be nothing, I have felt worse." He caught Moor's eye. The barest hint of a smile flickered on the paladin's face.

Simon put a finger of his free hand on the straight end of the hook to hold it down and gave a sharp tug.

To his credit, Daniel did not flinch as the hook came out.

"Aye now, that's how it should be done when they're buried," said Scupper. He took a cloth, poured some strong-smelling vinegar on it and handed it to Daniel. "Here. Put that on the hole and squeeze out some more blood to bring the dirt out of there. The vinegar will make sure it don't turn septic."

Daniel tried to get at the wound, but it was too far back to reach.

"Can I help?" asked Rachel in a shy voice.

"Yes. Please do," replied Daniel, handing her the cloth. Daniel caught the dark look Moor gave him as the girl went to his back and applied the cloth.

He smiled back at Moor. "Well, today didn't go as badly as it could have."

Chapter Ten
EARS AND EYES

He who planteth the ear, doth He not hear?
He who formeth the eye, doth He not see?
-    **The Book of Psalms 94:9**

Days tend to run together at sea. One day, after the midday meal, those of the crew who were not on duty sat on the deck swapping tall tales while they mended rope or did other small tasks. Moor was near the forecastle holding a low stance in exercise. Simon sat on a stairway, his hat off, enjoying the sporadic sun when it peaked out from behind the clouds. Daniel and Rachel strolled, as much as space allowed, across the deck.

Scupper, among the sailors mending lines, recognized the prince as someone who, unlike the rest of the crew, had not heard all of his stories many times, and so waved him over.

"Here, lad, bring the lady and we'll tell of tales like ye shall never hear stuck on shore."

Daniel loved a good story and came over to listen.

"Well, now," said Scupper rubbing his chin. "What should it be first—the sea, the ship or the men who sail her?"

He snapped his fingers, "Aye, I knows the tale to tell ye." He turned his head and gave his comrades a wink. "Did you know that our good skipper was a pilot, navigatin' and chartin' and such for other captains for many a year before gettin' his own ship? He swears to know the waters round Asulon like the palm of his hand, he does. Well, one day, on this very ship, while we was still two days out from Eboracium, the captain gets himself real sick and has to stay below in his cabin. Now, he don't trust his ship to the first mate and get some rest like he should. No, he has a fathom line put over the side every hour to get the depth and see what the bottom is made of, so as he'll know where we are."

"Wait, please," said Daniel. "I know how you would tell the depth by counting the knots on a fathom line, but how can you tell what is on the bottom of the sea?"

"Oh, then you have never seen a fathomer's line up close, have you lad?" said Scupper. "Well, then, 'tis a wondrous invention, it is. Here there, Dolf," he called out to a nearby sailor. "Hand me that line you've spent too much of the day working on." He took the long line with knots at every fathom. A lead weight hung on one end, about a cubit in length and as thick around as a man's wrist.

"See this cupped end here?" asked Scupper. "See now the wax set into the bottom of the cup? When we throws the line over the side, the weight goes to the bottom and whatever is down thar, be it sand or marl or mud, will get itself stuck to the wax and tell us over what kind of bottom we be sailing."

Daniel nodded. "Certainly an ingenious device. But how does that help you know your way?"

"Well, lad, I know ye now for a true land lover," came back Scupper. "Do ye not know that the bottom of the waters round Asulon be mapped out as good as ye please by fisherman and such? How else could they find their fishes, for some fish like sand and some rock and some likes the mussel beds. But that is another story altogether.

"See now, Captain Njorthr, being the great navigator that he is, knows that certain bottoms are found at certain depths and in certain places and those things mean we are a certain distance from our harbor. Well, each hour he has a line put over the side. The weight is taken to him and he dabs a finger into the wax, tastes it and then says 'Come to starboard three degrees.' At the next reading he says 'Come to port two degrees.' And don't ye know that he is right on the mark each time.

"Well, this begins to annoy our first mate to no end, so he decides to play a little trick on the captain. The next morning we come near the small islands just east of Eboracium, ones with nothing on them but a few small farms with sheep and cattle and such. Well, the captain asks for the first fathom of the day as usual, saying as we should be seeing them islands I just told ye about. The mate says they are not yet in sight. The captain says the mate must not have followed the course the captain gave him and the mate, he swears that he did. The captain, angry now, orders the mate up topside to get a fathom. The mate has us sail near the shore of those very same islands he just told the captain were not in sight. Well, as we draw close, the mate himself swings the fathom weight round and round over his head and sends it way out to land on one of the islands. He hauls it back and brings the weight down to the captain. The captain dabs his finger into the wax, takes a taste and, quick as that, spits it out. 'My apologies, sir' he says to the first mate. 'You are right. The barrier islands are not in sight because they have been sunk by a flood. We are sailing right now over old man Willet's cow pasture!'"

With that, the entire crew fell all over themselves with laughter.

"Scupper, you are a right scoundrel, but what a tale!" Daniel said, realizing that he had just been told a fable.

One of the men near Scupper, repairing a rope with a thick needle and line, doubled over slapping his knees and then straightened up, just as Scupper bent over to hand the fathom weight back to Dolf. The man's hand shot up and caught Scupper high in the face.

"My eye," Scupper cried out, "my eye!"

"Let me through," said Simon, coming through the sailors crowding around the stricken man.

Scupper held his hands tight over his eye.

"There now, Scupper, let me see your eye," said the priest, gently removing the sailor's hands. "Now open your eye." The sailor did so, but immediately closed it in pain. Simon had seen enough, though. A slit had been made in the center of the eye and clear liquid ran from it when the eye opened.

"What is going on here!" demanded the first mate, having just arrived from his place at the wheel.

Simon drew the mate aside. "His eye has been pierced by a needle."

"How bad?" asked the mate.

The priest shook his head. "Damage has been done to the pupil. There is nothing I can do."

The sailors pressed round Scupper, trying to comfort him or just to get a better view.

"Can I help?" asked a small voice from beyond the circle of men. It was Rachel.

"No lass, no one can," replied the first mate.

"Give her leave to try," said Simon. "She is in God's service as much as I."

"Do what you can, then," said the mate, making space for her.

Rachel knelt beside Scupper. "Peace to you, sir," she said, laying her small hands over the two callused hands of the sailor.

At her touch, Scupper settled down. His pained breathing slowed and he sat still, waiting for... no one knew, but a hush had fallen over the men.

Very softly, so that the sound could barely be heard at first, Rachel began to sing. She sang in a voice like that of a child, soft and pure, but carrying within it, like a scent caught on the wind, a note of comfort and of strength.

No man on board understood the language, but, as each heard it, each man saw in his own mind the place he loved most in all the world. Some saw the hearth in their home, the captain saw the sea at sunrise, the first mate saw the mountains where he was raised, but to each the vision brought peace, healing and joy.

Rachel removed her hand and said to the sailor. "Sir, please open your eyes."

Hesitating at first, Scupper opened his eyes a crack. Feeling no pain, he blinked several times, then opened his eyes wide and looked around at the faces of the sailors before him.

"Well, bless me! My eye is right again!" He took Rachel's hands and kissed them. "Thank you, lady, thank you."

"Do not thank me," replied Rachel, "thank the Lord God." She leaned in and whispered to him, "Do now what He tells you to do."

Scupper nodded, a knowing look on his face. He ran off down below decks.

Rachel rose to her feet and the men moved away from her in awe. She approached Simon. "It is best that I return to my cabin now," she said in Abramim.

The priest escorted her below. A moment later, Scupper came running back to the deck, a small bundle in his hand. He went to one of the men.

"Birt, this is been burning my guts since the day I done it."

"What are you jabbering about now, Scupper?" asked Birt.

Scupper handed him the bundle.

The sailor opened it and whooped in surprise, "My best pipe! I thought I'd lost it ashore."

"That ye did, Birt. Ye lost it in that tavern the night before we left port. I found it on the floor and recognized it right off as yours, as no one can carve ivory like ye can. But since it fell ashore, I figured I could keep it. I didn't know it would be bothering my sleep all these nights, but by that time I was too afraid to return it."

"Well, you did the right thing now, Scupper, so I'll not be holding it against you," said Birt. "Now let me have a look at your eye."

Just then a terrible screeching came from the skies above them. Every man looked skyward. A black shape streaked towards the ship from the low-hanging clouds. As it neared, they could see it was a bird, and, a heartbeat later, a hawk. It pulled up just before it hit the deck. Moor held out his arm and Theol landed upon it. The bird, breathing hard, repeatedly screeched at him.

"I would say that your bird is dead afraid, sir," said the first mate, "but what could scare a hawk out of the sky this far to sea?"

"I do not know," replied Moor, as he returned his gaze to the skies.

Chapter Eleven
THE LEVIATHAN

May those who curse days curse that day, those who are
ready to rouse Leviathan.
- **The Book of Job**- 3:8

The day before Moor stood on the deck of the
Prydwen seeking things aloft, the general members of the Builders Guild held a council. Sargon
stood at the head of the table.

"The unfortunate death of the king does bring us
some good news. As you know, before he died Argeus
pushed through the High Senate this foolish law
declaring gold, silver and copper the only metals to be
used in Asulonian coin. This deceptively simple law hin-
ders our plan to bring our medallion and our new mod-

ern system of commerce to Asulon—a system without the need for gold in the hands of common men and all the evils that that entails."

"Why not make the medallions out of copper?" asked a man across the table from Sargon. "That would allow us to get around Argeus' law."

"Unfortunately, the makers of the medallions tell me that they must be made of bronze for the black boxes to function properly," replied Sargon, "I do not understand all that goes into the making of the boxes. Our friends in the Brotherhood say very little about how these devices are constructed. Well, if the medallions must be bronze, so be it. What the Senate takes away today, it can give back tomorrow. We still have some senators friendly to our cause who will be looking for funding during the next election. Here is what I propose..."

Later, after discussing some small matters to which Sargon paid little attention, the council adjourned. As the members rose to leave, Sargon silently signaled three of them to stay. Sargon considered these three men, the oldest members of the Guild, as close to being his friends as a man with his ambitions and appetites could allow.

"Gentlemen," began Sargon, "I must ask you for you support."

The three men gave him quizzical looks but said nothing.

"For the last three years," Sargon continued, "my position as head of the Builders Guild has been under attack. Ferragus, the King of Gaul, is not content as leader of the Guild in the Unicorn Kingdoms. He has been attempting to usurp my rightful place in this organization. But it is a man of Asulon that must rule the Guild. Asulon, three times the size of the Unicorn Kingdoms, produces three times their wealth. With oceans to the east and west, a jungle to the south and a frozen waste to the north securely protecting our borders—

Asulon is the logical country to lead the world and, one day, to control it.

"But Ferragus believes that the ten kingdoms should rule the world, due to nothing more than that theirs are the older realms. I know you will agree that I have brought us along a course that has been profitable for us all. I have shown my value time and again. The untried Ferragus, holding his position because of his birth rather than his wits, believes himself my better simply because his is an older house. Well, we know that gold cares not for the age of the storehouse in which it lies. It gleams just as brightly on a new counting table as on an old."

A merchant with gray hair nodded in agreement, "Headship belongs to the man who can bring the most wealth into our storehouses. That wealth depends on stability in the world. No king in the Unicorn Kingdoms, with their constant border wars with the Magog, is in any position to poke his fork into our stew pot. If Ferragus wants your job, let him show us he can do as well as you have. Until then, let him see to his own house. No less than you, we desire to see Asulon take its rightful place in the world—with our hands providing the right guidance, of course. Should Ferragus lead the Builders Guild, whom would he choose as his lieutenants? I think it will *not* be men on our side of the sea. We will support you, Sargon, have no fear of that."

"Thank you, sir," replied Sargon, keeping a suitably humble expression on his face while his mind weighed how far he could rely on the word of these men.

Probably just as far as they could rely on mine, he thought, *which would be as far as they saw an advantage in it for them and no further.* Well, his newest venture would prove him still the right man to lead them.

"I have a plan that will knock Ferragus down a peg or two," said Sargon, *"and* bring us more gold in a year than any other venture has in ten." Sargon knew he had their full attention now, so he continued.

"My sources among the Magog tell me that a great discovery has been made. As you know, for the last three years they have suffered a drought, leading to famine and unrest. The emperor must deplete his treasury to buy food for his people. The empire cannot last very much longer under these conditions. Now, the shoreline of their great inland sea has been receding steadily for the last three years as the drought has dried the land. Recently, commoners discovered gold ore on the newly made shoreline. Here we find the problem for the Magog and the opportunity for us: the main vein of gold runs below the existing water level. It will be difficult for the Magog to mine profitably. They lack engineers and workmen experienced with this kind of mining, whereas we have been profitably mining under similar conditions for many years. I propose that we offer the Magog a loan to buy food until the drought has passed and a skilled workforce to help mine the gold."

"All for a fair percentage of the profits, no doubt," said the gray-haired merchant, warming to the proposal.

"Wait, it gets even better," said Sargon. "The gold will be mined far into the interior of the country. The nearest Magogian seaport lies many hundreds of leagues to the south.

"The Magog can get their gold to the sea by going westward, through Scandia. Of course, the Scandians have no love for the Magog. But it just so happens that I own a good percentage of the best seaport in Scandia, so I can use my influence there to open the port for the Magog's gold, which, of course, will be shipped on our ships, to our refineries, refined by us for a fee and stored in our storehouses so that the Magog may buy western food and goods."

As Sargon laid out his plan, he could see excitement growing in the other men as they calculated the percentages they held in each stage of the venture and what their profits might be.

The meeting ended with the merchants reiterating their loyalty to Sargon and leaving in a far better mood than they arrived.

A hidden door hissed open behind Sargon. *Oh, not now,* he thought, but he turned with a well-practiced smile nevertheless.

"My dear Aesculapius, to what do I owe this honor?"

The sorcerer emerged from the doorway and glided towards him, eyes hooded and hateful.

"You have allowed the son of Argeus to leave Asulon alive. Why?" demanded the sorcerer. "Did I not order you to kill him? Great powers are abroad; the age will soon change, and we must not fail our Master at this critical time. You do not know the peril you have placed us in."

Sargon raised his hands in a gesture he hoped would placate the old man.

"We do not know for a fact that the prince has left Asulon," Sargon said. "We know only that he has left the fortress. He could simply be away hunting. I have a good many of my best men out searching for him as we speak, and they have seen nothing to indicate the prince has left the country."

He knew that was not exactly true. Some of the new men he had hired had disappeared, but that could simply mean they had lost their stomach for the affair and ran off with the money already given them. Sargon did find the report from the two more experienced men worrisome. They claimed to have found the prince, but had lost him when 'a flood of rats', had prevented their attack. He found the tale too incredible to believe, perhaps an attempt to cover up their failure in eliminating the prince. Overall, something about the reports suggested the paladin Moor's handiwork. Sargon feared that old warrior far more than the untried boy.

"Sargon, know this," continued Aesculapius, interrupting Sargon's thoughts, "my brethren do not tolerate failure. You have dealt only with me and so you think you have seen the heights to which my order reaches, but one has scaled the mountain far higher than I. He it is who will decide your fate."

"Is that a threat? I would have thought you knew me better than to waste your breath on such things," said Sargon, allowing some of his anger to spill into his voice. "Please remind your fellows in the Brotherhood of my generous gifts to them. Our relationship has always been one of mutual benefit. I provide them funds and they provide me information. Remind them that they tell me what they *know*; they do not tell me what to *do*. I shall remove the prince at my convenience, as a favor to them. I am not under their authority."

"There you are wrong," said Aesculapius, his voice as lacking in warmth as a serpent's, "for you came under our authority when you invited us into your house. You of the Builders Guild often boast how easily you to place agents in every palace in the world. Do you think it too difficult for the Illuminati, who hold our servant's loyalty with a bond far stronger than gold, to place them into *your* homes?"

You shriveled old worm! How dare you! thought Sargon, but what came from his lips was, "This meeting is over. I think it is time for you to leave."

The sorcerer turned without a further word and departed the way he had come. As the hidden door hissed to a close Sargon called out, "And I am going to have that door sealed!" He looked down and found that his hands trembled.

"Fools, madmen—Hades take them all!" he shouted. Now he would have to completely replace the staff at all of his houses on the off chance that Aesculapius had been telling the truth. He made a quick decision and left the chamber. The meeting house was large enough that it had its own stable. His coach and driver waited for him.

"To the eastern house," he ordered. The driver cracked his whip and the horses moved off in a smart trot. The coach bumped over the cobblestones while Sargon seethed and chewed over his plan.

On the east side of the island of Eboracium, a causeway spanned a saltwater marsh, linking Eboracium with the islands that lay further to the east. On the first and largest of these islands, Sargon owned an estate set up on a cliff on the southern shore. Night had fallen by the time the coachman pulled to a stop before the large oaken doors of the stone manor house. A manservant already held the doors open for Sargon as he stepped from the coach.

"I am going straight to my bedchamber and do not wished to be disturbed," said the merchant. "And I want the main house empty of staff for the next week," he called back to the man as he raced through the great hall and up the stone staircase that led to his private quarters. Once inside his bedchamber, Sargon locked the door and stood a few moments, listening with his ear pressed against the wood. Satisfied that none of the servants had followed him, he strode to a large mirror mounted on a wall. He slipped his fingers behind the frame at two particular places. The mirror swung inward with a click to reveal a dark stairway beyond. Sargon took a lamp and stepped through the frame, careful to close the mirror silently behind him. He descended the stair, keeping a firm hand on the rail, knowing that the stairway curved far down into the bedrock below the house.

He had chosen this house because it offered a way of escape, should he ever need it. The house sat on a cliff overlooking the sea. Below the house, a cave cut into the cliff face at the high tide mark. The cave did not reach very far when he first brought the property, but it did give him an idea. He had the cave deepened and a shaft cut from the cave leading up into the house. Originally he had kept a small sailboat in the cave, to use if he ever needed a swift departure. Now he had far better means of escape. A great deal of work had been done to enlarge the cavern to accommodate his needs. At the far end of the cave, strong iron gates were set into the rock beyond which lay a large chamber. Sargon walked slowly towards the gates, chanting the words he had been taught.

Here he found a thick rope tied to a ring set into the wall inside the gates, the free end of the rope severed as if by a sword. The floor beyond the gates slanted upwards towards the deep shadows at the back of the chamber. Sargon saw that, behind the gates, above the high tide line, blood bespattered the walls. Every other day at low tide, two of Sargon's servants would come from the seaward mouth of the cave leading a pig. They would open the gate and tie the protesting animal inside before hurrying away. When next they came, they would find the rope cut, the pig gone, and more dried blood on the walls.

Sargon set his lamp down on a ledge. He called out the words he had been taught louder now, more boldly.

A harsh noise, somewhere between a hiss and a growl, came from the darkness beyond the gates, then a sound like a very heavy sack being dragged across the floor. Drag-stop...drag-stop...drag-stop. The sound came closer. A long reptilian head, as large as a man's torso and resembling something between a crocodile and one of the great serpents, came out of the gloom, moving back and forth on its long neck. Sargon took a key from his belt and unlocked the gate. The creature slithered out from its cage and came further into the light. A neck, nearly three fathoms in length, rose up off the floor. The creature drew itself forward and its great wings came into view. Folded now in the tight confines of the chamber, they would measure six fathoms from tip to tip when fully extended. Two legs, far too small to support its weight, lay tucked up against its belly. When the Magog had first showed him the creature, they had called it a dragon, but, from the first moment, Sargon had thought of it more as a winged serpent. Even the name the Magog had given it, *Nehustan*, he was told meant "Great Serpent" in some ancient tongue.

Sargon spoke the words of command again and the serpent lowered itself to lay flat on the floor before him, hissing in protest. The merchant wished that he could trust a servant with this next task, as he took the large saddle and placed it upon the dragon just behind the place where the wings met the body. He spoke another word and the dragon lifted itself up enough for Sargon to secure the straps. The merchant climbed onto the saddle and spoke the word for 'out.' The dragon slithered to the mouth of the cavern and then out into the fresh night air. It turned left, following a path that led up the cliff face. Sargon always hated the ride up the cliff. The side to side gliding of the serpent as it slid forward made him nauseated from the first turn. The dragon now came to the very edge of the cliff. Here Sargon had had a downward sloping ramp cut into the rock, much like the sled runs he played on as a child. Only here, the ramp ended fifty fathoms above the rocky base of the cliff where it met the sea.

Sargon steeled his nerves for the next part. "Fly, Nehustan, fly!" he commanded.

The dragon slithered forward and off the edge of the cliff. It gained speed as it slid down the ramp and then came a sickening drop as it fell towards the sea below. At the last moment, the dragon extended its wings, skimming so close over the surface of the water that Sargon could taste the salt spray. Then they were flying, the dragon beating its great wings to pull itself into the sky.

An hour later (and well out of view of the Asulonian coast), Sargon turned the dragon northeast, aiming for the first of the island way-stations he had set up for these journeys. He would be traveling far indeed before he reached his destination. Seabirds scattered as the dragon's shadow passed overhead. A high flying hawk almost collided with the beast as it came out of a cloud. The bird plummeted away from the dragon, screeching in terror. Sargon wondered at a hawk, so far out to sea, then dismissed the bird as unimportant. His thoughts returned to what he would say when he came before Gog, emperor of the Magog.

* * * * *

At that moment, far above Sargon—in fact, many millions of leagues above him—a small collision occurred. A comet passed through the asteroid belt between the planets Mars and Jupiter. The comet's path had long ago been mapped by ancient astronomers, who gave it little notice since it never came near the earth. A collision so far away would normally have little earthly consequence, but the comet moved one of the larger asteroids out of its regular orbit. Not by very much, but enough to make it collide with a cloud of smaller asteroids and send them flying like sparks towards the sun. The great majority of these small bodies would be drawn into the sun's gravitational field, where they would eventually fall into the great furnace and add themselves to the sun's fuel. However, a number of these lesser asteroids would strike a planet. One day they would shower down upon the small world that men like Sargon inhabited. None were large enough to completely destroy the planet; many were so small that they would make nothing but a few bright flashes as they burned in the planet's atmosphere. But one among those hurtling through space were much larger than the rest.

This one would still be the size of a mountain when it passed through the earth's atmosphere.

This one could kill a city.

But Sargon knew nothing of this. He continued to make his plans and thought himself secure.

Like warships that sailed, unknown and unseen, from a land over the horizon, the asteroids came, deadly and silent. It would take them all more than three years to arrive on the earth.

But still, they came.

210

Chapter Twelve
THE PRINCE

As if a man did flee from a lion, and a bear met him;
or went into the house, and leaned his hand on the
wall, and a serpent bit him
- The Book of Amos- 5:19

Three days later, Sargon could see the Magogian capital of Meshech far below and, at its center, the fortress of Maroth-Beria. He turned the dragon into a slow spiral downward. Sargon knew he need not be so secretive with the beast in Meshech, for in Meshech it had been bred. Maroth-Beria sat near the top of a dormant volcano, its rock sides hard and smooth and blackened from the ancient fires that formed the cone. Sulfurous smoke still issued here and there from fissures along the mountain, though the volcano had not erupted for the last thousand years. Nothing grew upon the cone, even in the years before the drought, because of this smoke, but that suited the men who ruled from Maroth-Beria—all the better to strike fear into the people they ruled. The fortress, many times larger than any in the west, housed ten thousand men under arms and twice that number in support.

Sargon landed the dragon in a courtyard near the high watchtower and dismounted. The dragon slithered into its usual hiding place in the shade of a covered portico and curled up to sleep. Trained men would remove the saddle and feed the dragon while Sargon made his proposal to their masters. A servant appeared in a doorway and beckoned him inside. Sargon followed, remembering the first few times he had flown here. He had found it a bit disconcerting that the Magog always anticipated his coming, but he supposed that one could see a creature as large as a dragon a long way off.

Sargon climbed the long winding stairway up into the watchtower where the emperor held his councils. He felt a bit winded when he reached the level of the council chambers. *I wonder if their fat emperor came up here in his youth and never came down again,* Sargon thought to himself, slightly annoyed at this indignity. *The Magog must believe this gives them some advantage during negotiations. Well, I have the gold they desire and that is* my *high tower.*

The soldiers guarding the doorway to the council chamber allowed Sargon entry and the door closed behind him. A young female servant led him to a small table set before the raised dais where the emperor and his ministers would sit. The high seat at the center of the dais, was called the "Gog," and gave the emperor his title. Sargon sat down and noticed that the table before him was bare of any food or drink.

"Child, I would like a cup of wine," he said, in what he knew was passable Magogian. The girl had her back to Sargon and seemed to be ignoring him. He sighed. Giving him a surly servant made a poor negotiating tactic. He tapped the girl on the shoulder. She turned towards him, her long hair swinging aside to reveal the cause of her silence. Her ears had terrible burn scars within them, as if they had been pierced with a hot iron rod. She gave Sargon a blank stare. Sargon thought she must be drugged as well. She would not be reporting anything that was said here today.

"Nothing, never mind," he said.

The girl left him.

A door behind the dais opened and the emperor's ministers entered the room. With none of the pomp and ceremony that would greet such men at a western court, they silently filed into the chamber. Sargon recognized most, but not all, of the men, so he knew that there had been some changes since his last meeting. A tall, slim, silver-haired old man dressed in somber black robes entered last–Smyyon, minister of the emperor's spies. Sargon knew his background only from a patchwork of reports, for though he had stood behind the thrones of five emperors, his reputation was that he preferred to keep to the shadows himself. The ministers took their seats. To Sargon's surprise, Smyyon took the emperor's chair, with a young man, clothed in white robes and a self-important air, taking the seat at his right hand.

So the old vulture finally decided to take the reins himself, thought Sargon, but said aloud, "Well, it appears that congratulations are in order. When did this fortuitous event occur?"

"My predecessor had an unfortunate accident while at his summer residence," replied Smyyon.

"May he rest in peace, then," said Sargon. He bowed before Smyyon, "Long life to Gog, emperor of all the Magog." The moneylender knew how often 'accidents' befell rulers in this country, but he also knew it wise to keep his thoughts to himself in this place.

"I have come to offer you..." began Sargon, but a voice cut him off.

"We know why you have come and what you think you know about our situation here," said the young man seated next to the emperor.

Keeping his eyes on Smyyon, Sargon said, "He who sits upon the throne may change, but it has always been the emperor himself who speaks for the Magog, in all the many years I have been dealing with your country."

Smyyon met Sargon's gaze, his cold features unreadable, and said, "This is my nephew, Prince Rosh. He will deal with you."

"You have come to make us an offer of 'help'," Rosh said, "but your help, as usual, will come at a high price. We have someone here who can help us more while demanding less." He signaled to a servant and the door behind the dais opened once more. A figure came into the room.

"Ferragus!" said Sargon with more alarm in his voice then he would have liked.

"Greetings, my Asulonian friend," Ferragus said, before adding another shock. "How goes your country since your king has died?"

Sargon sat speechless. *How could news of Argeus's death have reached here weeks before any ship? Could the Magog have another dragon?*

"We have ways of conveying information to one another that you can only dream about," Rosh said, seeming to read his thoughts.

Sargon decided it was time to regain some lost ground.

"Well, the Magog might be ahead of Asulon in ways to bring words across an ocean, but there are other areas, such as bringing gold up from below that ocean, in which no one in the world can surpass us."

"When I spoke of 'we'," Rosh said, "I spoke of my order. One which you know, and one whose voice you should have heeded."

"*You* are an Illuminati?" managed Sargon. This was not going as he had expected. A chill of foreboding swept though him.

Red anger flashed in Rosh's eyes. "I am not *an* Illuminati, you fool, I am *the* Illuminati. Those you have seen up until now have been but my servants. Now you must answer to me!" he roared. "Do you have any idea what you have done? Were you not told of the prophecies given at my birth, that I am to be 'the sword arm of the Magog?' Have you not heard what is foretold of Argeus's line? Why have you not done as instructed and, instead, let the prince of Asulon leave your country alive?"

Sargon felt fear, an unaccustomed emotion, and this made him angry.

"What, that foolishness about prophecies again? Spare me. I want no part of your madness," said the merchant. "It is plain that you do not want my help. Just remember that it is *my* gold that has seen you through the famines until this day. You will need much more to feed your people and hold back revolt until your mines can bear fruit." He stood up hastily, his chair scraping on the stone floor. "Contact me when you come back to your senses."

He turned and started for the door.

"Hold!" commanded Rosh. Sargon tried to move, but unseen and inhumanly strong hands seemed to hold his arms and legs.

"Here," commanded Rosh again. Something lifted Sargon into the air and turned him to face the Magogian prince.

"Unhand me! Put me down!" cried Sargon floating above Rosh, terror now in his voice.

"As you wish," replied Rosh. "Put him down," he pointed to the far wall, "there."

Sargon was turned horizontally. He found himself gliding, feet first, towards the wall. When he saw where he was bound, all courage left him and he screamed.

"No, you cannot! I am Sargon! No! I have gold!"

He struggled, trying to free himself, but whatever held him had a grip like steel. Rosh smiled with cold satisfaction, seeing that the narrow window was just a bit too small for Sargon's body.

No matter, he could be made to fit.

Screaming in terror, Sargon was pulled feet first through the window. His legs fit easily enough, but he

215

stopped as his hips caught on the stone edges. Sargon pushed against the stones, struggling not to be drawn out further. A sour smell invaded the room as Sargon soiled himself, but he was long past caring about such things. The unseen hands pulling him, pulled yet harder and his hips squeezed through the window. Sargon stopped again when the first of his ribs caught in the opening. He gasped, eyes wide with pain, as he felt first one, then another, then another of his ribs breaking.

* * * * *

The older of the two soldiers waiting in the courtyard slapped the back of his companion's head and grabbed the younger man's shoulder, pulling him back from his path towards the dragon.

"Fool! Do you wish to become a steaming pile of dragon droppings?" asked Volodya, the older of the two soldiers.

"But we have said the words," protested the other soldier, called Vanka.

"The words don't always work when she is as hungry as she must be now, flying as far as she did," replied Volodya.

"So that thing is a she." Vanka bent down, trying to look under the dragon's belly. "How do you tell?"

That earned Vanka another slap to the back of the head.

"Well, it has to be either a he or a she, now doesn't it?" Volodya said. "Since she is big enough to carry a man, she is a female dragon, as females grow bigger in dragons, as it is in most creatures that lay eggs. The male we have is below in the breeding program."

Vanka rubbed the back of his head to take away the sting. He was beginning not to like this new post. "We are making more dragons then?"

"We try, but it is difficult. Dragons are the meanest of all the creatures we make—most days they would rather kill each other than mate."

216

Vanka fell silent for a time. Then a thought came to him. "Hey, Volodya, if the dragon is so hungry, why don't we just feed it the pig now? Then we can safely move it to the cage."

Slap. "Fool!" Volodya said, "Do you feed a horse that is still hot from a race the moment you get it back in the barn? No, because its stomach will bloat.

"If we feed the dragon too soon after a flight, it will give her cramps and a dragon with cramps is not something you want to deal with, let me tell you. Besides, what if that moneylender must return across the sea after his meeting in the tower? After a pig or two, our girl here would want to sleep her meal off and would refuse to fly. Come sunset, when we know she will spend the night here, *then* we will get her a pig."

"Wait," Vanka said, "you said 'all the creatures we make.' You mean we have made more things than dragons?"

"Yes, all kinds of creatures," replied Volodya, lowering his voice to continue. "The wizards taught us how. We make them more than simple beasts, breed them to walk on two legs, give them a man's intelligence and make them useful for war. The masters are very proud of their new army."

He stole a glance upwards towards the top of the tower and lowered his voice still further. "You should see the things they are not so proud of—the things that didn't come out so well. It would turn your blood to ice."

"I know how to breed things; my family used to breed goats," Vanka said. "It seems to me that once you get the stock you want, it is not too hard to breed more."

Vanka managed to duck the slap to the back of his head, so Volodya, a senior man with much experience, backhanded the junior man across the ear.

"Oaf! Do you think we can just mate a bat, a snake and a crocodile with each other and 'poof', we have a dragon?" demanded Volodya. "You haven't seen how this all started, but I have. I cannot tell you the secret—for you cannot normally breed one kind of animal with another far different one—but I will tell you it is a most unnatural process. No, it has taken us years and years of careful breeding to get where we are now with the dragons and, even then, all we have is this one flying female and a smallish male whose wings are not large enough to support his own weight, let alone carry a man in flight.”

“Well, then,” Vanka said, after thinking for a moment, “this small male, can he at least breathe fire?”

“Breathe fire!” laughed Volodya. “Of course not. Where would you get such an idea?”

“Well, all the dragons in the fairy tales breathe fire,” answered Vanka.

“Well, our dragons are not from fairy tales, they were bred from real animals, and since no animal can breathe fire...”

Just then they heard a terrible scream coming from the heights of the tower. A short time later, a body fell to the courtyard, landing in the thick straw near the dragon.

“Well, Vanka, look now,” Volodya said, recognizing the clothing covering the broken body. “If it isn’t the great moneylender himself. I guess he won’t be flying back to Asulon tonight after all. *Now* you can get the pig.”

Vanka tore his gaze from the mangled form of the moneylender and hurried off towards the gate.

The dragon’s tongue flicked out and its eyes opened in interest. It saw the body of Sargon and slithered forward.

“Vanka, wait,” Volodya called out. “Never mind the pig.”

* * * * *

“Now that our entertainment is over,” Rosh said, “we have work to do. Ferragus, explain to the council, as you explained to me, how we shall take the gold from the seabed.”

Chapter Thirteen
BEGINNINGS

Whoso findeth a wife findeth a good thing, and obtaineth favour of the Lord.
-The Book of Proverbs 18:22

Many a young man dreams of a life at sea, traveling to exotic lands and having great adventures, but, in truth, most time spent at sea on a merchant ship like the Prydwen entails days upon days of hard work for the sailors and watching the endless waves go by for the passengers.

Each morning, when the day's winds blew the calmest, sailors brought the horses on deck to get some fresh air and sunlight. Daniel saw to the traveler's horses. Rachel worked at Daniel's side, helping to brush the horses' coats and singing to the beasts to calm them.

Daniel decided he would spend his afternoons learning Abramim, the language of Rachel's people. Gifted as all in his house in the learning of languages, he needed to hear a word only once to remember its meaning. Rachel, in turn, improved her understanding of Westerness. As they learned together, Daniel and Rachel found a bond forming between them. An affectionate smile here, hands that met accidentally on a railing there, and love crept up on its victims with silent feet— though, to those around the lovers, it came as secretly as a herd of galloping horses. As the weeks passed, the two young people found that they thought of each other, from their first thoughts of day to their last thoughts each night. Though neither would dare to say it aloud, Daniel and Rachel both knew that they were falling in love.

One morning, Daniel and Rachel stood on the deck, watching the sky and sea. The wind pushed a lock of hair across Daniel's eyes. Rachel brushed it back looking up at him. "Daniel, tell me about your people," she said in her accented Westerness.

The prince smiled and replied in Abramim. "Thy people and mine have been allies for hundreds of years, what more could I tell thee that is not already known to thee?"

"Many things, I think," replied Rachel. "Anak is your grandfather and the grandsire of all your kings. I know Anak has never been a friend to my people, but I also know that what I have been taught at home has been shown through a glass colored by the hearts of others. Let me hear the story of Anak and Asulon from an Asulonian."

"As the lady wishes, so it shall be done," said Daniel, bowing with a flourish.

"The story of my people began over a thousand years ago. Five hundred years after the Long Winter ended, the great sheets of ice that had covered the northlands for so long finally receded. The common people call the end of the old world 'The Fall', mistaking it for the beginning of man described in scripture, but the learned in Asulon say rather that we suffered one of many cataclysms that have struck the earth since its beginning. Whatever the cause, people scattered in fear and the search for food. What knowledge that survived was only that which a man could carry around in his own head."

"And yet your house survived," said Rachel.

"Yes, we survived, but it was a very near thing," replied Daniel. "Simon told me that a great war brought a terrible plague just before the Long Winter came. Because of this, the survival of my house rested on just one family. Asher, the second son of the King of Asulon, was traveling in the Ten Kingdoms with his wife, children, guards and servants. A scholar and a lover of old texts, he was making a study of such in a small monastery high in the mountains of southwestern Hibernia when the war began. The order at this monastery was charged with the preservation of ancient copies of scripture, so the chief priest ordered that food and water be stored up when word reached him of the war, for he knew how wars can spread to countries far from where they begin. When the plague came, the monastery, so small and remote, was forgotten and spared contact with the sick. The descendants of that prince and those with him became the House of Asher."

"Why did they not return to Asulon once the plague had ended?" asked Rachel.

"Simon, who knows more about this era than any man alive, told me that the years after the war were ones of turmoil; not only for man, but for the earth as well. Earthquakes and great storms were common. Perilous even in the best of times, imagine trying to cross the ocean when storms commonly brought forth waves that towered high above a ship's mast and then came down upon the ship with crushing force. Near the war's end, an earthquake far out to sea brought a tidal wave one hundred fathoms tall and thousands of leagues long, crashing onto the coastlines of the west, crushing all the ships in their harbors. Along with the ships, so did this great wave destroy the harbor towns that built the ships and the craftsmen who did the work in building them.

"Then the Long Winter came. A winter lasting for centuries covered all the northlands. Great glaciers crushed the remnants of the northern cities. Many years passed before the earth warmed and the seas returned to normal. By that time, the knowledge needed to return to Asulon was long forgotten."

Daniel paused to look out into sea.

"But Asulon itself was not forgotten by my people. Though years passed and Asulon went from a memory of the old to a dream of the young, when the sun set, my people would look to the west and sing songs of their return to Asulon.

"Centuries passed. My people grew in numbers and strength. Asulon became a name of legend, rather than of fact. The people of Hibernia thought that Asulon, if it ever had existed, must now rest below the waves like so much else of the old world. And still my people looked for a way home. Then, as is often the case, just when my people began to wonder if their hopes really were just a dream, the dream became real. On the first day of spring, in the thousandth year after the war, the Father of Giants came to the House of Asher."

"Anak?" asked Rachel.

"Yes, Anak," Daniel replied. "And he came with a tale hard to believe, but made believable by what he knew and who he was."

Daniel paused, thinking for a moment, then reached into his belt for a coin between his fingers. He tossed the coin into the sea.

Catching the look in Rachel's eye, he said, "No, I am not a pagan that I need purchase their god's protection lest Anak hear me. It is just a custom among my people. We rarely tell this tale, so we lose a coin when we tell it, to remind us to keep its telling rare."

Daniel returned his gaze to the sea. Rachel waited patiently for him to speak again, for she knew that he was about to tell her the heart-story of his people.

"Anak said he knew all the things that the House of Asher desired to learn most," continued Daniel, "How to make a true compass and how to navigate by the stars to find the land west across the sea. He knew how long the voyage would take and how to build the kinds of ships needed to cross an ocean. He tantalized my people with just enough of a glimpse under the tent to see the treasures stored therein, but not to see all. Why, I shall tell you in a moment."

"That is what he knew, but what of who he was?" asked Rachel.

Daniel smiled. "What do your people say he is?"

The princess thought for a moment. "Many tell tales of the kind of creature *Anak the Undying* might be. Some say he is the last of a race of titans that ruled the earth before the coming of man, one of those whom the ancient pagans worshiped as gods. Some say he was an evil spirit who repented and was made flesh as a reward; others say he was a good spirit who sinned and was made flesh as punishment. Some say he rose from the bowels of the earth and some that he fell from the sky. But I have never heard the tale from one who has seen him. What do you know of him?"

"I know only what he has told my people," replied Daniel. "When I ask Simon, who has often been in Anak's court, our good priest says something truly illuminating like, *'In the story of Anak there is more left unsaid than said'* and then changes the subject.

"The story, as it has been passed down from father to son in the House of Asher, begins when Anak first came to my people a thousand years after we had come to Hibernia. He rode up to the castle of my people saying that he wished to see our king (at that time, a descendent of Asher named Asa). In those days, any traveler who came through our land would be brought before the king to tell of news of far-off places and peoples, and be given a hot meal and a bed for the night. Even if that had not been the case, Anak would have gained an audience with the king.

"He rode up on a sunlit spring morning, seated on a great white unicorn, his breastplate of purest gold, a rich silken cloak, green as new grass, set about his broad shoulders. He stood a fathom and a half in height, with flowing copper-colored hair, a thick beard and eyes the color of bright emeralds. He appeared exceedingly strong and spoke in a voice sounding like thunder. Anak claimed to be an angel, one of the warrior hosts of heaven, made flesh and sent by the Lord God Most High in the days when the earth was young, to be mankind's guide and protector. Men called these creatures 'The Mighty Ones.' A fitting name, my father used to say, once you have seen even their sons in battle. They called themselves the *Bené Elohim,* 'Sons of God,' for they were made by His hand.

"When God sent the Great Flood to wipe evil men from the land, Anak and his fellow earthly angels were scattered to hidden places deep within the earth, to sleep until they might be called forth. Anak said he had come because the Magog gathered all the old allies of the Scythians for war against the West. He said he had come to lead the kings of the west against the Magog. To that end he proposed this contract. He wished to form an army of warriors, trained by himself, armed with weapons of his making, and paid from his own treasure (for he had been hidden with a great hoard of gold and gemstones). He would command this army for seven years. In those seven years he would bring peace to the nearby Isle of Logres and its ever-warring chieftains and become its king. Once king of Logres, Anak would gather the other kings of the west together in an alliance against the Magog. In exchange for their aid, Anak would build the people of Asher the ships needed for their journey back to Asulon, and teach them the seafaring skills they would need for that journey."

"And your people believed this?" asked Rachel.

"My father told me that Anak has a way about him when he speaks. That he can make you see as if seeing with his mind's eye while he tells you the tale. But he did not offer only words as proof; he asked that he be tested as well. Anak bade any man who would, try to cut his head from his shoulders. He took his armor off and knelt down, baring his neck. One of Asa's warriors came forward and tried a cutting stroke on the giant's arm. The sword made no mark. Heartened that he would not injure the king's guest, he made a good stroke at Anak's neck. The sword bounced off and Anak laughed, saying that he once had daughters who could strike harder. This emboldened all of Asa's men to make their attempts. With sword and axe they struck, but Anak's head remained firmly attached to his body. He stood while archers shot quivers of arrows at him, to no effect. The king came forward and examined Anak. His flesh felt like that of any man, but all had seen that no weapon could injure him.

"'What about fire?' asked another warrior, believing that evil things cannot abide fire. So Anak bade them make a great pyre of wood before the castle and set it alight. When the fire blazed fully, so that the flames reached up into the sky, Anak disrobed and climbed up the burning wood. All those present could see him in the flames as he climbed to the top of the stack and sat down. He looked perfectly comfortable, and even made as if scrubbing himself in a bath. He climbed down from the fire with no harm done him, not even smelling of smoke, though his hair and beard were now trimmed to within a finger's width of his skin."

Daniel smiled, remembering the way his father had always told this part of the story, mimicking Anak scrubbing himself in his bath of fire.

Rachel's eyes shone watching Daniel tell his tale. "And so your people believed Anak and gave him all he asked."

Daniel nodded.

"And then?" asked Rachel.

225

"And then," said Daniel, taking a step back. "I ran down to my saddlebags below deck while the lovely lady Rachel waited in the fresh sea air." And off he ran.

Rachel wondered at that, but, amused nonetheless, waited as asked in the fresh sea air. Soon Daniel returned with a leather-wrapped bundle in his hands. He unwrapped it to reveal a book.

"This is my history of Asulon," Daniel said proudly.

"You wrote this book?" asked Rachel, very impressed—and only partially because she was in love, for her people held scholars of any type in high regard.

"I have been working on it since I was a lad and made my latest entry just a few days before I met you." He turned to a page a quarter of the way through the book and, pointing to a spot halfway down, handed the book to Rachel. "The story continues here."

Rachel nodded. She began to read.

Anak and the House of Asher sealed their agreement. For seven years Anak and the House of Asher fought, and finally subdued, the tribes of Logres. Grateful for Asa's help, Anak gave to the young man his daughter Sari in marriage. Anak, now king of Logres, had an armada built for the House of Asher's return to Asulon. The Asherites sailed for Asulon in the spring of the third year of the Reign of King Anak.

It took six weeks for the heavy warships of the armada to reach the coast that, by charts Anak himself made, should be Asulon. The Asherites sailed along a forested coastline for two full days, but saw no inhabitants. On the afternoon of the third day, they came upon the mouth of a great river and turned in to explore. Once on the river, they found a battle being fought. A dozen seagoing, oared longboats, each carrying twenty armed warriors, tried to make the shore, but were repelled by forces from within the forest. Arrows from unseen archers and stones from unseen catapults rained down on the longboats. The longboats divided their attack, some going north and some south to outflank the defenders.

Asa had seen longboats like this before, having fought their like along the coastlines of Logres. Not for carrying cargo or for fighting ship to ship, these boats were built for raiding shoreline villages. With a shallow draft, they could be beached on a riverbank while their crews silently came ashore to steal goods and take captives away to slavery. Asa made a quick decision and ordered an attack on the longboats. The fore and aft decks, and each side of the Asherite ships carried great longbows designed by Anak himself, stronger than any five men could pull, mounted horizontally on a swiveling pedestal and drawn by a winch. These bows shot arrows more like spears in size, designed to be set afire and bring flame to the sails of enemy warships. They would put fist-sized holes in the bottoms of the much smaller longboats, while passing clean through any man unlucky enough to be in the way. The Asherites sank three of the longboats before the rest ran for the sea.

Men emerged from the forest and met with the Asherites. Asa told them the tale of the House of Asher and wonder overcame the men of Asulon. The Asulonians agree to take Asa and his lead ship into the hidden port city of Eboracium.

They tell Asa that, after the Long Winter ended, the people returned north to the place where tradition said their capital of Eboracium lay. There they discovered the remains of their city. Whether intentionally or the result of the Long Winter or some other calamity, the city now resembled no other. They found great walls of broken stone, as wide as they were high, but not one house, shop or palace. The formation of the walls was strange as well. Every wall ran north and south separated by just a few paces, but with hardly a cross tunnel between them. The people dug into the sides of the walls for their homes and cleared the spaces between for their streets. They dug cross tunnels through the walls, though they left the vegetation atop the walls and on their seaward faces, so that the city resembled a forest from afar. They cut only a single entrance giving onto the river, concealed around a bend upstream.

The Asherites sailed into the port of Eboracium with the banner of the lost king, an eagle bearing arrows in one fist and an olive branch in the other, at the mast. The people of Eboracium cheered and led Asa and his men to Aidraugal, their Warlord. Aidraugal, seeing the tokens of Asa's kingship and, moreover, seeing the great multitude—including his own guards—cheering, decided to welcome Asa.

Asa learned that all the villages and ports along the coast of Asulon had been plagued by the longboat men from the far north, and their ships at sea assaulted by pirates from the south. Asa, eager for a quick foothold in Asulon, told Aidraugal that he would protect Eboracium in exchange for some nearby land on a cliff overlooking the river. Aidraugal agreed, for Asa asked for rocky, steep land, considered worthless for farming. Asa built a fortress there, called Maôz Thabera, 'The Fortress of the Burning', for they found evidence on the site of a great fire in ancient times. Asa began the long, slow process of unifying Asulon.

In those days, Asulon was divided among several autonomous city-states, running along the coastlines and rivers, with much wild country in between.

Asa sent messengers to the rulers of the nearest cities to join him in council to choose a king. "We are free men," they said, "why do we need a king?" Many of the rulers did come, though, for they had heard of the men from across the great sea and the wondrous knowledge they brought with them. Asa must have learned some gift of speech from Anak, for he spoke such fair words of a great vision for Asulon that all the rulers sat in awe. Seeing all that the Asherites could do for them, and weary of the raids of the longboat men and pirates, most of the city rulers agreed to form alliances with Asa. They also agreed to bring together a council to form a central government with one king to lead them in battle. Many, however, did not agree to these things, fearing one all-powerful king. "One great king may do both great good and great evil to all, but many small kings can do only a little good and a little evil to a few" they said.

The people of Asulon, the rulers said, were mostly hunters, farmers and craftsmen, proud men used to ruling themselves. They would not willingly become the subjects of any earthly king. This led Asa to agree to the "Great Compromise" dividing power in Asulon. From that time on, four pillars of equal strength upheld the freedom of the Asulonian people.

The first, the Senate, would write the laws. The second, the king, would carry out the laws made by the Senate and command the army in times of war. The third, the High Court, would interpret each new law based on its compliance with the Elder Laws of Asulon. The fourth pillar, the people of Asulon themselves, proud of spirit, as well as proudly armed, would make a force superior to the small standing army that the king commanded in peacetime. Each held a power that balanced the powers of the others. All four groups were subject to the Elder Laws of Asulon, which the House of Asher had kept as a treasure down through the centuries. In Asulon alone of all lands on the earth, the will of the king was not the absolute power in the land. In Asulon, the ultimate power rested in the Elder Laws.

In the winter of the year that Asa became king, Sari bore him a son. They named him Adom, after the first father of men, for he was the first of the House of Asher born on Asulonian soil in a thousand years. The kingdom now reached from the jungles far to the south to the ice-covered northern wastes, from the Peaceful Sea in the west to the Great Sea in the east. Growing in prosperity, the realm began to sell grain and goods to the traders of Logres.

When Adom reached twenty-five years of age, his father sent him off to study in the court of Anak. There he learned the languages of the Unicorn Kingdoms, the ways of sea and stars, and the methods of war. The latter proved the most to his liking, as he learned all manner of warfare from single combat to the fortification of cities. Anak, taken by his grandson, gave the prince the hand of his youngest daughter, Adelia, in marriage.

Anak told the prince that there would be no madness in the children of such a union, as would be the case in mortal men, as Anak's descendents carried the pure blood of an angel, and Adelia's mother was not the mother of Sari. Anak also told Adom that, if he wed Adelia, the children born to them would have life spans twice that of common men. Adom wed Adelia and spent ten years studying at the court of Anak. Then he returned to Asulon with his wife and children, and told his people all Anak had said. And Anak's word proved to be true. The sons of Adom and Adelia all lived past one hundred and fifty years, their daughters nearer two hundred, while most fully mortal men in Asulon lived less than half that. Ever afterwards, the sons of the House of Asher traveled to the Court of Anak to learn his arts and seek a wife among his many daughters. Anak encouraged this, for it strengthened the bond between the two countries.

The men of the House of Asher began to differ from common men in ways other than length of life. While having the strength of any well-trained man, they possessed the endurance of the sons of Anak, the Anakim, and could fight or run or swim all day without tiring. No disease would harm them; no venom from snake or spider could fell them.

When Adom returned to Asulon, his father, weary of the unending political battles necessary to rule, immediately gave up the throne to his son. Ever since, the kings of Asulon have given up their throne to *their sons once they return from their ten years in Logres.*

King Adom started the great war college at Caurus, where the sons of the House of Asher study before they travel to Logres. The young men who graduate from Caurus, called paladins or "Peers of the King", are the guardians of the king, as well as the realm's military officers and first line of defense in times of war.

Across the sea, Anak begat sons to aid him in his many wars. The sons of Anak are the Anakim, giants among men. They stand nearly as tall as Anak himself and are stronger than any ten men. Anak and his sons succeeded in bringing the kingdoms of the west together to face the threat of the hoards of the east, the Scythian tribes, made up of Gomeria and Togamah and greatest of all, the Magog.

The Magog, of late, had returned to the worship of their god of old, Moloch, and begun to lust after the riches of the west. The worship of Moloch required the people of Magog to surrender all personal property to the "Son of Moloch", the Emperor of Magog. Even the lives of the people were forfeit. Each spring, before sowing the fields, one child from each town would be thrown alive into the fires of Moloch, then the ashes spread over the fields to bring fertility to the crops.

In those years, only the generalship of Anak held the Magog and other Scythian tribes at bay.

Many centuries passed in the west with little change. Asulon grew in power and wealth, second only to Logres. And still Anak ruled. After one thousand years of his reign passed, he appeared no older in the eyes of the world. But the angel who had witnessed eons pass like changing seasons sensed a difference. Anak had begun to age. He said that the age of man was passing and man would soon have no further use for him. Anak began to turn over more and more control of the realm to his ministers. Then the wives of Anak stopped bearing sons. Asulon surpassed Logres in strength, so that the young, which had been second, carried the old, which had been first. Asulon began to be called "The True West".

This period of peace and prosperity for Asulon did not last forever, as something changed within the people. Some of the wise later would say that the people of this age fell because times of ease test the heart more truly than times of hardship.

The change became apparent during the rule of King Absalom.

Absalom came to the throne promising to be the most moral of kings, yet became the most evil ruler Asulon had seen. He amassed great wealth by selling trade treaties to foreign kings and promises of title to the wealthy. He did this, not for the good of Asulon, but for his own greed. Though he kept a harem of concubines around him, these did not satisfy him, and no woman that caught his eye was safe from his groping hands.

Many in Asulon did not complain, though, for the wheat still flourished in the fields, the cattle grew fat and the harbors stayed full of trading ships. "Why should we care what the king does to others?" they would say. "Our bellies are full and so are our purses."

Later, many of the wise speculated on whether a corrupt people led to an evil king or an evil king led to a corrupt people. For, whatever the reason, the Death Cults came to Asulon during those years: the cults of Moloch (which killed any newborn child with a defect), Vanth (which led the old to suicide), and Pan (which led the young to indulge their lusts, spreading pox and plague). Chaos ruled the land, for every man did what was right in his own eyes.

The king allowed all manner of abominations in Asulon, and the realm grew weaker. Droughts came, trade grew thin, croplands lay fallow, men roamed from city to city seeking work. To hold on to his power, Absalom set the people one against the other, poor against rich, young against old, city dwellers against country folk.

A wise man wrote of this time, "The people became weak and fearful of strength, but rather than
seek to make the weak strong, they sought to make the
strong weak."

The Magog grew bolder. The lands of Alogna,
Sedor, Kyberia, Adanerg, Augaracinia, fell to the Magog while the king of Asulon stood idle. While many—
mostly the Molochite Senators who supported him—
called Absalom "The Father of Peace" for keeping Asulon out of these wars, many more called him "The
Mighty Eunuch" for lacking the courage to use the vast
power of the armies of Asulon. The people's militia
grew slothful and ill-equipped. The people divided into
those who hated Absalom and his ways, and desired a
return to the old ways of Asulon, and those who simply
hated Absalom. As the realm waxed worse and worse,
more and more people came to pledge themselves to the
worship of the Lord God.

A remnant of the Lord's people remained in the
land and they knew that the Lord God would not re-
strain his anger much longer. Finally, hundreds of
thousands of common men and women put on sack-
cloth and ashes and appeared on the battle plain before Maôz-Thabera. They came not to assault the fortress, but to plead with the king to return to the old
laws of the land and to pray for the realm's repentance.

And they came singing a song of the Lord.

> If My people which are called by
> My Name shall humble themselves
> and pray and seek My face
> and turn from their wicked ways
> then will I hear from heaven
> and will forgive their sins
> and will heal their land.

Absalom ignored all manner of warnings and supplications and continued in his evils. Soon painful, leprous sores developed on him. He spent the last months of his life wasting away in pain and then he died.

Absalom died childless, so a new king was sought.

Next in succession was Argeus.

As king, Argeus had all temples of Moloch, Vanth and Pan destroyed and their priests banished. New laws were made that restored the Eder Laws of Asulon.

Soon the realm began to edge back from the precipice Absalom had brought it to. Though the land had not yet returned to its former glory, the people could again hold up their heads. They had a true king.

* * * * *

Rachel handed the book back to Daniel, her eyes brimming with tears.

"Rachel, what is wrong?" wondered the prince. "I did not think that I wrote *that* well."

She stared at Daniel for a moment longer, then turned away crying and went below decks.

"What's got into her?" the prince asked aloud.

"I would have thought you possessed sufficient intelligence to see this coming." Daniel turned and saw Moor standing near the main mast.

"What are you talking about?" asked Daniel.

Moor approached the prince, shaking his head. "Where do we land in a week's time?"

"Logres, of course."

"And what, pray tell, did you expect to do with the princess once we arrive? You journey to the court of Anak and she must return to her people."

"Well, I, ah...I thought that perhaps she would not have to leave right away. It is a long journey, after

234

all. And I thought it would be good for her to see Anak's court and stay there awhile."

"And then what?" asked Moor, eyes boring into the prince.

Daniel just shrugged his shoulders.

"Well? You were not thinking of marrying the girl, were you?" demanded the Etruscan.

"And if I were?" Daniel said, returning the hard look. "Am I not now a man, free to do as I choose?"

"Yes, you are a man, but no, you are not free to choose in all things," replied Moor. "You are a prince of the House of Asher. Anak would surely take it as an insult if you did not wed one of his daughters. Relations between the two countries would suffer, and Asulon needs Anak's support now that it is left without its king."

"But not all the men of my house have married daughters of Anak," Daniel said, angry now that Moor had brought his father's death into the argument. "Two widowed kings married commoners." He thought for a moment. "Even some paladins have wed before they made the voyage to Logres."

"Yes," said Moor, "and that brings me to the reason that the girl ran from you in tears. She saw clearly in a moment the problem that you seem to have conveniently overlooked."

Daniel grew impatient. "Then you must educate me. The sea air has made me a bit dense today."

"Would that it were only today," Moor said. "You showed me your history while you were working on it at Caurus. In your history book, you accurately describe the benefits of wedding a daughter of Anak."

"But Rachel is just as beautiful as any princess of Logres!" protested Daniel.

"Perhaps she is," replied Moor. "But tell me this, historian, what happened to the children of those Asherites who wed commoners?"

Daniel thought for a moment. "The sons of the kings were killed in battle during the Gomerian wars. I do not know what happened to the children of the paladins."

"I will tell you then," Moor said. "They died. They died as common men die. Not at a hundred and fifty or so, as other Asherites, but in their seventies or less, and not peacefully in their sleep, but taken by the diseases that put most men in the grave. Some died quickly when their heart failed, or when a blood vessel burst in their brain; some died a little at a time through slow senility, spending the last years of their lives being fed and washed like an infant. They died of viper's bite and scorpion's sting and infections that you and your house have not had to worry about for a thousand years. They died, you fool, just as most men die. And now you would doom your children to that fate all because of a girl. Well, that girl has more sense then you and wanted no part in that doom. *That* is why she ran away."

Daniel's legs suddenly felt weak. He sat down heavily on a crate and buried his head in his hands.

"How can such blessing be such a curse?" he asked aloud, his head swimming. Then a thought came to him and he looked up at Moor.

"But, wait—perhaps after all these years of having Anak's blood in our veins, my children will still be as long lived as the rest of my people."

"No, Daniel, they will not," replied Moor, more gently now. "The last man of your house to marry a commoner lived just three hundred years ago and his children lived the life-spans of common men. If seven hundred years of breeding did not suffice, then a thousand years will be no better."

Daniel's eyes showed that the truth of Moor's words had struck home. "Oh, Moor, what have I done?"

"To the girl? Not as much as you may think. Many a girl her age has loved and lost. She is young and will soon heal because you did nothing to consummate your love. No, Daniel, it is *you* that I am worried about."

"Me? I will be all right."

"Will you? I think not. Your people can be as single-minded as salmon returning to their home stream when you believe you are in love. Why do you think your parents always ship you boys off to Logres just as soon as you come of age?"

When Daniel did not respond, Moor leaned closer. "Why?" he asked, tapping a hard forefinger against the younger man's forehead to emphasize his words.

"So that precisely this kind of thing *does* (tap) *not* (tap) *happen* (tap): that is why."

Moor clasped his hands behind his back and paced back and forth before Daniel.

"Now I am worried that you will pine over this girl your whole stay at Anak's court. Oh, you will wed one of his daughters to protect the lives of your children, but your heart will always linger on this girl. That is not wise for you and not fair to the maiden you will marry and who will one day be queen of Asulon. No, we cannot let that be. But what is the cure?"

He continued pacing for a time then suddenly stopped and snapped his fingers.

"There is a school of philosophers in my country, called Stoics," said Moor. "They believe that for a man to have peace, he must first control his emotions. If you will let me, I will take you through their training. It will give you peace in this matter."

"Peace," Daniel said. "Yes, I would like that, for now my heart has no peace."

"Then follow me," Moor said and he led them below decks.

* * * * *

"Child, what has happened to make you weep so?" asked Simon. He had been praying in his cabin when he heard Rachel dash into her own room and fall upon her bed, crying. He entered and sat across from her on the unused bunk, trying to comfort her.

Rachel buried her face in her pillow. Then she looked up at the priest, her eyes red, her face anguished.

"I have allowed my heart to love a man who can never return my love."

"Oh, there now, child, just because the prince is not Abramim does not mean that you and he cannot, well, cannot go where this seems to be leading. Alliances between kingdoms are made through marriage every day."

"It's not that he is not of my people," Rachel said. "It is that he is not of *any* people but his own." She lowered her voice. "He is not like us. I had heard that the people of the House of Asher lived longer, but I thought that they carried that gift within them, not that each of their men must marry one of Anak's daughters or else lose this gift for their children. Even though I love him, I cannot marry him. It would mean cutting his children's lives by half."

"I knew all about Asherite history when the two of you met," replied Simon. "And yet, when I saw your feelings for each other grow, I felt no warning in my spirit." He took the sleeve of his robe and gently dabbed an errant tear from her eye. "Are you not under my protection while we travel? So then, I think the Lord would have told me if your heart were in any real danger."

Rachel brightened "Then you think it is still possible that he and I...?"

"Little one, I cannot guarantee that anything, well, *permanent* will come of it. But I do know that the Lord brought you to Asulon for a reason, and that He would know beforehand that you and Daniel would love each other as you do. Therefore, have faith that the Lord both knows what He is doing and loves you more than you could know. Does not scripture tell us that 'All things work together for good to those that trust in the Lord'? We do not have a God who plays with us as the pieces in a game, but loves us as His own children. Have faith. We have not seen the end of this."

Chapter Fourteen
FIRES

And I will bring the third part through the fire, and will refine them as silver is refined, and will try them as gold is tried: they shall call on my name, and I will hear them: I will say, It *is* my people: and they shall say, The LORD *is* my God.
-The Book of Zechariah 13:9

It is best to get through the hardest part of the training first," Moor said. He and Daniel sat across from each other in their cabin, on two bunks bolted to each wall, with just enough distance for a man to stand between them. With little enough room here for mundane tasks like getting dressed, Daniel wondered what kind of training Moor would give him in such tight quarters and why it had to be done in the privacy of the cabin. Moor took a lamp from its holder on the wall and held it before Daniel.

"Roll up your left sleeve and hold out your arm."

Daniel did as he was told, stretching his arm out before him. Moor lowered the lamp and brought it under Daniel's limb.

"Tell me when you begin to feel the heat."

"Now," Daniel said, the flame about a cubit from his arm.

"Good, now hold still," Moor said as he raised the lamp half the distance.

Daniel jerked his arm back. "Hey! You nearly burned me."

"To burn you is the whole point," replied Moor. "We will use pain to focus your mind and make your body do what it does not want to do. Do you wish to have control over your heart and forget your feelings for the girl, or do you not?"

Daniel hesitated for a moment then thrust his arm back out and held it there. Moor brought the lamp up and held it under the prince's arm. Beads of sweat came to Daniel's brow as he gritted his teeth to bear the pain.

* * * * *

Simon looked for Daniel on deck, but did not find him. So he made his way back down the ship's stair to their shared cabin.

"Daniel, I think we should speak..." Simon began while opening the cabin door, but stopped in mid-sentence at the sight within. Moor was holding a lamp below Daniel's outstretched arm while the prince remained still as stone. The smell of burning flesh came to Simon's nostrils.

"What in God's name is going on here!" demanded Simon.

Moor replaced the lamp in its holder and handed Daniel a wet rag from a bucket on the floor. The prince took the rag and pressed it onto his arm, his face white.

"Stay here," Moor ordered Daniel. "Priest, I will speak to you outside."

Moor led Simon to the opposite end of the passageway.

"What do you think you are doing?" Simon said.

"Protecting Daniel's claim to the throne," replied Moor. "Daniel has fallen in love with the girl you insisted on bringing with us. Anak would not take kindly to a prince of Asulon rejecting his daughter for a girl of mortal blood. Only two kings of Asulon have wed commoners and each of these did so after their first wives, Anak's daughters, died and after they had become kings. With Argeus dead, Daniel's succession depends on his wedding one of Anak's daughters and spending ten years at Anak's court. Daniel would have jeopardized this if he wed the Abramim girl."

Simon's eyebrows bristled when he got angry. They bristled now. "Did you have a hand in what happened between them today?"

"What, and have the boy mope around this ship for the remainder of our journey with a long face and a heavy sigh every time he saw the girl, which he could not help doing several times a day? No, I am wiser than that. He did this all by himself.

"My plan, once I saw the path they were starting down, was to wait until we reached Logres. There I could have spoken to the girl privately. Once aware of all the ways that a marriage between them would have hurt the prince, I am sure that she, from a royal house herself and knowing its duties, would have left Daniel of her own accord. Women, despite their outward frailties, are much more practical in these matters than are men. She could have left him a note, perhaps telling him of her responsibilities to her own people," Moor gave his half smile, "or something noble like that, I hadn't had time to write the note yet.

"In any event, my way would have been less painful for Daniel than what he has brought on himself. But now I must accept a change in plans, for they have realized their folly and know that they have no future together. No doubt the girl will heal soon after she departs for her country, but the prince is an Asherite and they do not forget affairs of the heart as easily as other men. I am taking him through the training of the Stoics so that he can control his feelings for the girl. Do not interfere. I am helping him."

"Helping him! How, by hurting him?" asked Simon.

"One pain washes away another," replied Moor. "He must learn to control his emotions by first learning to control his body. Do not worry, though. The worst part is over. I had to shock his body. Now I must wear him down."

"And how do you mean to do this?"

"Leave that to me," Moor said. "Much of what he will go through he has gone through before in his regular training, save that now he will go though it in a shorter time. Remember, the queen put the prince under my protection and command. He is my responsibility, not yours."

This last statement seemed to satisfy Simon. "You will not harm him, then? No more of this torture with the lamp?"

"No more lamps. You have my word," replied Moor.

"Well, I still think that all this is unnecessary, but I will leave you be on one condition."

"Oh, and what is that?"

"You have said rightly that the queen has put her son under your protection, but you only concern yourself with the physical. I would like your permission to see to his spiritual training."

Moor nodded his head, "As you wish. As you say, such things are not my concern. Now, may I get back to my training of the boy without further interruptions?"

"Yes," said Simon. "Now that I have your assurance that no further harm will come to him, I will not stand in your way."

Moor gave the slightest of bows, spun on his heel and strode back up the passageway.

* * * * *

When Rachel failed to come to the evening meal, Simon brought her a bowl, though, as he anticipated, she had no appetite and only picked at her food while the two of them talked. Late that night, Simon took his leave of her and returned to his own cabin. Inside he found Moor lying in his bunk and Daniel doing push-ups and dripping sweat on the cabin floor.

"What are you doing, lad?" asked Simon.

"Push-ups," replied the prince.

"I can see that, but have you almost finished? I can't get around you to my bunk."

"Oh, sorry," Daniel said, coming to his feet and stepping aside.

Simon removed his boots and climbed into his bunk opposite Moor. The paladin lay under a blanket, his face hidden in shadow. He looked asleep. Daniel began doing his push-ups again.

"I have never liked these passenger bunks," said the priest. "We would do better with the hammocks that the sailors use. Hammocks can be tied against a wall when they're not used, so that the floor space is free for other things. I suppose the ship builders did not wish to risk a passenger breaking his neck getting in and out of a hammock, but I find them more practical at sea and much more comfortable." Simon put his hands behind his head and lay back, continuing to speak. "Ah, yes, the motion of the ship taking the waves as you lie in your hammock becomes like your very own mother rocking you in your cradle."

Daniel continued his exercises as Simon spoke. After a time Daniel rose, took down a water bag from a peg and took a long swallow. Seeing that he would get no conversation from the boy this night, Simon rolled over to face the wall, ready for sleep. Then Daniel's deep breathing indicated that another exercise had begun. Simon rolled back over and saw Daniel pulling himself up on ropes hung from hooks in the ceiling.

"And now what are you doing?" asked Simon.

"Pull-ups," replied Daniel, his body rising and falling steadily.

"Yes, well how long are you going to do those?"

"Master Moor is having me do one thousand each of four different exercises, push-ups, squats, sit-ups and pull-ups."

"So you have almost finished, then?"

"With this cycle, yes. When I have finished the last exercise, I begin again with the first."

"You are not going to do this all night, are you?" asked Simon

"Yes, those are my orders."

"Well, I cannot sleep with you breathing like that; it's near as bad as snoring. Go out in the passageway if you are going to be doing that all night."

"Go," came Moor's voice from his bunk. "Do what you can in the passage and let the priest get his sleep."

Moor did not bother to open his eyes. Simon guessed that the paladin woke as soon as he had entered the cabin. Daniel took his water bag and left. Simon knew it would do no good to question Moor about his methods, so he set his mind on sleep.

The next morning Simon woke at dawn to pray, as was his custom. He saw neither the prince, nor Moor in their bunks. After his prayers, Simon went topside and found Moor doing his morning exercises on the deck, as was *his* custom. Moor had taken a ballast stone and tied a rope around it to make a short handle. He was now swinging the stone up to shoulder height and then lowering it in a half squat. He spent a half hour each morning on such exercises and an equal amount of time slowly stretching at night. Each afternoon, he spent an hour on his sword technique.

Would it that all men prayed as regularly as this man does his exercises, thought the priest with a sigh.

"Where is Daniel?" Simon asked.

Moor cocked his head upwards. Simon looked and saw the prince doing some exercise in the ship's rigging that involved hanging by one arm. Simon just shook his head and walked away.

Rachel came out on deck after the morning meal and found Simon sitting on a barrel, reading scripture.

"Simon, have you seen Daniel? I knocked on his door this morning, but no one answered."

Simon pointed up the main mast. Rachel spotted Daniel in the crow's nest, apparently taking the watch for the sailor who would normally have been there.

"What is he doing up there?" asked Rachel.

"Moor has him engaged in some strange training ritual," replied Simon. "Daniel exercised all night and now I think Moor has him taking the sailor's watches to keep him awake through the day."

"But why?"

"It is supposed to give him better control of his emotions."

Rachel hung her head. "So that he can forget me."

Simon was reminded how very young she was and how fragile were the hearts of the young. "That may be Moor's intent, but it will come to nothing. Such training may enable a man to keep his emotions from showing on his face, but it will do little to prevent him from feeling them in his heart. Do not despair. Have faith in the Lord and in His wisdom and love for us. All things work together for good to those who love God, even if it is a good that we cannot foresee."

* * * * *

Simon kept watch over Daniel as best he could, though for the next five days the prince's training continued much the same. Daniel did not eat or sleep or shave or bathe. Drinking water was the only bit of normalcy Moor allowed him (and this Simon knew, Moor did out of necessity, as even an Asherite would die with-

245

out water). The prince spent his days up in the crow's nest (to keep away from Rachel, Simon suspected) and his nights in exercise. A common man training in such a way would have collapsed or even died, working his body without sleep or food for so long, but angel's blood ran in Daniel's veins and angels are not known to collapse or die.

True to his agreement with Moor, Simon did not enter the cabin during training sessions. But, on the evening of the sixth night, he needed a book from his bag. He went to his cabin door and saw a dim light coming from under the door.

Moor must be asleep by now, thought Simon as he opened the door.

Simon saw Daniel kneeling on the floor with his arm stretched out over a candle, the flame nearly touching his skin.

"My arm will not move," he said, a stone-like expression on his face.

Moor sprang from his bunk, blocking Simon's view as he came to the door.

"You are too early. Leave us."

"What is this?" demanded Simon. "You swore that there would be no more burning."

"No, I did not," replied Moor. "If you recall, I promised no more lamps, and I have kept to my word. Now you must leave. I will not have the last night of his training disturbed."

With that he shut the door in Simon's face.

Simon felt anger rise within him and contemplated breaking the door down, but, no...his instructions had been not to interfere just yet. He decided he needed some fresh air.

Two hours later he returned to the cabin. No light came from under the door, so he entered. Both Moor and Daniel lay in their bunks. The prince looked more unconscious than asleep. Moor's eyes were closed, but that meant little.

"Is his training over?" asked Simon.

246

"For now," replied Moor. "I will let him rest for a day and then see if the training has taken."

Simon shook his head. "Is it worth all this?"

"What is a kingdom worth?" Moor said. "Now let me sleep. I have gotten little rest myself while he trained."

Daniel slept all the next day. The following morning Simon and Rachel sat with the captain in the mess cabin, taking their morning meal, when Moor and Daniel appeared. Rachel's breath caught in her throat. The prince entered the cabin dressed like his teacher, all in black with leather armguards on his forearms, his hair swept back and his face neatly shaved save for the mustache and chin beard growing under his sunken cheeks and hard eyes.

Daniel caught sight of Rachel and paused. When he spoke, he spoke in slow, measured tones without emotion.

"Good morning to you, Lady Rachel. And to you, Captain." He nodded to Simon.

"Daniel, are you well?" asked Rachel.

"Yes, I am very well. Thank you for asking."

"Well, I for one am hungry this morning," Moor said, rubbing his hands together as he and Daniel sat. He took bread, cheese and meat from the main platter, putting some on his plate and some on Daniel's. Moor began to eat, but Daniel just stared at the food. Simon could see his lips moving and realized that he was counting to himself. After what seemed a very long time for a man who had not eaten for a week, Daniel picked up his fork and brought a piece of cheese to his mouth. He bit the cheese and closed his eyes, chewing slowly. The rest of the table watched in silence as a tear formed at the corner of his left eye and rolled down his cheek. He swallowed and opened his eyes. Spying the meat, he sliced off a chunk and brought it to his mouth.

Rachel waited for Daniel to notice the rest of the table staring at him, but, if he did notice these things, he was too absorbed in his meal to show it.

The tears continued to roll down his face as he ate.

* * * * *

"Logres," said the captain as he manned the ship's wheel, "should be sighted in three days if the weather holds. Figure most of a day to round the southern shore of the island and we should be at the port of Albion four days from now."

Simon had led Rachel on deck after the morning meal, which had not gone well. Rachel had tried repeatedly to engage Daniel in conversation. The prince had answered formally, as if speaking to a stranger. With each cold answer he gave her, Rachel looked as if she had been struck a blow. Simon felt he should get her out of there as quickly as he could and so brought her up into the sunshine.

Now Moor and Daniel practiced with wooden swords on the foredeck. Rachel came to the deck's rail, leaned upon it and stood waiting for Daniel to look her way. Simon walked up beside her.

"Why are the hearts of men and women so different?" she asked.

Simon remained silent, knowing that she did not expect an answer.

"I cannot blame him for not telling me we must go our separate ways once we reached Logres. I think we both knew that to be true, but chose to ignore it while we traveled together. But once I read the history of his people, I knew that I could no longer live in a world made of clouds and mist. I knew this, yet I hoped that we could still spend the little time we had together as friends. But now he acts as if he does not know me. Why does he treat me this way?"

"Men are hard, proud creatures, little one," replied Simon. "Because they are hunters at heart it is difficult for them to see and not hold, to taste and not eat. For them to hope for love and then settle for friendship feels like spending all day in their mother's kitchen,

248

smelling their favorite meal cooking and then knowing that they cannot eat it. With the forbidden food in front of them, its smell tortures instead of pleases. Daniel would rather put his feelings for you out of his mind altogether than be reminded of what might have been each day he sees you. He hopes that an untouched wound heals swifter."

"What am I to do then?" she asked. "Do to him as he does to me and pretend he is not there?"

"Do what we have always been instructed to do in difficult times," replied Simon "Pray, trust God and have patience."

Rachel smiled a wan smile. "You keep giving me the same answer."

Simon stretched out a finger and touched her gently on the tip of the nose. "That is because *you* keep asking me the same question."

Two more days passed with no change in Daniel's behavior. Simon spent his mornings praying in his cabin. Rachel spent much of her time in her cabin as well, for she understood now what Simon meant about a wound best left untouched. They sailed on.

The wind remained in their favor and so, on the morning of the exact day the captain had predicted, they sighted Logres. The captain gave orders to follow the shoreline north and east. They reached the port of Albion just before sunset.

Daniel stood beside Moor at the rail, anxious for his first look at his grandfather's city, Albion, which differed from Eboracium in many ways. Though both at the mouths of rivers, Albion was not concealed, but openly built. A large wharf area with docks, taverns and warehouses greeted them here. Beyond this, a tall stone wall surrounded the city, which was topped by strong guard towers and pierced by an imposing city gate, wide enough to drive four wagons abreast through. Beyond the city gate, a jumble of buildings climbed up the hillside towards the fortress that gave the city its name. Each structure in Albion seemed to be built at a different time and of different materials—some of stone, some of wood and some of brick. Even when two buildings sat close to each other and seemed built at the same time, their roofs never quite met at the same level. The narrow streets twisted this way and that, in contrast to the regular grid that made up Eboracium. In the distance, above the port, gleamed the white fortress of Caer-Albion, as large as a city itself.

Daniel stood at the bow of the ship in formal attire, the leather of his boots and sword scabbard polished to a high gloss. "It will be good to put my feet on shore again," he said. "Now, more than ever, I wish to see the wonders of my grandfather's court."

"It is said that no one who comes to Anak's court can leave unchanged," Moor said. He lowered his voice. "It is also said that the measure of a king lies in the difficulty of his decisions. You did the right thing, my prince. You will know that once you have spent some time here."

Two longboats rowed up to them, flying the flag of the harbormaster. The sailors threw lines and towed the Prydwen to a dock at the center of the wharf. "Make her fast," called out the captain and the crew cast lines to dockhands standing ready. The ship was tied and the gangplank lowered.

"Finally," said Daniel. "This journey has taken far too long."

Just then a clamor came from the city gate. A group of men wearing heavy plate armor charged towards the gate from the city above. Arrows rained down on them from the battlements atop the wall, but the men ran through the barrage, immune to the arrows in their armor. Just as they entered the gate, the great iron portcullis came crashing down, blocking their path. The men took hold of the portcullis and incredibly, began to lift it.

"Anakim!" Daniel said.

"Yes," Moor said, "but why do Anak's soldiers attack them?"

"They are my kinsmen. We should help them," Daniel said.

"How?" asked Moor, pointing to the gate. The soldiers atop the gateway now poured flaming oil into the street below. The Anakim let go of the portcullis and fell back before the flames.

"We must do something," Daniel said.

"There are forty or more archers on those towers," Moor said. "We would be cut down before we got halfway to the gate and, even if we did make it there, what then? *Blow* the flames out?"

He pointed up the hillside. The gates of the fortress had opened and a column of heavy lancers riding great armored warhorses came at full gallop, aiming for the Anakim at the gate.

"Once the lancers reach them, they are finished," Moor said. "The lancers will trap them against the gate and then the men atop the wall will pour flaming oil upon them."

Daniel drew his bow from its cover.

"What do you think you doing?" asked Moor.

"If I can get within bowshot unseen, maybe I can shoot down enough men to stop the oil from falling," Daniel said, pulling a bowstring from his belt.

"Those archers will pin you to the ground before you get halfway there," Moor said. "We do not know who is at fault in this. Stay here. It is not our affair."

Daniel searched for some other way to bring the Anakim to the ship or warn them about the lancers. He looked along the dock, measured distances and knew that Moor was right. There was no safe way to get to them.

"**STORM!**" came a voice from high above. The ship shuddered with the sound of it.

"**STORM!**" it cried out again.

Daniel and Moor looked up in unison and saw the priest Simon standing in the crow's nest, his arms outstretched to the heavens. Dark clouds rolled across the sky above him.

"**STORM!**" Simon cried a third time. A bolt of lighting flashed with a deafening thunderclap. Rain poured forth from the sky as if every cloud in the heavens released their burden all at once. Rain fell so thick that Daniel could no longer see the dock; rain fell so heavy that he could barely breathe and not drown where he stood. In a few moments, giant shapes appeared out of the darkness. The Anakim ran up the gangplank and staggered onto the ship. As suddenly as it started, the rain stopped.

Making a quick decision, Daniel drew his sword and cut the rope that tied the bow to the dock.

As the prince dashed to the stern to do the same to the aft rope, Moor untied a line near the main mast and ran it to the nearest Anakim.

"If you want us all to live, raise this sail."

The Anakim took hold of the rope and pulled the mainsail up so fast the rope drew smoke from its pulley. A final gust of wind from the storm turned the ship away from the dock and far out into the river's current.

"What goes on here?" bellowed Njorthr. "Who are these men? Who gave orders to put out from the dock?"

"I am Gath, son of Anak," said one of the giants, unbuckling his helmet. "And these are my brothers. None gave the order to flee the dock but dire need. If you had stayed dockside, you would all be dead."

Daniel counted seven of the giants on board. One by one the Anakim removed their helmets. Each had green eyes and thick red beards. They wore their hair in long braids, which they had wound atop their heads as cushioning for their helmets. Several had dents in their armor, but gave no sign of wounds.

"If you are Anak's sons, why, then, were you fighting with your father's troops?" asked Njorthr.

The Anakim looked at his brothers before speaking. When he spoke Daniel felt his world unmade.

"Those are not my father's troops," Gath said. "My father is dead."

Chapter Fifteen
LET THERE BE GIANTS

There were giants in the earth in those days; and also after that, when the sons of God came in unto the daughters of men, and they bore children to them, the same became mighty men, which were of old, men of renown.

-The Book of Genesis- 6:4

A nak dead?" Njorthr said. "That is not possible."
     "I am Gath," replied the giant, "eldest of the living sons of Anak. I would not speak such words if they were not true."

     The Anakim towered over the captain, standing a cubit taller and weighing twice as much as any man on board. His voice was like the deep rumblings of the earth.

The rest of the Anakim had gathered around them, all armed with a pair of long-handled axes in scabbards upon their backs. In addition to the axes, Gath also bore a short-handled war hammer, tied on a long lanyard and thrust into his belt; another Anakim carried a thick boar spear and the largest of the giants rested a great two-handed broadsword over his shoulder. Each of the six younger Anakim wore a gold chain around his neck bearing the Tau symbol of the worshipers of Yeshua.

"The bigger you are the more trouble you cause," called Simon, as he climbed down from the ship's rigging. When he reached the Anakim, the giants sank to their knees before him.

"Once again, old man, we are in your debt," Gath said.

Simon nodded. "It is good to see the sons of Anak again, but things do not go well in Logres, I think."

"No, they do not, Friend of Anak, for Anak breathes no more."

If these tidings surprised Simon, he gave no sign. "Come below and we shall speak," said the priest.

* * * * *

Njorthr, Moor, Simon, Daniel and the Anakim crowded into the ship's hold, as no other space would accommodate them all. Njorthr lit a single lamp and they stood round the circle of its light.

These are my brothers," Gath said. "As men say that all giants look alike, I will give you elements to remember our names by." He tapped the symbol on his breastplate, red rubies in the shape of a flame. "I am Gath, leader of the Anakim. Fire is my symbol."

With the back of his hand Gath struck the steel breastplate of the Anakim beside him, making the armor ring. "He on whose breastplate you see the image of a sword being forged between hammer and anvil is Eleazar, the second eldest of us and my right hand. Iron is his symbol."

Gath pointed down the line of his brothers. "My brother Benaiah wears the golden breastplate."

"Next comes Abishai, the wisest among us. Upon his black breastplate is etched a mountain, the symbol for 'earth'." In addition to his axes, Abishai carried a long boar spear, its shaft as thick as a man's wrist.

"The white cloud symbol for wind adorns Uriah's breastplate. If something breaks aboard this ship, tell Uriah and he will repair it."

Gath shook his head as he came to his brother who had taken a small book out of a bag that hung from his shoulder and was writing in it.

"He whose breastplate bares a likeness of a scroll is Asahel, our scribe, who even now must scribble in his book all that we have done this day," Gath said.

Asahel just nodded and continued writing.

"And the big fellow on whose breastplate is the blue water symbol below a silver moon, is my youngest brother, Shammah," continued Gath. "As he is the largest of us, he feels he must wield the largest sword." Shammah grinned and patted his great sword as it were a pet wolf.

Daniel now stepped before Gath and bowed.

"Sir, I am Daniel of the House of Asher, son of Argeus, late king of Asulon and Queen Isoldé, your sister. I greet you, uncles, though I wish we had gladder tidings for each other."

"Well met, kinsman," Gath said. "But the last news from across the sea was that Argeus sat strong as king in Asulon. What has befallen him?"

"My father was murdered, poisoned under the orders of the merchant Sargon."

"I knew your father well," Gath said. "Just as he was great in council and courage, great also is the loss to Asulon. I hope you fared better in vengeance than we, but that tale will have to wait. Ours is the older tale, so we should tell it first."

Gath nodded to the Anakim writing in his book. "Asahel will tell it. Start, brother, at the beginning of all things, where our father's tale truly starts."

Asahel replaced the small book with a thicker one from his bag, turned to the first page and began to read aloud.

* * * * *

In the beginning was The Elohim, The Creator. All that is came from Him and, without Him, nothing that was or is or will be, would have been. Before this world, before the universe, before even time itself, there was The Elohim. Men would later call Him The Lord God, The Most High, The Holy One and The Ancient of Days, but those who first knelt before Him, when the universe was young, knew Him as The Elohim.

He first created the Mighty Ones, the servants of the Elohim that men call angels. And the greatest of these angels was Azazel. Of all the angels gracing the fair heavens, none were more beautiful than Azazel, guardian of the throne of the Most High. For long ages uncounted Azazel, Captain of the Seraphim—the angels of flame—dwelt in the highest heaven, content with his station, joyfully serving The Elohim.

And it came to pass that The Elohim revealed His plan for the universe.

The Elohim spoke: "LIGHT, BE!" and the energy from His words slowed and matter was, where once it was not. And this matter exploded into a great number of burning orbs and light was. The Elohim spoke again and smaller bits of matter were drawn out, formed into spheres, cooled and made to circle the orbs of light. Upon one such sphere, The Elohim breathed and caused living things to come upon it. And this sphere was created in perfection, for The Elohim does not create in vain.

The Elohim created many different kinds of living things upon this sphere, but only one creature had an eternal spirit like unto those in the heavens. To this creature with the eternal spirit, The Elohim gave the greatest gift in the universe, the desire to love Him.

He chose Azazel, as the greatest among the angels, to go down to this sphere and lead the creatures with an eternal spirit in the worship of The Elohim. Because of his station, Azazel was given great gifts when he was sent down into the world. Every precious jewel was his covering and his head was helmeted in gold. He walked among the stones of fire upon the Holy Mountain and led the living creatures in praising The Elohim day and night.

Then it came to pass that The Elohim revealed more of His will. He would elevate the creatures with an eternal spirit to rule over that sphere and thus be more like The Elohim than even the angels, created only to serve and not to rule.

As he dwelt on this news, Azazel became prideful and angry.

How could he, the greatest of all created beings, guardian of the throne of the Most High, a spirit of fire and of might, have no realm to rule, while these lowly creatures, so weak they would die should they even glimpse the face of The Elohim, be given a whole world to rule?

And so it came to pass that Azazel conceived an impossible thought. *"I will ascend into heaven, I will exalt my throne above the stars of The Elohim. I will sit on the mount of the council in the sides of the north; I will ascend above the heights of the clouds. I will be as the Most High!"*

To this end Azazel gathered to himself a third of the hosts of heaven, claiming that The Elohim had given him a portion of His power and made him the equal of The Elohim. If they followed him, they would share in his rule of the sphere and its creatures. And a third of the angels followed after Azazel, and these came to be called the *E'gori*, 'The Fallen Ones.'

All the living creatures with an eternal spirit on the sphere followed after Azazel, worshiping him and making sacrifice before his altars, for he told them that he would give them power and make them like gods themselves.

Then The Elohim sent forth His warrior angels to do battle with Azazel and his hosts and Azazel and his hosts fell. The E'gori were banished to the earth and the airs that surrounded it, the moon set to mark their prison. The Elohim sent a great cataclysm, first of fire and then of ice, upon the earth, to destroy all the living creatures who worshiped Azazel. Thus the living creatures became unclothed spirits that walked to and fro upon the earth. These spirits would ever after try to enter those that lived with an eternal spirit, but who had not the protection of The Elohim, so that these spirits could once again touch and taste and breathe. Men would come to call these unclothed spirits demons.

For many ages after this first of wars, the world was without form and void and darkness covered the face of the deep ocean.

Then it came to pass that The Elohim, in His Mercy, decided to create anew. He brought forth a new creature with an eternal spirit—man, the children of the first Adom. And He set man in a protected place, a garden, to keep it and tend it and walk with the Lord there until man could learn to rule the whole of the earth.

Azazel however, remained a spirit of the air, having no realm, yet desiring a realm to rule. He had no realm, until he deceived man of his birthright and took the right to rule the earth away from man. Azazel became known as Abaddon the Destroyer, for he sought to destroy man's relationship with his Creator.

Now while one third of the angels followed Azazel and rebelled against The Elohim and one third of the angelic host obeyed The Elohim and did battle against the rebels, one third yet remained who refused both of these ways. They would not rebel against The Elohim, but neither would they to do battle against their brother angels. This angered The Elohim and He exiled them to earth for their disobedience. These banished ones came to be called the *Grigori*, the Watchers. The Elohim promised that, so long as the age of man lasted and the Grigori turned not to the ways of Abaddon, they would not die by His hand. Thus the Grigori were shown mercy, for The Elohim still had compassion on His creatures and was loathe to doom them.

And the angels who remained in the heavens sang this song:

> *Weep, ye heavens, for the Grigori*
> *Who cannot weep at their fate.*
>
> *When but two choices they were given,*
> *Said they, 'Perhaps there are three.'*
>
> *Know all who still dwell in the heavens*
> *In not choosing, a choice they have made.*
>
> *Know all who still see God face to face*
> *Never shall they return to this place.*

The Grigori came down to the earth, in a form like man, though greater, as a reminder of where they once dwelt. The Grigori knew many secrets unknown to man and did wondrous works, building cities whose gleaming towers reached into the sky and ships that traded goods across great oceans. Alas, after not many centuries passed, many of the Grigori fell to the temptations of Abaddon, calling themselves gods and requiring sacrifices made upon their altars. They fell from their place and sinned as men sinned. When men of old speak of gods who fell to earth and lived among men and yet sinned as men sin, they speak of the Grigori and the children of the Grigori.

Many abominations walked the earth in those days, monsters created when the Grigori lay with the beasts of field or forest: centaurs, satyrs, gorgons and the like. Many heroes walked the earth as well, for the offspring of the Grigori and mortal women were giants and mighty men. Hear now what killed the Grigori and learn from it, for as their sins grew, their strength lessened, so that even a mortal man might slay them. Thus Abaddon lured them to their destruction, promising them life, but giving them death instead.

Man also sinned greatly in the eyes of The Elohim in these days, so that He sent the last of the ancient cataclysms, the Great Flood, to cleanse the earth. The Elohim caused His servant Noe to build a ship, larger than any that had ever been seen before, for the saving of mankind and all the animals that took breath. Even the Grigori wondered at the building of it, for the oceans were always gentle in those days and such a large ship was not needed to travel them.

Then the floods came.

First the mists that surrounded the earth and protected man from the aging rays of the sun condensed and fell as rain. Then the ancient rivers that lay deep within the earth rose to the surface and began to pour forth. And last the lands of ice to the far north and south grew warm and released their captive treasures into the oceans of the world. The earth itself shook as if in distress and the seas became as mountains that crashed upon the shores. The Grigori who followed Abaddon took to their ships to escape the flood, but these were not built with the knowledge of such storms. All of the ships and all of the Grigori in them were lost to the waters.

All of the Grigori who had sinned, perished; but even among the watchers there were watchers, one third of the Grigori who did not fall into these evil ways, but remained neutral.

As the waters rose, screams could be heard from outside the ship of Noe as men tried to gain entrance. The Elohim spoke to the remaining Grigori, charging them to guard the ship of Noe from the doomed men trying to enter until the waters came and swept them away. This they did. Then The Elohim Himself took the Grigori to sleep in caverns set under the mountains of

Urartu to await the receding of the waters. With them went their mounts, the unicorns, the last surviving creatures of Eden.

Every living thing that dwelt upon the earth perished, save for the eight among mankind, the animals with them and the Grigori and their unicorns under the Urartu.

The earth moved from its place and tilted, so that its poles no longer held to true north and true south. After a time, the waters began to recede, returning to the oceans, the skies and the deep places of the earth. Ever after those days, each year was five days longer than the earth had first known, and the seasons more severe, the seas no longer at peace.

The Grigori slumbered under the mountain for many generations of men until an earthquake opened their cavern and the fresh air awakened them. They rose up and said, "Let us disperse to the four corners of the earth, each living among every tribe of man, so that when we have sons they may not make war among themselves." And so the Grigori went among men, and took wives, and had sons and daughters and became great rulers in their lands. And their sons grew much like unto them in size and strength, and their daughters became the most beautiful of women, so that all men went in awe of the Grigori and their children.

But, one by one, the Grigori fell to the temptation of Abaddon and so, one by one, they fell.

The Grigori who ruled Grecia fell first. His own sons slew him when he began to seek after their wives. They divided his body and ate it and were themselves forever cursed.

The four Grigori who went to the Chaldeans became great kings over all the land of Chaldeia, but soon jealousy moved in their hearts and they made war against each other to divide the kingdom. Men rose against them, tricked them and buried all four alive, deep in a ravine at the headwaters of the river Euphrates.

One by one the Grigori fell as they tried to make themselves into gods, weakening themselves, and were destroyed by the One True God. Until only one was left: Arakel, who had made his way west into the land of Canaan.

When Arakel came to live among the men of the land of Canaan, the people gave him wives and soon he had many sons. Most of the sons of Arakel stayed with him the length of their long lives, but some scattered to other lands, becoming kings of those countries, ruling mightily and bringing forth sons themselves, who were the heroes of old. Arakel taught the people of that land what he thought proper for man to know, but man did not wish to farm more abundantly or heal ills. Man only wished to build fortresses and great cities to bask in the reflection of his own power.

Man, hungry for more than Arakel was willing to give, turned to Abaddon. Abaddon corrupted the knowledge Arakel had given to man so that the arts of healing turned into sorcery; astronomy turned into astrology and the arts of the smith turned to war.

Fearing the wrath of The Elohim should he be blamed for what men did with the knowledge he had given them, Arakel secluded himself in a deep cave on the coast of the Internal Sea, forsaking all contact with man. Kings sent their sorcerers to Arakel, still seeking his knowledge, but he slew them. Men began to speak of him as *Anak*, "The Tall One" for his true name was forgotten.

Meanwhile the sons of the Anak in Canaan grew strong and proud, calling themselves *Rephaim*, that is, 'Those who fall upon you', and saying, "Who can stand against the Rephaim and who can defeat us?" As the numbers of the Rephaim increased, they built more cities: Gath and Gaza, Ashdod and Ashkelon.

But Abaddon, never far away, whispered quietly to the Rephaim, "Do you not wish to be great among men?"

The Rephaim began to hire themselves out to the kings of the land to fight their wars, for no man could stand against them in battle. Seeing their victories, the kings bade the Rephaim lead their armies. When the Rephaim grew tired of serving the kings, they slew them and took their thrones as their own. Abaddon seduced the Rephaim to his ways, recreating evils not seen upon the earth since before the Great Flood and spreading these evils across the land. They took as many women as they wished for their wives, so that no woman was safe in the land. The Rephaim made the people worship them as gods and took all their crops and herds to feed their ravenous appetites.

Then a people came up from the south, a small people, the children of Abram, and they made war against the inhabitants of the land near the sea, to call it their own. And the Abramim made war with the Rephaim. And the Rephaim, those who could not be defeated in battle, fought to retain their lands, but were themselves defeated.

Anak saw the hand of The Elohim in the victories of the Abramim and despaired. When even a shepherd boy among the Abramim could kill Anak's strongest son in battle, he turned his back upon Canaan and sailed north, far away from the lands where he had lost so much. He traveled up the western coastline of each country for a season, for the red of the setting sun above the green sea reminded him of the colors that clothed him in the heavens. In each country he would leave his seed: red-haired sons, tall and strong, and daughters desired for their beauty. Finally he came to Scandia. He took wives, had sons and soon became king. He remained there, content, for many centuries until a war set his sons at each other's throats. Brother fought brother until they were no more.

With the burial of his last son, Anak traveled south into the land of the Goths. There he lived alone, in the ancient forest of Thuringia, grieving for his sons for a hundred years, until his time for grieving ended. Anak came out of the wilderness intent on winning a kingdom and, for this, he needed sons. He went to the king of the Goths and offered him treasure for one of his daughters as a bride. Most kings would have gladly accepted Anak's offer, but this king remembered tales of the north and how Anak's sons had destroyed a kingdom in their own war upon one another. The king of the Goths refused Anak his request. And so Anak, for whom the lives of men passed like a single day, went back to the wilderness to wait for the king to die and a new king to take his place.

But the Goth king's daughter, a headstrong girl named Burgenda, heard stories of the mighty sons of Anak and desired above all else to have sons by him. She rode out to Anak's lodge in the wilderness and told him that her mother the queen had sent her to Anak, saying that the king would relent once he had seen his grand-sons. And so Anak took the girl to wife. When the king of the Goths heard what had happened, he cursed his daughter and all sons given to her. And the curse was this:

> *Betrayed you your father*
> *Lied you your mother*
> *Hoped you for greatness*
> *Upon you fall sadness*
>
> *Anak's sons you wish to bear*
> *Tall Ones, Mighty Ones, Great Ones all!*
> *Sons you shall have, but not so fair*
> *Small Ones, Little Ones, Lesser Ones all!*

And the curse fell true upon the king's daughter, for kings in those days–even among men– held greater power in their words than they do now, so that the race of dwarves was born from her deed.

Burgenda bore six sons and, though none of them stood above two cubits, they grew stronger than men and lived longer lives and had many of the gifts of

Anak's blood that their taller brothers had. The dwarves delved the mountain Kyffhauser, finding a vein of gold there, very pure, that ran deep below the skin of the earth. And so Anak lived in the wilderness of Goth with his six dwarve sons for many generations of men.

Then came a time when the world changed.

It is said that most animals can feel an earthquake coming long before men feel the actual violence in the earth. Anak, eldest of all living things that then walked in the world, now felt the tremors of an approaching earthquake—not one of earth and stone, but a shaking of the spirit. He knew the cause.

The Elohim was coming.

The Elohim had always been in all things, of course: in air, earth, stone and water and among all creatures that drew breath, but this was different. Prophesies spoke of The Elohim coming to walk among men, clothed in the likeness of a man and living among them. Anak knew that the time of His coming drew near and despaired.

Would not the coming of The Elohim mean the end of the Age of Man? Had not The Elohim told the Grigori that they would live among men as long as the Age of Man lasted? When The Elohim came to live among men, what would become of Anak?

Anak knew he could not hide from the eyes of The Elohim, but he hoped he might be spared the fate of his brother Grigori if he hid himself from men while The Elohim walked among them. Therefore Anak shut himself and his six dwarf sons and Anak's mounts, the last of the unicorns of the old world, deep in the mines beneath the mountain Kyffhauser, in the forest of Thuringia, in the land of the Goths. Anak placed all into the long sleep of Edenhom, the sleep possessed by all creatures before the Flood, so that they should not age while they slept, but live on no matter how long.

And so the seven sleepers and their mounts slept thus for centuries untold, as Anak's red beard grew round about them all. Three times the beard circled them and still they slept on. Then, one day, after many centuries of slumber, Anak heard a war horn and a man's voice calling him forth. He came out from under the mountain full of wrath, desiring to slay those who had awakened him. Out in the open air he found not an army, but an old man, a servant of The Elohim who spoke to Anak words of power. The old man spoke to Anak in the language of heaven, charging him in the name of The Elohim Who Was and Is and Ever Shall Be to hear his words. The old man told Anak that The Elohim had come among men disguised as a man, but that men had rejected Him and that the end of the Age of Man had been postponed until the chosen number of men, a number known only to The Elohim, should worship Him and welcome His return. The old man then told Anak of the House of Asher and their desire to return to Asulon. He gave Anak this charge from The Elohim, to aid the House of Asher in their quest to return home. The House of Asher in turn would provide him warriors, which Anak would use to conquer of the Isle of Logres.

Anak agreed, for he desired a realm from which he could unify the West against the Hordes of Scythia, whose rising up figured in prophecy, heralding the end of the Age of Man.

The Magog, Gomerians, Togarmahians and other Scythian tribes had lain scattered when Anak first began his long sleep, but now they had returned to their lands and made ready for war. Anak still feared that, once the Age of Man ended, so would his life. Anak believed he could keep the end of the age at bay by keeping the Scythians at bay. He dared not interfere with the worshipers of The Elohim Come as Man, Yeshua, lest he anger The Elohim, but Anak still sought to delay Yeshua's return by holding back of the Scythians and especially their largest tribe, the Magog.

When Anak left Goth for Logres, the dwarves stayed behind to work their mine, saying that they had no desire for war. Here, then, is the origin of the dwarves that rule Svartalfheim and the six dwarvish sons of Anak who founded that kingdom. The dwarves did not inherit their father's height, but they did inherit his love of working metals and jewels and mining the deep things of the earth. Anak had left with the dwarves six unicorns as brood stock, which the dwarves kept more because of the animal's worth, than the dwarves' love of riding (of which, all men know, the dwarves have none).

Not long after Anak had conquered Logres, the vein of gold at Kyffhauser ran out. So the dwarves set out south to seek new places to mine. When they came upon a high mountainous region between the land of the Goths and the Etruscans they knew they had found a land desirous to them, for they could smell the gold and jewels that lay hidden within the earth there. Now the Goths and the Etruscans disputed over this land, so the dwarves went to both kings, offering three of their father's unicorns to each as payment for the land. In the end, each side felt they had gotten the better of the other. The dwarves knew that the land they now owned would be rich in gold and jewels, and they had no use for unicorns in their mines. The kings, for their part, had never seen creatures as proud and strong and noble as the unicorns and were happy to sell some mountainous, disputed land, in exchange for the beasts. These two kings bred the unicorns and used the offspring, as kings in other lands would betroth their children, as a bond between them and the surrounding kingdoms. Ever after this, only these kings and their heirs bred the unicorns. Their kingdoms became known as the Unicorn Kingdoms.

As for Anak, after the wars that brought him to the throne of Logres, he took a wife and had a son, whom he named Gath, after a city his sons founded long ago. His kingdom grew strong as his sons grew in number, for they were great warriors, unmatched in battle by any living man.

Then, after nine hundred years as king of Logres and many more millennia upon the earth, Anak began to age.

His hair, once all the color of burnished copper, now showed streaks of gray; his brow grew lined by troubled thoughts. Each passing year saw Anak turning more and more of his duties over to his ministers. He told his sons, "I had thought this day could be put off, but the end of the Age of Man nears despite my efforts. Soon you will see me no more."

Disturbing reports began to come from the eastern border of Goth. A hunting party led by Anak's second son, Ashkelon, had disappeared in this area years before. Now strange beasts plagued the borderlands, killing livestock and seizing maidens to drag them into the forest, never to be seen again. Anak wept at this news, though he would not say why.

The Magog began to test the will of the Unicorn kingdoms with raids across their borders. The Magog grew bolder, sending spies and assassins into Logres to test the strength of Anak's rule. Anak's ministers grew fearful and began, one by one, to restrict the freedoms the people had once known, sending out men to spy on the people of Logres, banning commoners from owning sword or bow, and raising taxes ever higher to pay for these many new laws, saying all these things were needed to guard against the Magog. The people blamed Anak for his ministers' heavy hand, but the king had lost his will to rule in the last hundred years and gave his ministers free rein to do as they wished.

In the Year 1025 of his Reign, Anak called for a high council of the Unicorn Kingdoms to be held on the summer equinox. The council met in the great hall of Witenagemoot within Anak's fortress of Caer-Albion. Anak took his place at the council table, preparing to greet his guest lords. Each carried a token of their people.

First Volundr, King of Scandia, entered, bearing a shield with a white stag upon a blue field.

Next came Anshelm, King of the Goths, bearing a heavy shield of the finest tempered steel, set with a black raven on a red field.

Then came Wae'can, King of Iberia. His shield bore the likeness of a white-sailed ship.

Next entered Vanir, Lord of the Dwarves of Svartalfheim, who guard the gold of the Ten Kingdoms. He bore no shield, but had two short throwing axes on his belt and used a long-handled battleaxe as a staff.

Next, Cuchulain, High King of the isle of Hibernia entered. A great two-handed broadsword lay in a half-scabbard across his back.

Then came Dionysus, King of Grecia and the Mountains of Javan. His shield bore the likeness of a tall mountain with lightning bolts coming from the summit.

Next came Gareth, King of the Belgae. His shield bore the likeness of waves upon the sea.

Next entered Ferragus, Lord of the Gauls, master of the House of Red-Shield, prince of the moneylenders of the Unicorn Kingdoms. His shield was of pure gold and bore a red hand emblazoned upon it. A servant who went before Ferragus as he walked, carried the shield.

Finally, Antiochus, King of the Etruscans entered. Antiochus, a tall man in his sixties with silver hair and gray-blue eyes, was new to the council, having only recently risen to the throne. He carried no shield as his emblem, but bore a trident with an ancient bronze head fitted to a oak shaft intricately carved with strange runes. The end of the oak shaft was shod with an iron cap, which he struck on the stone floor as he walked so that it rang to announce him.

Anak called his fellow kings together to discuss a treaty with the small countries to the east, collectively known as the Glacis Lands. The Glacis Lands, lying between the Unicorn Kingdoms and the Magog, act as a buffer between them. Of late, the Magog had taken to raiding the Glacisii at every harvest. The Glacis kings had sent a proposal, seeking a treaty whereby the Unicorn Kingdoms would send troops and protect them from the Magog. The council came to order at the round council table and Anak rose to speak.

"Great Lords of the West, welcome," began Anak. "Long have we met here in Caer-Albion and longer still have we sought to protect the West. But what is 'The West?' Are our mountains greener than in eastern lands, our skies any bluer? Is it simply the land that we occupy, or is it more? Is it not the ideals that occupy our hearts? What are green mountains without the freedom to go amongst them, what are blue skies without the freedom to walk under them on a path of your choosing? But freedom has a price. It is not given to us, but must be earned and re-earned with each generation of men."

"But should we provoke the Magog by aiding the Glacisii?" asked Ferragus.

Anak looked at the Gaulish king. "I have lost more sons to war than all of you put together. I have seen wars fought to grand victory and bitter defeat. I have seen battlefields awash with blood and dead men lying in parts and pieces, as if a scythe had cut through red wheat at harvest. None here wish war less than I, and still I counsel strength."

Anak paused, searching their eyes for agreement or challenge. Could he lead them one last time, or would the courage in men's hearts fail them once again?

"No, strength does not guarantee peace," he continued, "but it does give you a choice. When you are weak, the choice of when to fight is not yours, it belongs to the invader. When you are strong, fear of your strength holds the invader at bay, for men with evil in their hearts are like wolves, calculating which elk in a herd to attack. Do they attack the elk with sharp antlers and a strong neck, or do they attack the antlerless and weak in the herd? Now the Magog test us by making raids against the kingdoms that separate west and east. Long have we been at peace with these lands and their presence has served us well, for they keep the Magog away from our own borders. We owe these small lands our aid now. If we build garrisons among them, we will be protecting ourselves as much as them."

"What these border kingdoms ask of us is a considerable outlay," offered Ferragus. "Garrisons cost money, monies that could be better used here at home. The armies we already have cost us too much. As you know, I favor reducing their size. The Magog are in no position to attack us. They have enough to do just to keep their own people from revolt. We need fear nothing from them."

Cuchulain now stood to speak. "My brother lords, should we speak of giving up the race with the finish line in sight? Should we allow our own armies to falter at this crucial hour, while the Magog, though their own people suffer for it, strengthen their own hand? We have allowed ourselves to chase riches rather than tend to the safety of our people. Yes, famines have gravely wounded our enemy. He may not have much more time left on this earth. But now we must be even more vigilant over him, for he is like a bear wounded and cornered –a bear at its most dangerous. The Magog grow bolder, more aggressive in their attacks on the Glacis Lands. In the face of this, many of us allow our craftsmen to apprentice the Magog in the war skills of the West and sell the Magog the grain that keeps their armies fed. Should we next sell the keys to our prisons to highwaymen and cut purses? Shall we sell the plans to our treasuries to thieves?"

Anshelm rose in protest. "Lord Cuchulain, would you have our craftsmen go idle in their shops or let our crops rot in the fields? What do these little border countries offer us for our help? Grain. Why we already grow more grain than we can eat. That is why we sell the blasted stuff to the Magog in the first place! The Magog give us gold for our grain. What gold comes from the Glacis kingdoms? The only gold they have is in the color of their wheat fields."

"Only by trading with the Magog and offering the benefits of commerce," added Ferragus, "may we cool their more warlike tendencies. Lord Anak, I ask you, would you rather we back them into a corner where their only choice is starvation or war?"

"They have a third choice, even if they will not take it," replied Anak. "They maintain a great army, both to keep us out and to keep their own people in. In truth, they have a far larger army then they need for their own defense. For the most part, that army quells dissent and prevents their own people from fleeing the country. Their emperor may be told there are only two choices left open to him, make war or face a revolt, but they need not go to war with us to get our riches. Instead of invading us, they would do better to become us."

"*Become* us, Lord Anak?" asked Anshelm. "How can the Magog become us without taking our lands *from* us?"

"There is a way," said Anak, "and it would cost them far less in both men and gold. None of your kingdoms are old enough to have record of this, but, once, the West did not sell the Magog grain, rather, the Magog sold their surplus to our kingdoms. That was many years ago, before Moloch came to them and stole their prosperity along with their children. If the Magog abandoned Moloch and allowed their people the same freedoms that our people enjoy, then they, too, would be as rich as we. It is our people's toil, not our soil, that makes our farmland so productive.

"The Magog do not understand that a man will only work as long as he sees profit in it for himself. The farmers and craftsmen of the Magog labor all day for Gog and then receive a pittance back from that as reward. 'From each according to his labor, to each according to his need' is the saying in Magog. If you tell a man that he will get paid a few coppers if he breaks his back working hard all day and the same if he works only hard enough not to be punished, which do you think he will choose?"

"But, Lord Anak, what of the armies of the Magog?" countered Anshelm. "They far outnumber our own. Who will come to *our* aid should the Magog attack in force? Will the Glacis kingdoms? They will be swept away by the Magog in the first week of battle.

"Will Asulon? Asulon lies far across the ocean and has grown weak under Absalom. Argeus may have strengthened his realm somewhat, but Asulon is far from ready to send us men in sufficient numbers to make a difference against the hordes the Magog can throw at us."

Anshelm looked around the room to gauge the tempers of his fellow kings. Most nodded their heads in agreement with his words.

He continued. "How long will Argeus remain king? Just ten more years, until his son returns from study here at Lord Anak's court. Kings come and go in Asulon, and their policies come and go with them. Here in our kingdoms, kings rule for life, making stable policies. Can we trust the Asulonians to aid us when their policies sway to and fro like a ship in a storm? No, I think not. Let Argeus see to his own country. The Unicorn Kingdoms can look after our own borders, our own people and our own peace. We have more money to spare then we have men to spare. Lord Ferragus is right. If we cannot win war, let us then buy peace."

"But at what price does this peace of yours come?" asked Cuchulain. "None of us desires the horrors of war, but I fear a fate far worse than war; I fear enslavement of our people under the Magog. They do not need their armies to enslave us, though. I worry more over the gold of the Magog than their swords," he looking pointedly now at Ferragus, "for gold can cross a border long before an army can. Oh, Kings of the West, have we relied on the courage of Lord Anak and the long sword of Asulon for so long that we have lost our own courage? Indeed, have we forgotten what courage is and now blame Asulon for that also? You now speak as if Asulon were our enemy rather than Magog. Is it because we have become as an old man, jealous of the strength of the young? Does seeing the courage, the vitality, the hope for the future you once had, now in someone else, move you to hatred?

"Do you know what I smell in this room, oh great kings? Two things I smell, greed in some and fear in others. It reeks from your very pores and surrounds your heads like a cloud so that your vision fails you. Well, greed may not be swayed by mere words, but words have often given courage to a weak heart, so hear me now, oh, faint hearts.

"'Buy peace for today and let tomorrow see to itself,' you say. Well I say, 'what of tomorrow and tomorrow's children?' Are we to abandon them for our own comfort? Shall we let the flood waters rise, but not see to the dam's repair, trusting that it will not burst in our lifetime? Is that what leaders of men do?

"Some would say that your love of gold makes you trade with the Magog, but I know better. A young man dreams of great foes fought and great deeds done. He seeks a name for himself and would risk great failure in the hope of scaling great heights of glory. But as a man grows old and nears the end of his days, he begins to feel Death's cold breath on his neck and his courage wanes. He risks less and less; his great hopes and dreams of glory turn into the hope for just a little more time, a few more days, one more breath.

"Oh, great Kings of the West, do you seek to put off the fate that awaits all men by hiding within a fortress of gold? You hire the strongest bodyguards and the finest physicians in the West. You purchase elixirs and visit the mineral baths in the vain hope that these will prolong your lives. Do you think yourselves able to buy more days for your life if you have all the gold in the world? Do you think to buy off your fates and somehow bribe Death? No, not even a single day shall you add.

"But I tell you that, though your body shall not live on in this world, your name *can* live on, if you are willing to take courage and do great things for your people.

"Do not despair. You cannot regain your youth, but you can regain the courage you knew when young. Let us do the deeds that require courage, for I tell you that courage left too long unused will atrophy like a broken limb, bound and unused for too long. Whether a young man drawing forth a sword in defense of his country, or an old man, speaking out in defense of a truth few wish to hear, courage is still required. Be as you once were. Unbind your courage and let it feel the weight of a sword in its grasp again, not on a battlefield, but here in this chamber. Let us take hold of a sword far stronger than one made of steel; let us take hold of the sword of truth. Do what is right for your people, even though they cry out against you today. Tomorrow their children will call you wise, for you have saved them from slavery this very day."

Silence hung long in the air. Many of the kings looked uncomfortably at each other.

"Lord Cuchulain," said Anak finally, "you humble us with your words. Such I have not heard from the lips of man since these halls were young."

"Lord Anak, may I speak?"

Anak turned his head and saw that Antiochus asked to speak. "Yes, Lord Antiochus. Though you are new to this table, you have just as much right to speak as any here," said Anak.

Anak wondered where Antiochus would come down on the issue of the Glacii. Couriers sent by Anak to find this out had returned with letters from Antiochus, then newly made king, that spoke of many things but committed to none of them. Antiochus, before his elevation to the throne, had been head of Etrusca's large diplomatic corps. Anak's ministers who had dealt with him had described Antiochus as courtly, with the smooth speech one would expect from a career diplomat. His ministers had liked the man, but that was neither here nor there, perhaps no more than professional courtesy among bureaucrats.

Anak knew that there had been a contentious fight for succession in Etrusca. Ambrosiano, the old king, had fallen ill the previous winter with a sickness of the lung. His son had been away hunting when he heard that his father lay on his deathbed. In his rush to return to his father's side, the prince had killed three horses and finally himself, as the fourth horse fell and threw him, breaking the young man's neck. After the loss of both king and prince, the king's two brothers had indulged in much bribery and no little bloodshed, to influence the members of the Etruscan Senate, who would choose between them. Antiochus, the youngest brother of Ambrosiano, had emerged victorious, but it was a near thing. Anak believed Antiochus would be looking to solidify his hold over the throne by emerging from this meeting with a trade agreement beneficial to Etrusca. Anak had already calculated what he could offer to sway Antiochus to his side.

Antiochus stood and took his wine goblet from the table. "Lord Anak, your guests are as noble as your hospitality," he said. He raised the goblet as if about to make a toast, but then stopped to examine the clear glass of the vessel.

"From Hibernia, is it not?" He gave a slight bow to Cuchulain. "The people of Hibernia are rightly known for two things: fine speech and fine glassware. Fair words you spoke, Lord Cuchulain, fair as this glass, but just as fragile."

Antiochus let the goblet slip from his hand. The vessel fell and shattered on the floor, splashing wine and shards of glass across the stones. Some of the wine stained the hem of his cloak a bright crimson, but he took no notice. He turned his gaze to the kings at the table.

"Kings of the West," said Antiochus, his voice now as commanding as iron, "do you really believe you can ever unify against the Magog in your present state?"

"And what state may that be, Lord Antiochus?" asked Cuchulain, folding his arms across his chest.

"A state of disarray," replied Antiochus. "Not one state, but many states, many realms, fighting if not on a battlefield then in the marketplace and at this table. You cannot be as one against the Magog in war if you do not act as one in peace."

"But are we not as one," asked Anak, spreading his arms wide to indicate all at the table, "joining together here to come to one mind on this matter?"

"Only one," replied Antiochus, "as a flock of geese travel as one. But when the hunters let fly their arrows, the geese will scatter. Your kingdoms cannot act as one until they are forged into one."

"And how shall we do this?" asked Vanir. The dwarf had held his tongue so far, reading faces for surprise at this thinly veiled proposal of Antiochus's or for a careful stillness that betrayed a prior knowledge of it. "For a thousand years the kings of the west have come together in council. Yet in all that time we have not sought to merge our kingdoms into an empire, for to do so is to invite revolt.

"For our peoples will follow no one king," the dwarf nodded to Anak, "not even the great Lord Anak."

"They fear Anak and what he would become," said Antiochus. "They fear that he would climb from the throne of Logres to the throne of Emperor of the Unicorn Kingdoms and never leave it. A mortal man, good or evil, will not live forever. Emperors may die, but Anak does not die. The people fear that Anak, as Emperor of the Unicorn Kingdoms, would demand that he be hailed as a god."

"If I have not done so for the thousand years I have sat upon the throne of Logres, why should I do so now?" asked Anak. "And yet, Etruscan, on your very first day at this table, do you not propose just such an Emperor? For what is an emperor, if not a man ruling as if he thinks himself God?"

"An emperor, yes," replied Antiochus, "but one unlike the emperors of old and their follies. We have spoken of the weakness of Asulonian kings, which comes not from the short time they wear the crown, but the limited powers they possess while wearing it. We lords in the Ten Kingdoms possess great power in our own realms, but lack the ability to act as one when the need arises. I propose that we merge the laws of Asulon and the Ten Kingdoms. I say we choose among ourselves an Emperor. Let it be written that he shall serve for no more than seven years. The other remaining kings shall make up a High Senate. During his reign, the Emperor's word shall be law over our lands and can only be challenged if the High Senate votes unanimously against him. In this way shall we have the unity we need against our enemies, while preventing the Emperor from having so much power that none can stand against his will."

As Antiochus spoke, it seemed to the men present that they had never heard any speak with such power and authority. All nodded in assent to his words save Anak, Vanir and Cuchulain.

"Aye, you're a bold one Antiochus, I'll give you that," said Cuchulain, slipping into his home accent, "Here you come and propose a thing never done in all our history, and on the very first day you set foot in the door. But how can such a contentious lot as ourselves ever choose one of us as emperor, even if it is for seven years? If put to a vote, you know each man will vote for himself–if not for pride, then to see that his people are not treated as second class citizens by a foreign emperor. Do you think we would be content to draw lots for such a great prize, or perhaps you would like us to revert back to trial by combat?" Cuchulain laughed. "We may as well hand the emperor's crown to Lord Anak, if that is to be our test."

Antiochus regarded Cuchulain for a time and then seemed to come to a decision. "Lord Cuchulain, you call me new here, for so I am. But we need new ideas, for it is only by new thoughts that new deeds shall be done."

He nodded and the doors to the chamber opened. Two servants entered, rolling a tall object draped in a sheet out into the room. Antiochus gestured and they removed the sheet to reveal the statue of a man beneath.

"Behold the Great God Man!" exclaimed Antiochus.

The statue was made of fire-baked clay, painted in a lifelike manner and clothed in the purple robes of an emperor, (many could not help but notice the resemblance to Antiochus). It bore on its iron pedestal the words, "ONE GOD-ONE KING-ONE PEOPLE".

"What foolishness is this?" demanded Anak.

"Does it really matter which god our people worship?" asked Antiochus. "Have not the wars over such things been as useless as they were countless? The borders in our hearts divide us more than the borders between our lands. One third of our people worship the god of the Yeshuans. Another third worship their ancestral gods, be they Apollius, Woden or Tor, and a third worship no god at all."

A knowing smile came to his lips, as if he included them all in a great secret. Antiochus had always been an effective diplomat; he had a way about him that made those he spoke with feel as if they joined a group of chosen wise men simply by being included in conversation with him. Most found themselves nodding their heads in agreement with his words, for to disagree with him would be to cast oneself into the outer darkness of ignorance and exclusion. He could not seduce all men this way, of course. He found this manner most useful with those who worried what other men thought of their intelligence, dressing themselves up with wise words that were beyond them, in much the same way that some midlevel merchants dressed themselves in rich clothing beyond what the truly rich themselves wore.

Antiochus continued.

"It has been said that, to the common man, all religions are true and, to the philosopher, all religions are false, but I say that, to the king, if he is wise, all religions are *useful*. I propose, gentlemen, a new religion. One that merges all these gods into one god, whose high priest will be our new emperor," said Antiochus.

"Sure and you are going to be telling my people, 'Surprise! We've just discovered a new god. Come and worship him'," laughed Cuchulain, the warrior-king of Hibernia. "I don't think they'll be forming any long lines to board that ship."

"And why not?" said Antiochus. "Have not all religions begun when some shaman suddenly has a 'vision' and tells his people to worship a god that only he can see? Why should this god of ours be any different?"

"You forget something, Antiochus," said Anak, rising like a mountainous wave pushed up by a storm. "I have seen The Elohim, the Lord God, Creator of the universe and have worshiped in His very presence. I know that there is one true God and no other. I know, therefore, that who our peoples worship matters as no other thing in this life matters."

The eight other kings sat silent, for Anak in his anger was terrible to behold.

Antiochus smiled. "Oh, does it really?" He turned to the others. "You fear Anak because he claims to be an 'Angel of God.' But what if I were to tell you of his true nature?"

Anak's face grew dark. "Take care, mortal man, I will not be insulted in my own house."

Antiochus ignored Anak and continued. "Have you ever looked into a night sky and wondered if any other beings look at the same stars, but from a different angle, under a far different sky? I have and can tell you that there *are* such beings."

A murmur went round the room. Antiochus raised his hand for silence.

"No, great lords, hear me out, I would not waste your time with vain tales. Give me but a moment and I will prove the truth of my words." The men in the chamber went silent, some with faces showing interest, some puzzlement and, on Anak's, an angry watchfulness.

"Our astronomers tell us," continued Antiochus, "that the stars in the sky are fiery globes, much like our own sun. From my youth I have wondered if, perhaps, in the vastness of the universe, there might be other worlds like our own circling one of those many stars. If such worlds exist, then perhaps beings live on these worlds as well. Much tells us that the ancients contacted beings not of our world. Writings tell of 'gods' coming from the sky and ruling over men, carvings on temples show men in winged ships, flying though the air, tales describe creatures unlike any we see today. All these things and more led me on a search, a search for a way to communicate with these beings. I began to study the ways of the great men of old, whom we would call 'wizard' and 'shaman' today, but who were hailed as the great men of their day.

"What if all that we now dismiss as 'magic' and 'sorcery' was simply the efforts of the ancients to communicate with these beings once they had left our world? The ancients did communicate with the creatures for a time, for they lived on a world close to our own, a sister planet in our solar system. But after a time, only silence met their entreaties, for a great meteor killed all the creatures that had lived on that world. But I, using the same methods as the ancients, reached out to other, even greater beings, beings who live near a sun larger than our own, yet so far away that, to us, it is the faintest of stars."

"Wait a moment," said Cuchulain. "If the stars are as our sun, then they must be a very long way off to look so small. How can you speak to ones across so great a distance? Take the fastest ships we have, multiply their speed a hundred times and it would still take a thousand lifetimes to reach that far."

"To physically travel that distance, yes—that and more," said Antiochus. "There is but one thing that can travel such a distance, to the end of the universe and back, and not in a lifetime but in the blink of an eye."

"And what might that be?" asked Cuchulain.

"Thought," replied Antiochus. "You gaze upon the moon and wonder what it would be like to walk upon it, not realizing that you already have. Your mind stretched out across the great void to reach the silver orb at the very moment you first set your thoughts upon it. From my youth I have studied the methods the ancients used to contact their gods. Many would call these strange potions and monotonous chanting the foolishness of primitives, but I have discovered their true purpose: to open your mind to communication with beings from other worlds."

Cuchulain laughed. "Sure and when I have had too much of a certain potion that comes in a tankard, I myself am 'communicating' with the fairy folk, too. 'Tis nothing new you are telling us, Antiochus."

"I am not speaking of the delusions you see when you are drunk," said Antiochus, his eyes aglow, "but visions of worlds far greater than our own, inhabited by shining beings made as if from light itself, giants larger than this fortress, who ride in ships that fly among the red clouds of their home planet. We have spoken long, they and I, and they have taught to me the secret history of our own world."

He stood and walked a circle round the council table, leaning upon his iron trident as a staff. It rang against the stone floor, adding emphasis to his words. He stopped halfway round the table.

"And they have told me the true nature of the creature who has led the West for far too long." He pointed at Anak. "He has told you that he is an 'angel of God', but I know the truth. Anak is the last remaining member of the race that ruled our sister planet, stranded here when the meteor struck his home world, destroying all creatures there, and any way for him to return. He has created this tale of 'angels of God' so that you may fear him. But I tell you that it is *he* who fears *you*. He fears that, once you know the truth, you will drive him from his place and destroy him. He fears..."

"Enough!" bellowed Anak, striking the council table with his fist and splintering the thick oak planks with a sound like the breaking of a ship's mast in a storm.

"Etruscan, the Deceiver has clouded your mind with lies," said Anak. "Sit down now and my temper will cool. If you continue speaking thus, I will grow angry." Anak turned to look down upon Antiochus. "And you would not like me when I am angry."

Antiochus smiled. "But Anak, I do not like you now, so what have I to fear?" He walked over to his own chair as if to sit, but took off his cloak instead, and threw it on the floor between himself and Anak. Men gasped.

"Antiochus, do you know what the throwing of the cloak means among us?" asked Ferragus.

Dionysus tried to rise, but Ferragus restrained him. "Antiochus, do not do this," pleaded the king of Grecia. "No mortal man can stand against Anak."

"My friends," said Antiochus, "the beings I spoke of have foretold that I am to be the first Emperor of Unicornia and have told me that they would give you a sign by which to know I am worthy of the crown. That sign will be my defeat of Anak, for they have told me how this shall be done."

Anak came out from behind his chair slowly, as if with reluctance. "It has been nearly four hundred years since this chamber has been stained with blood. If you insist on staining it with your own, I will not stop you, for I think I will be doing the people of Etrusca a great favor by killing you." He drew forth his sword, its hilt richly jeweled and heavy with gold. Anak bore it as a symbol of his kingship, for a being whose skin could not be pierced by any weapon made by earthly means did not need weapons of steel. Nonetheless, the sword was sharp and, with Anak wielding it, could split a man in two.

Antiochus lowered his trident awaiting the attack. Anak stepped across Antiochus's cloak, leading with a thrust. Antiochus met the thrust, turning the sword point aside with the head of his trident. With a speed surprising for his great size, Anak seized the trident's head with his left hand, wrenched it out of Antiochus's grip and tossed it aside. Antiochus turned to run, but Anak caught him by his collar and raised the Etruscan king off his feet so that they were eye to eye, Antiochus's face a mask of fear, his hands on Anak's chest, struggling to push himself away.

"Mortal man, have you anything to say before I end your life?" asked Anak.

Antiochus stopped struggling and his face became calm. "Just this." He placed one hand over Anak's heart and began to chant, "MENE', MENE', TEKEL, U'PHARSIN."

Anak looked amused. "Mortal, do not waste your last breath on useless spells." He drew back his sword, about to strike, but paused, a puzzled look coming to his face.

"MENE', MENE', TEKEL, U'PHARSIN," chanted Antiochus again.

Surprise and then shock came to Anak's eyes. He stared at Antiochus a long moment, then his mouth fell open and his eyes rolled back. Still holding Antiochus, Anak sank to his knees.

"MENE', MENE', TEKEL, U'PHARSIN," cried Antiochus a third time.

Anak's arms went slack and dropped to his sides. Antiochus stepped aside as Anak fell forward, slowly, as a great tree falls, to crash face down on the stone floor. Anak's body spasmed once, then lay still. Antiochus backed away from the fallen giant, keeping a wary eye on the body.

284

Vanir ran to Anak's side and felt at his neck. "He is dead," he said in disbelief, "You have killed First Father!"

Vanir sprang up, drawing a hand axe from his belt and hurled it at Antiochus. The Etruscan raised his robes and caught the axe harmlessly in the loose folds. Antiochus snatched his trident from the floor and parried the second axe the dwarf threw. Vanir took up his battle axe and charged Antiochus, aiming a blow at the taller man's thigh. The Etruscan caught the axe in the tines of his trident and pulled, wrenching the weapon from Vanir's hands. In the next motion, Antiochus thrust the trident forward, catching Vanir in the chest, burying the tines deep within him. Vanir struggled to push himself off the trident, but then life left him and he collapsed to the floor.

"Bloody-handed murderer!" shouted Cuchulain, "I will cut you in two, I will." He charged forward with his great sword held high.

Antiochus had just time enough to put a foot on Vanir's chest and pull his trident free before Cuchulain fell upon him. Cuchulain brought his sword down in a blow designed to split Antiochus in two. Holding the trident's shaft near its head, Antiochus raised the weapon up like a sword, parrying Cuchulain's blow and sidestepping his charge. Antiochus turned and brought the shaft of the trident down upon Cuchulain's head. Cuchulain staggered away. Antiochus drew back his trident and threw it like a spear, catching Cuchulain in the back. Cuchulain clutched once at his back and then the king of Hibernia fell dead.

"You will all bear witness that it was they who attacked me," said Antiochus. He pointed to the body of Anak. "Come here, there is something we must do to finish this." The remaining kings rose and came to stand around the body of Anak, staring down at him coldly. Antiochus retrieved his trident from the body of Cuchulain.

"Turn him over and expose his chest," ordered Antiochus. Each man taking hold, the kings turned the great body of Anak onto his back. Antiochus drew an ancient bronze spearhead from his robes and fit the socket onto the steel cap at the end of his trident. He set the spear point over Anak's heart.

"All of you place your hands upon the trident's shaft," said Antiochus to the kings, "for what we now do, we must all do together."

They each took hold of the trident.

"For the good of mankind, I banish thee from this world," said Antiochus. "Now all of you push." The kings put their combined weight upon the trident. Slowly, as if piercing the strong wood of an ancient oak, the spear point entered the chest of Anak. As the spearhead sank fully, a long sigh came from Anak's lips and the body seemed to lessen, as if Anak's spirit had just then left it.

"There, it is finished," said Antiochus. He pulled the spear from the body, leaving the spearhead within it and then waved his servants to him. "Take the body away. I want it hung on hooks from the fortress wall so that the people may see that he is truly dead. You may leave the body there till it rots away."

The servants went to the body, staring fearfully down at the great king.

"Take your ropes and pull him from here," ordered Antiochus.

"But, my lord, the body—it smokes," said one servant.

"What?"

The kings looked down and saw vapors rising from Anak's body, seeping from the pores of Anak's skin as mists rose from the earth early on a summer morning.

The kings backed away, fearing that the giant might rise. Only Antiochus stood unmoved. He prodded the body with the end of his trident. At the touch of the cold iron, the body sank in on itself, fading to a fine powdery dust. Antiochus stirred the clothing with the trident. Nothing remained of Anak but his robes.

Antiochus stared at the empty clothing for a long moment, and then returned his attention to the kings. "There, my friends, that was not as difficult as you feared it would be, now was it?" he said.

"When you first came to us saying that you would kill Anak," said Ferragus, "I must admit some of us doubted that you could bring it about. After all, that giant has sat on his throne for a thousand years and lived far longer than that. I thought you had discovered some poison that would work against Anak. I never thought you would fight him, man to man."

"With Anak dead, all Unicornia will follow you," said Anshelm.

"Yes, all hail Lord Antiochus, Emperor of the Unicorn Empire!" cried Ferragus.

"Hail! Hail! Antiochus," sang out the kings.

* * * * *

Anak's chief scribe withdrew from his hiding place above the chamber and fled the fortress. He brought word of the king's murder to Anak's eldest son, Gath. The call went out for the Anakim to gather at Gath's stronghold in northern Logres. Word came to them that Antiochus had gathered the wives and daughters of Anak and put them to sea on a ship bound for Iberia. The ship was later reported lost in a storm, along with all lives upon it, but no other ship sailing that route reported encountering such a storm.

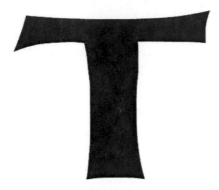

Chapter Sixteen
OF MEN AND MAGIC

And the Lord said to him: Go through the midst of the city,
...: and mark Tau upon the foreheads of the men that sigh,
and mourn for all the abominations that are committed in
the midst thereof.
-The Book of the prophet Ezekiel 9:4

Bitter frustration came to Asahel's voice. "While Antiochus fought Father, his men captured our chief ministers. Once Father was dead, Antiochus had the ministers brought before him. He killed half and the rest became like sheep. He had them order the fortress garrison, and all the young men of the House of Asher studying at our father's court, to board troop ships and sail east, to 'help put down a revolt in Gaul'. By the time we moved south, Antiochus had the fortress manned with his own troops. But this did not matter to us. We came with ten Anakim and more than one hundred of our sons."

The captain shook his head. "I have seen the fortress of Anak up close. How did you think to assault such a place with so few men?"

"You do not know the Anakim," replied Asahel. "Our armor cannot be pierced by any weapon made by the hand of man. No man's shield can withstand a blow from our axes. And most of all, Captain, we do not tire as men do and can fight all day if need be.

"Our sons were only half as strong as we, but still strong enough to be worth five men each. Even so, we did not try to storm the fortress by force, but tried an assault by a secret way that Father had built under Caer-Albion. But Antiochus awaited us. He poured burning oil down the tunnel as we came up under the fortress. We entered the tunnel with over one hundred of the best warriors on earth and retreated with only the seven you see before you left alive. We sought the harbor. The rest, you yourselves have seen."

Asahel ended his tale and fell silent. No one spoke for a time, the shock of the news of Anak's death leaving them without words.

Simon broke the silence first. "Captain, we should think of where we will sail next."

"Sail next? Where?" demanded Njorthr. "Somewhere where the wrath of this new emperor cannot reach us? Where in Unicornia is that?" He looked up at the Anakim. "Since we have taken his enemies aboard, we have become the emperor's enemies as well."

"There are other ports beside those of the Unicorn Kingdoms," Simon said.

"Yes, but I loaded food and supplies for the passengers and crew I *originally* left Eboracium with, expecting to sail no farther than Logres. We must put into a port soon for more supplies. How shall we pay for them? We would not last three days at any port, trying to sell our cargo with one of the emperor's warships sure to follow."

"Are these horses your only cargo, captain?" said the Anakim Benaiah.

"Yes," replied Njorthr, "and I would have gotten a goodly purse for them at the markets in Logres."

"How many horses have you to sell?" asked Benaiah.

"Twenty and five."

"Warhorses such as these would have brought you between ten and twelve sovereigns each," Benaiah said.

"Maybe," replied Njorthr, rubbing his chin. "Why do you ask?"

"I will pay you nine sovereigns each," Benaiah said. "Right here, right now."

"You carry that kind of purse around with you, do you?" asked Njorthr, eyeing the giant skeptically.

"Always," replied Benaiah.

"Well, you yourself said they were worth between ten and twelve sovereigns, which I think a bit low," said the captain. "Why should I sell them for less than twelve?"

"Because I will bear all the risk and expense for their continued journey," replied Benaiah.

"Eleven, then," Njorthr said.

"Ten," countered the Anakim.

"Eleven," Njorthr said.

"Ten and a half," Benaiah said, "and free passage to market of my choice if I pay for the supplies."

"Done," replied the captain, putting out his hand.

"Done," said Benaiah, clasping the offered hand. The captain was no small man, but his hand looked like a child's in that of the Anakim.

"So, then," said the captain, "twenty-five horses at ten and one half sovereigns each would be…"

"Two hundred and sixty two and one half sovereigns," Benaiah said.

"Why, yes, it is," said the captain, "You are quick with your sums, sir. Were you just as quick carrying such an amount while dodging Antiochus's arrows? That would be quite a purse to carry into battle, but I see no bag large enough on you."

Benaiah smiled and unbuckled the top straps of his breastplate. He lowered this down like a traveling merchant opening his wagon to display his wares. Thick leather lined the inside of the breastplate. The Anakim unhooked the clasps that held the leather to the steel, peeled the leather back... and suddenly the ship's hold was lit as if by starlight.

"Are those...? asked Njorthr.

"Yes, Captain, they are diamonds," replied Benaiah.

Row upon row of diamonds lined the inside of the breastplate. Benaiah selected two and withdrew them from their mounts. "These are worth one hundred sovereigns each." He handed them to the captain. He unbuckled a greave plate from his shin. From this, he retrieved an emerald. "This is worth fifty." He reached into his belt and pulled out a pearl. "Here is another ten." He opened a small leather bag and drew forth some coins. "And here is the rest."

"You seem a man always prepared to do business, sir," Njorthr said, admiring the treasure that weighed down his hand.

"That I am, Captain," replied Benaiah. "May I suggest that we sail for Tarshish? It is far enough that Antiochus's ships will waste time searching several other ports before they come there, yet close enough that your remaining supplies should last until we arrive."

"Aye, they *would* have lasted the voyage to Tarshish if I put all on half rations, but that was before we brought all of you big folk on board," Njorthr said.

"We will need no food on the voyage," Gath said.

"But even if the winds favor us, we will need a week to round the south coast of Iberia and sight Tarshish," Njorthr said, "What will you do without food?"

"We shall sleep for that week, Captain," Gath said.

"But no man can sleep for a week," Njorthr said.

Gath shrugged. "We are not men."

All at once Daniel felt ill, the walls of the hold seemed too close and the air too warm for him to stay below a moment longer. Without a word he turned away and left the hold.

Simon watched Daniel's face as he left. *Three wounds in so short a time,* thought the priest, deciding to follow the young man.

When Simon reached the passage, he found Moor waiting there, fists on hips, legs braced.

"Come with me," ordered the paladin. Without waiting for a reply, he entered their cabin.

"Now what?" asked Simon under his breath, but he followed, knowing Moor would not be put off.

"Do you want to explain to me how you did that?" demanded Moor without preamble.

"Not really, I have things to do," replied Simon. He looked at the paladin standing there silent and immobile. "I suppose that you mean the storm. Would it satisfy you if I said it was just a trick I had picked up over the years?"

"No. Snake charming is a trick, walking barefoot across hot coals is a trick," Moor said, rising anger in his voice. "Maybe I can accept that what you did in the tavern as some kind of mind trick, perhaps even summoning every rat in Eboracium *just* when you needed them was also a trick, but calling forth a storm out of a cloudless sky in time to save the giants—no, *that* was not a trick, *that* was magic."

He gave Simon a suspicious look. "Just what kind of priest *are* you that you can do these things? I have heard of people able to do magic down through the years, but none were actually able to do much when challenged."

Simon shook his head and sighed. "No, it is not magic. What men call magic is merely a poor imitation of this."

"Oh? If it not magic, what then?"

"Authority," Simon said. "Something that mankind had over creation as our birthright, but lost when the first man fell and the earth was cursed."

"So why did you not use this 'authority' of yours earlier?" demanded Moor. "You could have saved us a good deal of trouble at several points."

"I do not have the mantle of authority all the time," replied the priest, "I do not know ahead of time when I will be able to command the beasts or the elements. The times I may do these things are limited–so that I will not become proud, I suppose.

"Only when the Lord leads my spirit can I command creation, and then only specific things within it. For instance, I have never held command over any man, woman or child, for we are all co-heirs to this authority, though few realize it and fewer still use it."

Moor raised an eyebrow, even more skeptical now that he had Simon's explanation.

"So that is what happened in the tavern and with the rats and the storm? You used this *authority* of yours?"

"The rats, yes, and also the storm, but the vision we saw in the tavern surprised me nearly as much as you," Simon said.

"Are you saying that you had no hand in it?" asked Moor.

Simon thought for a moment before he spoke. "When the guard marshal was questioning you at the tunnel and the Anakim were under attack at Logres, I saw the danger and knew what must be done. In Asulon, I called for any creatures nearby to aid us and, it being Eboracium, rats came. As for the Anakim, fire threatened, so rain came. But the vision in the tavern– that was different. The Lord spoke in my spirit, saying, 'Bring the girl to the hearth and support her in prayer.' I was as surprised as you by what followed. For her part, Rachel told me that the Lord spoke to her and said, 'Go to the hearth and sing'. I did not know what would happen, only that the Lord's hand was at work in it. We are in strange days and stranger days are yet to come."

"All this still sounds like magic to me," Moor said.

"Argeus told me that you were married once," said the priest.

"Yes...once. A lifetime ago," replied Moor.

"Then you should understand this analogy. The difference between magic and the authority I use is much like the difference between the wrong and the right times people have sexual relations."

"Oh?" Moor said, wondering where the old man was going with this.

"An old man may buy the services of a prostitute, a young man may sleep with a girl he is fond of, though not wed to, or a young couple may come together on their wedding night. All have sexual relations, but it makes a great difference whether the act is under God's law and therefore protected.

"The sex act is powerful and, like all powerful things, dangerous. Prostitution is unlawful because it puts you in danger of physical and spiritual infection. God's law forbids fornication because an act that holds so much power is dangerous outside the safety of the fortress of marriage. The sex act carries the power of binding and, once an unwed couple go their separate ways, their spirits are torn apart and wounded.

"Men seek magic much like most of them seek sex, chasing something unlawful or, at least, premature in this age. Those who follow what is commonly called 'black magic' want only raw power and I have no use for them. They use magic to satisfy their lust for power, as a man uses a prostitute to satisfy his physical lust. But I *do* feel sorrow for those lured into what is mislabeled as 'white magic.' They seek something they know once must have been, but they do so before the time for its return."

"And what do they seek?" asked Moor.

"A return to Eden," replied Simon, a note of longing in his voice. "What attracts most people to magic is an innate desire in the human heart to regain the world as God first made it, before mankind fell. We instinctively know what we lost and long for its return.

"We all long for a time when we had power over creation and were its caretakers, when we could command the wind and the earth and the waters in a place where death walked not and sickness was unknown, where we could understand the speech of the animals and none would do us harm. That is why children are so fond of magic in their fairy tales, for they know that the world *should* work that way, even if it does not now. But all of us long for Eden, whether we know that name or not. We seek to satisfy our homesickness for a land we have never seen, but know, as surely as we know our hearts beat and our lungs draw breath, once existed and will exist again.

"But, as I said, that birthright was stolen from us. Those who practice magic, whether they realize it or not, attempt to buy back a portion of that birthright from the very one who stole it. Of course, he will never give up such power willingly, so they receive hollow shams and counterfeits, phantoms of the power man once had. What you see me doing is possible because God has lifted the curse for a moment and given me back man's birthright for a time. Magic seeks to carve a creature out of stone before the true birth of the living child that will be the new earth reborn and Eden returned. That is the difference between magic and what I do."

Moor stood staring at Simon, silent for a long time.

"You are a strange kind of priest," said the paladin finally. He opened the cabin door and walked away.

* * * * *

Simon found Daniel on deck, standing forward at the bow. Tears ran from his eyes and Simon knew that they were not caused by the wind. The prince gripped the ship's rail so hard that his knuckles were white and he trembled as he struggled to master himself. Simon stood silent, waiting for Daniel to speak first.

"First I lost my father, then Rachel's love and now this, the death of the Grandsire of my kindred," Daniel said. He looked down into the waters rushing below them. "I feel like a ship that has lost its way in a

storm, with my mast broken and my sails torn. I am adrift on the open sea." He stood silent for a time, in thought, and then a bitter laugh escaped his lips. "And to think that a month ago I had my life laid out before me like a well-marked road.
I knew where it would lead and I looked forward to the journey."

"Life is not as safe and secure as men like to think," Simon said. "Men may believe they know what path their lives will take, but that belief is an illusion." He eyed Daniel carefully. "All the more so when the Lord's hand is upon you, for those the Lord calls seldom follow a predictable path."

"I would hope the Lord's hand is stronger than that," replied Daniel. "Were I truly called by Him, I think I would not be in such pain."

"The Lord indeed has a plan for you, Daniel, son of Argeus," said the priest. "If that were not true, you and your house would not be under such attack. It is said that a king's son is called to do great works. Truly, I tell you that a believer's son is called to do good works. As your parents both led the land and loved the Lord, I know you are being called to do works both great and good."

"That all sounds very noble," Daniel said bitterly, "but this great calling seems to offer little protection from great suffering."

"Your father was my very dear friend, Daniel. I also grieve for him," Simon said, wishing he could bear Daniel's pain in his stead. "And Anak knew that this day would come, though he did not know how or when.

"I know that your wounds are very fresh and will need time to heal, but store my words in your heart so that later, when your pain no longer occupies all your thoughts, you will remember them and know their truth."

He paused, looking out to sea a few moments before continuing.

"Daniel, a man may see a tree struck by lightning and wonder, 'why?' Why was that one tree struck, and not any nearby? But men, especially men of God, do not fall as trees fall. We are at war, Daniel and your father and Lord Anak were casualties in that war. Sargon and Antiochus wield the sword, but another mind ordered the sword to cut: Abaddon, The Great Deceiver. In the war between the Lord God, Creator of the universe and Abaddon, the enemy of all that is loved by God, our world is the battlefield."

"Then perhaps it would be wise to keep our heads low and wait for the war to end," Daniel said. "Surely God will win and needs no help from us."

"If we spoke of a war between two earthly kings," replied Simon, "that option might be open to us, but there is no safe hiding place in this war. And, even in an earthly war, the land between the opposing armies makes the most dangerous place to stand. I speak of a spiritual battlefield, all around us and even within us; there is nowhere to hide. Those who serve the Lord are under attack from Abaddon, yes. Yet, as Abaddon is the enemy of all mankind, even those who openly side with him shall also suffer. Those who serve Abaddon may be spared his wrath while they live, but serving him poisons their hearts so that they know no peace. And later, once they are dead and thoroughly in his grasp, they will know the full measure of his hatred and his malice towards all creatures that God loves."

Simon placed a hand on Daniel's shoulder.

"Had Asulon been at war with another country and your father fallen in battle, you would still have grieved, but would not have wondered at his death, for that is the nature of war. I tell you truly that mankind is in a war far more deadly and of far greater importance than any that has ever been fought between men. It started before God first breathed life into man, but with Anak's passing, I think we may be nearing the time of the last great battle before the end.

"Daniel, your father and Anak are dead. You can do nothing for them now. But you have a third wound and with that wound I may be able to help. Rachel has been hurt, but it is a hurt of the heart and of a kind that can be healed. If you listen to me you may yet win back her love. Now, here is your first step..."

And so the old priest and the young prince spoke long into the night.

Printed in the United States
209490BV00002B/160-183/P

9 780980 105803